SECOND IMPRESSIONS:

A NOVEL.

IN TWO VOLUMES.

BY THE

AUTHOR OF "DILETTANTE'S DICTIONARY,"

&c. &c.

VOL. I. & II.

CHELSEA:
PRINTED FOR CHAWTON HOUSE PRESS.

2011.

Chawton
House
Press

Published by
Chawton House Press
an affiliate of the Chawton House Library
and the
Centre for the Study of Early English Women's Writing
Chawton, Hampshire, England GU34 1SJ
www.Chawton.org

P.O. Box 599, Upperville, Virginia 20185
www.SecondImpressions.US

Library of Congress Control Number:

ISBN: 0-97816136475-0-9

PRINTED IN THE UNITED STATES OF AMERICA

First Edition

To

THOSE MOST CONSTANT AND

DEVOTED JANEITES,

THIS WORK IS,

FOR THEIR APPROBATION AND DIVERSION,

MOST RESPECTFULLY

SUBMITTED,

BY THEIR

DUTIFUL

AND OBEDIENT

HUMBLE SERVANT,

THE AUTHOR.

ACKNOWLEDGMENTS.

BOOK LAY-OUT AND COVER ART: Judy Walker
EDITOR: Robert Lesman; ASST. EDITORS: Michele Middleton and Linda Cirba
RESEARCH ASSISTANTS: Anna Klenkar, Mary Channel, and Nicola Hislop
MENTOR: Jan Neuharth
ERRORS: The Author
FONT: Coldstyle
COMPUTER: 28 years of Apple. Thank you, Steve. Like Jane, you were taken from us long before we were able to let you go. Like Jane, you have added immeasurable joy and enrichment to the lives you too-briefly shared. I know, wherever you are, they are all typing into Macs, talking on iPhones, listening to iPods, dancing to iTunes, and Gabriel is calming the angels in the aftermath of Lion. And, as we all know, there's no such thing as a Windows-friendly attachment.

This is the place to thank everyone who has been a part of bringing this book out of darkness, and into light. The path has never been direct, has always been long, and largely one of unending questions, leading to yet more research. This book is the product of nothing so much as tenacity, for which I thank my Aunt Doris. She taught me the only lesson better than Nothing is Impossible: that Everything is Possible. They are not the same, and the latter is more powerful than the former.

I wish to acknowledge my debt and gratitude to the many others who have given so generously and graciously of their time, experience, and knowledge: Gillian Dow, Janine Barchas, Gilly Drummond, Jocelyn Harris, Joan Ray, Sarah Kernochan, Barbara Frank, Laurie Kaplan, Len Bosack, Graeme Cottam (a.k.a. Haggerston), Susan Staves, Stephen Lawrence, Elizabeth Garvie Rodgers, Laura Clark, Roger Trilling, Amber Denker, and Juliet McMaster.

Last, but certainly not least, thank you, Jane, for the years of pleasure, escape, inspiration, pithy quotes, guidance, and especially for reminding me that Everything is better with Humour.

VOL. I.

CHAP. 1.

A PERIOD of ten years' time usually brings many changes, and the Bennet family at Longbourn in the county of Hertfordshire—whilst believing themselves, as families do, to be generally very interesting, and on occasion, extraordinary—was, perhaps to their collective mortification, quite unexceptional. Mr. & Mrs. Bennet and their five daughters, a coachman, a cook, and all of the various servants thought necessary to a large and respectable country family were now reduced to just Mr. Bennet and his youngest daughter but one, Kitty, living in the village manor house with the few attendants who had not retired or followed to the houses of his married daughters. Mrs. Bennet had, alas, been suddenly carried off at Longbourn one particularly nervous afternoon, requiring Mr. Bennet to admit the possibility that her ailments had not been *quite* imaginary, and consider that he had not actually treated his old friends, Mrs. Bennet's nerves, with the compassion they merited after all.

Mr. Bennet consoled himself with her loss and subsequent domestic tranquility by spending as much time as possible with Elizabeth, his second daughter and long his favourite, and, occasionally, with Jane, his eldest and most beautiful. Jane, whose beauty and gentle, engaging manners had captivated even her censuring father, now lived with her husband, the rich and amiable Mr. Bingley, and four young children on a creditable estate in the county of Yorkshire. About a year after their marriage, the Bingleys removed from Netherfield in Hertfordshire to Holtham Hall, a low, modern-built house with requisite parallel wings and colonnaded, pedimented front, terraces and gardens, and parkland reaching to the banks of the Don. Elizabeth was now mistress of Pemberley and the wife of Mr. Darcy—though untitled—a man of vast fortune and great consequence, whose seat was not far from Holtham, across the border in Derbyshire. There, she lived with pleasure amidst the best of life's blessings with her husband and his younger sister, Georgiana.

Always fond of his library and ever-vigilant over its seclusion from the noise necessarily attending a family of "all silly and ignorant" girls (as he had described them, much to the vexation of his wife), at the time when four of his five daughters were married and removed from Longbourn, Mr. Bennet must now be supposed content, and possibly even happy. As a pleasure wished is often a finer thing than a pleasure gained, instead of rejoicing in his solitude, Mr. Bennet found that he did not relish domestic felicity in so unusual a form, and was, as a consequence, often making a visit to some one or other of his married daughters.

The business of Mrs. Bennet's life—of getting her five daughters well-married—was, at the time of her death, nearly accomplished. Her occupation had been regarded by her family as meddlesome at best, and frequently a positive evil to her two eldest and most rational daughters. A more practical view would have acknowledged the reasonableness of her concerns—if not their form—as, at the event of Mr. Bennet's decease, his house—indeed his entire estate—was entailed away from his own family on a distant cousin, Mr. Collins; this relation was a clergyman in Kent, currently enjoying the living at Hunsford and its comfortable parsonage. The success of Mrs. Bennet's stratagems for marrying her daughters well was, therefore, their surest preservative from want and the *ennui* that must attend a very contracted stile of living; if left to exist on their own unhappily small portions, they were destined to lose not only their home, but their comforts as well.

Of the five Bennet sisters, Mary, the middle sister, had the greatest and most unexpected change of state and fortune. Mr. Collins's first wife, Charlotte Lucas, was the eldest daughter of Sir William and Lady Lucas, the Bennets' neighbours in Hertfordshire. Sir William had been a successful country tradesman, and upon receiving a knighthood, retired with his wife and large family to Lucas Lodge on a modest income, and a newly acquired distaste for his business. Charlotte had been Elizabeth's particular friend and companion before Charlotte's marriage, when at the desperate age of seven-and-twenty, she had accepted Mr. Collins not for love, but for the security of an home and comfortable establishment. Charlotte had died the following year in child-bed, leaving Mr. Collins the legacy of an infant daughter.

Charlotte's marriage to Mr. Collins, for all of the differences in their reason and understanding—his obsequious flatterings and pompous absurdities, and her good sense and strength of mind—(and contrary to the general expectation) had been an happy one. Charlotte's intelligence, taste, and method had promoted Mr. Collins's respectability as well as his happiness, adding method and œconomy to his way of living. He had been attached to his steady and capable wife, and felt the loss of his companion and benefactress of everything that resembled domestic comfort and companionship, with a genuine grief. While absurdity is no armour against proportionate pain, few of Mr. Collins's acquaintance could appreciate the form of his sorrow—insupportable as was his usual conduct—now made infinitely worse with his grave retrospections and dolorous countenance. His heavy features and unfashionable dress, rendered even more unflattering with the addition of mourning bands, and lugubriousness occasioned by a self-pity unmitigated by reason or reflection, unfortunately united to make empathy less likely than ridicule.

Even Lady Catherine, Mr. Collins's patroness and mistress of the Hunsford manor of Rosings, was unable to redirect Mr. Collins's grief through the usual mechanisms of insult and interference. Arrogant, dictatorial, and disdainful of the feelings of everyone of inferior rank and consequence that—as the widowed daughter of an Earl and the present Mr. Darcy's aunt—encompassed nearly everyone of her acquaintance, Her Ladyship had been so affable and condescending as to advise Mr. Collins of his unsuitability, respecting both situation and aptitude to the raising of his daughter, and very generously recommending that Charlotte's people should have the care of her. Even the deferential Mr. Collins had been deeply shocked by Lady Catherine's frank assessments at such a time and had, for some days, not called at Rosings with quite his usual frequency. However, as it was impossible Mr. Collins's behaviour could be otherwise than that which Lady Catherine vouchsafed to advise, he accordingly went into Hertfordshire for assistance and sympathy. Had Lady Catherine foreseen that the product of her officiousness would establish another Miss Bennet, this time as the new mistress of the Hunsford parsonage, she willingly would have left off all such congenial hints in the future.

In the months following his Charlotte's death, when able to depute his duties to some parishless curate, Mr. Collins filled his days in solitary walks in the pathways adjoining Lucas Lodge in Hertfordshire. There, his perambulations would often take him near to the park at Longbourn. In this place he would—with a remarkable frequency—discover Mary Bennet seated in the copse reading one of her accustomed tracts on religious subjects and self-improvement. As she read from Fordyce or More, or some other writer of a serious stamp, he would gratefully spend many an hour listening to that which he should already have known, and, in the solemn recitation of those thread-bare proverbs and platitudes, received what assistance he might to assuage his present affliction. For the first time in his life, Mr. Collins's reflections produced a consciousness of his *own* want of attention to those instructions best suited to the restoration of his peace in those hours of change and loss. Had he attended with greater industry to the philosophy of his religion, he began to understand, he might have spared himself some portion of suffering. He honoured Mary for her application and taste, and believed himself indebted to her as the mechanism of his apperception, and the more secular benefits found in her singular sympathy for his grief.

In short, just after a year had closed following Charlotte's death, Mr. Collins was convinced that he had again found his true partner in life, one whom he could admire and respect for the improvement of her mind, as well as the gentleness of her temper. A more rational view might describe Mary's amiability as preoccupation, but the difference is of little consequence; it suited Mr. Collins's views of feminine virtue that Mary provided empathy as a balm to his sorrow in the form of those admirable books which contain the most common-place of wisdoms. Mary, often the object of ridicule within her own family for her peculiar turn of mind and unfashionable pursuits, rejoiced in having found a friend who could appreciate the value of her studies and the unusual nature of her accomplishments. In as short a time as could be considered decent, Mr. Collins brought Mary to Hunsford as his wife, and mother to his child. The Lucases must have had their disappointed hopes in Mr. Collins's second marriage, but more's the pity that Mrs. Bennet did not live to see Longbourn restored to its rightful ownership, in recompense for the grievous choice of his first.

It might be expected that Mary would make a very sober and ridiculous parent. But as is so often the case, necessity made a virtue. Mary found that in being a mother to Miss Collins, she had an opportunity to put her studies into practise, and to be of real use. She was an endless source of comfort, inspiration, and information to her husband and, if the parsonage at Hunsford did not have the same elegance that it had under Charlotte, it now had the benefit of an union of equal intellect, similar turns of mind, and a genuine mutual respect. In less time than he scarcely could have thought it possible, Mr. Collins was once again the happiest of men, and, in a form she could never have imagined, Mary was the mistress of an home, a wife, a mother, and a necessary addition to her parish. In time, even Lady Catherine came to be so persuaded of Mary's abilities as to ask Mary to help her with a specific quotation, or assist her in writing some little speech. These requests pleased and delighted Mr. Collins, and were a source of supreme pleasure to Mary, although it is perhaps best that these requests were never so frequent as to turn Mary's vanity to writing more than the occasional paragraph for the benefit of the public.

Of all the Longbourn family, Lydia and her husband were the least changed by the passage of time, if an exchange of one cheap situation for another, and increase in domestic discord can be discounted as change. Mr. Bennet's youngest daughter, Lydia, had foolishly eloped with a man of no fortune and less honour. Mr. Bennet had subsequently endeavoured to suppress all recollection of Lydia, due to the iniquity of her elopement with Mr. Wickham several weeks before they could be forced to marry. It was Mr. Darcy who, well previous to his engagement to Elizabeth, had seen to the proper regulation of the scandalous behaviour of the young and foolish couple. Wickham had long been obliged to move from regiment to regiment, each time staying only until the good-will of his fellow officers had been superseded by disagreements over his debts, imprudence, and extravagance. Lydia had learnt nothing of either prudence or gratitude, and lived in constant dependence upon the generosity of her sisters—the Darcys aware that, if they did not contribute further themselves, the Bingleys would be unable to refuse yet more expense in the discharge of the Wickhams' interminable debts—as the accepted expedient for their very survival. Lydia, if not her husband, was only barely welcomed even by the generous, good-natured Bingleys, and, through Darcy's love for his wife and the civility of his sister, was occasionally tolerated at Pemberley.

Whilst Lydia lived at Longbourn, her constant folly and unchecked imprudence had led her elder sister, Kitty, into emulating her habits of idleness and ignorance. Once removed, however, from the principal disturber of her reason and the constricted mind of her mother, and in the frequent company of her two older sisters and their husbands, whose regulated tempers and liberal minds produced the welcome effect, Kitty became more susceptible to remedy. In less time than could have been anticipated to effect a complete reversal of every notion of behaviour, Elizabeth ceased to have any apprehension of Kitty's arrival and could look forward to seeing her at Pemberley with almost as much pleasure as the visits of her favourite sister, Jane. Left with the responsibility of directing Kitty's happiness, Mr. Bennet now wished earnestly for his remaining child a suitable match with a respectable gentleman of sufficient means, or failing that, a lawyer or man of business, or even a yeoman farmer with a creditable property and a generous temper, a wish surprisingly similar to her mother's ambitions.

Kitty grieved most over the loss of her mother, naturally being most similar to her in temperament. Once the initial shock and melancholy had faded, Kitty learnt to value the increased consequence of Miss Bennet, mistress of Longbourn, and came to regard herself as not the loser by the exchange. In the absence of comparison with Elizabeth's intelligence and lively wit, and Jane's grace and beauty, all that remained to cloud Kitty's joy was the prospect of her father dying and she being unprovided-for, perhaps an unreasonable concern with two sisters well-married. She was heiress to other collateral blessings as well. Her father could praise the change in her mind, which had an effect that many might not consider wonderful: Kitty became less frivolous, less insipid, and more rational to the point where her father could scarcely remember a time when she was otherwise than his favourite daughter. And, although every year that passed lessened Kitty's chances of finding an husband, each year like-wise increased Mr. Bennet's comfort in having an agreeable companion in his old age, who was heard to say, "Now, Kitty, we may thank your mother for our being so comfortable and content; had she greater success, you would be carried away by some squeamish youth or another, and I would have been left to sit miserably all day alone in my cap and powdering gown!" Kitty would rejoin, "Oh! Dear Papa! That must never be!" usually several times of a day.

Jane and Bingley became the delighted parents of a little boy within the first year of their marriage. The Bingleys were natural parents: fond, indulgent, and attentive. Indeed, Jane had always been sure of a large family, and her own had answered every expectation. There were four healthy children within eight years, each valued as the best of blessings. Jane was very comfortably situated with a loving husband, a generous income, and the assistance of as many servants such a fortune provides; yet Elizabeth could see that Jane was obviously very tired. As the years went on and Jane became a mother to one, and then two, and then three, and then four, and now looked forward to the expectation of a fifth child in twice as many years, Elizabeth found that she could not discredit the effect of such a succession of children that had dulled Jane's mind and restricted her liberty. The constant confinements and loss of sleep and leisure must surely be a trial to even the most fond of mothers.

If Elizabeth had any expectation as to the extent of her future family, her fortune was to take a different turn. In the early years of her marriage, Elizabeth had been sadly grieved that she and Mr. Darcy continued childless. Not of a nature to give herself over to lamentation and bitterness, especially over a circumstance that was in the hands of Providence, Elizabeth sought other employments to fill her hours. She had always been a great reader, and took pleasure in walking in the Pemberley park, driving out with her husband or sister, and visiting the other families—particularly the poor—within Pemberley's parish. And, although she was a married woman, she saw no reason to neglect her music, her correspondence, or other accomplishments she had pursued with pleasure before she was become Mrs. Darcy.

To add to her better resignation on the subject was Mr. Darcy's own philosophy, that repining over the inevitable was foolish. To his credit as a rational man and a compassionate husband, he assumed the disappointment of childlessness on himself:

"Elizabeth," he said, "your family have their share of children; it seems an habit of my own family to produce few offspring: Lady Catherine has one child, Colonel Fitzwilliam has one brother, and I continued an only child for many years. I have always been of the opinion that our lack of issue was no fault of yours, but rather the propensity of our line to be parsimonious in the family way. If no other source of consolation is available," he added with a smile, "we may look to Dr. Malthus for approval."

With her husband's solemn assurances that he did not regret his marriage to her as the cause of no heir, his generous and reasonable reflections on the matter, and his half-jest that, "should Georgiana never marry, one of the Bingley boys will do very well," Elizabeth could have no further cause to repine. She had daily the very pleasant female society of Georgiana, and could visit the Bingleys whenever she chose. Mistress of her days, spent in the informed intercourse and agreeable companionship of her husband and his sister, Elizabeth regarded her own as the best of blessings. Elizabeth was as happy as even the wife of Mr. Darcy should be.

CHAP. 2.

IT IS WISDOM long-accepted that a man cannot serve two masters; it must be considered equally improbable that there exists an house in England of sufficient size to serve two mistresses. Yet despite the common expectation, Georgiana and Elizabeth Darcy not only shared Pemberley, but found great happiness in doing so. When Elizabeth was first come to Pemberley, all order had been nearly over-thrown by an unusual punctiliousness for the feelings and consequence of the other lady, each wishing to shew the greater deference and courtesy.

On Elizabeth's part, never before had she cause to regret her own studied inattention to her mother's house-keeping at Longbourn. On Georgiana's side, she was extremely anxious to shew Elizabeth deference, so keenly did she feel the inferior status of sister, as opposed to that which must necessarily attach to Elizabeth as wife. After several weeks of unremitting attention to the most trifling of courtesies, each lady more guilty than the other of over-scrupulousness, Mr. Darcy resolved to speak with his wife, concerned that Elizabeth felt the duties which attended the mistress of Pemberley burdensome, or otherwise unpleasant. Or, he gently enquired, was Georgiana inadvertently making things awkward in her general desire to please? Elizabeth had been nearly over-set, and could not immediately credit which imputation caused the greater share of her confusion: the indifferent performance of her duty which must have occasioned Mr. Darcy's observation, or her shame at such a mistaken attribution of guilt. To be so easily seen-through! Elizabeth, usually so quick to find diversion in the follies and inconsistencies of life was, at that moment, humbled and contrite. She could readily believe herself responsible for any deviation from the accustomed order and operation of Pemberley; her own sense of justice as to Mr. Darcy's concerns, and the *injustice* to Georgiana—whose daily exertions saw to their every comfort—made the very subject mortifying! With unaccustomed solemnity did Elizabeth endeavour to assure her husband that Georgiana was all that could be wished in kindness and more—a few minutes' reflection were necessary to both compose her thoughts and decide upon a more reliable plan.

Elizabeth was not formed for misery and vexation, instead having an opposite inclination to comfort and the ready relief of such very unwelcome sensations. She immediately sought Georgiana, at last finding her in the garden enjoying a solitary walk after an evening of rain. Elizabeth took her arm and led Georgiana to a seat that was reasonably dry and removed from the main walk. She laid her shawl down on the bench so that they could seat themselves safely and began thus,

"Dear Georgiana, I fear we have been very guilty, indeed," said Elizabeth in a grave tone.

"Guilty? I am sure I do not know what you mean; and, I can certainly recall no transgression to earn *you* such an epithet. Whatever the offense, Elizabeth, I assure you I meant nothing unkind."

"Indeed it is not of any particular evil," began Elizabeth in a doleful voice, "but a more general frailty: excessive civility—yes, that is our charge." Elizabeth could not help laughing at such an absurd pronouncement, and took both of Georgiana's hands to reassure her. "I owe you an apology: in my effort not to trespass on your excellent system of managing our household, I fear that I have occasioned us both to commit that rarest of sins, excessive civility."

"Elizabeth, you must have some incident in mind to prompt such an unnecessary apology. I beg you tell me what misunderstanding..."

"Misunderstanding! Dearest Georgiana—nay, it was a positive dispute! I recall only yesterday a most lamentable disagreement over the pudding! Mr. Darcy (and we may excuse some partiality on his side, for the present) complimented *me* on the pudding, and when I disclaimed all knowledge of there being such a thing in the world prior to having eaten it, and that his pleasure was all of your devising, you remonstrated with me most violently about the pears! As if a simple mention of the pears being ripened should secure me the laurels for the ingenious employment of our surfeit, not to mention carrying the day with Monsieur le Cook!"

Georgiana simply smiled and shook her head.

"Now, continued Elizabeth, "I mean to atone for my share of the offense by speaking with you quite frankly on how we are to contrive it so that Pemberley returns to its former, well-regulated ways, and my own inabilities no longer imperil either Mr. Darcy's happiness or his supper."

This speech had the unhappy effect of again making Georgiana respond in earnest, "Oh, Elizabeth! I am sure that if any fault is to be found, the fault is surely mine."

Elizabeth gently but firmly stopt her, and said in an equally serious tone, "You need not be concerned that I mean to apportion to myself any real inconvenience. Pray, let me continue—I am not afraid of being carried away by remorse; my feelings will resume their cheerful course in another moment. Allow me to me recollect that I was a visitor at Pemberley when it was under your care, and your care alone. I assume for myself only the credit due an acknowledgement of my own inabilities that prevent me from ordering *any* household properly, much less an establishment such as Pemberley. Your domestic management is not only able, but done with an ease and grace that I am sure I should never attain."

"My appreciation for my other talents—to order people, as opposed to suppers—is, in contrast, so complete, that I have no scruple in advancing a solution for a problem that I have so charmingly occasioned for us both," Elizabeth continued with a laugh, "and that I hope will meet with your ready approbation. I want to assure you, dear Georgiana, that I have given this matter much reflection—as long as the last ten minutes—and hope that you will see the matter as I do, without regard to the incontrovertible fact that my ideas are always without error."

Here Georgiana interrupted, "Oh! My dearest Elizabeth, I am sure..."

Elizabeth pressed her hand and said, "Now let us have an understanding—as sisters—that nothing shall ever come between us, much less something so common-place as dusting. My proposal is simply this: you continue to run the house at Pemberley as though it were your own, which, my dear Georgiana, it rightfully is. Pemberley shall, if you please, have one master and two mistresses. You, however, must continue to bear the daily burthen of its care and order. I, on the other hand, as recompense in some small measure for the trouble to which I so amiably propose to put *you*, agree merely to act the part of hostess, and, of course, take all of the probable credit for it. What do you think?"

Georgiana looked at Elizabeth with a countenance that spoke first of surprise, followed by a significant sigh of relief, and finally, a smile. "Elizabeth, how did you know? I was afraid of doing too much, and also of not doing enough."

Elizabeth replied, "Well, have I not the advantage of what I flatter myself is a superior acquaintance with your brother? And, I find your way of thinking much the same as his, which is perhaps not to be wondered at, as in many families—although not in mine—there exists a similarity of mind between brothers and sisters. It is more remarkable in your case, as you are so different in age, but, in truth, I find you very much alike. I know how it pains Mr. Darcy to appear at ease with many who would claim his time, when he would much rather be attending to other matters; I believe you to be much the same, is it not true?" Georgiana readily confessed she had forever felt unequal to the demands of being *seen* as the mistress of Pemberley, but her reticence disclosed itself chiefly in what appeared to others as shyness.

Georgiana's nature, like Mr. Darcy's, was meticulous. Her years of solitary study from a young age made the keeping of household accounts and the supervision of the servants—in short, the day-to-day demands of a large and social household—not toilsome, but a comfortable habit of employment since the early decease of her mother. Usefulness gave a direction to her thoughts and a purpose to her activity, and, most importantly, enabled her to be of assistance to her brother. Whatever small contribution she might make to relieve him of the domestic portion of his cares would necessarily allow an increase in the hours of leisure for the pursuit of his own employments and enjoyments. If there were another motivation—that of shewing herself worthy of his love and esteem—this supposition defied even Elizabeth's sagacity.

Elizabeth had neither talent nor inclination for sums or the management of service, and so determined that the charade would exactly answer for their collective comfort. Elizabeth spoke with Mr. Darcy about their conversation that evening: "So, Mr. Darcy," began Elizabeth, "I have spoken with Georgiana to-day concerning my plan for management of the house-keeping at Pemberley."

Mr. Darcy looked his concern and replied, "I had no idea that you should trouble Georgiana with my interference. I fear the subject may have been the cause of some distress."

"Well," replied Elizabeth with affected solemnity, "I confess that I took your comments this morning about the house-keeping seriously, indeed, and have consequently devised a plan which must necessarily be found agreeable to everyone concerned. This follows not only from the perfection of my own ideas, but because it most advantageously displays the abilities of the two women with whom you choose to live. In short, Georgiana and I have agreed that it is eminently reasonable that she continue to manage the household at Pemberley in her excellent way, and I have amiably agreed to wear all of the borrowed feathers. That is, I am to play the part of the hostess, whilst she, in reality, must arrange the hospitality."

Mr. Darcy smiled, immediately comprehending the wisdom of the plan, as well as its novelty. "The only trouble I can foresee," answered Mr. Darcy, "is how to communicate your plan to the servants; whilst I certainly see the merit of such a plan, it is unusual, in that the servants naturally expect to take their direction from my wife. How do you suggest we proceed in *that* matter? I am apprehensive particularly as to Mrs. Reynolds, who I know has been waiting for Mrs. Darcy for some time."

"I well remember her statement that there would be no-one good enough for you," replied Elizabeth. "I flatter myself that she has been so generous as to alter her opinion of *this* Mrs. Darcy. I am hopeful, however, given her strong reliance on your judgement, that she has done so, and that she would, perhaps, be more inclined to the arrangement if she were to have all her ideas over-thrown by yourself. We usually meet just after breakfast; would you find a meeting with three women regarding house-keeping trivialities disagreeable?"

"Not at all," he replied, kissing her forehead. "Not at all."

It may be reasonably wondered why Miss Georgiana Darcy, handsome, accomplished, and the mistress of thirty thousand pounds, might be an object of compassion. It is true that she had grown to womanhood surrounded by everything that money and the kindest of brothers could give; she was provided with superior masters and sent to the best establishments to be found in the Kingdom; and there, she had attained not only accomplishment, but true proficiency in those arts which become a woman of breeding and refinement—music, drawing, dancing, modern languages, as well as an uncommon inclination for such pursuits such as natural philosophy and mathematicks—thus securing her usefulness at Pemberley. Lest it be concluded in horror that Miss Georgiana Darcy was returned a blue-stocking or a prodigy, she was neither. Rather, she had the gift of a fine natural understanding, a preference for quiet pursuits and study, and a prodigious amount of time spent without the company of a parent, other children, or anyone else with the exception of kindly servants to look in on her from time to time. It should, then, be regarded as not very wonderful that Georgiana would find the demands of a noisy and capricious society at-large an uncomfortable *milieu*.

Her nature was a quiet one; she was very modest and shy, with an uncommon sweetness of temper. She had a timid, blushing smile that encouraged its pursuit, and clear, soft eyes, which revealed a mind of intelligence and probity, unclouded by art or affectation. Her brother spoke little to others outside his small circle of friends and family, for the simple reason of disliking the trouble. Georgiana's diffidence arose out of a settled disinclination to have attention drawn toward herself. She felt uneasy in company and unequal to those easy and graceful arts as would otherwise render the activity of common intercourse pleasant. This might well suffice for a description of Georgiana's persistent shyness, but it will hardly do for an explanation of its cause.

Miss Darcy lost her mother at an age when she could only just remember her countenance or her caresses. Her mother was succeeded by no-one in a capacity to love her and guide her; the few years following in which her father also lived, were insufficient in this case to secure a replacement to her father as a wife, or to Georgiana as a mother. Her father had been, indeed, all that was generous and kind, but he was not so young as to enjoy a child's company, and, as a father, he had little to say to her; her education was not his sphere. Her brother was of the same liberal and benevolent disposition as his father, and Georgiana had loved him in the place of a father, with full as many tremblings, and with so much respect, it might as well be called reverence at once. His pride she saw as disapproval, and his aloofness as detachment, and a distance that was entirely beyond her small powers to surmount. And, as children often do, she blamed herself not only for her own loneliness, but also in some inchoate way, for both the loss that procured it and her feebleness in resisting it. As a consequence, she never risked her own opinions for fear of losing such occasional companions, and when she did have company, it was her paramount endeavour to be pleasing to others, and always in agreement with whatever was said. Her years of application admitted much that could have been safely hazarded with sense and erudition, but the idea of being found disagreeable and losing the regard of her few friends entirely overwhelmed any idea that she might put herself forward; and, as her opinions were never ventured, she was left in perpetual doubt as to their merit, as well as her own.

At Pemberley, Georgiana could occasionally find diversion and companionship in her cousin, the kind and agreeable Colonel Fitzwilliam. Colonel Fitzwilliam's father, the Earl Hallendale, and step-mother, Lady Sarah, had an ancient seat within Derbyshire not above twenty miles from Pemberley. Lady Sarah had inherited the charge of her lord's two young boys, Viscount Dunfield and George Fitzwilliam, upon her marriage. The Hallendales were fond of their niece, and encouraged her happiness

by

by every means in their power, but, Lady Hallendale, being every season preoccupied with the care of the estate and His Lordship's two sons, was not able to visit at Pemberley as often as she would have liked, or indeed as frequently as she thought was necessary for the comfort of the motherless Georgiana. The eldest son, Viscount Dunfield, was only with the family occasionally, it being his habit to spend his time chiefly in London. His younger brother, George, not having the means of an elder brother, was at Pemberley more frequently. It was George Fitzwilliam who played hide-and-seek in the shrubberies in fine weather, and spillikins by the hour when it rained; who watched Georgiana ride on her pony in safety; who posed for Georgiana's crayons and exclaimed over her drawings; heard her music, and praised her childish copying-out; encouraged her journal, and guided the little hand making its letters; and when any volume was sufficiently complete, sent all of these works of genius off to London to be handsomely bound, with her cipher on the spine.

All who made the acquaintance of Colonel George Fitzwilliam found him to be everything that was gentlemanly and good in person, manners and address. He required some little association before his qualities could be discovered, yet his manner had a very engaging humility that rarely failed to prepossess every acquaintance in his favour within the first few minutes in his company. In appearance he was not as handsome as Mr. Darcy, but his conversation was a charming combination of wit and quickness, gentle and soft-spoken kindness. He possessed the happy ability to converse with equal readiness and ease with those to whom he was a superior, as well as those who looked down upon him as being the younger, untitled son of an Earl. Further, his judgement was sound, his mind rational, and his disposition liberal. Despite his birth, he was remarkably unaffected by rank or fortune, much preferring country air to the stuffy atmosphere of a card room, and more inclined to walk than use a carriage. His chosen vocation was the army, and, most unusually for a man of his rank in life, he had acquitted his commission with valour, and a strict adherence to honour and duty.

His temperament and worth had been recognised and valued by his aunt and uncle Darcy, with the result that Colonel Fitzwilliam had been appointed as Georgiana's guardian upon the death of her father, a duty he shared with Mr. Darcy. And, as with his other obligations, the Colonel was most assiduous in the discharge of those duties. Every spare afternoon and every leave from his regiment, he was sure to visit his little cousin, bringing her small presents and books, and assisting in the formation of her taste and education. Mr. Darcy's was a time of life which saw increasing engagements, taking him from Pemberley more often and for longer periods. Without the same independent fortune for travel, Colonel Fitzwilliam stood more in the place of a brother; he was at Pemberley whenever his studies—or later—his commission, did not require him elsewhere. The young Georgiana loved him with all her heart—the entire quantity of the love that would have normally been parcelled out amongst mother and father, sisters and brothers, was saved for her cousin and his visits. Unfortunately, as Georgiana passed through the difficult years in which a young girl changes into a young woman, her cousin's opportunity for visiting decreased, with the result that Georgiana, for many weeks at a time, had no friend to soothe her, or help her laugh her way out of the little tribulations of childhood, and later out of the confusion of feelings which accompany adolescence.

It is not surprising, therefore, that she did not naturally acquire the proficiencies of other young ladies: easy, graceful conversation; how to manipulate the attentions of young men; how to secure wanted attentions and discourage the undesired; how to dissemble when convenient; and how to maintain an air of unimpeachable innocence throughout. She had no mother to guide her through the tangled web of society and its contradictions, or to give her those lessons which could form her own confidence to do so, no mother to lead by example, and no mother to follow in safety. Until her own brother married many years later, there were no examples before her of the happy and easy relationship between husband and wife, and no brother or sister to shew her the rules, joys, and sorrows of courtship. Neither Mr. Darcy nor Colonel Fitzwilliam could see Georgiana as a young *woman*; she was always regarded as a younger sister, and a *much* younger sister at that. Their love was not the love of a lover, and the love that they excited in turn was, as it often is in interrelations between unequals, confused with both obligation and deference.

What began as a grateful affection for her cousin was grown into love, as Georgiana changed from a young girl into a young lady. But this was a secret known only to herself, certain as she was that the Colonel would never see her as anything but his young, callow cousin. And now Colonel Fitzwilliam had found a woman who possessed all of those arts and elegancies that Georgiana knew she could never attain. Indeed, the Colonel was enchanted by her ease and grace, her conversation, her wit, her dress—in short, Miss Crawford appeared to be everything worthy of such a man. Georgiana reflected, as she stroked the cat's silky white fur, that she had only to inure herself to the inevitable, and wish them happy with all of what was left of her heart.

CHAP. 3.

In the same year that he and Georgiana had lost their father, it happened that, in honour of her tenth birthday, Mr. Darcy gave his sister a kitten. He was sensible that the loss of a parent could be but insufficiently recompensed by the substitution, but wished nevertheless to shew his sister by gesture—where words were inexpressible—that he understood her loss and was eager, as her brother and ward, to do anything which might help to soften her sadness. Mr. Darcy was aware of the advantages a companion would secure to Georgiana, in his increasingly frequent and lengthy absences. At an early date soon thereafter, he conferred with the house-keeper, the kindly Mrs. Reynolds, secured her approbation, and the kitten was duly got and established at Pemberley.

The animal had been born to a tenant family, and was remarkable in being all white and having one eye of blue and one of green. The kitten was also completely deaf, a defect apparent to Georgiana within a few days of her having acquired it. What the little creature lacked in hearing was more than recompensed by the sweetness of its temper and devotion to Georgiana following the loss of its own mother. Georgiana, to the approbation of her French-mistress, had named the kitten Mademoiselle Blanche. From the very first hour, little Blanche was become her constant companion and confidante, superintending masters, reclining on the piano-forte, and accompanying Georgiana to her apartment in the evening. Her brother was pleased, and, it must be owned, relieved to have such comforts for his sister so perfectly secured.

Mr. Darcy knew well that Georgiana had neither the natural volubility nor the confidence which must attend her situation in life, without which her natural diffidence would render the demands of her position as mistress of Pemberley inordinately arduous when those duties became her own. Her brother understood that Georgiana's quiet, private nature belied an excellent understanding, a sweet, patient temper, and an affectionate heart. However, the difficulties that must necessarily arise in a world that judges hastily made him sensible, also, that she must acquire the easy manners she did not naturally possess, and so arranged to send her to Mrs. Fortesque's establishment in London, where emphasis was laid on the acquisition of those graces considered indispensible to the well-bred lady of fashion and taste. Mrs. Fortesque was a kindly, motherly woman who—most unusually for one in her line of business—wished her charges not only accomplished, but also happy. Accordingly, upon her understanding that her new pupil's sadness could not be entirely attributed to her history but was, to some degree, due to her recent separation from her beloved companion, on the next return journey following a convenient holiday, Mademoiselle Blanche became the newest inmate at Mrs. Fortesque's establishment, to Georgiana's immediate improvement of spirits and the other girls' delight.

Georgiana's progress under Mrs. Fortesque's tutelage was productive toward the attainment of that ease and accomplishment anticipated by her brother, and happier than she herself had reason to expect. Miss Darcy returned to Pemberley, after her time away, with a quiet grace and an extraordinary range of accomplishments, including a prodigious talent for music. Mr. Darcy had occasion to congratulate himself on his choice of establishments, as Georgiana's mastery of the piano-forte and her naturally charming voice had added something to her confidence, as well as her qualifications for her post.

Such was the life of Miss Georgiana Darcy from age five to fifteen, when a disappointment of the most dreadful kind occurred. George Wickham was the son of her late father's steward, raised at Pemberley, and given an education through the generosity of the late Mr. Darcy. When the young Wickham was not away at school, his holidays were perforce spent at Pemberley. As a consequence of having little else to do, the attention he shewed to the young Georgiana following the loss of her parents established him firmly in her affections. Wickham, a man of her brother's age and a favourite of her own father, had been artful and dissembling as a young man, and was become idle, insinuating, and unprincipled as a grown man. He followed Georgiana to Ramsgate in the summer of her fifteenth year, in fresh resentment over the present Mr. Darcy's refusal to furnish him with additional funds to squander in idleness and dissipation.

At Ramsgate, having been sent thither in the charge of a Mrs. Younge for an holiday, Miss Darcy was intercepted by Mr. Wickham. The latter so prevailed on her kind heart and unwillingness to disappoint anyone she loved, that she was convinced he was come for her because he loved her, and soon believed herself in love in return for such appetent sentiments. She esteemed her brother too highly to take such a step without his concurrence, and so sent him word of her joy, with the unsurprising result that he arrived immediately and removed her from Ramsgate. Georgiana could scarcely credit that such villainy could exist, as her brother communicated in his description of Mr. Wickham's intentions. More awful for Georgiana, however, was the realisation that she had *not* been loved; he had been after her considerable fortune, and, most likely, the added inducement of revenge against her own brother.

Mr. Darcy did not scruple to disguise his anger at the perpetrator of the offense, or even moderate his expressions of abhorrence of such iniquity in the presence of Georgiana. Not surprisingly, such immoderate language had the unfortunate effect that Georgiana heard only her own failings in his opprobrium, and in the few words they exchanged on the subject, she concluded nothing other than the acutest, irrevocable disappointment in herself. She was abased, abject, and miserable. At such a tender age, to have her virtue and propriety called into question! Such is an heavy burthen for a girl of fifteen: with no experience against which to gauge her error; no knowledge of others, with far more contemptible histories, who had found salvation; and no mother to value her and to say those words of understanding, heal her wounded heart, and put her innocent error in a proper perspective. Georgiana was left alone in her disgrace, and a repentance unrelieved by any information that might have secured a better understanding of her true portion of the offense. And, unaware that her brother had informed only her cousin Fitzwilliam, she had the additional mortification of believing everyone in the world to know the depths of her frailty and imprudence.

This unfortunate incident occurred at that age when a young woman is most vulnerable, when the accomplishments of youth had not yet been learnt so long so as to have solidified into the more enduring, confident grace of womanhood. Guilt and shame left a lasting mark: such confidence, as might otherwise have flowered, was swallowed up in the humiliation of her brother's evident disapprobation and disappointment. At the time of life when Georgiana should have found herself completely happy—happy in the improvement of her mind, accomplishment, and felicity, which naturally attends birth, fortune, and—if not the beauty of a fashionable kind—the more enduring attractions of a pleasing figure and regular, pretty features, by the time of her coming of age at sixteen—Georgiana was become more, rather than less, diffident. Although the shameful episode was all but forgot by the few who knew of it, she was become inured to the fallibility of her own judgement and the paucity of her own powers of attraction. Approving and constant through the years of sorrow and change, Mademoiselle Blanche alone was privy to the enduring affliction of her mistress, framed as it was by the certainty that no amount of subsequent probity and kindness could ever atone for her deficiencies of judgement, self-assurance, elegant airs, and easy conversation.

It was Mademoiselle Blanche, therefore, who held the position of comforter and approver in the loneliest days of Georgiana's childhood, keeping away the terrors of the night, exploring the rooms of Pemberley when the weather was inclement, and the gardens around the house if it was fine; was daily her audience at the piano-forte, and followed her to the paddock to see her pony; supervised the masters, glaring disconcertingly when she judged they were too severe; and stood as confidant and friend whether doing sums, reading novels in the safety of the bed-cloathes, or writing poetry as consolation to an imaginary lover. And, in Georgiana's womanhood, it was Blanche who gave Georgiana courage to resist, sweetly but steadily, attempts from all quarters to marshal potential suitors, by being a symbol of all she loved about Pemberley and a reminder of the deprivations she would face in leaving it. And so, Georgiana Darcy, possessing birth, beauty, accomplishment, and all the credentials which any gentleman of sense could wish for in a wife, and in spite of the best efforts of her friends, remained through her five-and-twentieth year unmarried, and quite likely ever to remain so. Unlike her Aunt de Bourgh's officiousness on behalf of her daughter, Anne, Georgiana had no horror of a future as a single woman. She was genuinely content to remain unmarried so long as her family went on as it always had; the family circle, as in Mozart's opera, was of exactly the right number—any additions or diminutions to its number must render it imperfect.

CHAP. 4.

THE RECTOR OF PEMBERLEY'S PARISH was a dignified, sensible, middle-churchman, the Right Reverend Mr. John Franklin, who tempered his sermons with only as much religion as would ensure its digestion in the minds of the brusque Derbyshiremen, whose characters could be cold as the clay and brittle as the coal. Reverend Franklin preached in the Pemberley church for most of his ordained life and was on an easy, intimate basis with the Darcys, being a regular visitor at the Pemberley table, and a participant in most of the usual celebrations and ceremonies, major and minor, of the Pemberley family.

Reverend Franklin made a journey each summer to see his relations in the south, and, in the same year that Mr. Wickham had been unreasonably disappointed by not receiving the living at Kympton (as he had resolved on not taking orders), the new rector of that parish was engaged to fulfill the parish duties whilst Reverend Franklin was away. Parson Overstowey was an heavy, happy young man, in florid health, and of earnest good humour, enough so as rendered an exterior agreeable to which nature had not been generous. Having the habits of a much older man, he preferred large, lengthy dinners, was fond of wine and country company, and liked nothing better than taking meals with his neighbours at their houses, or, as second-best, dining with as many them as would fit into his tidy parsonage. His evening pleasures were of cards, and the delights of his days were in fishing and visiting. Whilst never negligent in fulfilling the duties of his parish, he was sure to finish his dinner before attending to any service, and on at least one occasion, the sacrament was nearly denied a parishioner because the deceased had timed his dying so ill as to coincide with Parson Overstowey's supper.

Parson Overstowey was, however, most vigilant in the care of his tithes. The Kympton living was good, being about £600 per annum. Such that his income and table allowed, Parson Overstowey was the first to offer a six-pence, or to contribute in some small way to any subscription for the relief of some parish family in distress, the militia-men, or a larger national cause. The farmers of the glebe lands were steady, respectable tenants, who paid the parson annually at his rent-supper. In this gesture, the parson was as generous to his tenantry as to his peers; for their payments on tithe-day, they were treated to all the bounties of Glebe Farm and whatever he could add for their merriment. In short, Parson Overstowey was adjudged by many to be a generous neighbour, a respectable land-lord, a careful friend, and, in conclusion, a fitting clergyman for the home parish of Pemberley when that time came.

He was not, however, reckoned so charitably by all. Possessed of a sharp mind and a sharper tongue, his commentaries could be idiosyncratic and censorious, and his unfortunate prolixity when describing the defects—particularly in visage or habits—of his parishioners was disagreeable to some who believed that a parson should be more tolerant of the varieties and vagaries of human nature, and set a more tolerant example of Christian charity. Whilst Mr. Darcy was undisturbed by the speeches of the outspoken rector, being content in his conscientious discharge of duty to the parish, Elizabeth found him to be an exception to the peace of Pemberley. She went to unusual lengths to avoid conversing with the rector, including the expedient of an inconvenient detour in returning from the village, and on more than one occasion, caused tea to be later than its usual time.

There was no avoiding Parson Overstowey on every outing, however. Having been informed by the reliable Mrs. Reynolds that the parson was to be out of town for two days altogether, Elizabeth and Georgiana confidently drove past the rectory to visit one of the families of the parish whose wife had recently been brought to bed of a child, and was poorly. No sooner had Elizabeth expressed her relief that they were spared the parson's insights on that day, than they were greeted with the sight of the parson himself, hastening from his rectory with such hurry as his bulky form would allow. He had, no doubt, espied the Darcys from his usual position at the front window of his study, and was now rushing outside to arrest their flight. Elizabeth's attempt to satisfy the parson with a cordial wave, a slight change of course, and a quickening of pace went unnoticed by the voluble parson, and common decency prevented them from fleeing entirely. In a short space of time the ladies found themselves within the parsonage, being ushered into

the

the drawing-room and plied with offers of cake and tea by a delighted Parson Overstowey, who relished the opportunity of an *impromptu* entertainment on such a grand scale.

"Well, 'pon my honour it is a pleasure to see you here, Mrs. and Miss Darcy. Such goings-on in the village as I have to impart to-day require a large slice of cake, Mrs. Darcy; allow me to pour your tea now before it gets too strong. Miss Darcy, may I suggest that you try one of these delicious Bath buns to accompany your tea? I think you will find both flavour and texture in every way delectable. I am particularly partial to a Bath bun. In fact, I wonder whether anything of higher worth can be found in that city, for I certainly cannot believe in any benefit from the water there. Water! There is no sustenance at all in water! All these invalids might daily imbibe a Bath bun instead, and feel their strength growing as a result, with only the small-side effect that their waist-lines might begin to grow alongside, ha ha! But I cannot speak ill of the large-boned, for I suffer from that particular affliction myself!" rubbing his ample belly with fond pride.

"Now, we must start with poor Mrs. Northrop. The sad thing, you must have heard about the unaccountable circumstance of losing her brother and her child born upon the exact same day, and has been suffering a melancholy as a result; she cannot bear to look at the child, and has had to employ a nursemaid to bring the baby on, which—as you know—she can ill afford. There is no reasoning with her, for as all the parish knows, he was good for naught, and we can say nothing of him but that he lived and died, for he scarce stirred from the house, being altogether in his cups night and day. His nose, as you remember, was objectionably large, and I always wished he had a better. Mr. Seward was certainly unkind to his own wife and children, but there is no accounting for that extraordinary indisposition called love. I have been offering what help a single man can, but am ill-equipped to provide her with more than a little money for her bread."

"Speaking of tipplers, to be sure, I should value your view on the matter of my new man-servant, Mrs. Darcy, for he seems to me to be continually out of humour, and always ascending from the cellar whenever he is wanted. I have given him a jobation on several occasions, but he insists that I am mistaken. 'Young man,' I said, 'you are a sot and a disgrace, and might as well have your bed in the cellar for all the time you spend down there.' He assured me that his time in the cellar is spent on attending to the safety of the provisions stored thither, which I believe to be a tall story, indeed. 'Young man,' said I, 'objection is not in

your

your power, for I know you to be drunk, and you shall have your liberty at the end of this very month.' The saucy fellow proceeded to walk as straight as a die along the stones to prove his sobriety, and so I have kept him on. If I am being ill-used by the scoundrel, I should like to know it."

"Would you like some more tea, Miss Darcy? I rather think I must have eaten too high myself last night, for my face is inflamed somewhat and the side of it is painful. It was the funeral of Mrs. Symonds yesterday afternoon, a small and sad affair, despite the family's pretensions. They sent me neither hat-band nor gloves, which I thought scandalous, and so I did not wear my best gown as a mark of my lack of respect for their carryings-on, but poor Mrs. Symonds was—I admit—a kindly and good-natured soul (as compared with her family), although—as might be expected—she had a great deal of the Symonds physiognomy, which, I am sure, was a disappointment to herself as well, but this could not be helped—everyone cannot be favoured, or who would be plain? The younger Symonds girl has a bump upon her head, most disturbing in shape and size. She is the same age as my niece—have you not seen my niece, who is come to stay with me? She is a sweet girl, but does not ride, and speaks in a disagreeably shrill tone, which my kind sister imputes to a common failing on her husband's side. She is reckoned quiet in her own home, I believe, but is certainly not regarded so at the parsonage for she continues her chatter all hours of the day until the blessing of bed-time is arrived."

"May I press you to take another bun, Miss Darcy? I saw old Mr. Timmit wandering amongst his cabbages yesterday, so he is not dead. Last week, I was called to his bed almost every day, and he solemnly assured me of his imminent decease. His miraculous recovery is due, I am sure, to the fact that he was never ill in the first place, and enjoys the effect of giving his relations the inconvenience of a daily visit. As you well know, Mrs. Darcy, a Derbyshire man is a funny breed, hard and soft in equal measures."

Mrs. Darcy seized the advantage of the briefest of pauses occurring at that moment, and, rising, took up her reticule and cloak so as to make it impossible to misinterpret the gesture. In little more than ten minutes, Mrs. and Miss Darcy found themselves outside and being waved off by the loquacious parson, but neither could speak for several minutes more, until they were well clear of the Rectory.

Elizabeth laughed, "That man is preposterous! I cannot endure his ramblings! To sit without the power of making some dissenting remark makes me feel somehow complicit, however unwillingly, in his views, and I cannot keep pace at all with the changes in topic. It is like attempting to take breath in a whirlwind." As they drove on in silence, Elizabeth noticed that Georgiana looked a little pale and did not laugh at the parson's foibles with her usual gentle excusings; but as she did not venture any complaint, Lizzy had to be content to impute any indisposition to the parson's excess of both opinions and tea-cakes.

"Elizabeth, do you think we might make our drive shorter to-day, and return home by the fields?" asked Georgiana, "I suddenly feel quite fatigued and have a little of the head-ache."

"There is little wonder to that, you poor dear," said Elizabeth as Georgiana gave the horse the direction toward the home farm. "I will be completely quiet all the way home, and promise to offer you no tea-cakes for a week."

That evening, Georgiana was still indisposed and took her supper in her apartments. Elizabeth was still not sanguine on the nature of the illness, but, again, with no explanation offered other than the general indisposition of the head-ache, it was not possible to enquire further.

At length, it was again Mr. Darcy who secured the respectability and comfort of the last of Mrs. Bennet's unmarried daughters, although in this instance, not with perhaps such universal gratitude. In the course of Mr. Bennet's frequent visits to the Darcys', he and Kitty were often in company of Parson Overstowey when dining at Pemberley, at church, or at some one or other of the parish assemblies. To the surprise of everyone excepting the two most concerned in the business, Kitty accepted an offer from the sociable parson. Mr. and Mrs. Collins had not long adjusted to Mary's elevated state of importance at Hunsford, when she was called upon to change her station again within a twelve-month for one even loftier—mistress of Longbourn. Upon Mr. Bennet's removing to the parsonage at Kympton with Kitty and her husband, Longbourn was appropriated by Collins and his family, without requiring the melancholy circumstance, and the concomitant displacement of residual daughters, that had formed the most prominent portion of Mrs. Bennet's anxieties.

CHAP. 5.

Lady Catherine's late husband, Sir Lewis de Bourgh, had acquired a substantial fortune in shares at a young age and had risen, as a consequence of his success, to a knighthood. Sir Lewis was a tall, spare man, bookish, and industrious. His father, having sufficient insight to recommend his son to an elderly bachelor relative in business in London, had sent the boy to apprentice; whilst other young men would more likely have viewed a London education as an opportunity for vice, Sir Lewis was diligent in attendance, careful in his appearance, and quick in his study. The result of such responsible discharge of his duty was such that, upon his attaining his majority, his superannuated relative was disposed to take him on as partner, so as to relieve himself of the necessity of attending the business on a daily basis. The relative lived not long after this change in responsibilities, at which time Sir Lewis became the sole proprietor of a respectable and prosperous trading firm.

It might be assumed that such a material change in his fortunes would be accompanied by a reversal of his habits; this did not take place. On the contrary, Sir Lewis applied himself to his business to an even greater degree. Before he was one-and-thirty, Sir Lewis had been approached by a partnership wishing to purchase the concern, with the result that Sir Lewis was now very rich, indeed. Possessed of a fortune and the leisure with which to enjoy it, Sir Lewis was in want of a wife. All that remained for the completion of Sir Lewis's happiness was the encouragement of a suitable and willing Lady de Bourgh. Worldly and intelligent as he might have been in other matters, Sir Lewis was not well-schooled in the arts of ladies, and although he was attendant in London society as a bachelor, his serious nature did not endear him to either the society beauties or their mothers. His natural diffidence and disinclination to fashion decreased his chances with the fair sex to the unfortunate extent that, instead of dancing or flirting in the happy manner of the other single men, he invariably found himself in some distant corner with the married gentlemen, indulging in the far more comfortable topics of business, politics, and the weather.

Fortunately for Sir Lewis, not all of the eligible ladies were quite so reticent and modest as himself. Lady Catherine Fitzwilliam was the daughter of the Earl Hallandale, whose patent was owing to the time of Elizabeth, and whose fortunes had been in decline ever since, such that Lady Catherine's father had little but the title of "Lady" to pass on as dowries to his daughters. To the young son he bequeathed the additional burthen of an estate heavily mortgaged, and the necessity of providing for the dowager Countess and his two sisters in a respectable stile. Her younger sister, Anne, had recently secured an extraordinarily good match with a wealthy heir from Derbyshire. Lady Catherine, not being of a disposition to relish the obligation attendant upon her sister's assistance, felt all the more impatient for her own good fortune. She had already seen several seasons in London occupied in the ardent pursuit of a suitable match. In possession of a good title but poor fortune, her task was made yet more unenviable by a surfeit of handsome, well-dowered daughters of tradesmen, and a corresponding dearth of titled, single men not in need of a large portion.

Fortunately for Lady Catherine, she was able to congratulate herself as possessing the parallel virtues of tenacity and a rational mind, accomplishments she considered—perhaps uniquely—to be prized even above beauty, modesty, and amiability in a woman. Indeed, the less generous were inclined to view her intrepidity as a masculine virtue and therefore, the very reverse of feminine reticence; similarly if reason and intelligence were acceptable substitutes for beauty in the male canon of feminine charms, it would be wonderful, indeed, that the entire nation of mothers would be at such pains to conceal all traces of the former in their daughters. Whatever may be the general opinion of society, having noticed the shy gentleman who earnestly watched—but dared not approach—the ladies at every *salon* and *soirée*, rout and revue, ball and ballette, she directly ascertained Sir Lewis's position as to fortune, and settled upon this gentleman as the happy applicant for the hand of a modestly handsome daughter of a penniless Earl. She managed to keep well enough hidden her art to secure the attentions of the serious-minded Sir Lewis, by using the manifest allurements in the possession of every young lady: she professed a passion for all in which Sir Lewis took an interest, complimented his taste, echoed his opinions, and, in short, convinced Sir Lewis that Lady Catherine Fitzwilliam promised as fair a portion of happiness as he was ever likely to command. Her birth did much to offset the want of fortune, Sir William having none of the first and much of the second. Neither party being romantic, the mutual benefit of such a match, once apparent, was enough to encourage its fruition. How little happiness was likely to attend a marriage produced by art on one side and resignation on the other cannot be much in doubt.

Having secured her prize, Lady Catherine was not one to rest on her conjugal laurels. She worked diligently to establish the de Bourgh's place in fashionable society to every extent possible by giving Sir Lewis those hints as to dress and conversation which he was likely to adopt to please his wife; and, in time, she succeeded so far in her reformation as to persuade Sir Lewis of the necessity of obtaining an acceptable town residence, in addition to a country estate worthy of an union of wealth and family. A terrace house of four stories, a garden, and mews expeditiously replaced Sir Lewis's original London habitation at the request of Lady Catherine. Sir Lewis had long lived in the city, for the practical purposes of attending his business in Threadneedle Street; to promote Lady Catherine's happiness, soon after his marriage, he acquired a large house in Mayfair, off Curzon Street. The house was of the best quality, and the first and second floors permitted a sufficient view of the Serpentine and Rotten Row such that Lady Catherine could determine instantly if activity in either required her notice. The general din resulting from the low company of the corner was generally considered more a deterrent than an attraction, especially when any speech or parade would attract throngs of noisy spectators, or if a squall should arise, the scores of open carriages dashing head-long through the crowds in an effort to preserve the silks and bonnets of the fair atop the box, and heedless young men come from Rotten Row in their curricles, trampling over old and young, fair and poor, animals, carts, and tents in their flight, all protesting in the loudest (and frequently coarsest) accents their lungs would produce. Amidst such harmonious murmurings and illustrious scenes, Lady Catherine had been heard to repeat,

"My sister's house is detached, and this a terrace, but Sir Lewis's is four floors full above the ground—not to mention the attics—two detached buildings for the kitchens, and the entire width of the garden for the mews. My sister must suffer the inconvenience of walking to the second floor to see even so much of the Park as Broad Walk, and even then may do so only in winter, whilst I may see the whole of the corner, and that year-round, from the window of my own sitting-room, not to mention that hers—I must add—faces full north, most inconvenient in exactly the months one would wish to use it."

Not being content to tolerate the ignominy of remaining in London for the twelve-month, she had successively persuaded Sir Lewis to take a country property on a short-term let, whilst they sought out a suitable permanent estate, could engage an architect of suitable stature, and complete a residence of suitable expense. After some months, the de Bourghs secured a tolerably large property in Kent and began the construction of an imposing modern house. The old manor house was relegated to the future—to the distant time that a dower house would be necessary—but ignored for the present, in favour of amending the natural situation of the land to conform with Lady Catherine's own views on the picturesque, an endeavor hindered only by Sir Lewis's desire not to dissipate his entire fortune in a fruitless attempt to insult nature completely; indeed, his last rational act had been to dismiss the London gentleman hired for that purpose. In a surprisingly short space of time, made possible by the expedient of unimpeded ready means, Rosings had been established: a large house and a respectable park, although the shades of Pemberley suffered naught by comparison. Being modern-built, Rosings lacked both the situation and elegance of the former. Nonetheless, the expense of Rosings well-satisfied Lady Catherine's notions of a sufficiently imposing retreat for the wife of Sir Lewis de Bourgh: the result of much money, little taste, and no restraint.

For all of Lady Catherine's selfless endeavours, her one deficiency as a wife (and it was a serious omission, indeed) was that she failed to provide her husband with a son. However unlikely to begin a dynasty, she did bless him with a daughter, Anne. It is commonly regarded as unusual for a father to be sincerely attached to a daughter; however, in Anne, Sir Lewis found one with a disposition most like his own: quiet, more inclined to sufferance than forbearance, grown comfortable in the assumption of being constantly ill-used by Lady Catherine, and a willing and understanding commiserator. Neither had any inclination to see their own errors: Sir Lewis's in the impropriety of infusing a daughter's mind with derision and contempt for her mother, and Anne's in forswearing her mother's natural claim to gratitude and respect.

Whilst her father lived, Anne had been the source of comfort and relief in the few stolen minutes of any day when Lady Catherine happened to be busy elsewhere. Then, they would share misery, blame, obloquy, and dejection, one with the derision of a disappointed choice, and the other with the censure of a disappointed child. Lady Catherine was not sufficiently well-pleased with either to interrupt these tête-à-têtes of father and daughter, who were consequentially and agreeably left in peace, excepting at meal-times, or when Lady Catherine felt obliged to demonstrate the existence of her husband or daughter in accepting a general invitation, or when Lady Catherine had nothing else to do or no-one else to disturb.

Upon Sir Lewis's early and unexpected death, Lady Catherine, a woman unhampered by deep feelings, was able to continue in her daily occupations of improving Rosings, settling regular disputes amongst her tenantry, harrying her servants, and bullying her daughter without interruption. Never happier than when surrounded by a society that reflected the imagined status of her drawing-room, she cultivated a coterie of dependents, the Reverend Collins amongst them, and diligently offered alternately useless advice and unstudied insults to anyone so unfortunate as not to be Lady Catherine of Rosings, or possibly Anne. These scenes of domestic harmony and its extension throughout the neighbourhood of Hunsford continued throughout Anne's transition into womanhood. Only once had the congenial consistency of her days been threatened, occasioned by the marriage of her cousin, Mr. Darcy, to Miss Elizabeth Bennet. Lady Anne had been long-deceased by this time, but her interest—at least as represented by her sister—exactly coincided with the views of Lady Catherine: Mr. Darcy should marry his cousin, Anne. Lady Catherine had been so little satisfied by her nephew's following his own inclinations in the matter that, for many weeks, Anne's daily portion of misery was augmented by her mother's abuse of her cousin, and of herself for the dereliction of her duty to her mother and the entire Fitzwilliam family in failing to secure the affections of her cousin so as to pre-empt his choosing elsewhere.

The differences of physical size and demeanour in mother and daughter produced an instant impression that Anne de Bourgh resembled her mother not at all, but a more thorough knowledge would reveal some similarity of character. Anne de Bourgh possessed the same firmness of purpose as her mother; from her father, Anne inherited a pessimistic view of marriage and attachments in general, the sad but natural consequence of such an unhappy union. Anne was generally pronounced to be sickly and cross, and even her companion, Mrs. Jenkinson, could not discern the studied resentment that had precluded the happiness of childhood and the usual diversions of youth.

Anne had long resolved that direct opposition to Lady Catherine only aggravated the measures that her mother would perforce adopt to secure her submission. Rather, Anne fixed on her father's expedient of a sullen indifference to all things as the best method of resisting her mother, and putting any chance for pleasure out of the reach of both.

Anne had grown up with no expectation of release until the day she would marry her cousin, Mr. Darcy. In this one matter, she had no difference of opinion with her mother, finding something like contentment in the expectations of both freedom and privilege. The exchange of the mother's tyranny for that of the husband must be a material improvement. She had decided (it must be confessed, with some accuracy at the time), although her cousin Darcy was far too proud and conceited, his wife would necessarily have pleasures denied to Lady Catherine's daughter. Therefore, when this mixed blessing had been put out of her reach by the marriage of her cousin to Elizabeth Bennet, Anne had been forced to seek a new method of release. As yet, however, Miss de Bourgh had been unable to settle upon any plan that had a convincing chance of success, and which did not include the potential of finding herself in a worse situation by choosing ill, as had her father. Her own fortune was large, and Rosings itself was quite valuable, but her mother shewed little sign of letting go her grip on life, and seemed more likely to live forever than not.

One day, as Anne and Mrs. Jenkinson were returned from taking the air in the pony Phaeton, one of the servants hailed them to say that Lady Catherine desired the presence of her daughter in the drawing-room upon immediate receipt of his message. Making a face at her companion, Anne alighted from the carriage and walked in a desultory fashion past the servant into the house, at last making her entry into the drawing-room, where she found her mother.

"Anne! There you are. You have been quite an age arriving since I sent for you, which I do not think shews evidence of the respect to which I am naturally entitled. However, I would never mention such a *trifling* slight, as you know I never regard my own feelings. I have decided our plans for the next several months and wished to give you information so that you may begin your preparations. Instead of removing to Bath or Tunbridge, we will go up to London. We may then be in Bath by the autumn and—if I carry my way—in Derbyshire for Christmas. I am interested to see what a confusion that Bennet girl has made of Pemberley. As you well know, she is far too spiteful to invite us to stay with them, feeling—as she must—that her innumerable failures as mistress of the estate will encourage me to regard her as unworthy of her situation, but such apprehension on her part is unnecessary; I cannot possibly view her with more contempt and disapprobation than I do at present. We will travel to London, and then I will write to my brother, the Earl, to inform him of our intended arrival late in the year at Derbyshire."

Hearing no response, for indeed there was none either required or any that would admit of opinion, Lady Catherine continued, "Very well, then, you may return to Mrs. Jenkinson, and this afternoon I would like you to call upon the Collins family and announce our plan of being away, for I am far too busy with these arrangements, which I have undertaken on your behalf, to consider making a visit to-day. Whilst you are there, *do* remember my instructions to Mrs. Collins regarding the shrubbery at the parsonage."

Anne affected astonishment, and replied when Lady Catherine had done, "But Mother, you did not explain *why* we are to go London. I did not think that you found London at all agreeable. On our last journey thither, you decidedly expressed it to be full of ne'er-do-wells and cheats."

"I would have thought the reasoning behind my decision is quite obvious, child. You still need to find an husband, and you are getting rather old to be unmarried and living at home. At least one of us still knows your best interest! I have every reason to believe that you may yet find a suitable husband in London, and the coming months may procure an arrangement. Above all, you must be willing to take your own measures to prevent your gratitude and esteem for me from ruining your chances of ever making a match. I cannot find that you have made any such effort in the past, but that is neither here nor there. You may go now. Will you tell Purvis to bring my hat and shawl? Of course, you will not go to Hunsford on your own; I must accompany you. It will give me an opportunity to ask Mrs. Collins about her preparations for the village fête. The poor thing is quite dim underneath all that book-nonsense and will say nothing worth-while, but as you know, I like to shew a proper condescension to my neighbours whenever it can be done without inconvenience, and she will be most grateful for my notice. Come, child, why do you make me wait? It is precisely such inactivity and indecision, which makes my duty to you as a mother all the more necessary, yet at the same time, all the more tiresome."

C H A P . 6 .

HAVING SECURED the proper address for her visiting cards and augmenting that title to which she had been born, the wife of Sir Lewis entertained in grand stile. Every detail calculated to excite admiration and envy had been attended to with a punctiliousness that defied any natural elegance. With innumerable servants, an house laden with gold and damask, and a superfluity of mirrors and candles, the effect achieved was more likely to illustrate the adage that, in some things, too much is worse than too little. Lady Catherine had been vastly pleased by her success, and daily contrived to increase her joy by inviting the most fashionable sets in London to balls, *soirées*, and the occasional breakfast, in multitudes so oppressively crowded as to ensure that few escaped being crushed, having their dress trampled, or some evidence of their dinner on their cloathes; this, she knew, coloured these aristocratic gatherings with a very desirable exclusivity. Even the *élite,* who scorned to invite Lady Catherine to their own houses, courted her diligently on account of the excellence of her entertainments, whilst making both her ambition and lavish hospitality a frequent object of their gossip and derision. In time, as her daughter became of a presentable age, these ostentatious gatherings lost their focus on her own victory in having secured Sir Lewis and his fortune, and turned instead to the display of her daughter, and the search for another equally qualified husband for Anne.

When Sir Lewis was alive, his journey to town was undertaken immediately with the opening of Parliament, a practise which accorded with his own pleasure in visiting his former associates, and watching for any indication that an unfavourable bill might elude his vigilance and become law against his interests; his ladies would arrive after Easter with the fashionable set. When Anne was younger, her father often took her to the balcony in the House and interpreted the action on the floor below them for the benefit of her education, ensuring that she would have her opinions correctly formed as to party and issue; Lady Catherine did not chuse to accompany her husband and daughter, as attendance did not enhance her own personal prestige to be seen amongst the others in the gallery, and she had no intention of obliging her husband by feigning an interest in a subject not immediately before her own ideas of advancement.

Following the death of Sir Lewis, the de Bourgh ladies were in London before Christmas in the transparent misfortune of having nowhere else to go, excepting the dullness of a country house in the winter without either sport or sportsmen. They arrived to a London deserted by those having winter engagements, and no plans to return any earlier than the following spring. Lady Catherine and her daughter had spent several seasons in London without attaching a suitable object, despite the former's assiduous efforts in the form of schemes and entertainments. Anne had now reached her majority, and, at one-and-twenty, remained as unlikely as ever to secure an husband, despite a tolerable person and an extremely attractive fortune. In this endeavour, Anne had to balance the competing claims of satisfaction derived through impeding all of her mother's plans for removing her from Rosings, against the penance of continuing there as Lady Catherine's daughter. At present, Anne had met with no dependable replacement for Mr. Darcy's fortune and situation; and so she remained with her mother as the best-known of ills.

Days spent in London soon devolved into a wearying sameness that could test, but not surmount, the resolve of both: Lady Catherine intent upon directing Anne through the labyrinth of intrigues and deceptions necessary to secure an advantageous match, and her daughter's determination to the contrary. Neither was popular with their acquaintance, so after breakfast at ten o'clock, their mornings were usually spent in the stupidity of dressing or other frivolous employment, and afternoons abroad, if they happened to secure an invitation to tea. Shopping was always an available diversion, but as Lady Catherine enjoyed it not and, as her daughter's apathy extended universally, the merchants of Mayfair were poorer than otherwise might be expected through their want of custom from that quarter. Fine afternoons might be taken up with excursions to Ladies' Mile and occasional promenades around Mayfair in order to exhibit Anne's cloathing, which otherwise would have travelled no farther than her wardrobe. Anne could never be prevailed upon to drive herself, drawing the admiration of those gentlemen who rejoice in such accomplishments on the part of ladies, much less to trouble herself to return later in the afternoon for a repetition of the performance. Sometimes of a Wednesday or a Saturday, Lady Catherine and her daughter might attend the Parliamentary sessions, but these efforts were of limited value, as they only rarely produced the desired invitation to dinner. Anne might occasionally attend the Royal Academy, having no design to study the pictures, but rather to annoy Lady Catherine with her choice, and to be secure against her company. Most days, Miss de Bourgh elected to pass her unsubscribed hours at Hookham's circulating library in Bond Street. To that place she would come and go in an open carriage whenever the weather was fine, assuring her mother that she was promoting display from without, yet secure against any interposition sufficient for the examination of the intangibles within. In that borrowed sanctuary, she would pass her time reading novels, safe from her mother and society at-large, and relieved of the tedious imposition of pleasing either.

In the evenings, if the de Bourgh ladies were fortunate, of a Tuesday they would be invited to attend a private concert at one of the fashionable residences about Mayfair, occasionally thence proceeding to an assembly at another establishment of the *ton*, and, if *very* lucky, would have received a third invitation to a *soirée dansante*; the opportunity to appear on the following day with dark eyes, drooping eye-lids, and a general listlessness was not one easily denied. On Wednesdays, the scene varied from the infrequent drawing-room—or, for two weeks one year, the public rooms at Almack's—or some other less exclusive, private entertainment. Thursdays the de Bourghs attended the opera, theatre, or another *assemblée privé*. Fridays evenings were usually reserved for the Hotel Pultney, where, it was hoped, there were many unmarried men, and a great proportion of younger ones who were not too fine to dance.

In January and February, there was little to do in London, and, hence, few diversions offered in the way of private entertainments. Even those few willing to suspend their own pleasures out of deference of duty to the nation were just now returning to town. The papers had short lists of arrivals and a corresponding want of news, the most pressing items being that "the waggon carrying the goods of Lord M—— was overturned twice in going from his Surrey house down to London," or that "Lady S—— had taken an unfortunate tumble upon exiting her carriage and sprained her ancle." Even those paragons bound thither felt the need to explain their presence in so unfashionable a season:

"Oh dear, no; I never go to town in March; and at that early season, Almack's is not even named. But, this year I am much interested about a bill, which I hope will pass the House this session; and therefore, for a wonder, I will be in town 'til June." Only those punctilious about attending the House were in town, and of that illustrious portion, an even smaller share were so mutually attached to their wives that both would arrive to share the captivity of the sooty fogs and dark windows of London in winter.

All the play-houses were lamented as, "thin of company, thin of performers, thin of lights, thin of *figurantes*, thin of scene-shifters, thin of everything!" Always, however, there was the opera, should the de Bourgh ladies fail to obtain admission to a private concert. These early months, whilst securing a far greater proportion of men than ladies, afforded only a portion of the usual pleasures of the opera: the interminable wait for one's carriage in the concluding performance of the crush-room, where all of the fashionables in attendance were packed into a small antechamber to await the call of, "Lady C——'s carriage," "His Grace, the Duke of——
—— to drive off," "Sir H——'s servants are without," and other such harmonious strains shouted over the deafening din; starving above an hour where there was no food or drink to be had at any price; having one's skirts soiled, feet trampled, arms bruised by elbows and canes; ornaments caught in the finery of others in the mob; choking on the dust, and imbibing the fumes of expiring lamps and burnt-out candles, in a blowing draught of air; young ladies by the score shivering in their thin gowns, shawls uselessly arranged over only one shoulder so as to attract the notice of some exiting gentleman in the effort of a final flirtation, rendering it impossible that the man could refuse the office of handing them into their carriages (to be seen hazarding the small, wet steps unassisted was to broadcast a signal failure); the older ladies all near to expiring with the draught and cold, pleading with their daughters in weak tones from the sofas, "Please do let us leave, Sophia, the coachman has been waiting this past half-hour!"

The opera was always the destination of last resort. The name of Lady Catherine de Bourgh had been inscribed on the fans, making her subsequent object to appear only infrequently in the box, as attendance was a clear indication of having no invitation elsewhere. The de Bourgh ladies were not so charming as to be the universal first choice of company, but as there were few competitors in the lists, Lady Catherine could often contrive an invitation for some nights of the week. If this diversion failed, the ruse of particularly preferring *this* opera could provide some justification in a few extra attendances. If the performance were indifferent, the concluding ballet was usually interesting, and the diversion of watching the exquisites lounging and parading about Fop's Alley with their snuff boxes and affected lisps was always available, although at this season, they were also amongst the "thins." The dandies, having no business at the House, had—as was their practise—contrived to inveigle invitations to a succession of country houses sufficient to pass the time until one's appearance in London could be made in safety for one's reputation. The de Bourghs assiduously avoided the Green Room, the bargaining being too flagrant for the delicacy of an unmarried girl, and no charm remaining for a widow not in search of a younger man willing to exchange some portion of his freedom for the security of an income.

The crush-room was now sparse, affording hardly an injury or affront, and the opportunities for flirting and gossip were similarly circumscribed. The less-fashionables in residence employed themselves *faisant bien des riens*, making the usual purchases, visiting their usual set, walking in Hyde Park, and watching people in the Square. The Royal Institution offered lectures on various learned subjects and, for a time, the ladies of the first sets had sought a place, squeezed in amongst an hundred others of a morning, to listen with profound attention to a discourse on some difficult scientifical topic such as the Calculus or Chemical Philosophy, taking notes, and hoping to have an opportunity to display their erudition before it evaporated from their brains. The younger ladies had teachers and lessons in the mornings, whilst the older wrote letters, reviewed their visiting-books from the previous year, and paid morning calls to whomever they thought would not be offended by an early visit. If the weather were at all tolerable, a short turn in the park might be agreeable, and then maybe an afternoon call or two, and, if lucky, an invitation to stay the evening at some desirable residence after a dinner or entertainment to avoid having to go home in the wet and the dark.

In March, London was always very dull; those who had not been in town at that season were astonished at the change in a few months, and so looked forward to the future, in the hope it would not always be so, lest they be required to devise their own means to pass time. With little to do but a continuation of the previous months' synthetic industry, there was yet scarcely anyone worthy of being seen or any place of fresh interest to attend. Private dinner engagements comprised the corpus of the de Bourgh's activities, either at-home or abroad, but not one assembly was yet to be ventured upon. Lady Catherine contrived to be away from home almost every night, but such enforced employment is only slightly preferable to—or possibly less agreeable—than staying in. It was not always possible to give dinner parties and choose the company (although town was still so depopulated that one could imagine to fair certainty whom one would meet each evening); Anne and her mother would go wherever they could secure an invitation against each other's company.

At every gathering, the ladies all complained about the lack of *ton* at this season, graciously offending the other ladies present, before the weak after-thought, "Present company excepted, of course," and the gentlemen spoke of nothing but politics to other men. Amidst the meagre supply of aspirants in March, spending evenings in this manner ensured that the participants had fair claim to the title of *ton*, and, more importantly, had some reason to appear fatigued and dull, and could augment their conversations the next morning with a great many yawns, "Lady M—— said...," and "Lord W—— looked dreadful! The opposition to his bill is a great trial for his nerves. I assure you, I have never seen him in such ill-health." "I heard that Mrs. D—— actually *called* on Lady R—— at half-five, just to return her call made by mistake, and not wishing to be *uncivil!*"

By April, London was beginning to look a little more propitious, although the crush-room was not as interesting as it would be when the season was commenced; the assemblies had sufficient people to cause some general inconvenience, but the joy of not having room to stir, walk, or dance with safety was to be denied until June. When there is plenty of elbow-room from the thinness of the company, there is nothing to be said for the evening; when there is no time for conversation, everybody is fancied agreeable; and in fashionable life, the retailing of any evening to the unfortunate absentees is vastly superior to the actual event, whether chiefly consisting of complaints or commendation. Scandal is as thin as the crowd, and such insubstantial gossip as, "It was no such thing, I can assure you; for a particular friend of mine, who is extremely intimate with the nephew of a particular acquaintance of a friend of Mr. Jackson's, whose son is continually amongst that set who know everyone of any importance in the Kingdom, confidently assured me, from the most undoubted authority, Sir, that her father was a country attorney, and she had run away with a dancing-master."

During May, enough people had found their way back to London to make it tolerably gay at last. There were fine mornings to take a walk in the Park, where a few fair equestriennes mingled amongst the gentlemen on Rotten Row; others, stopt along Ladies' Mile, were busy in desultory conversation, or being witty and impertinent as required. The fashionable city assemblies, opera, theatres, routs, or what passed for pleasure in that place in that season had returned to their comfortable over-crowding, those in the mob either participating or observing an hundred little comedies, melodramas, and schemes. There is always a daughter waiting for the unapproved suitor, followed by an anxious parent; a less-anxious husband seeking to discover the trail of an inconstant wife; the impatient declaration of a successful match, with the hint in the loudest tones that "nothing is to be announced just at present"; the open flirtation in this place; weariness and "Please, let us go home now, Mamma!" in another.

The de Bourgh ladies filled their diaries with such events as, "Monday, The Opera; Tuesday, private concerts at Mrs. B—— and L. V——'s. Wednesday, dinner at the house of Lady G——, followed by an Italian singer at Lady de R——'s, where the drawing-room was a dreadful squash. Thursday, music at home, and supper at Lady M——'s; Friday, cards. Saturday, Opera. Monday, we arrived home from the ball at half-past six; we were very tired, cross, and dissatisfied. I heard that the rest of Lady G——'s party left by half-past seven, where they breakfasted before *they* went to bed. The next day was breakfast all the morning long, & very jolly *they* were; we had not been invited to stay. We had tea with Lady deF—— and heard all about it after-wards. Had a few of Lady M——'s acquaintance in for an informal supper. I had the misfortune to be seated next to a man whose conversation was as uncomfortable as his cloathes appeared to be. Thursday: Ball, arrived about nine. The ball-room was elabourately decorated, hung all-over with white Calico, which made all the ladies look dirty. 160-170 people, many men; dances were too long and too crowded, which made it unpleasant for those dancing, but I was not put to the inconvenience by being asked."

CHAP. 7.

WITH ANY NUMBER of predictably poor second sons at-hand, it may reasonably be considered wonderful that five years' time had found Anne unable to tempt even a single suitor. She was certainly prettier than her mother, and did not have the disadvantage of height to discourage some portion of the gallants. True, she was rather small and thin, but it is not an uncommon thing for a wife to be on a much smaller scale than her husband (nor, in Lady Catherine's judgement, had the contrary-wise been deemed a deterrent.) She had hair of a pretty chestnut colour, courtesy of Sir Lewis, and, although there was little of it, the deficiencies of one's own hair had long been a defect susceptible to remedy. It might be supposed to be her teeth, if an ill-favoured smile could deter the less desperate of suitors; but no, on the rare occasions when she spoke, a set of fine, even teeth could be briefly discerned by the acute. Her gowns were of the best silks and of the latest fashion, unblemished by such excessive decoration and immodesty as marked out those women whose age or poverty had made them reckless. Not a word could be uttered as to any history of impropriety, as she had never committed activity of any kind, and so was free from any suspicion of scandal. With such a catalogue of virtues as Anne possessed, what unconquerable disadvantage could endure so as to have kept her safe from even the most determined admirers for the astonishing interval of five years?

In truth, Anne's stratagem encompassed nothing more ingenious than silence. If her mother's overbearing heartlessness could be construed by society as masculine, why would invincible reserve and obstinate indifference fail to deter the greatest part of the male sex? Even the most resolute of aspirants must receive the occasional token of encouragement to maintain his campaign; thus, her plan answered every expectation of success. This method was exempt even from the censure of her mother, who could distinguish no alteration in Anne's conduct from that at Rosings, and the constancy and duration of her daughter's demeanor had long led Lady Catherine to reclassify Anne's studied silence as a becoming modesty, occasioned only by a most appropriate deference to a mother's superior judgement. It was fortuitous for Anne that her mother's expectations as to the manifold virtues necessarily comprehended in an husband worthy of the hand of Lady Catherine's daughter rendered the reserve of applicants very thin, indeed. Unsurprisingly, Anne had met no-one remaining in this highly exclusive fraternity who could shake her resolution against gambling with that minute portion of happiness that remained in a known evil and the security of a tenure that an unmarried daughter could command.

It must be remarked—in fairness—that Miss de Bourgh was more scrupulous in the exhibition of her feelings than many of the men who surrounded her. Such men laboured only to *look* the gentleman, whilst sparing themselves the inconvenience that a compatible morality would require. Their ambition encompassed only the minimal exertion required in arrogating unto themselves the right of self-adjudged superiority, despising everyone who sought honest accomplishment— dining, dressing, and cultivating ill-humour, insolence, and eccentricity to a degree unattainable by an English gentleman. The *modus operandi* of these illustrious exquisites was captured in an anecdote frequently related in the drawing-rooms of London: "In the course of the evening, the dandy told a lady a wondrous story, and upon her looking incredulous, he said vehemently, 'Upon my honour, Madam, it is true!' then added gently, 'When I say, *'Upon my honour,'* Madam, *never* believe me.'"

Anne's countenance never assumed the beautiful crossness of a young lady who finds herself seated away from a popular gentleman, sitting in a lovely state of *pique* watching others dance, or displaying a graceful *bonhomie* in making away with the lover of her friend. Anne possessed none of these superior refinements of sentiment, leaving her features to remain expressionless and impenetrable. And so, day-by-day, week-by-week, season-by-season, year-by-year, one of England's wealthiest and most advantageously connected daughters remained single. A mother of lesser determination than Lady Catherine might have despaired, or at least resolved on an alternate method for detaching her daughter, but as Lady Catherine valued tenacity in her own character to an higher degree than she comprehended as evil Anne's unmarried status, no substitute scheme could be considered.

For as long as either of the de Bourgh ladies could remember, the contest for the weekly allotment of tickets to the Wednesday balls at Almack's had produced a rivalry for the vouchers, blinding the *haut ton* and its legion pretenders with splendour and fear—in defiance of all reason—and certainly in opposition to any serious notion of salvation in the future. This judiciary decided the success or failure of all London society, and had done so by blatantly disregarding all claims to superior pretentions and interest; indeed the Ladies Patronesses declined to admit their own mothers and sisters for the inexplicable (and unexplained) epithet of *mauvais ton*. Instead, all favours were granted by those demi-gods to those supplicants as had evinced that this most desirable of spheres might retain its incomparable lustre, only if burnished by their own singular surfeits of personal merit, beauty, high fashion, graceful dancing, or exceptional wit—in short, by that ineffable blessing of *ton*. Every gentleman was required to dance for his tickets, or to remain within that temple of pre-eminence every moment in dread of eternal banishment, in favour of a more animated replacement. Young ladies without partners sat in uncomfortable chairs, in solitary mortification and pretended happiness for their luckier sisters, but could not obtain more than one evening of such desirable misery. Lovers, of all people, were to be refused: pale cheeks, sunken, black eyes, and an unhealthy thinness of form were indicative of an hopeless state of either consumption or love, and so to be rejected immediately as unsightly and—as lovers are proverbially stupid but to each other—unfashionable.

As an alternative to demand, Lady Catherine had gone so far as to appeal to every one of her acquaintance for vouchers to Almack's. Whilst known to the Lady Patronesses, Lady Catherine had never been honoured with a visit, and so could not approach that august tribunal on her own. Mr. and Mrs. Darcy had been provided with vouchers to attend, in spite of being married, but—in a singular disinclination counter to the universal opinion of all London—had no desire to attend. Their mutual description of that august assembly was that "it includes those who prefer admiration to respect, make lively conversation possessed of very little substance, humour, or taste, evince no pretentions to either education or reflection, and consist chiefly of second-hand opinions and prejudice, all masquerading as wits and philosophers." Elizabeth declared that she was quite content with the airs, folly, and conceit to be met with in the course of their usual invitations, and had no inclination to stifle in a room that—once a week—was stuffed with the quantity of bodies as the entire city of Derby; and Mr. Darcy was heard to declare that he had no pretentions to go where Wellington could not, repeating that frequent judgement, "Almack's is a system of tyranny which would never be tolerated except in a country ever-celebrated for its freedom; such complete freedom that people are at liberty to make fools of themselves." In addition to the protection of its lights from the shades of the unfashionable, the Ladies Patronesses took care to distinguish Almack's from private assemblies by providing scandalously poor refreshment, which would—in any other house—have resulted in a general condemnation as the most penurious of entertainments: a few slices of stale bread, dry cake, weak lemonade, and weaker tea was to suffice as sustenance for an entire evening of intrigue and exertion.

In general, such gentlemen as had voiced the above sentiment would perforce be found in the course of the following Wednesday, the victim of either his own wife or his own vanity. In those illuminating words of Mr. Luttrell,

> All on that magic list depends;
> Fame, fortune, fashion, lovers, friends
> 'Tis that which gratifies or vexes
> All ranks, all ages, and both sexes.
> If once to Almack's you belong,
> Like Monarchs you can do no wrong,
> But banished thence on Wednesday night,
> By Jove, you can do nothing right!

It must be hoped that the sentiments of the Darcys did not become more generally accepted, lest London lose its most irresistible attraction to bemused foreigners, grasping rustics, or the legions of would-be fashionables who would go to any length to secure admission to the assembly most calculated to expose their pretentions, and display their own inferiority.

Lady Catherine, after an unseemly series of attempts, had been successful in securing subscriptions. The blessed vouchers had been got through a connection of one of Lady S——'s family (as her own had very disagreeably not seen fit to seek the approbation of this tribunal). Ten guineas a year, and an additional 10s. a-week was sufficient to purchase the mortification of seeing Anne roundly ignored. The lights of Almack's shone in *décolleté* and rouge, knee-breeches and bicorns, and the dim presence of an unmarried girl, unwilling to speak, and in a plain (though very fine) dress could not be seen through the reflections of the

brighter

brighter stars. Lady Catherine had resolved on the maternal precaution of instructing Anne that she was never to accept any gentleman who had the effrontery to suggest a waltz or, if a quadrille, only with a gentleman of a truly unexceptional character; such an injunction was superfluous, as Anne could never be prevailed upon to dance, not even anything so safe as a reel. Less favoured ladies danced a good deal, and the only gentleman even to approach Miss de Bourgh was an infamous Bond Street lounger whose name was Stane; he desired a Lady Patroness to introduce him to a partner, stipulating, "Let her be charming!" and, as she had promised Lady Catherine that she would chuse a partner for Anne, he came scraping and lisping apace, with many flourishes and absurd sayings. Anne was vastly amused at his conceit and folly, and to her mother's horror and the Lady Patroness' boundless indignation, she declined, quoting a famous authoress with the line, "You are all kindness, Mr. Stane, but I must decline; 'I cannot approve this plan of settling partners unseen—the usual privilege the men have pleasing themselves I think far preferable, as only *one* can be dissatisfied then, but otherwise, *two* may.'" Anne's thinly veiled *ennui* had, accordingly, dealt Lady Catherine the mortification of having their subscriptions rescinded by the Ladies Patronesses after the second Wednesday, the collective wisdom of whom universally decreed that animated and attractive *behaviour*, in addition to family and fashionable dress, was *de rigueur*.

The masquerades were not to be thought of, although the censuring might have regarded such an omission as the most serious deterrent to Lady Catherine's chances of success, for a mask would have prevented any potential admirer from noticing the lack of animation of its possessor. Eventually, despite the criminal cost of a box, the elegant, extremely fashionable dress of the de Bourgh ladies could be seen regularly in the crowded tiers; one of them could be seen affecting amusement and acquaintance at the opera or the ballet.

In the wake of the failure of the illustrious Almack's to produce a suitor, Lady Catherine resorted to the desperate expedient of securing tickets for the less-fashionable, but well-attended, Argyll Rooms. Auguring no success even in this inferior quarter, Lady Catherine had written to the Chamberlain (where the credentials of her own family had been sufficient), and procured Anne an audience in that drawing-room which would secure their entrance to the unfashionable court balls, but, alas, to no avail. At the court balls, the reigning lights were not those who comprised the *ton*, but those of merely superior pretentions to birth, title, and unblemished respectability. The supplication to the tribunal of Almack's had at least been of a temporary nature; the widow of a mere knight, or even the daughter of an Earl, was of minor consequence at court, and every attendance was a trial for Lady Catherine's ideas of her own consequence. She had the collateral mortification of seeing Anne slighted in favour of young ladies with only the claims of birth, and as much beauty as bright eyes, a smiling face, and the attraction of a general wish to please and be pleased, is generally comprised.

CHAP. 8.

AT LONG LAST, Colonel Fitzwilliam's regiment was returned from the Continent. It had been above two years since he had last secured leave, and he spent his few weeks' leisure in Derbyshire. Colonel Fitzwilliam had, therefore, not paid his annual visit to Rosings for several years, as was long his custom. These visits were necessarily not so pleasant as formerly, occurring now, as they must, without Darcy's companionship. By an implicit mutual understanding, the Colonel's company without Mr. Darcy was not so agreeable to Lady Catherine, so his visits had been correspondingly shortened in duration, following the Darcys' marriage. As he had long been in the habit of attending upon his aunt each year, the Colonel's honourable nature would not admit of a complete amendment arising solely from a loss of pleasure to himself. Accordingly, he went to Rosings at an early opportunity with the conviction that a labour sooner undertaken is a labour sooner done.

A naturally more patient man than his cousin, Mr. Darcy, Colonel Fitzwilliam bore Lady Catherine's obtrusiveness and his cousin Anne's obmutescence with better philosophy, and hence better grace. Within a few days of his arrival at Rosings, Lady Catherine would abridge her instructions for his welfare to not more than three or four an hour, and Miss de Bourgh might proffer a few vapid remarks if Lady Catherine should happen to be momentarily absent. In the first instance, Colonel Fitzwilliam's very existence without such constant instruction was nothing short of wonderful, given his occupation as a military man; and in the second, it required the cunning of Ulysses and the strength of Atlas to produce the shortest of speeches from Anne, and these transitory rewards were delivered with neither information nor sensibility. The officiousness of his aunt had become too common-place to be wondered at, but Miss de Bourgh's inalterable habit of lapsing into a steadfast silence the moment Lady Catherine reappeared—regardless of the state of any proceeding conversation—never ceased to surprise the Colonel, who considered such behaviour as singular well past the point of incivility. More than once did Colonel Fitzwilliam compare his two cousins, concluding that one lady was silent from her great desire to please, whilst the other from her equally strong desire *not* to please.

One evening soon after his arrival, upon their finding themselves sitting alone after supper, Lady Catherine addressed him thus:

"Well, George, 'tis a dreadful business about Darcy, but as they *are* married, I suppose there is nothing to be done about it now. I have long been resigned to the disgrace attending this deplorable alliance but, as you know, my sympathy is never directed toward my own complaints. However, Anne yet suffers the disappointment attending Darcy's selfish violation of all claims of honour and duty due his family, an affliction I do not intend to brook any longer. As *my* first duty is to my daughter, I must no longer suspend decision as to the best alternate course for her happiness. These five years are now passed without any change in Anne's inclination to marriage, and it occurs to me, as the most sensible—indeed, as the only acceptable alternative—that I should give my consent to your marriage with my daughter. To be sure, you have no fortune and, therefore, no prospect of marriage with anyone of her rank and situation in life. Her beauty and person are superior, her accomplishments unsurpassed, and as my daughter, she would be a match far above any you could hope to make without the benefit of the interest which, as a younger son, you are unlikely to receive."

Colonel Fitzwilliam was taken entirely by surprise and could only stare with unaffected astonishment as she continued,

"In considering your own recommendations, I know your disposition to be good, and your family excellent. My own observation leads me to conclude that, as Anne cannot be the wife of Mr. Darcy, to become the wife of Colonel Fitzwilliam is not a situation to be regretted or otherwise looked upon as exceptional in any way; to be sure, there is a great disparity in fortune, which—in these times—is nothing very wonderful."

Colonel Fitzwilliam had coloured deeply during this last volley, making every attempt to keep his composure and recall the courtesy due his aunt, despite her being, in the present situation, little deserving of any such civil consideration. At the earliest pause, he quietly but firmly replied, "Indeed, Ma'am, you do me too much honour. As we are both aware, my low prospects as the younger son are not such that Miss de

Bourgh's birth or person should merit. Whilst I am not insensible of the compliment of your proposal, I must decline out of deference to my regard for Miss de Bourgh."

"Nonsense!" exclaimed Lady de Bourgh. "Whilst Anne is doubtless one of the most favoured of her sex, she is approaching an age when it is desirable to have her well-married. And, I am convinced that she could do much worse," said Lady Catherine in a rare moment of compliment abroad. "In addition to being a close relation, your modesty tells me you are sensible of your good fortune in securing such a wife. Therefore, we may consider the matter as settled."

Even the easy temper of Colonel Fitzwilliam was sorely tried by this latest affront, and he could hardly keep his mind and countenance calm as she continued, "All that remains, Colonel Fitzwilliam, is for you to inform your father. He and I shall meet, and everything quickly settled. I should think you might be married without any material delay."

"Indeed, Lady Catherine," cried Colonel Fitzwilliam, "your persistence after my reply is astonishing. Whilst I have no doubt that my esteemed parents would regard an alliance with Miss de Bourgh as in every way desirable, indeed, I must beg leave to decide my own feelings, to say nothing of the consideration which is due those of Miss de Bourgh, and her own views as to what course best constitutes her future happiness."

Lady Catherine now dropt any veneer of civility and, in a quite different tone of voice, responded, "Fitzwilliam you surprise me exceedingly. I should have thought that a man of your sense and experience in the world could properly credit the opportunity of such a connection."

"It is precisely the contrary, Lady Catherine: a man of sense and experience must be guided by his own judgement as to what constitutes his happiness, and mine is not to be directed by you or anyone else on this point. I will add, especially when this officiousness comes in the form of great imposition and insult to my own feelings, *and* most probably those of Miss de Bourgh."

"Fitzwilliam," said Lady Catherine, "you greatly mistake me. I did not call you here to enquire..."

Colonel Fitzwilliam could bear no more, and interrupted her with some warmth. "Ma'am, this application, in any form, is extraordinary, indeed. You say that your daughter has been long disinclined to marry. Would your approval of our marriage necessarily change her preference for being single? I have known Miss de Bourgh all of her life and have never once been honoured by any mark of distinction or esteem in her behaviour. Even *were* I to give my consent, would that make her consent more probable? In addition, I know not whether Miss de Bourgh might have consented to an union with our cousin. In any case, her acceptance of me—as a substitute—must make a poor basis for marriage, *if* she would accept me. No man would willingly stand in for another in such a case; the disappointed hopes of one and the declared inferiority of the other must render any chance for happiness wholly impossible."

"Fitzwilliam, unlike yourself, Anne knows her duty to me and will do it. She will rely upon my judgement," declared Lady Catherine, rising to her full height and speaking in accents of uncommon *hauteur*.

Colonel Fitzwilliam now stood and, picking up his gloves, replied, "Even if this is so, Aunt, I should never wish to marry wholly out of duty; nor would I wish any such sacrifice for my wife," replied Colonel Fitzwilliam, every feature marking his disdain for Lady Catherine's insolence in continuing to press the subject.

"Fitzwilliam, in *your* case it is more than duty. It is *interest*. As Darcy has refused the claims of family and friends, it is incumbent upon *you* to keep the fortune of Miss de Bourgh from being estranged from the Fitzwilliam line."

"If that is Your Ladyship's chief consideration," replied the Colonel with evident disgust, "I wonder you do not chuse my brother for this honour. With that expedient, you would preserve both the fortune and the title!"

Lady Catherine paused for a few moments and appeared to select her own reply with unusual care, and with a somewhat softer tone and an attempt at a smile continued, "George, you greatly mistake me. I have only the happiness of my daughter as my object. Pecuniary considerations must and will always take a second place. Your brother has the title, yes, but I judge your character to be the superior; your habits are unexceptional and your actions have always been those of a gentleman and a prudent man. A mother would always wish to see her daughter the wife of a respectable man."

"You mean to say, Madam," said Colonel Fitzwilliam angrily, "that you estimate my character to be more tractable than my brother's, that I am weak and malleable, and that you are, therefore, more likely to succeed in obtaining my consent. I assure you that I am neither so weak nor so malleable that my own future happiness is to be auctioned in this manner. Lady Catherine, I well understand that, as the second son, I must give some consideration as to fortune when and where I chuse to connect myself. I am, however, yet quite far from seeing my own prospects so blasted as to require the services of another in finding a wife, especially one who uses insult and offense to both parties as justification for interference."

"Fitzwilliam," cried Lady Catherine, "do you, then, absolutely refuse to marry my daughter?"

"Yes, Lady Catherine, I do. And allow me to say further that both the motive *and* the method with which this injudicious campaign has been waged has relieved me of any distress as may be comprehended in my refusal that I must otherwise have felt in your disappointment, or in any unintended disrespect for Miss de Bourgh. Pray give my regrets to Miss de Bourgh on not taking my leave personally, and my sincere wishes for her happiness. My refusal to accede to this preposterous plan is my best assurance for her being ever so."

With the briefest of bows, Colonel Fitzwilliam turned and quitted both the scene and, within the hour, Rosings.

C H A P . 9 .

COLONEL FITZWILLIAM'S father was the brother of Lady Catherine de Bourgh and Lady Anne Darcy, and thus the uncle of the present Mr. Darcy. Lord Hallendale had been the ideal son and heir in his younger life, giving an unusually small portion of the manifold anxieties which fall to the lot of over-fond mothers and fathers of sons, save in only one instance: that of his being so removed from the usual pursuits of young men of fortune and title, that he should never stir far enough from the family hearth to find a wife. Indeed, he had gone from Derbyshire up to University with his customary quiet cheerfulness, distinguished himself neither as a scholar nor as a rake, and returned to the parental abode just as agreeably as he had left it, and just as single.

His Lordship was a man of uncommon ability and intense energy when his mind was drawn to an interesting topic, regrettably united with an habitual lethargy of temperament that limited his achievement and advancement in the world. His sole passion was rocks, or, more precisely, the study of the various minerals and examples of stones as were to be found throughout the Kingdom and the world; his energies as a child— and now as a man—were in pursuit of new specimens for his collection and any new-written book upon the science. With the exceptions of family suppers and the occasional claims of the neighbourhood which his mother—in her natural occupation as teacher of those gentle accomplishments which mark good-breeding—would insist upon his attending with her, his cabinet had always been the first occupation of his morning and his principal companion throughout the day. His business at-home was comprised in writing to his brother collectors, enquiring, buying, and comparing; his pleasures in town encompassed the various societies of scientifical gentlemen, and his custom to one particular merchant who dealt in specimens of the highest quality.

The Viscount was a curious admixture of parts. His father had, without success, long wearied of trying to interest his son in the usual pursuits of a gentleman: hunting, fishing, and attending to the plantations and farms which comprised the family estates. Whilst it is not to be imagined that His Lordship actually wished for the more typical anxieties of a parent—gaming, duels, drunkenness, and the other regular pastimes of the sons of the neighbouring gentry—his inability to understand the occupation which so wholly engrossed his only son was a source of daily disappointment. His wife's chief occupations were to soften the displeasure of the father, and, if unwilling to steer her son into more manly employments, to ensure that his conversation was pleasing, his cloathing presentable, and his manners unexceptional, so as to render him fit for the society of gentlemen and, more particularly, gentle ladies.

His Countess, actuated as she was by love and not disgust, was also more likely to see success. She had an additional advantage: the neighbourhood was sufficiently generous as to encompass several families of quality, some with eligible daughters. Her son was found to be generally agreeable to all the neighbourhood, regardless of sex; however, it was not within the power of the most discerning observer to impute his partiality to any one of its daughters, owing simply to their being none. Her Ladyship at length grew discouraged in the pursuit and spoke to her husband:

"My Lord," she began one evening as they were sitting at the supper table, their son having already removed to his study.

"Yes, my love?"

"We have been to the Duttons' this day."

"Yes, and they are well?"

"Quite," replied his wife, "but our visit was for naught, I fear."

"Oh?" her husband enquired, catching instantly her meaning.

"Yes, their eldest daughter, Celia, would be a good match for Charles, as amiable and quiet as he, but he does not chuse to prefer her, or indeed any of these young ladies who could make him a good wife. I begin to despair of finding any young lady to rival rocks in his affections."

"I am wholly of your opinion, my dear," said the Earl, "but what are we to do? I hesitate to begin by forcing his choice in such a matter."

"Yes, my Lord," she replied, "but consider that he is now turned nine-and-twenty, and there are several eligible girls within our immediate acquaintance. In two or three years, his indecision will exhaust the small number of suitable young women who will, in any event, have chosen elsewhere. I understand and respect the delicacy which attends the matter, but I should be grateful if you would find a convenient time to speak with him—as his father—about his duty to the title, and the need to make his choice whilst there are eligible daughters near-by from which to chuse. These girls are from known, respectable families who will settle the daughters' shares generously. I dislike the necessity of putting the matter in such mercenary terms, but as an only son, he cannot be in doubt as to the necessity of his marrying. It may happen, that, in waiting too long to chuse a wife, a man will lose the chance of an heir."

And so it was that the Earl, at the first opportunity, spoke with his son on the delicate topic. Far from being resentful of the interference or contrary in receiving the hint, the Viscount was, to the astonishment of his parents, completely unawares that the unceasing round of visits amongst the neighbouring families had been for any purpose other than keeping his mother company.

"Indeed, father," the Viscount replied, "you must believe that I would never wish to give either of my esteemed and affectionate parents the slightest cause for uneasiness; I have been selfish and inattentive, despite the trouble and goodness of your endeavours to securing my happiness, for which I apologise with all my heart."

The Earl, who was at-heart an affectionate father, upon seeing the genuine distress the revelation had caused his son, earnestly began to wish he had never opened the subject. His son, whilst oblivious to the long passage of time that had occasioned the crisis, was nonetheless expeditious in its remedy. After consulting with his parents as to their inclination, and ascertaining which of the young ladies under study was most certain to promote his happiness, he set about his courtship of the chosen specimen with the enthusiasm customarily reserved for his other, less animate pursuits. The Lady Celia was a young lady of title, suitably pretty, suitably named, and suitably unmarried. An agreement was quickly reached between the fathers, and the church register, wedding-breakfast, and wedding-cloathes consigned to their various states of completion; the new Viscountess settled into the wing of the Earl's house from which her husband had ridden to the church. The arrangement was an uncommon example of parental solicitude and filial duty wonderfully united for the happiness of all parties. The Viscount was allowed to return to his rocks, and his quiet little wife to her books and drawings, albeit with the singular change that Lord Hallendale's study now had *two* silent occupants for much of the day.

Despite any general supposition by anyone who knew the habits of the couple to the contrary, the Viscount and his wife were, within the course of just over a year, in expectation of the much looked-for heir. The heir was duly delivered, and within the space of two further years, the addition of another little boy blessed the family. The joy, which usually attends such events, was most tragically abbreviated when Lady Celia, shortly after the birth, contracted a violent fever and died. The care of his children was necessarily consigned to his lady mother, and to all outward appearances, with the exception of the children, Lady Celia might never have existed. If the Viscount attended his cabinet even more diligently in the months after the death of his wife, the simple explanation was that he was grown accustomed to her quiet presence in the hours of his day, and missed her a great deal more than was generally imagined. The years passed with no change other than the Viscount became the Earl, a distinction not likely to be perceived by his closest associates—his cabinets.

The new Lord Hallendale had been in regular contact with a seller of a great variety of stone specimens and mineral books in London over the long course of years spent acquiring his collection. The rock-seller had been content that, upon his own decease, his daughter should inherit his business, she having for many years sufficed for his assistant, agent, book-keeper, and clerk. This daughter had not only acquired an uncommonly thorough knowledge of the minerals her father collected for sale, but managed the concern successfully, in that those gentlemen who had previously favoured his establishment with their custom had no occasion to complain of either the quantity or quality of objects which continued to be offered for their consideration. She, in that capacity, had occasion to correspond regularly with the Earl, and to meet with and shew him any new acquisitions whenever the Earl would journey to London for that purpose, which he now did with increasing frequency. At some time, the purpose of his visits became as much to see the lively, dark-eyed proprietress with the merry wit and agreeable conversation, as the contents of her ware-house.

If the Viscount had been amenable to follow the inclinations of his parents in the choice of his first wife, the Earl's feelings were so materially different, that he sought no-one's opinion other than his own in his choice of a second. His Lordship had no interest in running the affairs of his estate, as he had left the small portion of any such activity to his father; the estates continued unchecked in their certain decline, left solely to the care of a London attorney and a negligent steward. The

Earl's successful solicitation of the hand of the shop-keeper's daughter gained him, in the bargain, not only a capable superintendent, but the entirety of her father's collection, as well. In due course, the new Lady Hallendale was installed in Lord Hallendale's study, along with her father's best cabinets.

What the public may have felt upon the Earl's remarriage may be left to the reader's conjecture. Lord Hallendale had not, as might be considered customary in such a case, married a shop-keeper's daughter principally to disoblige his own family, but simply to please himself. In forsaking the opportunity to acquire a wife of birth and fortune, which his rank would otherwise dictate, the Earl had chosen a woman of sound intelligence and education, and one who had abilities which would make her even more valuable to him in the management of his estates than she had with her dowry of rocks. Society in general does not find favour with any influence of women outside the domestic sphere; however, as in the choice of his wife, the Earl was more inclined to prefer his own judgement to that of the world at-large.

Early in their marriage, Lord and Lady Hallendale had reached an agreement as unusual as it was practical; namely, that Lady Hallendale should cease her employment at her father's business and resume a somewhat similar occupation at the home of her husband, for the mutually beneficial purpose of emending the management of her husband's estates. Indeed, Lady Hallendale was genuinely grateful that she had talents which might, in some measure, balance the increase in her comforts and consequence attendant upon her marriage and would, she sincerely hoped, be regarded by her husband—even if condemned by society—as atonement for any disparity in her birth and fortune to that of her lord. Her habits of careful attention and intelligent application to matters of business were as necessary and as valued by her husband as they had been by her own father. Happily she applied herself to the oversight and improvement of the Hallendale estates with a diligence and care that had not been seen for many generations.

Appearing down-stairs, several hours before Lord Hallendale arose in the morning, she would use the quietness of the early hours to review the receipts and reports of the house-steward, and answer letters of business, as well as attend to the lot of domestic details that normally fall to the mistress of a large estate. Every fine morning, she would drive in her small Phaeton to inspect some distant part of the estate; in inclement weather, she would walk through the home farms, speaking with the servants, and viewing the order and industry of the

dairy

dairy, game-larder, still-room, &c. Lord Hallendale would later attend his Lady in the offices, where she would present, for his signature, the various letters and petitions. Lord Hallendale would approve these solemnly as though he had some knowledge of their content, and, when the house-steward appeared, his Lady would give instructions to him, all invariably prefaced by, "His Lordship desires. . ." Apart from this daily charade, Lord Hallendale might return to his rocks, his mind and conscience relieved of the obtrusions of every-day life, his house kept, his estates productive, and his hearth-side shared with his fond wife in the mutual pursuit of ever-more interesting articles for his cabinets.

And, whatever may be generally understood to be the consequences of such a choice for the children of the first marriage, Lady Hallendale proved to be an unusually good mother to the two boys, in that she was genuinely solicitous of their health and their happiness. Lord Hallendale had sent the boys off to school as soon as they reached a suitable age, and to University thereafter. On holidays, when the boys were at home, they found their new mother to have easy, kindly ways, and always willing to leave aside the rent-books or other business to take up those duties that more commonly fall within a mother's sphere. Apart from the early loss of their mother, neither boy had any cause for unhappiness, and none at all that could rightfully be imputed to their father's second choice. On the contrary, William and especially the younger son, George, found Lady Hallendale to be more ready with her time and attention than ever their own father had been, and this even though—as is most often the case—she had more claims upon the hours of her day. The Viscount's character was more inured to the preoccupied neglect of his father, and he was like-wise of an age when it was unfashionable for boys to be guided by a mother; the younger son's warm heart and gentle temper inclined each to the other—she as teacher, play-mate, and confidante, and he as a companion for that portion of each day, and often whole days altogether, when His Lordship was busy with his scientifical societies or otherwise engaged away from home. The man George Fitzwilliam was genuinely fond of his step-mother, and found occasion to return to Hallendale House more frequently than might otherwise be the case at his time of life.

Mrs. Darcy, too, liked Lady Hallendale. In her she found a woman of sense and use, and one whose penchant for uncommon domestic arrangements was parallel with her own. She greatly admired not only Her Ladyship's skill with matters of the estate, but the delicate diplomacy through which she spared the feelings of her husband in the discharge of those duties. Her servants treated her with respect and something more—affection. Elizabeth could not impute such attachments as owing to any other cause than Lady Hallendale's kind and grateful treatment of themselves. Elizabeth longed to be held in such esteem at Pemberley, respected and admired for her own merits, not just as mistress and wife. She genuinely wished to be useful to her husband—perhaps not to the degree occupied by Lady Hallendale—but to make some contribution, if only to increase the hours of leisure her husband might be spared away from his own necessary employments.

Elizabeth had long suspected Lady Hallendale of being an Hebrew; her name, Sarah, diminutive size, colouring, quick intelligence, and inclination to business naturally predisposed conjecture in that direction, but certainly did not decide the question. Whatever might have been her early habits, it was certain that Lady Hallendale never missed Sunday service, appeared sincere in her devotions, and was responsible for any such influence on her step-sons; to the extent that they received any serious instruction, it certainly proceeded from that source. The Earl, being of a scientifical persuasion, was never wont to spare time away from his own studies to attend to the religious education of his sons. Elizabeth could find no reason to declare Lady Hallendale irreligious or otherwise exceptional, whatever may have been the practise of her family, but remained undecided and unaccountably curious.

On one of Elizabeth's visits to Lady Hallendale, she one day felt secure enough of their friendship to introduce the delicate question. Upon Elizabeth's enquiry as to the faith of Lady Hallendale's family, Her Ladyship replied with a laugh and a sly smile,

"Oh Lizzy, my Lizzy, your penetration is not to be denied! You are right to regard me with suspicion; my father was indeed a member of the Jewish faith, or an Hebrew, as you would call it. However, my mother was born a member of your church, the Church of England. And, in this case, convenience met necessity, as—in my father's religion—one's mother determines the faith of the children, not the father, as in your tradition. Therefore, to a Jew, I cannot be a Jew, and am so neither by training nor inclination. I have attended Christian services since I was able to walk, my mother and father dividing my education such that my mother superintended my spiritual studies, and my father taught me from his scientifical books. There, have I accounted for my unusual ancestry and hope that you are now comfortable on this issue."

Elizabeth could only reply in an embarrassed way that she had never suspected Lady Hallendale of any disingenuity with regards to her faith, and the subject was never raised again.

Seeing Elizabeth's remaining confusion of spirits, Lady Hallendale continued in a soft tone, "It may be that the success of the unusual arrangement between my beloved father and myself made me sufficiently bold to adopt the present arrangement out of respect for His Lordship's talents and the pleasures he finds in his studies, and my natural willingness to undertake for my husband no more than I assumed to ease the burthens on my dear father. I am blessed to have learnt a few simple lessons which enable me to even partially repay His Lordship's kindness and generosity to myself."

Elizabeth could not oppose such modesty and felt that the true degree of Lady Hallendale's exertions toward the restoration of the Hallendale estates, daily providing a more dependable future for Lord Hallendale and his sons, might well go unknown to anyone but herself, and, perhaps Mr. Darcy.

CHAP. 10.

ELIZABETH OFTEN FOUND a reason to visit her aunt and uncle Hallendale, especially when Mr. Darcy was called away on some matter of business, and regarded Lady Sarah as ample compensation for the vexation occasioned by her acquisition of the other of Mr. Darcy's aunts, Lady Catherine. Elizabeth was not business-minded, but appreciated the large rôle the Countess had appropriated to herself in the management of the Hallendale estates. Her Ladyship was invariably to be found sitting of a morning before the large mahogany bureau in the estate office, across from the great field maps, torn and brown from years of use. She would come down before the others to work in her day-gown, a shawl about her shoulders, her curly, dark hair under a cap more off than on, surrounded by a sea of account-books and papers. Invariably, she would greet Elizabeth with a smile and an invitation to sit with her, if she were at leisure. Lizzy was well aware that any leisure in the present case was her own, and so attempted to pass through the offices on her way to breakfast, and stopt only long enough to wish Lady Hallendale a good morning.

"Lizzy, pray do sit down and visit with me. These papers have no end, so I may as well indulge myself in a little pleasure," replied Her Ladyship. "Lord Hallendale is gone to view some specimens recently come from America, and is likely to be gone the whole day. Are you finding your stay pleasant, my dear?"

Elizabeth replied in the affirmative, glancing about at the papers, littering Lady Sarah's desk, and tumbling from the various drawers and pigeon-holes of the estate cabinet behind her, open, shut, and in some attitude in-between, each with labels for receipts, notes and bills, writing papers, &c., all seeming to be ready to start an avalanche, which would easily be capable of burying her small person entirely.

The sheaves of paper appeared in no regular system, but Lady Sarah moved amongst the various deposits and drawers with a method and an assurance Elizabeth could only wonder at. Elizabeth asked what occupied her aunt this morning.

"Mostly letters of business, I am afraid, which are rather tedious, but which must be answered. Here," she said, pointing to a leaning tower of sheets, "is the pile of letters that have already been seen to and simply require my Lord's approval, and these here," indicating a sheaf of similar stature, "are hitherto unanswered correspondence which I have promised myself I will work through this morning before I allow myself the pleasure of unpacking the latest parcel of minerals we have got, and getting them labelled up in time for my Lord's return this evening."

Lizzy laughed, "I would be most pleased to assist you if I could be of any use this morning. You have set yourself a most challenging objective, and, selfishly, I worry that I will not see you at all to-day unless I can persuade you to accept the pleasure of my hindrance to your progress." Whilst wishing to be of use to her aunt, Lizzy's unstated motive was to understand those portions of Lady Hallendale's business that could be most easily learnt. By this expedient, Elizabeth's plan was to learn what she could to relieve Mr. Darcy of the most mundane of his labours, which for one reason or another could not be passed-off to the house-steward, the land steward, or the bailiff. Lady Hallendale gladly acquiesced, giving Elizabeth the employment of adding up a sheet of ledger sums, and copying several receipts into a more coherent hand in the large leather estate-book. As the two women worked together, Lady Hallendale, who had only infrequent opportunity of female companionship, relieved her feelings a little as she discussed with her friend the complete difference in characters of her two step-sons, Viscount Dunfield and Colonel Fitzwilliam.

"I cannot pretend that Lord Hallendale is not hurt by the treatment he receives at the hands of his elder son. William is constantly getting himself into one scrape after another, and is grown very wild ever since he returned from school. We thought that time might settle him, but he is become more heedless than ever, and seems entirely unimproved by the advantages which education should afford a young man. Perhaps he has had to bear too little responsibility in his life as the eldest son, for his disposition is far more spoilt than George's, who is always very steady. I tell you—in confidence—that I have ventured so far as to hint to Lord Hallendale that an improvement is unlikely if he does not cease supporting his elder son in so generous a fashion, for George asks for a very little, and can certainly receive little in comparison. This must be a severe trial, indeed, when we can all discern how the Viscount unconcernedly spends all he is given and probably, quite probably, even more. It seems unfair that it is the fate of younger sons to make their own way in the world, watching the elder one as he receives every advantage."

"I agree the fate of younger brothers is unfair," replied Elizabeth, "but what of the fates of daughters? It seems to me that we receive no advantage at all, and are destined for a life of certain dependence. I have not forgotten the entailment of Longbourn away from my family, to be bestowed instead upon a distant cousin whose only claim was his sex. When I was single, I was unreasonably intolerant of my mother's preoccupation with our marrying well, believing it only avarice and the employment of an unenlarged mind; I now understand her fears, and honour her all the more for them. Few women are as lucky as we, Lady Sarah, to find ourselves married to such rare men as are able to value women for our true merits—not only our faces—and encourage us. The fate of many women is to marry for security's sake, or—even worse—to remain unhappily single, and thus forced to endure society's scorn *and* poverty as they attempt to get their own living in whichever manner they are able, and often with children to feed as well."

"Of course you are right, Lizzy. If Lord Hallendale had not made me an offer all these years ago, I would have continued as a shop-keeper's daughter and never as a shop-keeper. I can know this and still feel immense gratitude to my father for leaving me the means to earn a respectable living, even though I could not then have imagined a quarter of the freedoms and pleasures which I daily take for granted. I have long felt that we, who enjoy more than our share of blessings, owe it to those less fortunate women to be diligent in improving our own natural talents, and promoting our usefulness in every way possible."

Elizabeth reflected on Lady Sarah's words, as she copied a bill for some mending into the page of Lady Hallendale's receipt-book, feeling that she was disappointing those many women of mean existence.

"Certainly there are women who are granted opportunity, but lack the abilities to exercise it? The running of an estate such as Pemberley is simply beyond my power, as I quickly learnt upon marrying. I am not a great organiser, and find no pleasure in instructing others. House-keeping comes naturally to some women, but not to me. I seem as hopeless of remedy as of use!"

"Your view is only too narrow, my dear," said Her Ladyship, as she reached across the desk to pat Elizabeth's hand affectionately. "Women need not be confined to the house. You will find that you have talents elsewhere. Darcy's estate is large and has many dependencies, but it is not incapable of improvement. The village does not, for example, boast a trade-school—an enterprise which would generate a great deal of good if someone were sufficiently energetic and apperceptive to formulate and carry out a plan for its institution."

Elizabeth immediately realised the merit of the idea, and further, all of the gratification as would attend the fruition of such a creditable improvement to her husband's estate and its tenantry. Yet above any selfish ambition for her own pleasure, she ardently wished to be as necessary in her husband's concerns as in his leisure. Certainly, Elizabeth had no inclination for a life of drudgery and self-denial; she was nearly as resolute in refusing an existence free from any larger responsibility. The improvement of mind, she thought, made possible by a continued and regular exertion for the general welfare, was an estimable ambition. In the next instant, she apprehended that Lady Sarah's indispensability was not a *part* of her happy marriage, it was, in some measure, both the cause and the effect of the congenial intercourse and mutual interests of the Hallendales. Elizabeth was very happy, very blessed, and—of all women—had no cause to repine. Yet, she now comprehended that the self-appropriation of some portion of her husband's—and Georgiana's—daily discharge of the obligations conferred by the blessings of comfort and privilege was the the surest plan for increasing her own extraordinary sources of happiness.

She resolved to discuss the possibility of a trade-school with Mr. Darcy. Later that day, however, she realised—to her shame—that Georgiana and Lady Hallendale, with their habits of steady application, were far more suited to the their rôles as help-mate than she. Not for the first time, she recognised a similarity between Lady Sarah and Georgiana, and discerned with a mixed satisfaction that she was so fortunate herself as to be surrounded by such friends as were too fond to see her faults. This was chusing well indeed! Undaunted by success, Elizabeth was in earnest to undertake the labour which attended the business of founding a trade-school, if her husband felt it to be of advantage to the poor of their area of Derbyshire. Lizzy, however content with her chosen lot in life, was resolved not to be downcast or defeated, and meant to speak with her husband about such a school of industry for the village, especially in light of his plans for the new cottages, as soon as she was returned to Pemberley. A school-building could be added with considerable

advantage

advantage to the plan, she thought. If her friends could not provide the necessary censure to confute her own accustomary idleness, she resolved to undertake both the change of habitude and the industry itself.

"Mr. Darcy," began Elizabeth as they met the following evening at supper, "Lady Hallendale and I were discussing the merits of a trade-school in the village. I would find great gratification in such an employment, first undertaking to study what has been done to advantage elsewhere. I am confident of the merit of Lady Hallendale's suggestion and your very reasonable reliance upon my genius to venture such an improvement along-side your plans for the new tenants' cottages. Do you find the idea interesting?"

"Much more than interesting, Elizabeth, it is laudable. I only wonder why such an idea has not come to our thinking before this."

Elizabeth replied, "As I now become a true proficient upon the subject—having studied for the entirety of this afternoon—I believe it probable that we are well-situated as to the neighbourhood where such a school of industry could be of great utility in improving the prospects of the poor." Elizabeth was scrupulous in imputing the idea—now that she was sure of her husband's approbation—to Lady Sarah, and re-iterated her own willingness to assist Mr. Darcy in the school's establishment and proper operation. Darcy was visibly delighted, but expressed his only reticence that, lest Elizabeth find such an undertaking to be more demanding upon her time and energies than she reckoned, perhaps Georgiana or Lady Hallendale would be amenable in assisting with the plan.

"My dearest, you quite mistake the matter," said Elizabeth with an unusually grave air. "It is precisely because I am ashamed of what I do *not* do, compared with your own exertions and the useful employments undertaken by your sister and your aunt, that I have given myself at least so much trouble as to *contemplate* what endeavour might lay within my limited sphere of usefulness."

Darcy looked at Elizabeth with a gentle scepticism and again reminded her of the amount of time and effort which such an undertaking would require. Elizabeth very thoughtfully replied that she would willingly compound for the necessary trouble, if she were assured that he would view the school as a beneficial addition to the new plan for the village. That it should be necessary to give an explanation for her attention to this undertaking was exceedingly awkward—Oh! How heartily did she now wish that she had compounded more diligently with Georgiana for some share in the house-keeping!—Elizabeth assured him earnestly and solemnly that she truly wished to be useful. Lest he be overwhelmed by the extent of her ambition, she concluded by smiling and saying, "It would be a great boon to my already prodigious conceit to walk about the building, pointing to 'what great improvement here,' and 'that stamp of genius over there.' It may be that your great improvers will choose to write about *my* building, in time!"

"Lizzy," he responded gently, "I think you could do anything you would attempt well, indeed, but there are many things to consider and much to decide. This is not a simple undertaking, but one which, I believe, would require more application than you anticipate. The design and construction of the buildings in themselves is not the most onerous portion of the scheme; the successful administration of the school thereafter is a never-ending labour, and one that would require considerable effort for many years. We live in a time of great change— of industry and of the skilled labour requisite for such industry; even if we should succeed in finding an able master, I think that we must necessarily be involved to some degree to ensure that the school maintain its usefulness and value to the parish. Is that what you wish?"

"I can readily believe that you discount my willingness to give myself *any* trouble at all, much less survive such a prodigious and prolonged undertaking, but the fact remains, Mr. Darcy, that you must attend to such immortal matters every day, and have for many years. As your wife, I have willingly engaged for at least a share of your exertions, however little suited to my indolent nature, or my poor example of such self-employment in the past," replied Elizabeth. "Your doubt is very reasonable, but in this case, ill-founded. I mean to be a full partner in such an endeavour, if you will but chuse both the project and the partner."

"I believe that my choice was made long ago for the partner of the bargain, but I should be delighted to have such a beautiful and capable accomplice for the *project*," said Mr. Darcy, smiling, as he rose to move her chair. As they walked to the library, Elizabeth smiled to herself at such an unanticipated end to her communication, and diligently set to work on the business of the trade-school.

Elizabeth had often paused at the portraits of the late Mr. Darcy and his wife, Lady Anne. Mr. Darcy's father's face was one of penetrating eyes, and an active, intelligent countenance. She did not appear as tall as her husband—that was likely the influence of the Fitzwilliam side, if Lady Catherine were an indication—but an English gentleman of the most respectable stamp—distinguished, attentive, confident, and straight as the great oak that could be seen through the window in the portrait. She could trace more of his features in

Georgiana than in her own Mr. Darcy, but in his eyes and the set of his jaw and mouth, Elizabeth could read his pride, and the habits of business and occupation: the prosperity of his family, his tenantry, and his fields. It was a countenance of purpose, but not likely one much given to pleasantries or mirth. He was wearing a simple buff coat—but not otherwise in the habit of a sportsman—over well-made, useful *English* cloathing for the out-of-doors. He was standing by a table, which Elizabeth recognised as the great reading table in the library, with an open volume before him: a book of columns and figures—not a tradesman's account-book, but a listing probably of the fruits or fields in the plantations and their bounty. Elizabeth had often seen her husband carrying similar volumes as he inspected the home farms.

To Elizabeth, Lady Anne appeared tall and angular, with a startling impression of resemblance to Lady Catherine. Upon a closer study of the face, Elizabeth could perceive a kindness and a gentleness that would never have occurred to the latter. Her hair was darker than Lady Catherine's, and she had the same gray-blue eyes; however, in Lady Catherine's face, those eyes had a cold, steely look about them, but in Lady Anne's visage, they were a soft sky colour, and added to the warmth of their neighbouring cheeks and lips. She was also dressed for the out-of-doors, in a gown of pale blue silk, and a straw bonnet decorated with a few small blossoms about the crown, and affixed to her head with long blue ribbands. She carried a basket of flowers and—to Elizabeth's initial astonishment, fruits and vegetables!—with an air of elegance and pleasure. This was a partnership, indeed! How far removed from Lady Catherine's useless officiousness! Mr. Darcy's mother was, judging from the *accessoires de portrait* she had chosen, evidently wishing to be remembered as her husband's pendant, in art and in life: useful, elegant, and noble, but with a feminine softness that at once made her seem kind and congenial. Elizabeth reflected on the blessings of such a mother, so different from her own; no, there would be no scenes of embarrassment to her children, no want of sense and propriety which could draw her husband's scorn. There was nothing in the portrait to bespeak anything but what Elizabeth could readily have imagined of Mr. Darcy's mother.

"I wonder what she would have thought of me. Would she have felt as Lady Catherine—that I am a stain on the family honour and respectability? When my portrait is here, will my own likeness portray me as her equal? Will I be thought kind? Frivolous?" mused Elizabeth. She shook off such unusual apprehensions of self-doubt with her customary cheerfulness—no, she would require no such exertions on the part of the portrait-painter; no, nothing other than capturing her own, remarkably fine eyes.

CHAP. 11.

As a result of her recent visit to Lady Sarah, Elizabeth returned to Pemberley full of ideas of usefulness. It might surprise her acquaintance that her initial enthusiasm for industry did *not* return to its accustomed course, and she went so far in her labours for the general good as to read the Derbyshire volume of *Rural Œconomy*. As she sat with her husband the evening before Colonel Fitzwilliam's expected arrival at Pemberley, in a valiant struggle with the pages of maps and figures in her own volume, she looked across to her husband, engrossed in his own broad-sheet. Acting on a sudden whim, she shut her own book and loudly proclaimed in a voice quite unlike her own, "How delightful it is to spend an evening in this fashion! I declare! There is nothing like reading to improve the mind and promote enjoyment. How much sooner one tires of anything but a book!"

Darcy responded by raising an eyebrow. "You are most impertinent, Mrs. Darcy, to ridicule the lady who might well be credited with causing me to fall in love with your fine eyes." The occupation of recalling their history of pride and prejudice occupied the couple so intently, they failed to notice the opening of the drawing-room door, and the appearance of a very welcome figure from behind it.

"Colonel Fitzwilliam!" exclaimed Elizabeth.

Immediately upon receipt of the warmest of greetings from Mrs. Darcy, the Colonel turned to his cousin. "You are looking well, Darcy. Marriage is still agreeing with you, I can see."

"George! You are welcome, indeed," added Mr. Darcy, with an hand-shake. The calm, abbreviated English greeting did not do justice to the depth of affection and brotherly attachment that had long existed between the two men. Mrs. Darcy rang for refreshments, and they seated themselves to hear the Colonel's explanation for his precipitate arrival. Colonel Fitzwilliam sank into a seat with theatrical flourish, and apologised for surprising the family by coming a day earlier than he had originally intended.

"Of a sudden, I could not stay in Northamptonshire a moment longer, and so I have been travelling since, and am glad to be arrived. My father will doubtless expect me to remove to Hallendale House in a few days' time, but with your consent," he said, bowing his head to Elizabeth with an air of mock formality, "I would like to settle here. I have missed Pemberley and its denizens, especially my little cousin—where is she this evening?" His question was answered by a pause, which, at that moment, permitted his hearing the sound of music echoing down the hall from the music room. With a bow that would do credit to the most accomplished of courtiers, Colonel Fitzwilliam stood up and left the room to follow the sound. He listened from the door, waiting for her to finish, but Mademoiselle Blanche, occupying her usual spot on the top of the piano-forte, caught a glimpse of her old friend and leapt across the music-stand to greet him, causing Georgiana to break off her playing mid-phrase and smile up at the unexpected visitor with delight. She took his proffered hand, and stood so that he could take her hands and kiss her cheek.

"I was not expecting you so soon, and you are a welcome surprise, indeed," she told him, taking his arm and tucking her head into his shoulder in an instinctive gesture. Upon the Colonel's answering her with a question as to her own health, she replied, "I daresay my brother will tell you that I have been quiet these past months, but now you are come, I am sure to recover my usual equanimity. You must have a great deal to tell me about your adventures with the regiment in Northamptonshire. Pray tell me, how does Miss Crawford do? And her brother? Your letters have been full of them, and I wondered you might bring your new friends to Derbyshire for a visit."

Georgiana recollected the Colonel's last letters, and was determined to shew no outward signs of the distress that had occupied her mind and oppressed her spirits since the arrival of the first letters, introducing his tentative praises of Miss Crawford. The succession of others that followed had been filled with little else than his admiration. Her feelings could not properly be called jealousy, as Georgiana so underrated her own merits as to believe Colonel Fitzwilliam entitled to such perfection as he had described in Miss Crawford; no—it was impossible that she neglect her duty to him as a friend and near-

relation

relation, to do other than approve his choice and rejoice in his happiness. The acknowledgement of a duty does not always produce sufficient resolution for its immediate execution, however. Georgiana steadied herself for the anticipated recitation of that lady's virtues. Upon her mentioning Miss Crawford, she saw a shadow cross her cousin's face, and abruptly began upon the alternative topic of having accompanied Lady Sarah on a recent trip to London.

It waited for next morning for Colonel Fitzwilliam to seek Georgiana and indulge himself in some relief of those feelings of wounded pride and unanswered affection. Depending upon Georgiana's natural tenderness and her reliable interest in his concerns, he was entirely insensible that the result of their long-established habits of companionship and confidence had produced any change in Georgiana's feelings, other than that she now appeared happier and more animated. Her spirits noticeably improved, as she resumed her usual employments in his company; and the peace of mind they procured led invariably to the natural, quiet elevation of her spirits. Her cousin would have been astonished to understand the true cause of the alteration in Georgiana's demeanour, and how intimately he was concerned in the change; he had not intended to impose upon Georgiana's feelings, merely to relieve his own. Other than the small circle at Pemberley, there were few who knew of Colonel Fitzwilliam's disappointment. News of his flirtation with Miss Crawford had not travelled beyond the confines of the neighbourhood in which they occurred; as a consequence, his misery— whilst possibly durable, or at least as constant as may be supposed for an active man at his time of life—was not increased by the circumstance of its being more generally known.

For some weeks, Colonel Fitzwilliam had thought himself in love with Mary Crawford, whom he had met in Norfolk whilst stationed there with the militia a year previous. Her vivacity and lack of reserve, particularly in her conversation, in which her own frank opinions and her sport with the feelings of others, would have been deemed serious defects of character, were not the whole combined with a loveliness of countenance and sweetness of manner that blurred any resemblance to impropriety. She had captivated him, and he had found himself in a very willing infatuation. Mary Crawford, in the rare moments when Colonel Fitzwilliam could secure her company alone, was sweetness itself; but in society, she had a tendency to a worldliness that seemed irreconcilable with sound principles. She was a puzzle, but a beautiful one, and Colonel Fitzwilliam felt certain that, if he could detach her from the fashionable set who so frequently surrounded her, and take her back to his quiet Derbyshire, she would make him very happy, and he her. In those moments spent apart from her friends, her tenderness toward him seemed entirely genuine, but those moments were infrequent and tormenting in their unpredictability.

Colonel Fitzwilliam had pursued the object of his affection for a number of weeks, but each offer was met with an ambiguous rejection. She would merely respond in a laughing manner and say, "if only I might," but could never be prevailed upon to describe the circumstances that would yield a positive answer, or conversely, what was invariably producing a negative reply. At last, the modest Colonel concluded that Miss Crawford had appeared very agreeable by making himself the object of her particular attention, for whatever her reason—likely a dearth of more interesting aspirants; all of her good qualities had instantly succeeded into view. He had been delighted by her notice. He had been mistaken in her regard. He had been disappointed through his own folly. He returned to the peace of Pemberley and the indulgence of Georgiana's company for a much-needed dose of sympathy, with pride intact, but an heart seemingly lost forever.

It was not in Georgiana's power to deny her cousin anything. He talked incessantly of Miss Crawford this, and Miss Crawford that; Georgiana bore her duty silently and patiently, making an allowance for some hurtful remark, or an explanation for some caprice of behaviour, but always steady in her compassion for his wounded feelings and regard for her cousin's happiness. Colonel Fitzwilliam had developed an habit of long-standing in his dependence upon Georgiana's willing ear and tender heart—indeed, more than he knew himself. By the end of the week, Colonel Fitzwilliam was able to console himself with the certainty that Mary Crawford's affections could not possibly be worth such pain and mortification, and a few more days of Georgiana's remedial company was sufficient that he could resolve to think no more of the lady, and was able to return to his regiment with his usual calm and cheerful spirits.

C H A P . 1 2 .

"ELIZABETH, would you like to go?" asked Mr. Darcy at breakfast one morning. "I am apprehensive that you might find the trip tedious and the destination disappointing."

"What? Go to Manchester to see the gas-light with Mr. Parker?" replied Elizabeth. "Does Mrs. Parker go?" Mr. Darcy and Mr. Parker belonged to a philosophical society in Richmond where papers were presented that reflected the latest thinking in the scientifical philosophies: medicine, geology, mathematics, and especially mechanics and chemistry. The two men quickly discovered that they were in agreement about many points regarding the scientifical method and the need to make the applications of the new inventions by Watt, Priestly, and others more commonly available; in addition, Mr. Parker, not having the capital of a large landed estate, had employed his intelligence in securing shares in ships, farms, mines, iron works, smelting ventures, and other industries and manufactories as diverse as steam engines, a brewery, and a soap-making business. Mr. Darcy had discovered in Mr. Parker a profound intellect, especially as regards the scientifical aspects of not only industry, but many other areas of natural philosophy. Mr. Parker was somewhat younger than Mr. Darcy, and had a first-rate education in the latest theories, but who had neither Mr. Darcy's property nor experience in its use and management. Consequently, each man respected the other for what he was not himself, and was bound by a friendship formed over a desire to experiment with new methods that held promise for bettering the working conditions, especially for the labouring class. Their correspondence had become more frequent, and their plans and ideas more collateral.

"I think that Mrs. Parker is agreeable to any plan," answered Mr.

Darcy, "If you and Georgiana chuse to remain at Pemberley, she would come here and stay whilst we are gone to Manchester."

Elizabeth was thoughtful for just a moment and asked, "What is your wish, Mr. Darcy? Surely it would be an encumbrance to your business to have three women along, and would complicate travel, surely. Manchester is not so very far, but I see no need to put you and Mr. Parker to such inconvenience, unless you especially desire we come."

Darcy replied, "I could never find pleasure in any journey without your company; however, we can surely travel much more expeditiously on horse-back than in the chaise."

"As I believe myself to be a rational creature, Mr. Darcy," replied Elizabeth with a smile, "I shall willingly compound for a few quiet days at Pemberley with Georgiana and Mrs. Parker in order to secure your sooner return, so long as you assure me," she laughed, "that you firmly believe me to prefer, in fact, bouncing along the mud and ruts the length and breadth of Derbyshire, to sitting in our elegant rooms at Pemberley. It is only your business and your earlier return that I consider in declining the pleasure. What sort of lady is Mrs. Parker?"

Mr. Darcy smiled. "I have not yet had the pleasure of meeting Mrs. Parker. I believe that she is a country-woman, and that she and Mr. Parker have several young children."

"Oh!" exclaimed Elizabeth, "Does she bring the children?"

"No," replied Darcy, "I believe the children remain behind in Sussex."

"Do I understand that Mr. Parker is acquainted with Mr. Lee? Is that why you go?" asked Elizabeth.

"Yes, Mr. Lee has made extensive use of the coal-gas to light his manufactories. Mr. Parker is very sanguine on the employment of the coal-gas for lighting and has been studying its use for some time. He is a partner with a Mr. Winsor in London, and they are looking for share-holders. And," continued Mr. Darcy, "as our estates encompass several collieries, we would naturally wish for the use of the coal-gas as a replacement for candle-light for the manufactories as well as in the domestic sphere—Mr. Lee's own house is already fitted with gas-lights. Apparently, according to Parker, the cost of gas-light is one-quarter of that for candle-light, and the coal-gas provides a superior light."

"Coal-gas must, indeed, then, be an improvement, as the cost of candles to the poor is a large expense. But, is it safe? Although it would be hard to imagine anything which does more actual evil than a lighted candle in a small, crowded room, it is still the danger that we know," replied Elizabeth.

"One would never wish to promote any new method precipitously, certainly. However, that Mr. Lee uses it in his own house must speak highly of his estimation of its safety. Indeed, since having the coal-light at his factory in Manchester, Mr. Lee has contracted to extend the gas-pipe in his spinning establishment, as well as to light the stretch of yard that separates the various buildings in the grounds. Only think, Elizabeth, of the salubrious results of gas-lighting along the streets of London: how different travel would be in the night-time, and the disability such light would cause the footpads and other criminals who depend upon the cover of darkness on the roads for their mischief."

"My dear Mr. Darcy," cried Elizabeth, "is such a thing possible? I know that London has had great success with gas-lights, but that is one town, albeit a large one. Do you imagine a plan which would encompass the highways, in addition to the towns?"

"Yes, Lizzy, it is not only possible, but I think inevitable."

"And, this coal-gas comes from the coal naturally?" asked Elizabeth.

"Yes, which is the logic of it all. The coal naturally yields the coal-gas when heated, but not heated sufficiently to consume the coal, providing the gas-light as well as the heat. The Pemberley collieries are profitable, to be sure, but the interest of public safety is, I believe, a powerful inducement to the adoption of gas-light. I would certainly wish to be a part of its wider general promotion, given proof of its safety."

Mr. and Mrs. Parker arrived at Pemberley late the following evening. Mr. Darcy and Mr. Parker set off for Manchester before the Pemberley ladies had made their appearance at breakfast. Elizabeth had only the short space of a few hours in the evening before to observe Mr. and Mrs. Parker. Her amazement at his choice of wife was complete. He was an excellent example of that new breed of scientifical gentlemen who had been raised on the newest theories and inventions, directing his own education from his earliest years toward those studies most advantageous to a philosopher concerned in the business of invention and industry. Mr. Darcy had been most impressed with Mr. Parker's mathematical turn-of-mind and his knowledge of the most recent advances in all areas of natural philosophy. He especially commended his application of those ideas that held the greatest promise of benefit to those whose suffering was the most acute—the working poor of the new cities. Darcy honoured Mr. Parker for his abilities and his liberality, his energies and his application.

Where Mr. Parker was a tall, slight, fashionably dressed gentleman of rapid thought, rapid decision, and rapid action, his wife was short, fat, and jolly. Her delight was to spend the entirety of her days being merry in spoiling her husband and children; and when this occupation was impossible due to the lamentable absence of one or the others, she spent her time describing their days and speeches to everyone within the sound of her voice with such exactitude, as to render imagination unnecessary.

Elizabeth, whilst generally not backward in finding humour wherever possible, was entirely unable to suggest any additional topic of interest to Mrs. Parker. She decided to invite the voluble parson and her sister Kitty to dinner, so as to spare herself the exertion of attempting conversation with Mrs. Parker; between the latter and Parson Overstowey, none would be necessary, or, indeed, even possible.

"Oh, what a lovely big room, Mrs. Darcy!" exclaimed Mrs. Parker, entering the drawing-room upon her arrival. "What a mess my children would make of it! They would have the cushions on the floor in a moment, and these China-men! Oh, dear me! Such lovely things! You are so brave to leave them about! Bless me! Mr. Parker and I have long given over having such lovely things just to be broken!"

Lizzy was scarcely able to reply before Mrs. Parker began again. "Upon my soul! Such a beautiful table and so much fruit! However do you contrive to have it at this time of year! And so far to the north of us! Mr. Parker and I have no time for tending to hot-houses, what with Mr. Parker's business, and how busy I am with the children! My dear mother had ten of us! I do not know how she managed, although, to be sure, even though I was the eldest, I was never wanted about the cooking or tending to the younger ones. It made for a sad business when I was taken to wife! Poor Mr. Parker was a bachelor, you know, and so must have been glad of even my poor dinners, though we had a proper cook."

Lizzy suppressed the idea of complimenting Mrs. Parker for her marriage to a single man, but took the advantage of Mrs. Parker's brief pause for breath to ask, "Surely, Mrs. Parker, your dear mother had help?" Here Lizzy was forced to stop her question as Mrs. Parker interrupted.

"La! Oh, I assure you, Mrs. Darcy, we country-folk do not hold with the ways of you city-folk with the governesses and masters! It was all my poor father could do to keep all us girls in gowns and the boys at school with the parson!"

Lizzy was at a loss to consider herself as any such thing, but fortunately for herself, she was spared the necessity of reflecting upon

the

the issue by such continual effusions on Mrs. Parker's part regarding the furniture, prospects from the windows, the length of the drive, the weather in Derbyshire, and so on, as to require any reply.

Georgiana had no opportunity for speech at all. Finally, at length, Mrs. Parker paused long enough on other subjects to remark on Georgiana's cat, which was sleeping all the while on Georgiana's lap, in spite of the noise of Mrs. Parker. Elizabeth was amazed at the undisturbed composure of the animal, but recollecting its deafness, was momentarily envious of the poor animal's defect. Georgiana thanked Mrs. Parker for the compliment, but got on no further at dialogue than had Lizzy.

After Mrs. Parker had retired for the evening, Georgiana came to Elizabeth's apartments to wish her good-night, and to ask if Elizabeth required her to attend with Mrs. Parker in the morning on a drive around the park. Elizabeth replied, "No, of course not, if you do not like it, and I do not wonder at your wishing a few hours' quiet. Do not you regard Mrs. Parker as very unlike her husband? For my part, I wonder at his choice."

"I have not thought about it before, Elizabeth, but no, I do not wonder. Mrs. Parker is a good-natured, kindly woman, and obviously dotes on her husband and children. To me his choice seems not only natural, but wise."

"Yes," replied Elizabeth, "but Mr. Parker is a worldly, reading man. How can such a man respect a partner whose mind is so dissimilar to his own?"

"I cannot disagree with your comparison, Elizabeth; however, remember that, in addition to her good nature, Mrs. Parker is very pretty, and I believe that gentlemen usually give such a virtue more weight in their choice of a wife than we might prefer to credit. In addition, Mrs. Parker has made him a very attentive wife and devoted mother."

"Oh yes!" cried Elizabeth, "She is so attentive that their house must be in perpetual derangement, as well as having no fruit!"

"Dearest Elizabeth," said Georgiana smiling, "I hope you are not so severe upon my house-keeping."

"Georgiana, as always you are right. No, you are not right, you are good, which is much better. I am humbled, and will allow Mrs. Parker to be Mrs. Parker in a bid to regain your good opinion. Have I any hope?"

Georgiana kissed Elizabeth good-night, and turned at the door saying, "I know you too well to believe that you could really mean anything unkind, so my good opinion can never be lost."

Upon their return, the gentlemen were confirmed in their enthusiasm for the advancement of gas-lighting, and the potential for a venture that depended upon the collieries of the Pemberley estate. The Parkers left that same day, eager for each other's company and the comfortable chaos of their own hearth. Pemberley was like-wise restored to its original fruit and peace.

Mr. Darcy had also extended an invitation to an agricultural correspondent, Mr. Knightley of Surrey, to accompany him on a tour of the Pemberley collieries, as well as its orchards. Mr. Knightley was due to arrive the following week. Mr. Darcy hoped to procure that gentleman's opinion on the endeavours in gas-light, as Mr. Knightley was a steady, reflective man, with a reputation as having uncommon success in agricultural experimentations.

"I believe we will all find Mr. Knightley most agreeable," ventured Darcy to his wife and sister. "It is sometimes difficult to discern the character of an acquaintance made through the medium of pen and paper, but he writes with such reason and attention to the details of his study, that I feel I already know him. He is married, Elizabeth, before you ask; it is a question ladies always ask. His wife is a young woman of respectable family and fortune from the village adjoining his own estate. His younger brother is married to her sister; he is an attorney living in London, and who I believe is acquainted with the Gardiners."

"Oh!" laughed Elizabeth, "that must have been very convenient. If only my mother had been blessed with a son, Georgiana might have made a match with him, and we all could have been disposed of with a very little inconvenience! But upon a prolonged reflection, I could never be persuaded to relinquish Georgiana, so we are happiest as to fortune as we are."

"It is a great shame that his wife does not accompany him," Darcy added, "for he writes of her as being both beautiful and charming—high praise from such a man, indeed—but she is in expectation of her confinement, so she remains with her sister and invalid father in Highbury. I was surprised to hear that Mr. Knightley removed to the estate of his father-in-law upon his marriage, and did not take his wife to his own house, Donwell Abbey. Her father, as I understand it, so disliked losing his daughter and could not, at his time of life, be expected to countenance so material a change to his habits and remove thither. A most singular arrangement, indeed, but I must honour Knightley for

being

being a man who would make such a change for the love of his wife and the feelings of her father."

"You surprise me exceedingly, Mr. Darcy," teased his wife. "You honour Mr. Knightley, but I do not recollect any similar offer to quit Pemberley for the comforts of Longbourn—such an omission is especially regrettable, as we might, by this time, all be living with Mr. Collins in the rôle of *pater familias!*"

Such a vision inclined even Mr. Darcy to laugh and rejoin, "I daresay, my dear, such a change might call for increase to even Mr. Collins's natural air of *gravitas*; we are, I believe, better situated at Pemberley."

Mr. Knightley was as agreeable and inclined to genius as his letters had announced him to be, and both Elizabeth and Georgiana were delighted with him. Like Mr. Darcy, he was naturally more prone to thought than speech, and the two men had many mutual interests and shared a strong sense of duty. Elizabeth later expressed privately to Georgiana that Mr. Knightley had reminded her of Colonel Fitzwilliam in his kind steadiness of character, and was surprised at the warmth with which Georgiana refuted the comparison.

"It is not that I think they are so very different," Georgiana attempted to explain, after apologising that her initial response had seemed immoderate. "But they are at such contrasting stages in their lives. Mr. Knightley is married and happy, and sees himself as an husband as well as a man of business. He has found a wife who complements his own nature and makes him settled and easy, as he said to us at dinner. I cannot view Colonel Fitzwilliam in the same way at all. He is so uncertain of himself, and, were it not for the affectionate nature which spares us any distress, I fear we would often find him out of spirits. When he marries, I believe we will see a more cheerful side to him, and his complete happiness will give him the ease and bearing of which Mr. Knightley is possessed. That is—I mean to say—that they are not different as to character, but rather Colonel Fitzwilliam has not yet risen to the same blessings as Mr. Knightley."

"Georgiana, you have a nicety in the comparison of character that must always incline me to your opinion. I believe you are exactly right; our Colonel Fitzwilliam is best of men, but he would do better for being married. Were he to be as content as Mr. Knightley when he does so, we must both, then, regard him as perfect—well almost perfect, for I cannot allow perfection in any man, as you know, save your brother," she smiled.

Having reconciled their difference with such success, they returned to the dining-room, and Lizzy and Georgiana spent the remainder of the evening, respectively, in studying Mr. Knightley and thinking of her cousin, Colonel Fitzwilliam. Over the next several days, Mr. Darcy and Mr. Knightley spent a great deal of time both above ground and under it, conversing with the land steward and mine manager, ascertaining the best plan for the creation of manufactories to extract the coal-gas; whilst the coal-gas had heretofore been seen as an adverse and dangerous substance, the new process of distillation had safely harnessed its utility, and its potential for good was seemingly limitless. Each evening, Mr. Darcy and Mr. Knightley engaged in very detailed discussions as to the methods for the best exploitation of the coal-gas, and, upon Mr. Knightley's departure for Surrey and his family, both men were entirely satisfied. A plan had been drawn up, which, after securing Mr. Parker's approbation, was to be implemented with all the availability of means and assurance of right.

CHAP. 13.

THE GREAT FRENCH WAR that prevented travel abroad confined the English at-home, the exploration of the houses of their neighbours as an enforced substitute. Legions of once scrupulously polite ladies and gentlemen assumed the duties of house-inspectors, boldly enquiring into the cupboards and corners of Pemberley—whether arriving for the day (as once an inquisitive Elizabeth Bennet had done) to view the furniture and trees, wander around the extensive gardens, and admire the lake, or—more troublesome still—if they were at all acquainted with the family, staying at Pemberley for what seemed interminable periods of time, consuming the contents of the Darcys' larder, shooting, fishing, and touring the countryside, tormenting the neighbouring families. At first, Mr. Darcy bore this trial with the tolerance of habit, but, even with the coming of the Peace, the visitors continued to arrive in such multitudes as to try even his inured patience. Elizabeth was heard to complain, "It is insupportable that we should constantly be incommoded by a public who wish to wander through our house and gardens, looking into cupboards, carrying mud into the hallways—actions which certainly *aspire* to incivility—preventing us from being easy in our own home. Is there nothing we can do to discourage this stream of intruders, Mr. Darcy?"

Not wishing to give Elizabeth uneasiness on the subject, at length Mr. Darcy replied, "As these visitors provide what can only be described as a second income for our house-keeper and head gardener—both of whom receive substantial remuneration for their enterprise of shewing visitors about the house and grounds—I believe there is very little we can do to limit those determined to see Pemberley that would not be regarded both as uncivil to respectable families, as well as illiberal upon the perquisites of valued servants, Elizabeth. However, you will be gratified to hear I have lately formed the opinion that the only alternative available to us is retribution. Should you like make a trip of our own? I have long wished to return to Scotland, to explore the Highlands and Moray; and, as you have never visited that part of the world, I should think we could—between us—make a fine job of outstaying our welcome in the homes of others, and simultaneously avoid the inconvenience in our own."

With Elizabeth predisposed to any expedient promising relief, and immediately feeling more complacent about the volume of footfalls she could hear descending the main staircase above them, the Darcys set about planning their route, engaging Colonel Fitzwilliam and Georgiana to accompany them. Besides a mutual inclination to please the other, the Darcys found a very agreeable diversion in touring the Kingdom, travelling whenever the roads and weather allowed for a tolerably comfortable journey. They did not spend the season in London, but went to town when Mr. Darcy had a meeting he wished to attend, or had some other business thither. And, as the Hallendales had little desire for travel, other than the few trips they now made to London, one or more of the Darcys accompanied them whenever Colonel Fitzwilliam was not able to secure leave at a convenient time to assist His Lordship.

As a matter of course, the family frequented the theatres, the Opera House, and the Lyceum, and occasionally the Pantheon when it held an agreeable entertainment, Vauxhall, Astley's, the great city parks, Oxford Street, Kensington Gardens, Leicester Square, and the other respectable amusements and diversions to be found in London. Oxford Street, with its broad, regular, clean pavements, street-lights, and beautiful shop-windows, was regarded by foreigners as the Ninth Wonder of the World, falling little short of Buonaparte's Simplon for exciting wonder and awe; so much so, that visitors—as would fain compliment England or the English in any other place—were eager in their praise of Oxford Street.

The Darcys visited the new picture gallery at Dulwich designed by Sir John Soane, which possessed a fine collection of pictures, as well as the unusual additions of a mausoleum housing the remains of its benefactors, and housing for alms-women. The interior was a splendid example of Soane's genius in creating a very plain exhibition space, focusing the attention of the viewer on pictures suspended on the walls, instead of the more usual ornate surroundings that seemed to compete with their attachments. Mr. Darcy especially appreciated the

new

new theory in Soane's plan of the gallery, and Georgiana found much pleasure in sitting in the various rooms and sketching the paintings. London provided an uncountable number of public edifices which also required the Darcys' enquiry: besides the usual route of St. Paul's, Vauxhall, Theatre Royal and Wren's smaller master-piece, St. Stephen's Walbrook, was to be seen with its dome and West's altar-piece.

The family also attended the exhibition of Buonaparte's carriage, built by the Belgians for the French Emperour to his personal specifications. It had been captured at Waterloo by the Prussians and sold on to the English government. Housed in the London Museum in Piccadilly, the carriage was a marvel of invention: the competing claims of safety, comfort, and elegance had been united with the utmost efficiency to convenience and magnificence. The carriage had a novel shape that prevented the coachman (or indeed, anyone else) from seeing the passengers within, but giving those within an unobstructed view of the horses and all the country surrounding the carriage. The body of the chaise was bullet-proof, and was attached to the pole by the action of an ingenious lever which kept the body of the carriage level in any terrain. Inside, a number of clever contrivances provided for a kitchen, bed-room, dressing-room, office, and dining-room. Most of the on-lookers were stupefied by the immense quantity of articles in solid gold, and a curiously small box no longer or wider than a woman's arm containing an entire bedstead! All of the items attached to the vehicle remained with it, but the immense quantities of diamonds, money, and Buonaparte's personal effects had all been appropriated by the Prussian soldiers upon its capture. Mr. Darcy remained some minutes noting the parts of the carriage that shewed the most superb mechanical ingenuity in the compactness and efficiency of design, making drawings in his pocket-book to record the contrivances and dimensions of the innovations he particularly admired.

Their town-house being in Mayfair, when the weather was fine, they took their carriage into the environs of London; travelled Beaufort Street along the Thames; rode southward as far as the water-mills of Croydon, and the orchards and Old St. Mary's Church at Beddington; and, dismounting, walked along the banks of the river across from Gravesend and watched the ships from above the old sea-wall. More frequently, they drove through the pretty fields of Hounslow Heath, interspersed with windmills and hay-ricks—*en route* to Windsor Great Park, to the broad *allée* of the Long Walk, to the glens and cool plantations with herds of deer, to the large, rambling castle near Brocas Meadow, or to the shore, with its vista of barques and barges and people fishing along the banks. They explored the Thames along the woods of Henley—where the wood-cutters could be seen with their horses and timber-bobs—to the scenes of Varley, with the barges and their queer sails, and the setting sun over the ancient church at Chiswick. The western end of the Thames to Richmond was become rapidly populated, and latterly the Darcys had perforce abandoned this part of the river due to the unwholesomeness of the vapours emanating from the tenements of the new towns. One place they did *not* venture was the Grand Menageries, Georgiana being violently opposed to the transportation of the animals from their original habitations and the extremely small areas of their confinements—all of which she believed to be a great offense against both humanity and nature. She was particularly discomfited by poor elephants in their chains, their being thought remarkably intelligent and almost human-like in their family groups. So unalterably was she decided against the practice of subjecting the wild animals, not only to the miserably cramped and filthy cages, but to the terror they must feel when displayed amongst such noise and crowds, simply to gratify the public's insatiable desire for spectacle, that she persuaded her family to be of her opinion—a surprisingly easy labour, as the misery of the animals was evident to any sympathetic eye; Georgiana so infrequently expressed any opinion, that the Darcys' immediate response was to concur whenever she would venture her view.

On those days when Georgiana was not present, Mr. Darcy took the cabriolet to drive his wife out on these excursions, celebrating the warm summer days and fresh air. Elizabeth gloried in the English landscape, the solidity of its houses, and respectability of the people she would see working in well-tended fields, mowing, reaping, ploughing, or herding; or, passing through the market towns, from the carriage she could see the bustle of tents, carts, livestock, laden donkeys, dogs, pigs, baskets innumerable—all expressively proclaiming the productivity and prosperity of the countryside. She spent long days in the company of her husband, looking at his handsome profile, watching him expertly guide the horses around the usual impediments—moving and inanimate—each calling the other's notice to something or other along the way, aware of their blessings, and obliged to the other for their mutual happiness.

The Darcys also enjoyed travelling to Bath and its environs, especially in the early spring and late autumn, when the weather in Derbyshire was less dependably pleasant. Whilst the Darcys were disinclined to attend the Pump-Room or the Assembly Rooms with any regularity, they delighted in taking a Phaeton around the hills of the city, admiring the architecture. They traversed the various valleys and streams that met at the Avon, and rode through the charmingly situated villages of thatch and stone, the fields where the yeomen farmers and labourers worked together with scythes and forks, gathering the hay in their rumbling carts, the hills criss-crossed with stone walls, keeping fat sheep and contented cattle. Somersetshire being a prosperous county, there were great-houses near-by to see, such as Dyrham Park, Ston Easton, and Homewood Park; the lovely water-villages such as Bathford and Milford—particularly agreeable in the summer—and those places as far as Wells, Longleat, Thornbury, Bowood, Cheddar, and Lucknam Park. The Royal Theatre, the Opera House, and every other amusement was to be enjoyed, but without the crowding and inconvenience of London. And, although the young and the Court now preferred Brighton or other of the watering places along the south coast, the Darcys followed their own inclinations and continued to visit their friends, despite any disapprobation on the part of the fashionable public.

Elizabeth particularly enjoyed her visits to Mrs. Anne Wentworth, with whom she was become acquainted some years previously. Mr. Darcy found her husband, Captain Wentworth, to be an active, sporting man, and an excellent companion for fishing, shooting, or riding. Mr. Darcy often of a morning joined Captain Wentworth at the Corn Exchange to review the news, later meeting their ladies in the promenade, Queen's Walk, or some other pleasant destination for conversation and exercise. If the weather were fine, they might take a walk to Beechen Cliff or Beacon Hill, Kingsmead Fields, or some other eminence to enjoy the view of the grand crescents and terraces. One year, the Darcys had persuaded the Bingleys to accompany them, for the first time leaving their children at home, with the prospect of providing Jane some much-needed restoration to her health and spirits. However, Jane was so often exerting herself either in writing instructions to the house-keeper about the children, or watching daily for the post in expectation of a reply to her instructions, and so little attending to any opportunity for diversion and rest, that she left Bath with little less fatigue than she had brought with her.

Travel farther afield encompassed a stay at Fort William, Inverness, and Dornoch, and a trip to John o'Groats with the Gardiners. Mr. Gardiner and Mr. Darcy continued on to the outer Hebrides, leaving the ladies on the Isle of Skye for a fortnight. The gentlemen were well-pleased with their accomplishment, and Lizzy and her Aunt Gardiner had very pleasant walks along the Highland trails and the coastline near their hôtel. Mrs. Gardiner was not her niece's equal to walking, so they engaged the hire of a donkey-cart to explore the island, including the ancient Armadale Castle on the cliffs, the home of the Lords MacDonalds. Turning homeward, they stopt to visit Lord B——, viewing the site of the ancient Christian monastery. *En route*, they crossed eastward so as to come through Arbroath, as Mr. Darcy wished to view Mr. Stevenson's Bell Rock Lighthouse, a superb feat of engineering that had saved untold lives when his successful plan to put the light eleven miles out to sea—and in more than a rod of water—had worked, against all odds and all wagers to the contrary.

A visit to Drummond Castle at Crieff was considered necessary to see the ancient building and its famed gardens, now in the possession of Lady P——. The latter was known as a passionate admirer of the property, and took great pleasure in not only residing there, but, to Georgiana's approbation, managing much about the estate. They returned through Edinburgh, viewing the splendid castle against the summer evening sky, continuing on to Northumberland to see the great wall of Hadrian. They turned south and visited Jedburgh, through the Yorkshire Moors, again eastward to the sea and the great Abbey at Whitby and the town of Scarborough, before turning back westward, to stay at York; they staid some days visiting the great Minster and the environs of the ancient city, before resuming their road through Doncaster, and thence, Derbyshire.

In the following spring, Mr. and Mrs. Darcy took Georgiana, Elizabeth's father, and Kitty to see the northern part of Wales. Mr. Darcy wished to visit the noted stable at Gronant, with a view of making a purchase of some Shire horses of that breeding. Continuing west and then south along the Welsh coastline, Mr. Darcy viewed the place chosen by Mr. Telford for the great suspension bridge to be built at Menai. They stopt at Conwy, Caenervon, and Harlech castles, before returning to Derbyshire via the great glens of Moel Hebron and the pass through the peaks of Snowdonia. The route through the peaks of Wales was entirely in the pristine state of nature, very quiet and very grand. The desolate route required careful planning, as the inns were less numerous than any place they had previously travelled. This trip was graced with exceptionally fine, clear weather; the gentlemen were able to indulge themselves in fishing, and the ladies in reading, drawing, and watching the rustics tending to their herds of small black cattle and

wiry

wiry mountain sheep. Georgiana spent many pleasant hours drawing the peak from the vantage of a seat beside the river near their inn, with the graceful three-tiered bridge spanning the water, the immense Snowdon reflected in its blue waters.

Wishing to see the modern wonders of the viaduct at Llangollen, Iron Bridge Gorge, and the great bridge across the Tyne at Sunderland, Mr. Darcy particularly found pleasure in viewing these marvels of human ingenuity, and canvassing the improvements to commerce and industry with his wife and sister, as well as his philosophical acquaintance. On these tours of improvements, more often than otherwise, Mr. Darcy would describe the latest wonders of the age, and his wife would often question him on some particulars or other, pleased at the end in finding their opinions, as usual, exactly coincided. Georgiana was the most moderate of the three, keeping her opinions to herself, pensive as to whether the hands of man were inevitably an improvement on the hands of God.

CHAP. 14.

ON A LONGER TRIP ABROAD to Dorset and Cornwall, the Darcys made for the western road, travelling first to Birmingham, thence Worcester, Gloucester, and Bristol. Reaching the coast, they drove southward along the vast expanse of the Severn, with its views of the Monmouthshire hills to the west. The tides were displayed for the convenience of travellers at the tavern in Old Sudbury, at which they stopt for a meal at mid-day. It was determined that they could, with only a little expedient, meet the packet-boat that afternoon; accordingly, the Darcys decided to make a short excursion across the Severn to Strighill, Sudbrook, Chepstow, and Tintern, before returning to their road south.

From the old passage-house at Aust, the Wye could be seen across the Severn, along with the remnants of Strighill Castle atop Wentworth Forest and the verdant valley spread before it. The crossing at Aust was about two hours at low tide, and could be made an hour before the new passage, the latter requiring an additional hour to reach Port Skewith at that time of day. They left the carriage and servants at the old Passage-House, and took the packet across the river. Arriving at Beachley, the Darcys hired a chaise. The late Mr. Darcy had taken his young son to see the excavations of the entrenchments built by the Roman general Agricola, but a few years after their discovery. It being high summer, the sunset faded slowly, allowing sufficient time that evening for Mr. Darcy to shew Elizabeth and Georgiana where the ruins had been found in a field near-by Sudbrook. They staid at Chepstow and Tintern, recommencing their circuit of the various castles and other ancient ruins before returning by the express the following afternoon, meeting their horses at the new Passage-House a mile-and-a-half down-river at Pilning.

The Severn's powerful currents were not to be described; the vast plain of water moved at an extraordinary speed, and the boats upon the torrent appeared to be toys incapable of either direction or resistance agains such forces. The tides in the immense estuary were increased by the sand-bars that constricted the flow of the water, the latter being visible only at low tide. Embarkation when the tide was gone out was particularly difficult, owing to the roughness of the lower shore-line and the force of the current in the narrowest points of the channel. The scenery, looking back up the broad Severn, was magnificent: the hills of Monmouthshire and their patch-work of hedgerows and trees, behind which rose the great peaks of Plinlimmon; the Wye, and the rocks at Piercefield towering above it, varied with hanging woods and jutting precipices, were all at once visible in the setting summer sun. To the south, the confluence of the Avon and Severn, and the Somersetshire coast extended into the distance. Mr. Darcy noted that the old woods had been felled and the commons exposed, wherein grazed fat sheep and black Pembrokeshire cattle, and a number of ditches had been new-cut into the fields for the purpose of catching shrimp as they were washed up the Severn by the tide.

As the Darcys walked along the embankment in the last of the day's warmth, of a sudden they were startled by a vivid flash of lightening to the west and a tremendous clap of thunder, accompanied by an heavy cloud that—in but an instant—covered the area. The various elements seemed spontaneously in a fury: the Severn began to roll with an awful roar, whilst the lightning that flashed continually from the black clouds, exposed alternately the frightful waves and foaming surf, illuminating and making the scene yet more terrible. Peels of thunder resounded on both sides, announcing a deluge with sheeting rain enough to cause the inhabitants of the four counties of the Severn to come floating helplessly by. In but a few minutes the storm vanished, and the sun appeared beneath the remnants of the clouds passing over the Monmouthshire hills. Their general relief, as the thunder and pelting rain subsided, was abruptly curtailed as were now heard the cries of people in an horse-boat that had been caught by the storm. The boat had been becalmed, and was attempting to reach the shore when the storm arose. The shrieks of the women, the bawling of the boatmen, and the incessant kicking of the horses against the boat were now perfectly heard. It was impossible to reach the poor victims, and they watched with horror as a woman, half-dead with terror and drowning was borne to the shore between two men. A terrified horse was next landed, dragging his keeper, who had

miraculously

miraculously maintained a steadfast hold upon the halter. The horse repeatedly slipped down the rocks, and made again to swim to the shore, before he finally clambered up the steep bank and broke away. After many unsuccessful attempts, all the passengers were landed, during which interval, the storm had passed and the serene, glassy surface of the Severn in the still moonlight erased any recollection of the violent storm just passed.

Bristol was a large, busy town, and the approach to the city was heralded by the smoaks and sounds emanating from numberless blazing furnaces, brick-kilns, and other manufactories, and by a ceaseless procession of over-burthened coal-horses. The coal-mines thereabouts were vastly numerous and productive, and the coal emerged from these mines covered in a black, stony substance that the inhabitants called "wark," which, when cleaved, split like slate, and therein was often found the print of a fern leaf, as if engraved. Georgiana had read that the original name of the town was "Brightstow," called so by the Saxon people. The city itself was very beautiful and conveniently arranged, but it lay in an uneven surrounding of hills, and the smoaks issuing from the various buildings kept the town in a grey blanket and the sky obscured for much of the day. Mr. Darcy regarded the docks and quays there as far surpassing those of London on the Thames.

The river Avon, rising with the tide to a depth of forty feet, was deep enough for ships of a thousand tons to sail all the way up to Bristol Bridge. The river Froome, dividing Gloucestershire and Somersetshire, led to the very centre of the city, now fairly regarded as equal to any trading-city in Europe. Bristol was the very illustration of a total occupation in trade: above twenty sugar-houses, an abundance of sulphur, turpentine, vitriol, and coal-works, brass and iron foundries, distilleries, glass manufactories, cloth-mills, and china-works—all incessantly in operation. It was wonderful, thought the Darcys, that such industry was equalled in that city by the polite arts, literature, and the liberal urbanity of the inhabitants, being come from many nations, rendered the intellectual and artistic life of the city as valuable as its commerce. The theatre in King Street and an Assembly Room in Prince's Street provided the citizens of Bristol with every diversion of a large city. They drove past the Cathedral, the great Exchange in Corn Street, the Council-house, and the Guildhall with its chapel. The smoak and noise were sufficiently unpleasant to promote no longer stay, and so the Darcys continued out of the city, passing over the Avon by means of the Rownham Ferry.

Stopping that night in Henbury, the Darcys chose to make another excursion down the Avon to King-road, waiting at the New Passage-House for the return of the tide. The inn was very good, deservedly reputed as amongst the best in the country. The following day, resuming their road southward, the Darcys passed many elegant country-houses of the Bristol merchants, then Blaize castle (it being a Tuesday, they were not admitted), before continuing toward King's Weston. Leaving their carriages and servants at the inn there, they walked to Lord de Clifford's seat in Shirehampton. They entered a small park through a broad gravel walk; the mansion stood surrounded by woods on a gentle rise sheltered by the King's-Weston down. His Lordship was at-home, and the Darcys very fortunately arrived in the forenoon, when they might be shewn the pictures. In the various halls were portraits by Kneller, Vandyck, Ramsay, Lely, and all of the other eminences, most notably including Holbein and Rembrandt, that properly adorn the walls of the best houses in the Kingdom. Thanking His Lordship for his civility, they continued along the high road that afternoon, taking the ferry back across to the Hot-wells, where they passed the night.

They quitted the environs of Bristol through the Durdham-downs where, in fine weather, a sufficiency of elegant equipages and expensively dressed ladies and gentlemen were present to remind on-lookers of similar scenes at Hyde Park, with liveried coachmen and their gold epaulettes driving pairs and teams of gleaming horses in their polished harnesses with silver bosses and pretty rosettes. The air of the downs was uncommonly pure, and a gentle breeze passed over it from the Severn. Riding along Wallis's wall, they had the view of a long vale, in which could be seen the several villages along the banks of the Avon. The Darcy carriage passed by the Bath road, and continued south-west into Somersetshire.

Mr. Darcy remarked sadly, "Bristol is rapidly expanding over the farms and parklands that previously surrounded it, and now that the Peace is come, it will not be many years before the terrace-builders will be as industrious in destroying the small villages and verdant farmland as they were in London.

"But, it is their right. I do not begrudge any man of sufficient industry a good house and comfort for his family, but it seems it might be done more conscientiously with respect to the countryside. I regret there can be no incentive to inform each other in an attempt to concert their plans, because any such effort would, I think, serve to raise the prices in anticipation of such intent, and act as a deterrent to any such agreement."

Georgiana replied in a thoughtful tone, "But, Brother, do not you believe that the general good of society must sometimes prevail, to the detriment of personal gain? I know not what Mr. Smith would say in defence of the hap-hazard manner in which these developments arise; possibly that the diminution in beauty of the countryside would promote a corresponding diminution in value, but I believe not. There is such an abundance of wealth consequent to this industry, that competition would render any other consideration subordinate to procuring the best house possible."

Elizabeth then proposed that Mr. Darcy take the part of Hobbes, Georgiana that of Rousseau; she would be Mr. Locke and mediate between them. However, Lizzy laughed, saying,

"I am more than willing to assume my share of this dispute, but I have always found that an empty stomach is not conducive to disputation, as it then involves too much of the *spleen*. Here we are come to Clevedon, and if we delay getting dinner, we will have to wait until Weston for supper."

The Darcys continued their road along the western coast until Highbridge, before turning south to Taunton. Their route took them through Tiverton, to the Vale of Okehampton and the ruins of its castle, skirting to the north of Dartmoor to Launceston, and into Tintagel, where they stopt to view the remains of what was reputed to be King Arthur's castle. It was windy and cold on the north Cornish coast; indeed, it did not appear that the old castle could ever have been comfortable and dry, no matter how many trees were burnt in the enormous hearths still evident. They continued past Bodmin, and into the environs of Truro. Mr. Darcy planned this journey to visit the mines in Cornwall, hoping to see first-hand the successful innovations and abandoned experimentations, assisting his understanding of the merits of the first, and the reasons for the failures in the latter.

As they approached into Cornwall, the Darcys were horrified at the devastation of the Cornish landscape. A few miles in from the lovely, temperate coastline lay an endless desert, composed entirely of hills of mine rubbish. There were few trees to be seen, but instead, everywhere people of a most miserable, wretched existence were observed in some state of subservience to the mines. Indeed, conditions for the lower classes was so deplorable, that many had turned to Anabaptism as a form of relief in their next life. Elizabeth was appalled at conditions which could turn men from their faith, and Georgiana was aghast at the causes—the horrible, furious hammering of the engines as they turned to keep the water from flooding the mines, and the filth and noise where the men, women, and children—all working digging, hauling, crushing, smelting—working as hard and ceaselessly as the engines—everything for the mines. Even the poor pit ponies, blinded by a life spent in the lightless passages of the mines, were haggard, thin, and miserable. To the Darcys, Cornwall looked as much like England as the moon. Darcy's brow was contracted and his air gloomy as he viewed the remains of the countryside.

"Oh, Mr. Darcy!" exclaimed Elizabeth in an hushed voice, so as not to draw the attention of their host, "surely we need not despoil Derbyshire and its inhabitants—man and beast—in our search for improvement."

"I cannot call this *improvement*," sighed Mr. Darcy. "The mines are not greatly profitable, there is much competition from the cheaper ore in Newcastle and other such places in the north, and the engines are costly. The mine owners are obligated to produce the best return for their investors; hence, we see the result of a focused pursuit of profit."

Georgiana was so discomfited by the scenes of suffering everywhere around her, that she ventured to add, "This, to my way of thinking, is not an example of the machine serving to improve the lot of men, but the reverse: the people are all made slaves to the machines. I wonder that it must always be so, as a general case."

Mr. Darcy replied grimly that he certainly *hoped* for the success of an alternative form of the industry, *replacing* the debilitating toil of men and animals as was inherent in the system before them, rejecting the abuse seen here as a requisite by-product of what was called by the euphemistical term "progress." "This desolation was certainly *not* the vision of Priestly, Darwin, Boulton, and the others at Soho, and I am shocked—appalled— to find Mr. Watt and Mr. Boulton involved in the partnership that has created the infernal scene before us, and is daily sustaining this atrocity. I am grieved, indeed, that the application and genius of these men would produce the very antithesis of their intentions."

They arose in the morning and agreed that the Cornish lessons were too hard-won; none had any stomach for continuing in the area, and turning homeward was decided upon as the most agreeable plan. They took a brief detour to Falmouth to see the shipping fleets as they were laden and launched to all ports of the world, happy to be, once again, amidst verdure and the gentle hills wrought by the generous hand of Providence. Following the road along the south coast to Plymouth, the Darcys took the opportunity of viewing Saltram House to see the works of Reynolds and Adams; from there, through an area of sheep-pastures and open countryside of expansive, picturesque views along the gentle south coast of England, the Darcys visited Ugbrooke Park with its rustic bridge over the River Ug and views of Dartmoor. Such scenes of comfort and prosperity were particularly welcome after the desolation they had just quitted.

The family continued on to the seaside destination of Weymouth, whose amenities, they understood, were of the first distinction (the sea-bathing being particularly commodious). At Weymouth, they spent several days enjoying the town and its shops and other diversions; the town latterly had been improved with assembly rooms, coffee-houses, billiard-rooms, and other manifold advantages, which secured its favourable distinction over other watering-places in the neighbourhood. They went as far eastward as Dorchester before turning north and toward home.

Despite the beauty of the seaside towns and the interesting scenes of the great houses and parklands, the return into Derbyshire was more solemn than usual, none in the family able to prevent their thoughts from returning to the devastation of the countryside, and the horrific memories of the people forced to such hardships as they had never before witnessed. Mr. Darcy was pensive, and Elizabeth reflected on her more perfect understanding of the benefits and injury made possible by the hand of man. Time had given Elizabeth a better understanding of the unceasing obligations of duty required of a land-owner during these times of change, and the care and liberality with which her husband daily discharged those responsibilities. Elizabeth had long been far from discerning any pride or other impropriety of expression in his manner; she now recognised only the countenance of a strict adherence to honour and duty. "With what a weight of cares and dilemmas he is daily burthened, not only to preserve Pemberley, but the many families who depend upon the success of his endeavours!"

At the time of her marriage, her first design had been to relieve the gravity of his expression by shewing him how to laugh at the follies and inconsistencies of daily life, and to view these absurdities with pleasure, instead of censure. She later realised that she could never infallibly distinguish between the ridiculous and the reasonable without first learning to share his burthens, and understand his concerns. Elizabeth had met these apperceptions with a coincident determination to preserve the pleasure and delight in their days—and to her mind, this was the greatest gift she could give to her husband—to keep his cares from overwhelming his earthly existence, by the simple expedient of remaining the woman he had married. He had been attracted to her—in part—for the playfulness of her disposition. No, she could not be dour and melancholy, but she *could* learn to better judge when her teasing was likely to ease his disturbance of mind, or when it would act contrary-wise and add to his affliction through her own ignorance and unintended thoughtlessness. Elizabeth daily rejoiced in the blessing of an husband that she could unreservedly admire and esteem for the strength of his character, his information, and his knowledge of the world.

The following summer, the Darcys had taken their holiday traversing the New Forest, through the ancient village of Lymington, and thence on to the Isle of Wight. Travelling as expeditiously as possible, Mr. Darcy had decided upon the use of post-horses, put to their travelling chaise. Georgiana declined to accompany the Darcys as she preferred to stay near Derbyshire, helping Jane with the Bingley's new baby, and visiting with the Hallendales. Mr. and Mrs. Darcy set off early one morning at the beginning of August, travelling the most direct route south, through Coventry and Banbury, and thence down the Winchester Road through Newbury to Winchester. On the last day of travel southward, they crossed Southampton Water and continued down the coastline to the estate of Mr. Darcy's acquaintance, Mr. Drummond of Cadland House. Passing the estuary of the broad Southampton Water, they saw the fisher-folk on the jetty mending their nets; small boats and barges anchored along the quays and shoreline, stranded upon the mud at low tide, looking forlorn and sullen, as if they never expected to float again; and sailing ships of all sizes, barely afloat in the middle of the channel, looking somewhat more hopeful. How strange was the human imagination, to conjure sensations as springing forth from a collection of wood and nails!

Cadland House occupied a very creditable property on the banks of Southampton Water, down the estuary from Southampton Castle, and could be seen just north of Calshot Castle. The father of the present Mr. Drummond had engaged Mr. Brown's son-in-law, Henry Holland, to design a *cottage orné* at Cadland, assigning the landscaping to Mr. Brown. At the hospitable Mr. Drummond's insistence, they staid at Cadland two nights, allowing Mr. Darcy to see the Cadland plantations, which extended over a large area of land bordering on the Solent, and Elizabeth to walk about the gardens with Mrs. Drummond.

The last morning of their stay, they breakfasted with the family before continuing through Exbury to Lymington, whence an horse-boat to the Isle of Wight embarked. Lymington, at the south of the New Forest, was a very old town, situated on the top and declivity of a gentle hill. The ocean breeze kept the air clean, and removed the humidity of the noxious damps common amongst the lower areas. One street of modest, neat houses sat upon the rise, at the bottom of which ran the deep and broad salt-water river, leading from the western Solent, separating the Isle of Wight from the Hampshire coastline. The inlet was of sufficient size to accommodate the great vessels of two and three hundred tons that, from time out of mind, had anchored at the large quays, delivering coal from the north of England, and returning with the sea-salt produced in the environs of Lymington, reckoned as the finest such in the world. As they walked through the town that afternoon, Mr. Darcy shewed Elizabeth the sad indications of the loss of the salt-trade to the area, which was recently being under-sold by inferior mined salt from Droitwich and Nantwich. At present, he noted, only the medicinal salts were extracted from the area, being of a requisite purer constitution, and, therefore, not so constrained in price.

The town boasted two bathing-houses, the best being located one half-mile from the town. As the ferry did not depart for Yarmouth until that afternoon, the Darcys spent several hours in driving out to see the baths and the grander houses of the area, including the admirable gardens of Walhampton. The town names, such as Bouldnor, Alum Bay, and Totland attested to the violent history of the area which had been variously under Saxon, Roman, and Danish rule before being united under Harald. The Roman encampment of Buckland Rings was still visible, although one end had been recently removed by an industrious farmer with a view to improving the pasturage for his cows.

At the appointed hour, the Darcys took a small-boat from Lymington port to Yarmouth, leaving their chaise with the servants to follow in the horse-boat. They sailed down the Lymington River, passing the salterns along the shore, coming about near the Light-house and Hurst Castle to cross the small distance to Yarmouth Castle, where they were to disembark. There were several neat, cheerful cottages on the shore within view as they crossed, along with a few more significant houses— some with pleasure yachts moored near-by. Arriving in Yarmouth, they went first to their inn, The George, near the quay to refresh themselves before setting out to walk about the town. Yarmouth was a busy place, not so large or prosperous as formerly, but there was enough intercourse between it and Lymington (the Solent being but one-half mile wide at that point) to keep the town in tolerable population and plenty.

The town all about was built to the shore-line with piers, ware-houses, quays, and the like, and many small boats and drays made their way about the harbour, in the first instance by water, and in the latter on the beach to meet the fishermen and carry their catch quickly to the port for sale on the mainland. Scattered about were the new houses built by prosperous merchants from Southampton, or captains and others who had made their fortune by the late war. The small hills and cliffs of the island made for many suitable locations for an house and small park, commanding a situation which afforded good prospects over the sea or the Solent. A few ancient buildings were in view, but the beauty of the area, indeed of the Isle itself, lay in the neatly arranged fields, houses, and farmsteads that were among the most well-ordered and productive in all England.

As they were to spend three nights in Yarmouth, the first morning, the Darcys hired horses for the duration of their stay and drove south toward Aston House, and, crossing the bridge, continued along the far western shore to view the singular sights of The Needles, The Shingles, and the White Cliffs. The road could not get immediately near to the cliffs; as a result, it was necessary to leave the carriage and walk a short distance to reach the shoreline. The light-house on the cliffs west of Freshwater Bay was a curious building, looking more like an ancient keep than a tower modern-built for the purpose. The English coastline from St. Alban's Head in Dorsetshire all the way to Lymington could be seen from the High Downs. The scenery of that side of the island was indeed sublime: the chalk-white of the cliffs, seen against the green edges of the down, with the summer sky above, and a calm sea below. Picturesque cottages and mansions were located at agreeable intervals, the natural beauty of the prospect enhanced by boats of many sizes and large ships passing in the middle distance; looking farther, the multitudes of sea-birds gave a sense of grandeur to the background. Walking eastward from Freshwater Gate, the Arched Rock suddenly appeared in the opening of the trees, an immense isolated rock with an arch-shaped void along its entire width, created by the forces of the dashing waves. It was necessary to make a short excursion by boat to properly view the extreme western cliffs, so the Darcys engaged the waiting owner of a small-boat at Freshwater Gate for that purpose.

From a distance of about a quarter-mile, the cliffs could be viewed in their immensity, to a very imposing effect. Numberless sea-birds flew along the height and breadth of the cliffs, caverns and chasms appeared to reach a great way into the rocks, and all along, small cascades issued forth from ground-springs, tumbling into the sea. The Needles soon rose into view. Mr. Darcy explained that these singular rocks had once

been

been yet more distinguished by one great, tall pointed rock which had risen one hundred and twenty feet above the water, until—within the memory of his father—it was become a victim to the waves, falling with a tremendous crash that had been heard as far away as Southampton, and then disappearing completely beneath the sea.

The following day, they travelled overland to Newtown, Carisbrook, and Calbourn, the principal towns of the westward island. The ancient church at Shalfleet was close-by the town of Newtown, the latter deriving its name from the circumstance of its being rebuilt, having been destroyed by the French in the time of Richard II. The town had been amongst the most ancient and populous habitations on the island, but was now very contracted, encompassing only about a dozen tidy cottages. In the centre of the Island were several very grand houses, all modern-built, surrounded by small, pretty plantations, seen to advantage against the dark lushness of the surrounding woods.

Carisbrook Castle could be seen for some distance, being situated atop one of the higher hills on the island. The strong outlines of its ancient ruins formed a most picturesque view within the panorama of downs, fields, woods, and cottages, viewed from the hill behind St. Mary's Church. Mr. Darcy noted that the grass was more forward on the island, and pointed out the rows of hay-ricks in the distance, and the small figures of people busy in getting in the grass. This area of the island was remarkably devoid of trees, making the mound and its castle more reminiscent of Sarras, than a scene in England. The castle was approached by a gateway that led across the moat, through the two great towers, and into the Court. The Darcys tarried some while in the chapel and the remains of the rooms where King Charles was confined before his execution; the building was now empty of every article save the few items of furniture necessary for the accommodation of the servant retained there to shew the castle to visitors. The rooms were dark and melancholy, as befitted their history; Elizabeth and her husband staid some minutes imagining the sad last days of the King. The pretty village of Carisbrook lay below, with its grand Gothic church tower, many neat and comfortable houses, and a sparking stream winding through the village and around the foot of the castle hill.

That evening was the last night of their stay in Yarmouth; the following day they rose early and took the Ashton road along the southern coast along as far as Shotwell, before turning north to Newport, where they were to spend the remainder of the week. Newport—now the largest town on the island, and its capital—enjoyed a situation central to all parts of the island, further improved by large streams on three sides, providing plenty of fresh water and power for mills and other manufactories, and its very clean, well-paved, regular streets adding to the town's general appearance of purpose and prosperity.

The next day being Sunday, the Darcys attended the ancient church. A large, respectable dissenter community lived at Newport, with two churches of considerable size belonging to the Independents, each with a valuable library for the use of the congregation. Newport also supported two public schools—one supported by the established church and the other by the dissenters, as well as Sunday schools at all of the places of worship—in a manner which well-reflected the liberality of the town. The permanent public library, being but several years founded, was supported by voluntary subscriptions, and there newspapers, reviews, and other periodical publications were available for the convenience and pleasure of the public. Altogether, the Darcys were very much of the opinion of Mr. Sturch: "There are few places where independence may meet with more sources of rational enjoyment, or where virtuous industry is better rewarded than in this clean, healthful, and elegant town." The inhabitants were sociable and kind, the inns large and commodious. For the cultural edification of the public, there was a large theatre, two assembly rooms, spacious and well-furnished shops, and a variety of other places of respectable diversion, that in the long summer evenings, kept the principal streets full with innocent bustle and activity.

On Monday, the Darcys drove out to Parkhurst Forest to see the House of Industry, a trade-school latterly built on a large piece of land granted by Parliament for the purpose. The large building was handsome, and provided windows sufficient for thorough ventilation and good work-lighting. There were accommodations for the seven hundred inhabitants, including a chapel, a pest house, a separate house for the small-pox, cells for delinquents, and a place of interment. The building was a model of thoughtful design and liberal intent. Mr. Darcy and Elizabeth spent much of this day looking at the various structures of the school, their size and shape, and the contrivances for the comfort of the residents, and efficiency in the education of the students.

"The circumstances of the schools and libraries of this town," said Mr. Darcy as they walked about the grounds, "demonstrate that the principle of the education of youth lies at the very foundations of private and social prosperity. The enemy of knowledge has always been superstition and bigotry. My last letter to Knightley dealt at length

with

with this subject. The affairs of the poor are so wretchedly managed in nearly every other part of England, creating generations of poor, who beget children born to continue a life of indolence and want. These children here are educated on Lancaster's method of instruction. As I understand it, this study has been proven remarkably successful, as judged from the rapid progress made by the students in reading, writing, and arithmetic, since beginning upon this plan."

"Certainly," replied Elizabeth, "the proof of the public liberality here in Newport and other places near-by is in every way exemplary and commendable; however, the generosity and forward-thinking of the principal families has been amply recompensed by the general comfort we see everywhere: the lack of want, the respectability and industry of all classes, as well as the evident increasing prosperity of the town, indicating—to my thinking—that this method should not be confined to this island, but must be the general rule for the Kingdom."

Elizabeth was very impressed with everything they saw, and concluded with her husband that their own school could not do better than emulate—to whatever extent possible in the northern part of Derbyshire—the plan before them. Again, Mr. Darcy had recourse to his pocket-book, and Elizabeth assisted his notes by sketching the various buildings and their details.

The following day was spent in the environs of Ryde and the eastern shore of the island, where Lord Spencer had latterly built an house for summer residence. Mr. Darcy remarked that it looked more like a horse-barn than a nobleman's seat. However, they were generally not to be disappointed, as the other grand houses in the neighbourhood were elegant and well-situated. Several very pretty thatched cottages were intermingled with the larger houses, which, with the shrubberies, hanging woods, fine groves of hardwoods, plantations of evergreens, and their fine views of the sea, assumed every advantage of the picturesque. On the road to the east, very agreeable views of Ryde, Spithead, Portsmouth, and St. Helens could be seen variously through the trees. Mr. Simeon's property contained a lodge of a new and singular description in the stile of Mr. Repton, giving the grounds a very natural-looking unnatural ornament, and to the visitor a very gratifying view of an estate perfectly situated within nature, placing each to the best advantage of both.

"I cannot agree this practice of first removing nature, then putting back the landscape in a 'natural' stile. It seems the work of both folly and conceit," said Elizabeth as they returned to the carriage after viewing the house and grounds, "as well as giving insult to the hands of Nature."

"Mr. Brown, and here Mr. Repton, certainly have a gift for creating the sublime. However, with such an example of natural beauty as is here on this island, he—and Mr. Simeon's purse—might have been spared their trouble to little, if any, disadvantage."

"I would venture further, Mr. Darcy. In the present instance, the very definition of 'success' would indicate that a viewer would be unable to distinguish the hand of the improver from a similar scene arising naturally and spontaneously through the workings of time and benign neglect, as advocated by Mr. Price. The only way to secure the accolades due such extraordinary effort is industriously to circulate the history of the grounds as being the work of Mr. Repton, which—as we both know—is but an indirect and indelicate boast of the costs of the whole-sale destruction of the natural, in order to reconstruct the picturesque 'as from nature.' Such an effort seems absurd."

"What did you think of Pemberley when you first saw it, on that day with the Gardiners? Did you believe it a scene of 'destruction?'"

"Of course not, Mr. Darcy. My opinion to-day coincides with my first impressions on that day—that I had never seen any place where natural beauty had been so little counteracted by an awkward taste. However, I am no proficient in the matter of landscape gardening, and did not know then, whether such beauty had been the result of a serendipitous placement of the house and park, or whether it had been done by removing the whole of the village, rearranging it, and setting it back down, only for the purpose of making a change to the original situation."

"Well asserted, Lizzy!" smiled Mr. Darcy. "This discussion gives me a great inclination to re-employ all of the gardeners at Pemberley in the fields, and leave the house and grounds to the 'gentle hands of time.' We will have realised a significant savings from sparing the gardeners the work, and—in some ten or twenty years—we will not be able to see the house from so far away as the lake!"

"Check-mate, Mr. Darcy," rejoined Elizabeth laughing; "you well know that I could never approve such a plan, and hence have shewn me the errors of my thinking quite ably, thank you."

On their last day before leaving the Isle of Wight *en route* homeward, they drove to the southeast to view the undercliffs, and looked across the British Channel to France. Coming abruptly to the termination of the walk at the edge of the cliff, they could see the rich border of land, a half-mile in breadth, through which lay the carriage road to Steep Hill and Bonchurch. On this road was found the cottage of Lord Dysart, long-known as the "Cottage at the Back of the Island." There were other very pretty cottages, but that of Lord Dysart was unrivalled in its situation. The thatched cottage with its white walls was of two-stories; the apartments within were comfortably well-furnished, and contained some very good pictures. However, the most admirable advantage of the cottage was in its surroundings: verdant fields, hedgerows, and woods, framed by the gently rising hills to be seen receding from the house. A fine spring appeared through a large, hollowed stone in the lawn, and over to the left an expanse of ocean was perfectly framed by the trees.

Coming back to Newport through Shanklin and St. Helens, the Darcys took the same road which led to the daily scenes of English sailors and merchant-men bidding *adieu* to their homeland, and sailing out to the most distant parts of the globe.

In the morning, they collected their servants and belongings, and drove out to Cowes. They had arranged to meet Mr. Drummond, who had very kindly offered to give them a day of sailing on his pleasure-yacht, delivering the Darcys back to the mainland at Cadland, whilst their servants met them that evening, returned via the horse-boat. The famous Mr. Nash had designed and built his own establishment in the neighbourhood of East Cowes on the summit of the hill above the town. The crenellated roof was interspersed with a succession of towers, which in turn commanded the prospect of West Cowes and the Medina. The parkland was not large, but very striking. However, Mr. Nash's aspirations to the pre-eminence of this residence had latterly been out-done by Norris Castle, which had been placed so as to be prominent from almost any vantage-point. At the summit of the road approaching from East Cowes now rose Norris, an immense pile of castellated turrets with its park descending all the way to the water's edge on the Solent, and with unrivalled views of the New Forest, Southampton Water, and the Hampshire coast all the way to Portsmouth. Elizabeth felt a momentary pang of regret for the feelings of Mr. Nash, but the bright sun and pleasant breeze made all disagreeable feeling evaporate in the exquisite pleasure of the scene.

Mr. Drummond spent so much time on the water that he was described by his wife as having webbed feet. There was nothing which gave Mr. Drummond more pleasure than shewing his friends (particularly the ladies) the principal sights of the Solent, describing their history, and attending to their raptures in response. In his earlier years, he had been quite the buck, and was much admired. Now, he was a ruddy-faced, smiling, gentle man who passed his good days on-board his handsome yacht, but when the weather was so disagreeable as to prohibit his favourite activity, he staid within, writing books about the sea and the Solent. His lady wife was a great gardener, to the extent that the Cadland estate produced a bounty of beauty and plenty throughout the year; yet her attentions to the flora of the estate were never so pressing that she would forego a sea-voyage with her husband. Throughout their married life, they had been so many places and staid so long at-sea, that her own foot-prints must have long ago assumed a similar outline.

Dinner at Cadland House was always a gay affair, with long tales of the sea, and the foreign places the Drummonds had visited. After several attempts to steer the conversation landwards to the Cadland farms, Mr. Darcy was forced to abandon his efforts at the tiller and climb aboard with the rest of the party, seeking the answers to his questions of the steward on the following day; Mr. Drummond was experimenting with the small, hardy cattle of the Scottish Highlands to see how they would fare on the meagre, salty marshes along the Solent. Mr. Darcy was interested in their progress, as he had been thinking along the same lines; although there were no salt-marshes in Derbyshire, there was certainly a dearth of good grass, very thinly and irregularly interspersed amidst a bounty of rock. The cattle were hardy indeed, the steward had related, but also very wild. Used to the great mountains and glens of Scotland, the animals had not been content within the confines of the enclosures, were proving a difficulty to keep in, and a near-impossibility to find and recapture once they had obtained their freedom. However, *if* they could be caught up, they were very fine eating. Mr. Darcy was grateful for the information, which gave him some reason to revisit his own ideas.

The Darcys elected to return to Derbyshire through the expedient of a detour to the west, viewing the great cathedral at Salisbury and the stone-henge near-by. Mr. Darcy asked his wife which she considered the greater accomplishment, the movement of the great stones—which had apparently come from as far away as Wales—or the building of the great Cathedral. Elizabeth replied,

"I could not judge otherwise than to find for the Cathedral, as it is an expression of the true faith, built by free men; they both attest to the strength of a people united to a purpose. I can easily understand the reasoning for the Cathedral, although its spire seems an excess to every proportion; however, the motivation for moving the large

quantity

quantity of immense stones to set them aright in a field in Wiltshire is beyond my comprehension!"

They turned north-eastward and examined the Chute's great Vyne in Basingstoke, and viewed the remains of Donnington Castle, once in the possession of Geoffery Chaucer's son and given in dowry for his daughter, the Duchess of Suffolk. Continuing up the Oxford Road, Elizabeth and her husband stopt to see the ancient buildings of the colleges and chapels, and walked along the river in Christchurch meadows to watch the sailing boats and sculls as they raced on the river. Turning homeward, they paused to view the great castle at Warwick, home of the King-maker Earls of Warwick, before concluding that they had incommoded a sufficient number of their peers and others, and were able to return to Pemberley with credit and satisfaction.

CHAP. 15.

MR. AND MRS. DARCY were invited to attend His Grace, the Duke of
B——at his seat in Gloucestershire for the racing season at Bibury
and Kingscote, to be followed by the sport in Marlborough, and ending
with the Epsom Derby in June. Neither of the Darcys was inclined to
the activity for the purpose of wagering, but the opportunity to travel
southward in April—when the weather in Derbyshire was likely to be
capricious—to more a propitious climate and the promise of pleasant
company was very welcome, indeed. Georgiana declined to accompany
them, as she wished to spend the months remaining in the season with
the Earl and his wife, who yet remained in town, and with the Gardiners.

The Duke was a peer of the old stamp. Of the middle age, he was
tall, dignified, still very well-looking, hale, hearty, endlessly sociable,
and thoroughly good-humoured. In spite of his rank, he was a man
whose ideas of pleasure were simple and respectable: hunting, racing,
shooting, fishing—in short—anything that could be done out-of-doors
with a dog or an horse comprised the pleasures of his hours. Like his
peers, he was fond of his wine, and fond of his table; yet unlike many
in his sphere of life, he was fond of his *own* wife, a devoted father to his
children (all of whom were the issue of his Duchess), and a kind master
to his servants, who neither took liberties nor tolerated the abuse of
privilege within his family. His Grace and Mr. Darcy, often together
at the various agricultural societies, were in regular, friendly contest
as to their abilities as producers of animals, crops, soils, machinery, or
anything else that could be grown, devised, or measured and weighed.

Mr. Darcy chose to leave the second week in April, Easter falling
later that year, so as to miss the several hunts which covered the area
between Derbyshire and Gloucestershire. Whilst not opposed to any

sport himself, Mr. Darcy had no wish to have his coach run through by the hunt, so frequently were leaders seen breaking their traces to bolt away with the pack, and the wheelers thrown down upon the pole, over-turning the carriage and subjecting the vehicle, its contents, and its passengers to much delay, disorder, and injury. Leaving Pemberley, the Darcys travelled through Burton to Lichfield to shew Elizabeth where the late Mr. Darwin had lived, and continued on to Great Barr Park to visit Mr. Galton. The present Mr. Darcy had not been of age to be a member of the Lunar Society of Birmingham, but had several times attended its meetings in the summer months with his father, and was on easy, friendly terms with many of its members. The Society was no longer extant, but the surviving members still enjoyed a regular correspondence, in which Mr. Darcy took part. Leaving Birmingham, and by passing through by the most expeditious route, they reached Gloucestershire within the week. This country was similar to Hertfordshire, thought Elizabeth, although less settled.

The last distance of their road went through the area of the Cotswolds, with its hills and villages of yellow stone, all built more or less of a piece in the century of Queen Elizabeth, giving them a very pretty, regular appearance. Elizabeth mused that she had never seen the equal of the picturesque clusters of houses surrounding the old chapels and the requisite gabled manors as they passed through the hills and wool-villages. The villages were becoming quiet now, with the cottage industry largely moved off to the great mills and manufactories of the midlands, but Elizabeth could imagine their noise and liveliness in the time of the Queen, when the villages were new, and England was yet to defeat the Spanish navy and acquire the wealth and power of the Spanish Kings. The places were now very peaceful and pleasant, but Elizabeth, with her love of humanity and its noise and bustle, felt that the quietude was come at a price, and she was herself of no firm mind as to the removal of the livelihoods of these villages being entirely a good thing.

The Duke's seat was—as expected for a Duke—very grand. The Darcys were cordially received by Their Graces, and given apartments overlooking the lake and deer-park. The Duchess was very tall, handsome, and slender (even after producing four children for His Grace), with an agile, decided walk that was the hallmark of someone who was much outside; her expression shared the same frankness and warmth of her husband. Elizabeth fancied that, should the Duke be marvellously transformed into a woman, he must necessarily be the twin

❧ of

of his wife. So strikingly similar were the pair, that Elizabeth could but imagine that their children, when younger, must have had trouble distinguishing one parent from another! Elizabeth was consequently not surprised to find that the Duke and Duchess were cousins on the mother's side, and had spent much of their youth at one of the family seats or other in pursuit of winter sports, or summer amusements in the company of one another. This accounted, reflected Elizabeth, for the easy, harmonious intercourse between husband and wife, and the remarkable similarity in their tastes and pleasures.

During the mornings, Elizabeth, the Duchess, and the other ladies of the house would either walk or ride; the Duchess was a keen horsewoman and not only rode with her husband at the hunt, but shot as well. Elizabeth admired her graceful figure and the ease with which she traversed the park, jumping over stiles, riding through the coverts, laughing and conversing with the other riders. She could lean from the saddle and shake hands as easily (and often more gracefully) as could many of the gentlemen, and even in her skirts could mount and dismount in an instant with no assistance save the mounting-block. Elizabeth thought of Jane and her proficiency as an horsewoman, and wished she could be here to ride with Her Grace and give the Darcy family some credit on the female side—but with motherhood had come a decrease of outdoor exercise and a proportional increase of figure, so Elizabeth was required to be content with her own accomplishments and conversation as recompense for the kindness of their hosts.

Mr. Darcy alternately rode out with the others, or went with one of the other gentlemen to fish, it not being the season for shooting; all returned promptly for breakfast at ten o'clock, and lunch at one o'clock. In the afternoons, there were races, games, or visits abroad. It being the country, the Duchess ordered tea for four o'clock, and supper at eight, as the Duke and his wife were fond of early mornings, and had no turn for the activities usually associated with later hours. They enjoyed their children in a stile that did not call for sacrifice on the part of their guests, and Elizabeth noted with an unusual approval that the children were grown up remarkably unspoilt and useful, respectful and obliging—in short, as happy and healthy as loving parents, plain food, exercise, and naturally good dispositions could form them.

"What a blessing to be in the care of such natural parents!" she thought. "An husband and wife of equal temperaments and talents, mutually fond—and more—*appreciative* of each other's society, and obliged by their companionship. How different from the common course of matrimony, where couples unite only to part for the best hours of the day, more careful for the approbation and comfort of their friends than each other. Or, like her own parents, inhabiting the same rooms, but totally separate in their thinking, any pleasure in the other's society arising from the amusement provided by the ignorance, folly, or frailty of their chosen partner in life."

"Mr. Darcy," began Elizabeth one evening of their visit, "Did your mother and father find the same pleasure in each other's company as I observe between the Their Graces? They seem not only very mutually attached, but so very alike! I have been used to believing such excessive similarity between husbands and wives results in so pervasive a tranquillity that *ennui* must soon starve any desire for the society of the other entirely away; although in my family certainly the obverse was true, but the result was the same."

"I cannot decide the general case, but, yes, my mother and father shared many interests and pursuits, and were obviously very happy together. That is not to say that happiness in marriage is only possible where the tastes of each exactly coincide with those of the other, but certainly there must be some communality of pleasure."

"Are you sorry that I am not more like Her Grace? She is His Grace's equal in so many ways, that they appear more like sister and brother than husband and wife in the pattern of their intercourse. Surely such coincidence of nature is agreeable," replied Elizabeth.

"Lizzy, I *have* a sister. I wanted a wife and, at the risk of congratulating myself, after some very humbling trial and error on my own part, I got the wife I wanted. I well remember your censure on poetry as the adversary of love, but I venture to repeat that old verse, 'My heart is fixed, it cannot range, for I like my choice too well to change.' Do you have regrets in your choice?"

Elizabeth laughed. "Mr. Darcy, you well know that you are the only man who, in your disposition and talents, your understanding and temper, could ever make me happy. My only regret is that I knew you for more than a year before I could recognise your perfection, and admit it to myself, not only unreasonably delaying my own happiness, but the education of the world as to the very picture of conjugal felicity. Is this assurance enough?"

Mr. Darcy put out the candle, saying, "A man can never have too much of example where the love and admiration of his wife is concerned."

The following day, the entire party was to leave for Marlborough, the seat of the late Lord and his relict, Lady Brookstone; Elizabeth

was

was initially not sorry for the change, as she felt that she had seen so little of the world, even the distance of thirty-five miles was enough to make her eager for the prospect of new scenery and new pleasures. The journey was accomplished through the expedient of post-horses and the generosity of the Duke: his servants were to bring the Duke's carriage horses into Wiltshire, saving the Darcy's horses the fatigue of pulling the large travelling chaise such a distance in one day by bringing them along as well.

Lord Brookstone's establishment was in every way more formal and less delightful whence they had come. Lady Brookstone, unlike the Duchess, proved to be enamoured chiefly of her own imagined consequence, and entirely disdainful of the feelings of nearly everyone else. Toward the Duke and Duchess, she was obsequious and servile. Elizabeth could hardly keep herself from staring, and could not imagine how they could bear such absurdity with patience. She wondered what could be Their Graces' meaning, by coming to stay for weeks in the company of one at once so ridiculous and unpleasant. Her question was answered in the course of the first day, in the Duchess making the statement, "It was a great change to their pleasure that Lord Brookstone was no longer alive." Lady Brookstone had understood the comment to mean that the Duchess was being civil in remembering Lord Brookstone to the company. Indeed, it required no great stretch of thought to understand Her Grace to say that the house without Lord Brookstone had lost much of its pleasures and all of its appeal. Whereas Their Graces were the picture of great consequence and a firmness of character which made them civil and obliging to the world, Lady Brookstone's low birth and fortune prior to her marriage resulted in a small consequence being thoroughly overwhelmed by a large conceit. The good-breeding and amiability of the Duke and Duchess made a contrast with the pretence, airs, and demands for precedence of Her Ladyship all the more striking, and a lesson for all as example to serve as warning.

It was fortunate that Lady Brookstone—unknowingly—supplied Elizabeth with such diversion that she paid this lady the compliment of attending to her speech, dress, and habits to a far greater degree than her performance could otherwise command. Elizabeth learnt that Lady Brookstone, a widow of the middle-age from the West country, had been living in a small way at one of the faded sea-side towns, when she had been singled out for intimacy by one of the comparatively more affluent ladies who frequented the town out of deference to the greater expense of the more fashionable watering-places. Lord Brookstone had

❧ seen

seen several wives come and go, for the various and usual reasons which are afforded those whose means place themselves beyond the reach of scandal. By the time he was introduced to the last Lady Brookstone, the gentleman had already suffered from a such a succession of fits as had left him unable to walk, almost blind, and without the power of speech; in this form came Lady Brookstone's lover. It was as well that Lord Brookstone could not see, as his Lady's visage was as transmogrified as the application of powders and pomatums could render a face as comely as nature had made plain. Her figure was like-wise unenviable, being short and stout, and her movements were entirely without any of those graces of which ladies are commonly possessed. She had early resorted to every art available to reconstruct where nature had erred, but with such an heavy hand, that the effect served more to accentuate the cause of her efforts, than to diminish the original defect. Lady Brookstone presented not so much a picture of any particular age or fashion, but a living warning to others as to the limitations of the cosmetic arts.

The uncharitable described the match as one in which one party had the power to refuse, but would not, and the other had the power, but could not. Lord Brookstone had lastly married, it seemed, for the sole purpose of disobliging his family. Lord Brookstone's issue by his previous ladies regarded each other with at least the veneer of civility, and had, as a sure inducement to familial accord, the existence of such an objectionable step-mother to unite them in some feeling of family connection. Lord Brookstone lived only a few years after his last marriage. When the will was read, he had left everything legally possible away from his heirs and his title to his last wife. Any morsel that had not been entailed by marriage articles upon the children of the various mothers was now the property of a woman of neither birth nor beauty, charm nor wit. Lord Brookstone had, for reasons of enchantment—or feebleness of mind—been persuaded by this lady to give her a life-estate on any property which was not actually in the possession of his own children! His only daughter had been left with nothing other than a small settlement that had been in her mother's gift. Elizabeth, looking at Lady Brookstone, was wholly unable to account for such an history. The disgust of Lord Brookstone's sons and daughter, when forced into the company of their odious step-mother, could be only partially imagined by those not subject to the daily diminution of comforts, owing to the enrichment of a woman who had no claim to fortune other than that she had seduced a man no longer in possession of his faculties to take her as a wife. The lady now passed her days in the company of a coterie of single-men of all ages, united—as it appeared—only in their fawning attention to Lady Brookstone and a singular disinclination to matrimony. These men gathered about her like moths to a light, which Elizabeth initially found unaccountable. Elizabeth later learnt of a rumour that Lord Brookstone had included a reversion in his will should his relict remarry, which might well explain Her Ladyship's preference of company.

Such visits and diversions occupied the Darcys throughout the first the ten years of their marriage. The family often recollected the delights of their travels: the views from Exe Bridge in Devonshire, from which could be seen ships of one hundred and fifty tons, and the ingenious contrivance of the flood-gates latterly placed to protect the towns along the river from flooding; Falmouth, in Cornwall, where the fleet of English packets were sailing regularly to Lisbon, Groyne, North America, and even to the West Indies from its docks; and, the Isles of Wight and Skye, Sussex, Wessex, Essex, Wales and the roads in-between. Having travelled as far as John o'Groats in Scotland, standing nearly a thousand miles' distance to the edge of Land's End, Mr. and Mrs. Darcy could claim with veracity that they had indeed travelled the length and breadth of the country. The pursuit of pleasures in their own country, riding along the post roads of Britain, had not requited their taste for travel, but rather the reverse. The Darcys found themselves ready for a trip abroad, the war being at long-last over and the Peace secured; enough time was now passed to heal the wounds, and bring regular commerce to a continent long troubled.

CHAP. 16.

"I MUST SPEND some hours to-day on business of the estate, Lizzy," began Mr. Darcy, "and, if you would not think it too fatiguing, I would be delighted if you would accompany me." Mr. and Mrs. Darcy had finished their breakfast and were enjoying that quiet companionship formed of equal understandings and mutual pleasures, sitting together by the hour, intent upon separate occupations, yet united by the blessings of contentment and attachment. Elizabeth was at the moment engaged in the very pleasant business of letter-writing to those whose delight in her news she could most confidently depend, the one being addressed to Bingley and Jane, and the other to the her Aunt and Uncle Gardiner. Mr. Darcy, meanwhile, was seated in his armchair, reading the latest publication of the *Annals of Agriculture*, and had been quite as fully absorbed as if it had been a novel.

"I would willingly sacrifice the pleasures of my correspondents to go with you, if you like my company, Mr. Darcy. With Georgiana gone to London with your Aunt Hallendale, I am quite at leisure. If you do not wish me to the slavery of an ungrateful piano-forte, and consequently perforce witness my feminine accomplishments to an even greater degree of perfection, you must give me some excuse to preserve my defects for yet another day."

"The case as you describe it is grave, indeed. I must save both you and the piano-forte from such a fate. You must, however, give me your solemn vow never to actually achieve perfection, for as you know, I married you for your faults and not your virtues." Mr. Darcy smilingly kissed his wife, and suggested that they take their coffee earlier than usual that morning.

As they walked out of doors toward the gardens, crossing the lawn that reached to the lake, Elizabeth discovered that Mr. Darcy had a motive for wishing her to accompany him.

"I would like to know your views on my latest ideas for the improvement of the Pemberley estates. Knightley has recently published a treatise on improvements to habitations for the poor. Taking John Harford's example, Knightley commissioned several single-storey cottages for benefit of the elderly and infirm, as well as some very tidy dwellings for the poor within the village surrounding the green at his Donwell Abbey estate. He has rejoined with some additional amendments for improvements to Harford's scheme, including a plan for some gardens within the properties." Such advancement for the general good had made an immediate impression upon Mr. Darcy, who set about writing to Mr. Knightley, enquiring on some particulars of construction; the only unresolved issue was placement of the buildings, and the details of the interiors, the subject that was to occupy the two on their walk.

Both gentlemen held *Kent's Hints* in high esteem, and Knightley had used Kent's agricultural plans and costings in the building of his labourers' cottages. Elizabeth listened to her husband's plans for improvements, and recalled with pleasure Mrs. Reynolds' warm praise of Mr. Darcy and the high regard in which his tenantry held him. Elizabeth, with less gratification, also recalled her very first visit to Pemberley and the mortifying self-acknowledgement of that prejudice that had led her unreasonably and uniformly to under-value the man who was become her husband. His every decision concerning the estate was made as much to secure the long-term prosperity and comfort of his tenants as that of his own family at Pemberley; Elizabeth felt that compassion was amongst his most admirable qualities. As they walked onto higher ground, Darcy continued to talk of the success of his new crop varieties, and improving the fertility of the poor Derbyshire soil.

"As you know, the cottagers' dwellings and the trade-school will necessarily be an enterprise of several years, so I wish to undertake the drawing of plans for their construction immediately. I mean to have a small orchard in the back of the dwelling, which will serve both to provide food, and to shelter the cottage from the worst of the winds and summer heats. I would much value your ideas as to where they might be most advantageously positioned, and what you think of Knightley's amendments to the interiors. My other investigation may take even longer, as it requires a trip abroad, and I do not know when such a trip might be convenient. I would very much like to obtain cuttings of the

true

true French 'Paradise' pear stock, which I believe would grow very well in our heavy Derbyshire soil."

"I had no suspicion you were become such an expert in the field of French horticulture, Mr. Darcy. Listening to you makes me quite ashamed that I spend any time at all reading novels, when I could be learning about things more likely to *yield* improvement," Lizzy said laughing. "Perhaps one day we will be able to make the trip abroad together. I have always envied gentlemen this aspect of their educations, and have reason to believe that the discomforts of a life on the road, as you know, suit me very well. As we walk on, extol, for my benefit, the merits of an asparagus," she said taking his arm, "for I am certain I espied you reading about that very subject this morning. And, to shew you I am in earnest, beg you enchant me with encomiums on plums or turnips, as you please!"

Mr. Darcy followed the pattern of many landed gentlemen in his avid interest in the improvement of soils, crops, plantations, livestock, practical buildings, mechanical implements, and such-like. His reading was broad, his numerous correspondents the chief agriculturalists of the day, and he attended scientifical meetings and academies when he was in town. Elizabeth had once enquired if his pursuit of new methods in husbandry was motivated by pecuniary or philanthropic interests, and he had replied, "Both, my dearest. It can no longer be assumed that ownership of land will be profitable; it is the ownership of profitable land that will ensure its preservation. And, in consequence of the capital raised from the land, we are able to improve the prospects for the tenantry, and, hence, keep the best of our tenants on the land when so many others are leaving the fields for the manufactories. It is a necessary endeavour on all counts: my effort is recompensed with capital, which enables increased investment in land and people. In these times of rapidly changing ideas and inventions, it is more complicated than in my esteemed father's lifetime, when sheep and wheat or barley were enough. Now, one must chuse between many industries that may be supported in any place at any time: mining, manufacturing, housing, crops, livestock, or timber. It is not to be supposed that the sale of land would ever be beneficial to the increase of the value of the estate for future generations, but even that is not now always the case.

"It is not all about capital, however," he continued as they walked slowly back up the hill toward the house. "I very much enjoy, as do many of our scientifical gentlemen, the discovery of those animals and crops that are considerably improved, and testing the various methods toward their betterment. I have been very fortunate in that my late father's steward, Mr. Wickham, Senior, and our present factor, Mr. Bakewell, have been scrupulous record-keepers, and very careful in their experimental methods. As with the library at Pemberley, the produce of the farms is the work of many generations of improvers."

Elizabeth stopt him just as they were about to enter and said, "But your favourite researches of all are the pears?"

Darcy smiled down at her and said, "Yes, how did you know? Was my enthusiasm for the asparagus and plums not what it ought?"

Elizabeth replied, "Your comment on the French pears. They must be very special, indeed, to surpass these at Pemberley."

Darcy laughed, "They are, my dear, just as are you."

"That may do very well for a compliment," replied Elizabeth, "but it will not do as a comparison: they must be even more special, as I did not require you to make such a journey into France to collect me, merely into Hertfordshire."

"Well said, Lizzy, but should you like to make a tour of Europe? I think that it may be a good thing for Georgiana, as her society is so little varied. We see the same families year in and year out. It is very pleasant to us, but you and I are not in need of enlarging our acquaintance for matrimony's sake."

"Yours is an excellent idea, for it exactly coincides with my own. I suppose it is too soon to leave to-day, but perhaps we may be gone to-morrow?" Lizzy replied, as they went in to tea.

"Lizzy," began Darcy as they were seated in the small parlour, "I know that you are not serious about to-morrow, but I am concerned that you do not comprehend the inconvenience and trouble of such a journey. For example, to carry our immediate necessities and our servants with us, I need to bespeak a travelling chaise large enough and heavy enough for the journey over the Alps. You and Georgiana must see to the packing of our linens and cloathing for the journey of several months, and for all vagaries of climate. I have my hunting flint-lock and my father's stag-rifle for under the box, but I would also like to commission a brace of new pistols for myself and Harmon— and a thousand other troublesome details which must be thought of and attended to before we can leave."

"Dear Mr. Darcy!" laughed Elizabeth, "you must be taking your lessons from my own book of sparing one's self all inconvenience. I am not so incapable or unwilling as you imply, and further assert that I would find such a project most agreeable. I have a great love of travel, having met with much success and happiness as a consequence in the past. Although I have already got my share of husbands, I may be so generous as to lend Georgiana some of my good fortune *en route*. I am not sure, however, what I may do for you, as your share of happiness is necessarily complete. I was thinking of a great German Cuckoo clock for the hall at Pemberley, or maybe a Venice-boat for the lake?"

Satisfied with having made Mr. Darcy laugh, Elizabeth continued, "I do believe that we might begin after Christmas, and the Bingleys could travel with us?"

Darcy replied that the Bingleys were most welcome, indeed; however, it may be difficult to persuade them to leave their children for such a long time. Elizabeth then suggested her father and Kitty, and Darcy made no objection. Colonel Fitzwilliam was added, and the composition of their party credited with perfection. Besides the family, it would be necessary to bring such a number of servants with them their present coach would not accommodate. Besides the ladies' maids, it was necessary to take Mr. Darcy's valet, Mrs. Reynold's assistant, a maid-of-all-work, the under-butler, the steward's boy, and two footmen to serve as postillions and out-riders, in addition to the two coachmen and a stable-boy, who could also serve at table, if need be.

Darcy began a correspondence the next day with his carriage-maker, one Mr. Birch of Great Queen Street, and ordered a travelling chariot and a travelling coach of large size to be ready the following February. Elizabeth saw that he frequently consulted his notes from the visit to the museum to view Buonaparte's chaise, and felt some complacency in the thought of travelling in the same stile as had the Emperour! Put to this large coach must be a team of four heavy carriage-horses for the mountain journey, requiring Mr. Darcy to direct Mr. Bakewell to find suitable horses. "We require an additional four for the servants' coach for the main part of the journey, and will put two of them to the travelling chaise for the road over the Alps. We can take post horses for the second coach when required. Two mounted out-riders will be necessary for safety, and in case one of the carriage horses becomes lame."

The Darcys planned an early departure for the continent, calculated not only to permit a leisurely tour through to Paris and Geneva, reaching the Italian Alps and Simplon Pass as soon as the snows permitted safe passage, but also to avoid the hordes of round, English faces who would descend upon Europe later in the spring. It was said that there was no refuge to be found where the picturesque or solitude was yet undisturbed by their innumerable compatriots, their chaises, and loud accents. Mr.

Darcy had been informed that prices had increased significantly with the invasion southward, and Elizabeth was given to understand the necessity of bringing all of their bed-cloathes, as the linens on the continent were not dependably clean. Georgiana ordered a new sketch-book, and her brother provided her with an ingenious folding easel that, when extended, included a chair! To his wife, he presented an exquisite travelling escritoire, inlaid with her initials. He presented himself with an handsome brace of pistols, and a new great-coat.

Elizabeth was energetically employed bespeaking linens and travelling cloathes; Mrs. Reynolds in ascertaining which of their trunks would fit on the coach most efficiently, and how to contrive to fill them with every imaginable article that might—in the most unlikely of circumstances—be of need to the Darcys on the road. Mr. Darcy wrote to his scientifical friends abroad as to their residence when the visit was likely to be paid, and to the loriner bespeaking large harness for the new coach horses; he asked the farrier to lay in extra shoes and extra carriage-furniture. Everything was to be in readiness for a departure in late February or early March, depending upon the vagaries of the English climate.

All of this industry and invention was nearly over-thrown when Georgiana announced that she could not possibly leave Mademoiselle Blanche, who, in her advancing years, appeared to be ailing. "She hardly eats anything, no matter what delicacy Cook sets before her, and see how rough and dull her fur is become? I am convinced that, in my absence, she may not eat at all, or, at any rate, will be much worse without my attendance." Both Darcy and Elizabeth tried to reassure her that Mademoiselle Blanche looked likely to exist for some time to come, but Georgiana was unusually obdurate.

"Mademoiselle Blanche was there to soothe my sorrow and offer me comfort in times of a most wretched loneliness and grief. I shall never consent to forfeit my duty to in her time of need."

There seemed an impasse until Mrs. Annesley offered to remain behind with Mademoiselle Blanche: "Georgiana, dearest, Mademoiselle Blanche may not love me as well as she loves you, but we have been three together these many years. I will answer for her comforts in your absence." Reluctantly, Georgiana was persuaded to yield to entreaty, with the declarations of all that Mademoiselle Blanche yet looked very well able to survive to see another twelve-month, at least.

CHAP. 17.

GOOD COMPANY IS INVARIABLY the best cure for a melancholy mind, and Georgiana had been unusually low since the Colonel's departure to the Hallendales', where he was to spend a fortnight before returning to Pemberley for Christmas. She looked forward to the Christmas holidays, bringing an house full of visitors and, therefore, diversion. Mr. Bennet and Parson and Mrs. Overstowey were the earliest arrivals, although travelling the shortest distance. Darcy had long since abandoned his habit of wonder at the eccentricities of his father-in-law. Elizabeth suspected that her husband rather enjoyed Mr. Bennet's spontaneous visits, giving, a larger share of pleasure than pain; Mr. Darcy was grown less censorious, and Mr. Bennet less capricious. Added to this, each looked forward to the opportunity to compare the latest acquisitions of their respective libraries. The Gardiners were next to arrive with their troupe of children, all smiles and presents, as was their custom.

Upon their first meeting, Georgiana had seemed to all the Bennet family as being not unlike her brother, but with more warmth and an obvious desire to please. A more intimate knowledge of her revealed that, beneath the intelligence, genuine accomplishment, and finely-bred manners, lay a very simple, generous heart, and not a little loneliness; she had been immediately claimed as one of their own, much to Georgiana's delight. Like-wise, Mr. Bennet saw with satisfaction Miss Darcy's sisterly partiality for Lizzy, and found her diffident, unspoilt, affectionate nature enchanting. He was grown fond of his new daughter, and ranked her in his estimation above at least two of his own. Hastening into the morning room, where Elizabeth had been writing letters, Georgiana was greeted by the sight of Mr. Bennet unceremoniously removing his great-coat, and Kitty and her husband smiling to greet her.

"Mrs. Overstowey, Parson, Mr. Bennet, you are welcome, indeed. We had not expected you for several days—how delighted my brother and sister will be to see you so soon as to-day," Georgiana said, kissing Kitty and shaking hands with Mr. Bennet and Parson Overstowey. "My brother is about, out of doors somewhere."

That evening at dinner, the conversation turned to the anticipated tour abroad. At Darcy's urging, Elizabeth had written to her father, desiring him to be of their party along with Kitty and Parson Overstowey, but Mr. Bennet had never been fond of travel and the prospect of more than four months away from the peace of the parson's library and the noise of his grandchildren was insupportable. Equally inconceivable was that Kitty leave her father for any length of time. Instead, both were content to listen to Darcy's plans for the route, to confirm the merits of a Dover to Calais crossing over the alternative of Brighton to Dieppe, and the dispensability of the entire north of France.

So engrossed were the whole company in their armchair journey, that Kitty temporarily lapsed in her self-appointed duty of vigilance over her father's dinner-plate, failing to notice it had been heaped with a second portion of venison and pheasant, the food being despatched by Mr. Bennet with evident pleasure. A momentary pause in the Alps allowed his younger daughter to glance in her father's direction, and the horror-stricken look he received, as her eyes seized upon his plate, could not pass unnoticed by the rest of the table. Darcy, with a quickness of mind that marked his good-breeding, asked whether the produce of Pemberley Woods had not met with Mr. Bennet's approbation. Before her father was able to answer beyond a splutter, Kitty jumped in with formidable emphasis:

"Mr. Darcy, I daresay your venison is delightful beyond comparison, but our family have made some salutary changes of late in consequence of Papa's misery with the gout. A book, which I have taken to carrying about with me, finding it extraordinarily useful for constant reference throughout the day—perhaps you would like to peruse it yourself?—has rather changed our table, has it not, father?" (producing the volume *On Food* from her pocket) "Here it is! It is as useful a book as ever I saw. Once I had read it, I vowed that our life was to change. There would be no more strong drink and no more eating of meat at the parsonage, for the evils of an high table, I have discovered by way of this book, cannot be underestimated. It has been not a fortnight since we changed our habits, and yet already our dear Papa feels better, is that not true? We would not go back to meat and strong spirits, not for all the world!"

Georgiana and Darcy looked meaningfully at the plates of Mr. Bennet and the parson, upon which were piled substantial portions of venison and pheasant, and tried to avoid one another's eye. Kitty, mistaking the fragile silence of the room to be the sign of a captive and convertible audience, continued, "You see, to my ready approbation, I find meat and spirits hazards to the health, and most especially to the constitution of a valetudinarian, as is dear Papa. You could not believe your eyes if you read all the delectable recipes for dining well without meat. Here, look at this one—it uses mushroom forcemeat instead of gammon and partridge. I own Cook was rather put out at first, but she is quite reconciled upon finding how vastly improved my father's leg becomes as a result of a plain diet."

Finding all the table looking at him for an unlikely confirmation, Mr. Bennet replied, "You may all well expect me to gainsay my daughter's experiments, but, if truth be told, my gout weighs less on me than before. However, my dear," patting Kitty's hand and smiling, "we may take a little liberty against the leg, now and again, lest we insult Mr. Darcy or—Heaven forbid!—the woods of Pemberley." Mr. Bennet then implored Mr. Darcy to consider exchanging abodes with him, at least for long enough to prevent himself and his son-in-law from wasting away altogether, gout and all, from lack of sustenance. Kitty momentarily looked as though she might be insulted, but for a kind look from Georgiana, who added, "It is altogether commendable, Kitty's concern for the comfort of her father."

Kitty, unused to anyone taking her part, replied, "Oh! Dear Papa! Yes, but you are quite correct in acting so as to avoid giving offense."

Mr. Bennet leaned over to his younger daughter, and, kissing the top of her head, gently said, "Kitty, my child, you know I could not do without you." With that, he signalled for the footman to take the plate away, declaring that the delights of Pemberley's woods were always worth a limp or two and, with a wink directed at Mr. Darcy, laughed with Lizzy and Georgiana. Parson Overstowey, in deference to the collective opinion, after cleaning his plate entirely, persevered in this laudable resolution to take no further additional servings of any dish but the puddings. After dinner, the gentlemen retired to the Darcy's library to consult maps, with the three ladies left to a comprehensive discussion of the myriad items that could not possibly be done without *en voyage.* Kitty, who, like her mother, was unable to comprehend that Meryton was other than the centre of the world, offered to lend Elizabeth her straw bonnet just bought on a visit to the Collins's. Elizabeth was so charmed by this mark of affection that she accepted, despite having no deficit of bonnets herself. The next day made Elizabeth yet more pleased with her own graciousness in taking the proffered hat, as Kitty exclaimed at breakfast her intention of writing to Jane, telling her of her pride in her own bonnet's being gone to Italy!

"My father and I made a visit to Paris when I was a boy, sailing to Ostende through Bruges, and Lille. I was fortunate enough to come of age directly following Amiens, although we all knew that the peace would not last. It lasted just long enough to require my tutor to over-throw all of our plans at the last moment, and avoid France entirely by travelling through Saxony. I was looking at my copy of Wilkinson," said Mr. Darcy, "but I find it now hopelessly out of date. It was my bible during the tour of my youth, but it seems hardly a place has survived with its name or boundaries intact since Buonaparte has finished with Europe."

"Come, come, Darcy," cried Mr. Bennet, "I am sure an atlas is still quite satisfactory, for, even if the names are different, the geography is the same. Even Buonaparte could not move the mountains!"

"That is a matter of some dispute," replied Mrs. Gardiner, "especially if you consider his great achievement over the Simplon. If he has not actually moved the mountains, he has surely made them less relevant to the traveller."

"Very true, my love," nodded Mr. Gardiner, "although I am not sure it was a great bargain from the point of view of the English—the convenience of the present company excepted, of course!"

The rest of the week continued fine and frosty, and Mr. Darcy, Mr. Bennet, Mr. Gardiner, Parson Overstowey and Colonel Fitzwilliam, recently arrived, were able to amuse themselves out of doors. The ladies walked, talked, and sewed. The Bingleys and all their children and servants arrived well before Christmas. Lord and Lady Hallendale, living much nearer, were due to arrive only a few days before Christmas Eve. Lady Catherine and her daughter, unable to command a sufficient audience amongst the other distractions and personages, declined to visit and remained instead at Bath, under the pretense of preferring it to all places at that time of year.

Family tradition at Pemberley dictated that there be performed a theatrical at Christmas time. Upon the arrival of the Bingleys, therefore, it took little urging for the plan to be concluded that a play be performed at Pemberley, although no-one could agree on *which* play, the family all talking ten to the dozen over one another. The children were charged with the task of the selection, and under the watchful

eyes

eyes of Mrs. Reynolds and Mrs. Annesley, the eldest of the Bingleys' and the Gardiners' children were allowed into the library of Pemberley to locate a suitable play. The Bingleys had been recently abroad on a family journey to Argyllshire and Inverness, which had included a sailing trip around Iona, Mull, Coll, and Tiree. The children excitedly alighted upon a volume of Joanna Baillie's *Miscellaneous Plays*, selecting "The Family Legend," for it included the requisite ingredients of night-time boat rides, sinister schemes, dramatical gentlemen's duels, and at least one hysterical lady abandoned on a rock.

The play was conducted with reverence to the hands of Colonel Fitzwilliam, to whom was deputed the assignment of cutting the play down from five acts to three, whilst necessarily retaining all its most horrid scenes. After a whole afternoon of employment for Colonel Fitzwilliam, whose every alteration was most anxiously superintended by the sea of children who crowded about the table, the play was declared fit for its purpose, and the preparations began. The good Mrs. Reynolds was prevailed upon to organise costume, props, and scenery, and Mrs. Annesley found herself charged with presiding over the distribution of speeches, as all the girls could see themselves as none other than the tragic Helen of Argyll, whilst the boys universally fancied themselves as her brother, Lorne, the deliverer of the fatal blow that fells the evil MacLean. Once these essential controversies had been resolved at last, rehearsals began in earnest, and Mrs. Annesley substituted her occupation as distributor of speeches for the less interesting and uncontroversial rôles of prompter and approver.

Welcome, indeed, was the relative peace that descended upon the great house as the children spent night and day in one of the smaller reception rooms, which had been allocated to rehearsal. Interrupted by frequent calls for the immediate attendance of Colonel Fitzwilliam and Mr. Bennet, who had been invested with the important rôles of Vassal One and Vassal Two and were, subsequently, much in demand, the other adults were free to enjoy the days at their leisure.

The eve of Christmas was settled upon as the date for the *début* of the Pemberley Players, and, with great anticipation, the audience collected in the Great Hall around the stage that had been erected for the afternoon's performance. The main characters had naturally been seized by the older children, but a great many smaller speeches had been left over, which Elizabeth, Georgiana, the Gardiners, the Bingleys, and the Overstoweys had been urged into playing, and so the spectators themselves were curiously costumed as befitted their various identities.

Darcy, content to view the production with the detached bemusement of the uninvolved, had been persuaded—under some duress—to assume the rôle of Fisherman Four, a part that demanded only a fleeting presence on stage and the delivery of a single line. For this appearance, he had steadfastly refused to dress himself in the garb of a boatman until the closing moments of Act Two. Even Mademoiselle Blanche had a part to play, having been written in by the agreeable Colonel Fitzwilliam as the ship's cat and, under Georgiana's watchful eye, allowed herself to be hoisted thither and yon with remarkable forbearance, especially in view of the fact that she had affixed upon her head a tiny b'osun's cap.

As hostess, Elizabeth reserved for herself the opening scene, reading the prologue, latterly added by Sir Walter Scott, as soon as the audience were seated—after many last-minute searches for pins, ribbands, lost hats, &c. "The Family Legend" was expected, alternately, to produce tears and sombre reflections on the faces of the audience. The tragedical efforts that were attempted, in spite of very earnest endeavours on the parts of the players (as well as some very doubtful attempts at Scottish speech) resulted in a near-pandemonium of hilarity, and any tears to be seen were the consequence not of affecting empathy, but rather the enjoyment of farce. Undeterred, the Pemberley Players carried on valiantly, and the scene reuniting the Earl of Argyll with his long-lost daughter would have been affecting indeed, had it not been for the muffled howlings of Mademoiselle Blanche, recently arrested and confined to a pic-nick basket to prevent her from appropriating additional scenes. By the time Mrs. Annesley had ventured onto the stage to deliver the epilogue, the entire company were exhausted from laughter, and could go about their afternoon's business assured that, even if the livelihoods of Mr. Kean and Mrs. Siddons were not threatened, all had acquitted their parts admirably.

The halls had been hung with yew and fir boughs, mistletoe, and holly-berry, and the largest logs were in readiness for the Christmas Eve fire. Pemberley was a scene of noise and disorder such as had not been witnessed in any recent time, and possibly never at all. The grand galleries were perfect for hoop-rolling, the parlours the scene for great games of hide-and-seek, and the old Great Hall for pantomimes and carol singing. That evening, whilst the children were left to the care of servants and their dreams, the rest of the Pemberley party attended church.

In the morning, there were little gifts for the children, and church again, before the great dinner of goose, venison, roast beef, bacon, black butter, and plum pudding. Elizabeth and her husband sat at each end,

doing

doing honour to their elegant table, carving and serving. There was much toasting, singing and gaiety after supper and into the evening. When the children had eaten all of their sugar-plums and gingerbread and been seen off to their beds, the rest retired to the library for coffee and the inevitable discussion of the Darcys' tour. Books and maps were again produced, and the entire evening spent in suggestion and conjecture. Colonel Fitzwilliam, Bingley, and Darcy told stories of their travels of years past, and of the Earl of the Grand Tour of his youth. Neither Mr. Bennet nor Mr. Gardiner had travelled extensively, but, having read a great number of the guide-books published in recent years, had fully as much to suggest as to routes and the principal sights of many of the places they planned to pass through. Parson Overstowey was warm in his praise of the wines of the various regions they might visit, and his conviction that the food of each land could answer as an end in itself, but did not seem actually sorry to be spared the exertion required to acquire it. All-in-all, it was a very agreeable day.

CHAP. 18.

Sɪʀ Wɪʟʟɪᴀᴍ Eʟʟɪᴏᴛ, of Marlborough Buildings, Bath, Somersetshire, had always taken great care with his appearance: as a young man, he was careful that he appear young and fashionable; as a baronet, he dressed to cultivate that air of respectability he felt was owing to a man of title, and one which was least disposed to incite exception. Indeed, his views at this time of life were to assume those niceties of speech, dress, and manners which would recommend himself to those whose notice he desired, and whose discernment was not so acute as to look further than the shine of his buttons or the height of his cravat. Upon this superficiality of judgement Sir William depended, as any deeper scrutiny would reveal the most astonishing lack of the true substance of a gentleman: no heart, no honour, and no taste, at least none for any pursuit occupation save the occupation of money.

His initiation into the state of matrimony had been motivated solely by the fortune of his wife, the heiress of a tradesman. His callous and neglectful treatment of her during their married life was so cruel that it had been generally assumed—by those who knew the couple—that she died of a broken heart, young enough to make her death unexpected, but old enough to have realised her own imprudence in marrying a man who, once he had secured her fortune, had not even the decency to feign the slightest atom of respect or regard for his wife. He had subsequently made the acquaintance of his cousin (the delay of which was owing to his distain for the acquaintance of her father, the previous baronet, from whom he obtained his title and estate). To his pleasure, he had found that his cousin, Anne, was very pretty, possessed of a sweet nature, and an excellent understanding—in short, she had captivated the heartless Sir William, or at least had created a feeling as close to love as Sir William was able to approach. He had been disappointed by the defection of his cousin for one Captain Wentworth, a man of no title or property, and who was superior to himself only in fortune, honour, valour, liberality, and a constant, generous heart. Sir William had resolved to return to his former pattern of marriage for the sake of increasing his fortune, as he had no remaining inclination for any experiment which might enlarge his sentimental feelings.

His manor of Kellynch being long-let to respectable tenants (and the creditability and regularity of the Admiral's bank-draught was as far as Sir William had enquired in that line), he had settled permanently in Bath, as its supply of lonely widows of ample jointure, and hopeful spinsters whose property could remedy the want of youth or beauty, were far more numerous than in the country neighbourhood of Kellynch. The Kellynch estate had provided him with little more than a title, the previous heir having been a man of more fashion than sense. Accordingly, Sir William had made the restoration of the Kellynch fortune his concern, and had scrupled to release the estate from its burthen of mortgages for at least the comfort of the present baronet. Sir William's method in securing the funds necessary to maintain his estate and his consequence was of the simplest construction possible: his myrmidon, Colonel Wallis, would travel to various parts of the country where trade was most in want of ready money; investors would be sought, and Sir William would receive an attractive percentage of the sum. The ultimate success of the venture was not the baronet's concern, only the delivery of those sources of unfettered capital. The fates of the investment and the investors were histories in which Sir William had no concern. His residence in Bath exactly coincided with his need of a steady supply of those who could be enticed to venture some or all of their fortunes with just such an amiable and handsome baronet as himself.

"Sir William," said Lady Catherine, moving closer to him on the settee, "Where can you have been these last three days? You have quite spoilt us! Anne and I were excessively disappointed that you did not dine with us, and we could not find that you had been at the Pump Room this week."

"It was unavoidable, I assure you Ma'am" he replied with a low bow and a smile. "There can be no inducement of a voluntary nature which could stand as recompense for the loss of the greatest of pleasures in seeing you and Miss de Bourgh. Regrettably, the harsh dictates of business must occasionally triumph over the sweeter voices of pleasure."

Lady Catherine and Miss de Bourgh had been in Bath since the preceding winter, as her brother, Earl Hallendale, had selfishly chosen to stay at his nephew Darcy's for Christmas with all his family, instead of remaining at-home with his wife to receive the de Bourgh ladies. The expression of Lady Catherine's continued bitterness over the Darcy's marriage had not been softened, even after ten years' time, with the result that, by general agreement, she was not welcome at Pemberley. Her stated preference for removing to Bath was a slight feeling of fatigue; her unquestionable motive was that Miss de Bourgh had seen yet another unsuccessful season in London, and her mother was grown apprehensive of her daughter finding an acceptable suitor. The relative retirement of Rosings afforded few eligible men, and Anne's long having attained her majority meant that time was not on her side. As always, Anne de Bourgh made no objection to any such plan; revenge being more akin than resistance to her philosophy, and, like her father, what she lacked in goodness, she atoned for with a surfeit of sufferance, and the firm belief in eventual gratification. Accordingly, they decamped to Bath, taking a creditable suite of apartments in the Grand Parade. In a matter of hours, Sir William Elliot had arranged to make the acquaintance of Lady Catherine and Miss de Bourgh.

Upon Sir Walter's untimely death in a fall from the pavements some years earlier (principally owing to his walking out in inclement weather in his court-shoes), his heir, Sir William, had secured his baronetcy and the estate of Kellynch. He was exceedingly proud of both his baronetcy and his person, and, with the exception of some acquaintance necessary to his business in the shares, kept only the best company and was seen to patronise only the most fashionable of routs, *salons*, and *soirées*. His good looks had, if changed at all, improved with age—he looked only more distinguished—and the illustrious circle with which he socialised knew only that he was a widower of good fortune; that he continued to keep his mistress, Mrs. Clay, was known only to his few particular friends.

Whilst taking the water one day in the Pump Room, Lady Catherine temporarily abandoned her daughter in order to pursue a slight acquaintance with one of the titled families with whom she had contrived to secure an introduction in the first week of their arrival. As her lapse in vigilance lasted only a few minutes, she was quite surprised to find, when she returned across the room, Anne engaged in conversation with an handsome and fashionably dressed gentleman unknown to herself. Having no scruple as to interrupting this tête-à-tête, she demanded an introduction.

"Anne, dearest," began Lady Catherine in her most gracious tones, "who is your new friend?"

"Mamma, may I present Sir William Elliot, an acquaintance of Arabella's?" and turning to Sir William, said, "My mother, Lady Catherine."

Sir William bowed low to Lady Catherine and, kissing her hand in the continental stile, replied, "*Enchanteé.*"

Sir William, Her Ladyship was to learn, was known to Anne's friend, Arabella, who was also then resident in Bath. Miss Arabella Randolph had been at Mrs. Heywood's Academy with Anne. At the request of her mother, Lady Randolph, Arabella was obliged to renew the acquaintance with Miss de Bourgh formed at school. Lady Randolph viewed the latter's family connections and fortune with a keener eye than her daughter, and so wished to encourage any friendship with those in possession of a greater share of both. Out of duty to her mother, Arabella was presently spending frequent, insipid afternoons in the company of Miss de Bourgh, although justice would demand the further explanation that Anne de Bourgh was certainly better company when she was not under the oppressive influence of her mother.

Sir William happened to drive past the two fashionably and expensively dressed young ladies in his curricle as they made their way along Milsom Street, and had, in his own description, "with every hour since he had known there was such a creature, been waiting with the greatest impatience to secure the honour of an introduction to Miss de Bourgh." Miss Randolph was neither so desperate nor so designing as to deprive him of an introduction to Miss de Bourgh, and the two ladies were, from that hour, more liable than not to meet Sir William during the course of the afternoon.

Quickly discerning that Lady Catherine's character was one which responded to flattery, rather than making the daughter appear to be the chief object of his attraction, Sir William immediately turned his charming and complimentary nothings toward Lady Catherine with such success that she was soon simpering with delight at the attentions of this eligible paragon. Miss de Bourgh witnessed this shift in approach, but was neither offended nor alarmed; she had heard that Sir William was a great speculator in the shares and that his income was chiefly derived from such endeavours of chance. Anne reasoned it to be highly probable that Sir William chose to court her mother as the more promising source of additional funds. In truth, she regarded him with a good deal more interest than the other eligibles, for his active part in

the

the unfolding charade, and the pleasure it afforded in watching the daily increase of his impositions upon her mother. She contented herself with observation: she was almost envious of the dexterity with which Sir William deflected Lady Catherine's ever-impertinent questions in such a charming manner that the lady did not comprehend his own answers to be merely cleverly disguised echoes of her own recent opinions. Such a superior example of flattery to the clumsy, worn-out phrases of the other gentlemen! How much more accomplished the instructor, and how much better the lesson! Anne was mistress of herself enough to acknowledge that she could learn a great deal from such a teacher. In Sir William, she could see her own studied detachment masked in a far more attractive combination of civilities. As she watched her mother daily succumb ever more deeply to his arts, Anne could see that his own heart was unlikely to be touched; she saw him as a bird of her same feather, and could discern without any great study that his heart was callous, although his manners were captivating.

That Lady Catherine not only allowed his daily attentions, but eagerly *wished* for such an enchantment may well constitute a source of wonder. However, it must be remembered that Lady Catherine had been widowed at a tolerably young age, and was quite disposed to find that an attractive and pleasing baronet was a suitable second attachment for the daughter of an Earl, in her present state and circumstances. She received Sir William's attentions and flatteries with pleasure and more—something approaching gratitude. There was some little difference in age, and on the wrong side, to be sure. However, this disparity was not so great as to be *very* exceptional, and there were other inducements on each side to confirm the suitability of the match: Sir William's name and title were respectable, his person and manners were pleasing, and, at her time of life, surely she might be allowed to think of her own pleasure? If her own fortune and title were a little superior, was that not, in itself, some apportionate balance to their little difference in age? And, reflected Lady Catherine, she was yet a quite well-looking woman; certainly Sir William was just tall enough that only the most astute observer would be able to discern some little disparity in height.

Sir William found his attentions on Lady Catherine arduous in the extreme. Like strong drink, flattery needs increase to remain effective; week after week, Sir William laboured to sustain Lady Catherine's growing expectations of amusement, indulgence, and compliment. Clearly more used to being pleased than pleasing, Lady Catherine's common-place expressions were infinitely more dull than diverting and, as she thought so much of her own voice, she was frequently an embarrassment in company. But the pain was, he reckoned, of a finite duration, and would be a penance only until he could command Lady Catherine's fortune. She, in evidence of her prepossession in his favour, returned him equal measures of coquetry, complaisance, and docility in such a degree as would astonish the entirety of her acquaintance. Anne found it unaccountable—but highly amusing—to see her mother the dupe of Sir William, her own mother whose self-avowed perspicacity and discernment of character seemed entirely forgotten.

Over the course of the following weeks, the three inhabitants of Bath were well-satisfied with their mutual society. Lady Catherine's consequence grew each time she was accompanied to some entertainment or other by such a gallant and handsome gentleman, gainsaying the customary epithets of being a single woman and unloved. Anne studied Sir William diligently with the cold impartiality of one who is at once both adversary and ally. Her admiration for him increased to attraction, and from attraction to inclination. Anne had learnt the peculiar lesson at an early age that, in marriage, the certainty of a known adversary was preferable to the small likelihood of finding that your chosen partner was either estimable or amiable.

What were Sir William's feelings? His first marriage made him prudent as well as rich; his first object upon meeting the de Bourghs was to establish the nature and extent of their ready fortune, and whether they could be of use to him in the furtherance of some one or other of his adventures in the shares that required capital—a great deal of capital—and he was scrupulous in preferring that the sums be as little derived from his own pocket as possible. How soon after meeting Miss de Bourgh did he re-adjust his ideas to include herself as well as her fortune is uncertain. That Anne soon became his intended object for a wife was, he felt, so well marked by his constant, although quieter, compliments, and his steady solicitude in the few moments they could speak together without including Lady Catherine, that she must be in no doubt as to the nature and respectability of his intentions.

Shortly after the turn of the new year, Sir William's associate, Colonel Wallis, having an acquaintance who derived his income through the procurement of information not obtainable through respectable means, related to Sir William the astonishing results of his enquiries; namely, that Lady Catherine's father had been able to secure on behalf of his daughter, upon her marriage, a jointure of no more than seven thousand pounds. The Earl had not thought to provide Lady Catherine with a life estate, as may usually be supposed, for the reason that there was neither town-house nor Rosings at the time of his daughter's marriage; Rosings had been the purchase of Sir William following his marriage, and he was, therefore, able to dispose of it as he chose. The only requirement made of Sir Lewis by his marriage was a clause that he provide Lady Catherine with a dower house for her life-time. Other than that vague stipulation, the estate was entirely unencumbered.

In consideration of the years of conjugal misery, frequently punctuated by Lady Catherine's reminders as to their difference in rank, that his fortune and house had been acquired by trade, that their consequence and respectability were owing entirely to her family, &c., the good knight had seen fit to settle the entirety of his estate upon his daughter, his commiserator, comforter, and confidante in the pathos and torment of daily domestic abuse. Sir William's enquiries also proved enlightening as to the particulars of Sir Lewis's will; namely, that Anne de Bourgh had been a wealthy woman since attaining her majority, the fact of which Lady Catherine had apparently kept her daughter in the dark. In short, that Lady Catherine was living on her daughter's inheritance and ignorance, Sir William felt with certitude. The entirety of the Rosings estate was now the property of Anne de Bourgh; the will of Sir Lewis left no ambiguity on that score. That no one of independent means, regardless of relation, would live under the iron thumb of Lady Catherine a moment longer than absolutely necessary was equally unequivocal.

In the week prior, this honourable gentleman deliberately cancelled several engagements with the de Bourghs in order to confirm his indispensability to both mother and daughter, so that when they next met, Sir William felt it highly probable, within the space of a short time, he would be master of seven thousand pounds to be pledged with Lady Catherine's ready approbation, in a most attractive speculation. With the pecuniary details all but secured, Sir William was now free to turn his attentions to Miss de Bourgh. It was extremely convenient, thought Sir William, that the mother was so disposed to the match; he would much prefer Lady Catherine as an ally—if necessary, to secure her daughter's consent—than an adversary, but this was of trifling concern. He was in no uncertainty that he would succeed in his suit, as, indeed, every time he was in the presence of Her Ladyship, she seemed almost wishing to introduce the subject! Anne's feelings toward himself were less definitive, but he had never yet failed to engage any woman's heart with his attentions. He anticipated little resistance, and resolved to lose no more time in securing Anne and her fortune to himself.

CHAP. 19.

IF SIR WILLIAM BELIEVED that Lady Catherine would be easily parted from her fortune, he was to be disappointed. Far from the familiar, sentimental pattern of their intercourse, when it came to pecuniary matters, Lady Catherine preferred to involve herself in the details of the speculation to an astonishing degree. She believed herself to have— either by absorption or marriage—acquired Sir Lewis's discernment for matters of business, and was not to be dissuaded from appraising the apparatus first-hand. Accordingly, amidst the mud and miserable weather of March, a travelling chaise-and-six set out from Bath on a tedious journey to the neighbourhood of Telford. The destination of this excursion was an iron foundry where the proprietor had installed a new system of steam-lights. The journey necessitated a stop in Worcester, and thence through slogging rain to the area of ——, close-by the town of Telford. The day was uncommonly unpleasant and the chaise unbearably tight, owing to the requisite discomfort of bringing Lady Catherine's waiting woman and a maid, besides Lady Catherine, Anne, Sir William and his associate Colonel Wallis, the latter having been gratefully liberated from the stifling confines of the coach by the conventions of rank, and the corresponding opportunity to sit in the cold rain on the box with the coachman. Although the party were going to be only three nights on the road, Lady Catherine was accompanied not only by her entourage, including an additional two out-riders for safety, but enough baggage for a month's sojourn. It was necessary for Sir William to remind himself repeatedly of the profitable speculation to be infused by Lady Catherine's jointure to keep himself in even the appearance of a tolerable humour. The rattle of the chaise and the pounding rain were the only audible relief from the Lady's interminable narratives, invariably concerning the affability of her temper and the condescension of her notice, as liberally applied of late to the trivialities of Hunsford and amongst her numerous noble acquaintance at Bath.

The evening at the Talbot Hotel was necessarily an improvement, as it afforded at least a comfortable place to sit and a cold collation, their having arrived too late at the inn to have a proper supper. The establishment was ancient, but clean, and the land-lady especially grateful to have the custom of travellers at this season and in such inclement weather. The land-lord was everything to be expected of the publican at a posting house: well-fed and rosy-nosed, generously assuming the arduous burthen of incessant conversation with his disinclined audience, leaving the lighter duties of cooking, cleaning, waiting, and house-keeping to his lady. At length the weary party were able to excuse themselves and apportion the rooms after much civil quarrelling as to who was to have the best room, and who was to share. In the morning, the party had a scanty breakfast and left before the land-lord was come down to further impede the progress of their journey. Owing to having slept poorly, Lady Catherine's garrulity of the previous day was now replaced with irritability, augmented with a pronouncement every five minutes of how disagreeable it was to travel in a closed, crowded chaise. The carriage groaned as it toiled down the rutted roads, and after another day of sheeting rain and seas of mud, they reached the inn in Telford where they were to stay the night.

The next morning, they had some leisure and the possibility of breakfast before meeting Mr. Roberts, who would conduct the party to the foundry. Lady Catherine had—to everyone's inexpressible delight—found this situation more to her liking and arose refreshed. With astonishing energy, she abused her fellow passengers roundly for their want of fortitude and spirit on the journey hither, and ate a substantial breakfast. Anne ate little and was silent. Sir William studied the news-paper, leaving Colonel Wallis to support whatever attempt remained at conversation before Mr. Roberts was to make his appearance later that morning.

The foundry was a great stone and brick structure adjacent to a stream of considerable size. Long before they could see the building, the din of the machinery and smoak from the chimneys announced their destination. Mr. Roberts had devised the mechanism of the steam-lights, and agreed some months previous to provide the foundry of Mr. Wainwright with several of them, in return for the privilege of shewing the invention to those who might wish to invest in the promotion of his apparatus. Upon removing from the carriage, Mr. Roberts, a

❧   small

small man of quick movements and dishevelled appearance, struggled in vain to shout over the clanging of metal and roar of the furnaces to introduce the party to Mr. Wainwright in the yard adjacent to the building. Contrary to Mr. Roberts, Mr. Wainwright was an enormous man, deliberate of speech, and dressed with all the dignity of a man in charge of his own manufactory. Inside the foundry, the cavernous room was entirely lit with the red glow of the molten iron and Mr. Roberts' wonderful blue steam-light. Each steam-light was comprised of a large globe, affixed atop an iron pipe, which, as Mr. Roberts shouted to the assembly, was pressurised to introduce steam into the glass globe. Within the globe was a turbine assembly (the scientifical description of which was scarcely audible and altogether incomprehensible), and a generator of an electrical flow, which was produced by the spinning turbine. What could not be heard could be seen, however, and the immensity of the foundry's interior was unquestionably suffused with a most peculiar—but not unpleasant—bright blue light.

Stepping outside, where the steady drizzle was now a welcome relief to the infernal heat of the foundry, Lady Catherine exclaimed that she would be much surprised if everyone employed therein were not stone-deaf within a week. Mr. Roberts explained that there was little requirement for communication in the foundry, but a great need to *see*, and hence Mr. Wainwright's enthusiasm for the installation of the steam-light. Further, Mr. Roberts added, "The steam, being water, is infinitely safer than the coal-gas within the foundry. It is not to be thought of, the installation of coal-gas in such a place which requires open fires."

Sir William nodded and added in a tone of thoughtful gravity, "And, similarly, the transportation of water is unquestionably safe, when compared to the risk of transporting the coal-gas; and certainly— as water is universally abundant—the need to install a system of pipes to carry it, such as is required for the coal-gas, makes the steam-light scheme highly œconomical."

Colonel Wallis respectfully waited until the other two had finished their encomiums on the apparatus before speaking: "And, the steam does not give off the noxious vapours as does the exhaust from the gas-light. As everyone knows, the steam reverts to water in the air, which, in such a place as a foundry, is a positive benefit to the health."

Sir William could not help interjecting that, "There were many places of manufacture which were already powered by steam, so the immediate advantage of a system of lighting without the trouble and expense of an additional combustible was a great inducement to its adoption."

Mr. Roberts agreed heartily with this insight, adding, "The steam-light is also of a pleasing shape, and being filled with water, will not blacken as do the coal-gas lights, which require frequent cleaning."

Lady Catherine enquired as to the merits of blue light, instead of the yellow of candles, Mr. Roberts declaring that it, of all things, was a benefit to the eyes.

And so the wonders and advantages of the steam-lights were canvassed and re-enumerated until it was time to depart for an early supper at their inn, in preparation for the return journey, first stopping at Romsley. The inn-keeper at the Rose and Crown regularly welcomed the custom of visitors to Mr. Wainwright's establishment, and so the party were treated with particular attention, and given an hearty, hot dinner before being left in grateful peace to go to their beds.

Lady Catherine enquired of Sir William if she might relay her good fortune to her nephew Darcy, as he would certainly wish to share in such a desirable new scheme. However, Sir William was adamant that secrecy was paramount to ensure the success of the business; accordingly, Lady Catherine postponed the important communication, and did not immediately write to Darcy of her new-found occupation in the speculation of shares. If she had some misgivings in keeping such a source of ready fortune from her nephew's knowledge, they were swiftly allayed by the assurances of Sir William, that there would be time after the patents were in-hand, and certainly this was not the only such opportunity—did not Lady Catherine trust him to superintend all of her family's fortunes as industriously as he was securing her own?

CHAP. 20.

SIR WILLIAM ELLIOT, having secured Lady Catherine's jointure, had nothing further to fear from that quarter. Whether or not she were aware of the fact, she was now dependent upon his generosity. Sir William was little disposed to wait any longer in attaching the larger part of the de Bourgh fortune through Anne. As with her mother, he did not anticipate that his wife would be in any way troublesome, or make awkward demands once they were married. Anne was not much given to speaking, in general, and—at any rate, as his information concerning her father's will having been the means of effecting her release from Lady Catherine—Sir William felt secure in the expectation of that form of conjugal felicity as conferred by obligation on the one side, balanced by an unremitting exercise of authority on the other. So confident was Sir William in the affection of the lady, that he determined to speak with Lady Catherine without even the customary expedient of securing the hand of his intended prior to addressing her formidable parent. Upon his being shewn into the de Bourghs' apartments, he was met by Lady Catherine herself and given a seat in the best parlour, an elegant and spacious room with full-length windows facing the river, through which she had apparently been watching for his arrival with some anticipation.

"Sir William," began Lady Catherine, "come and sit with me. I am delighted to report that my daughter is this afternoon engaged with some friends. It gives us an opportunity to converse alone."

"I am most pleased and grateful to hear you say so, Lady Catherine. I have also been wishing a chance to speak with you privately for some time."

Lady Catherine paused only briefly and continued, "I am celebrated for the frankness of my character, Sir William. One may, perhaps, be excused for some trespass on civility that would not do for matters of less import. On this subject, Sir William, I would have you speak with me quite plainly as to your situation and the extent of your property."

"I understand you perfectly Lady Catherine," said Sir William. "I could not do otherwise. It is the greatest of pleasures to be allowed the use of language delivered directly from the heart—to speak openly and without those locutions deemed necessary by a disingenuous society—and particularly gratifying to find that we are of the same opinion on this issue of particular delicacy."

Lady Catherine simpered and smiled.

"Lady Catherine, as you know," continued Sir William, "I was Sir Walter Elliot's heir to Kellynch, which passed to me these several years now. In addition, my first wife came to the marriage as the sole heiress of her father's estate. I am well provided-for; my circumstances are exceedingly comfortable. Whilst Kellynch is not a Rosings, it is my home and I would propose that it is the properest home for my wife. It is there that I propose we should live."

Lady Catherine blushed and smiled. "That is all to the good, Sir William, but we are, I believe, getting a little ahead of ourselves. Have you no other encumbrances? There are no children from your first marriage, as I understand it?"

"Yes, Lady Catherine. You have been correctly informed; my late wife and I were not blessed with children," replied Sir William.

"And her family? How are they situated?"

"Very well, Your Ladyship," he assured her most earnestly.

"Then there are no claims on your fortune other than your own?"

"That is correct, Ma'am; I am my own master, and my property is mine to dispose of as I wish."

"Well, that is all to the good," said Lady Catherine, moved perceptibly closer through the expedient of adjusting her skirts. She smiled and took his hand. "Then all that remains for us, Sir William, is to decide the day that shall be the happiest of our lives."

Sir William stared at Lady Catherine with unfeigned astonishment. "But Lady Catherine...," began Sir William.

"No, Sir William," interrupted Lady Catherine with unusual softness, "I will not have any impediments mentioned, for, indeed, as we are situated there can be none."

"But Lady Catherine, I insist," he began again. "Do not you believe, before we take such a step, we properly ought consult Anne?"

❧   My

"My daughter be consulted?" started Lady Catherine. "Whatever can you mean? What has Anne to do with our plans?"

"As it is her happiness as well as our own, I could never wish for our married life to begin with her feeling that such an important decision as concerns her own future had been made without consulting her own views," replied Sir William.

Lady Catherine looked at Sir William closely. "I am sure Anne will be amenable, whatever we decide, and that—certainly on this issue—we may please ourselves."

"Lady Catherine, I must be satisfied that—on so urgent a matter—I speak with your daughter and ascertain her sentiments, before we proceed to any such arrangements as she may not wholly approve."

Lady Catherine began to grow warm in her remonstrance. "Sir William, I assure you there is no mother with greater maternal solicitude for the feelings of her daughter than I. However, in matters such as these, I believe that ours is the only opinion which can be material!" She recollected herself in the next instant, and smiled demurely as she moved yet closer to Sir William.

A mortifying idea was beginning to enter the mind of Sir William. "Lady Catherine," he replied deliberately, "let us have a right understanding. I fear that we are on the precipice of involving ourselves in a misunderstanding of the most distressing nature."

"Sir William, what can you mean?" said Lady Catherine, patting his hand affectionately. "Certainly we are of an age and situation where we may decide such things for ourselves, do not you..."

"Lady Catherine!" interrupted Sir William, unable to restrain himself for another moment, "When I began this application, I earnestly believed you to be speaking on behalf of your daughter!"

Lady Catherine continued holding his hand for a moment and then abruptly drew herself upright. "Sir William, do I understand you rightly? You are making an offer of marriage not to me, but to my daughter?"

"Yes, Lady Catherine. I assure you most earnestly that I had no other object in view. Whilst I am extremely sorry, and no form of apology can erase the grievous misapprehension as has just occurred, I believe I have secured the affections of your daughter, and sought an opportunity to speak with you privately about making her an offer."

Lady Catherine rose and walked quickly to the window. Sir William could not see what she was doing except to note she had reached into her reticule and then put her hands near her face. "Sir William, please leave me now."

"Madam," he said, rising, "upon my honour as a gentleman, I would never have intentionally offended you in so cruel a manner." In so saying, he bowed to Lady Catherine's back and quickly and quietly left the drawing-room.

CHAP. 21.

WHAT SIR WILLIAM DID NEXT may be easily conjectured. Walking quickly through to the promenade where he expected to find Miss de Bourgh walking with her friend, he at length espied her in the crowd, and, coming behind her, touched her shoulder. She was startled, but upon seeing who it was, smiled and said, "Sir William! How pleasant!"

Sir William bowed to both ladies and pulled Miss de Bourgh a little aside from Miss Randolph and said in a confidential voice, "Miss de Bourgh, may I have the pleasure of a few minutes' speech with you? Will your friend wait? Do I put you to inconvenience?"

"I think she will wait." Turning back to her companion, she called, "Arabella, will you wait a moment whilst I speak with Sir William?"

"To be sure, Anne. I shall walk on to the weir," said Arabella.

"What is it, Sir William?" asked Miss de Bourgh with all the feigned concern she could muster on such short notice. "I am afraid you are unwell?"

"No, Miss de Bourgh. But I am afraid I have just had a most frightful interview with your mother."

"Oh, dear," said Miss de Bourgh. "I am ever so sorry to hear it, but what can *I* do to ease such distress? You know the little influence I have with my mother."

"Everything," said Sir William, "as the interview solely concerned you."

"Me?" Anne replied, assuming an expressive countenance of shock and wonder.

"Yes, you. I had gone to ask your mother for consent to offer you my hand in marriage. And—in an interview I will ever remember—your mother has these many weeks mistaken my attentions to you for affection for herself. When at the last possible moment the misunderstanding was discovered, she was become very angry, and I am afraid she will forgive neither of us easily."

"Oh," said Miss de Bourgh, turning quickly away. "This is wretched news, indeed." She spent a few moments in the business of arranging her face to speak less of amusement and something more like concern, but the images of her mother being so utterly humiliated at the hands of the unwitting Sir William raised her spirits to such a degree that she could not immediately recompose herself and assume her usual air of indifference—a most extraordinary event indeed. "And, pray, how was the unfortunate situation resolved at the close of your meeting? What were the last words you spoke to one another? It is necessary to be quite clear upon the matter, as at least one of us must be sacrificed in expiation of the sin."

"She would not look to hear my apology for the cruelty she had inflicted upon herself, and I must own that I was so shocked at the *dénouement* that I left as quickly as I could. I have always believed myself as perceptive as the next man, but her misunderstanding caught me entirely by surprise. In life, I aim for nothing but to render myself agreeable to all whose friendship I value, and had not an idea that your mother was grown attached to me as an husband, not as her future son." Taking both of Anne's hands in his, he continued, "My ardent affection for her daughter has long occupied my thoughts to such a degree, that any perception of feelings I might unknowingly be engendering in another heart was impossible."

Anne looked as beseechingly as was in her power, and asked with a smile, "Sir William, is this an offer of marriage? Or, merely an elaborate stratagem to insult my mother?"

Sir William then told Anne of the weeks of suspense he had endured at the hands of her mother until he could feel assured of success in both quarters. He sealed the impression of his sincerity by imparting to her the fact that she had long been a woman of independent means, and other particulars relative to her late father's marriage settlements, including his final act of leaving the entirety of the Rosings estate to his daughter. Upon Miss de Bourgh's careful questioning of Sir William, she was given to understand that, since attaining her majority, her own mother had knowingly withheld the particulars of her father's will. In this testament, Anne, not Lady Catherine, was the mistress of Rosings!

"Anne, as your father purchased Rosings and did not inherit it, it need not be entailed on any successor. His wife forfeited her dower rights with the marriage articles, as agreed between the Earl and Sir Lewis at the time of her marriage. As the Earl was not rich, the best he could reasonably secure for his daughter was a jointure of £7,000 without any life-estate, excepting an otherwise unstipulated 'life-time domicile,' which I venture to suggest—by your leave—to be habitation of the old dower cottage. I am sure that Lady Catherine's father did not have an idea of Sir Lewis leaving the entirety of the estate away from his widow to settle it upon his daughter, but it was done, and we may both easily guess his motive. In short, your mother has been living at Rosings these past few years at your pleasure, and her only source of income derives from her jointure of £7,000 in the four per-cents. In short, all she is left with is a little money and a little house."

The accumulated resentment over years of subjugation may well be imagined, but cannot be wonderful. Miss de Bourgh's marriage to Sir William would be the undoing of Lady Catherine, heart and home; Anne resolved, at once, to accept the hand of Sir William, and effect the ruination of her mother. And with what pretty words did Anne plight her troth to Sir William?

"I find my present situation unpleasant; any escape would be most welcome." Recollecting herself, she made a brief effort at better civility: "Indeed, I am honoured by your proposals, and accept your offer with all my heart." Here Miss de Bourgh was forced into a little falsehood, if the substitution of heart for design can be considered inconsequential. Anne may have had a momentary struggle in discovery that her own heart—under the careful example of Lady Catherine, and in the sincerest flattery of imitation—had room for no-one but herself. If Anne struggled inwardly at the exchange of one form of tyranny for the self-imposed shackles of revenge, she congratulated herself, on the whole, as getting the better of the exchange, renouncing the restraints of Anne de Bourgh—or even Anne Fitzwilliam or Anne Darcy—for the lighter bonds of Lady Elliot.

Such were Anne's musings, when she was at length roused by Sir William. Imputing Anne's silence as the embarrassment which naturally follows such a declaration, he looked most earnestly into her face. "Anne, I can provide your means of escape, and do so most willingly, but I fear your mother would never forgive you if we announced an engagement at present. She feels that she has been scorned as a result of this *contretemps*, and the thought that she might punish you for my errors is insupportable. Your superior knowledge of your mother must decide our next steps. Do you believe her resentment to be implacable?

I am eager to propitiate her anger by any possible expedient. What is your inclination?"

Miss de Bourgh found herself momentarily at a loss. Lady Catherine, she knew, would wish to pretend that the event occurring between herself and Sir William had never happened at all, and would rely upon Sir William's conduct as a gentleman to allow the occasion of her embarrassment to go no further. An obvious beginning, therefore, must be that Anne pretend to know nothing of the recent misunderstanding, and continue as before; Sir William must, in order to keep any semblance of domestic peace, not mention their agreement to anyone, and to all outward appearances, and certainly to Lady Catherine, they must exhibit no alteration of conduct.

"Had Lady Catherine really appeared to be in love? Had she certainly believed you to be offering for herself rather than for me?" asked Anne, more to the purpose of hearing it again, rather than being in any serious doubt of the matter.

Sir William's affirmations were that Lady Catherine had appeared entirely taken in by her imagination, and was most bitterly deceived. Anne's thorough knowledge of the conceit of her mother yielded an idea: after a suitable delay of a few days, Sir William was to write to Lady Catherine, apologising unreservedly for the misunderstanding, and assuring her that his own lack of confidence had been at fault; he had not dreamt that Lady Catherine could entertain any idea of preferring himself. Sir William had accordingly settled upon her daughter as a way to connect himself with the family he so admired. Her revelation that she had viewed him in other than the inferior status of suitor to her daughter had been shocking in the extreme. He humbly apologised that his distress and embarrassment had rendered himself unable to respond as he ought. His confusion and her immediate request that he leave her had forced him to withdraw in a most disgraceful way, namely, by confirming at that moment, that Lady Catherine's affections were not his object; his mind had since been a torment of regret and fear that he might lose any chance for the affections of the woman he esteemed and respected above all others. The blunder which had occasioned his foolish and clumsy behaviour was contemptible, and should, in any mortal heart, render him unfit as a friend. Yet he sought a release from his misery by begging her forgiveness, with the hope only that they might go on forever as they had prior to his inadvertent, wretched mistake.

Sir William listened to her scheme and readily acknowledged that her mother's high opinion of herself would likely encourage her to accept

such

such an explanation, but he could not agree its necessity, for the thought of indefinitely postponing his marriage to Miss de Bourgh was not conducive to his plans for her fortune.

"Anne, do you wish to punish both of us? What good can come of delay? Will denying our own happiness make Lady Catherine's feelings more apt to diminish? We will be lost to one another entirely, as your mother will undoubtedly increase her efforts to secure your marriage elsewhere."

"Sir William," she smiled, "for now, you need only to renew your place in my mother's affections, and divine a way to remain there. Is that in your power? Will you try—for my sake?" She took his hands and said, "At a propitious moment, we will secure her blessing."

Sir William had no alternative but to assure Anne that he placed himself entirely in her capable hands, and home he went, under strict orders to remain within doors for several days so as to avoid any early meeting with Lady Catherine. That would give him sufficient time, Anne reminded him, to compose his letter.

Upon her return to the Grand Parade, her friend having long been forgotten—and for all that could be known, was still waiting aimlessly at the weir—she observed to herself with some satisfaction that her mother was quite discomposed and displayed none of her usual *hauteur*. Anne betrayed no outward sign of being aware of the events of the day, only asking if Lady Catherine were feeling a little fatigued? Should she call for tea? She sat quietly beside her mother, took out her needle-work, and in a few words began describing her morning walk along the Promenade. She saw her mother's close inspection of her countenance, seeking confirmation that Anne was indeed ignorant of the day's events. Upon receiving satisfaction that Anne knew naught, Lady Catherine felt able to claim that she was somewhat distressed upon receiving a letter from her brother, which, in its retelling of the circumstances of his elder son's recent return from London, detailed the shock and horrors of fast company and the increasingly pressing demands for money. As Anne knew—without the reminder again on the present occasion—her mother held the respectability of all her family dear, and felt personally responsible for the Fitzwilliam family's good name and its honourable reputation; she was, therefore, severely affected by the news that her nephew persisted in his almost-certain descent. Her avowed consolation was in her proclamation that—despite a liberal allowance of advice for their benefit—her nephews seemed in a conspiracy against her, and were all, hence, reaping just rewards for their united iniquity. Darcy was beyond redemption as a result of his own folly; Colonel Fitzwilliam persisted in relying upon his own counsel as to his future happiness and was, in any case, not responding to her letters. And now, her only other nephew, the Viscount, was given up to a life of dissipation and depravity. Really, she felt quite ill-used by everybody; her brother's letter had quite overset her, for she was, as Anne surely knew, the most selfless woman in the world, and had devoted her life entirely to the improvement and dignity of all her family.

Anne heard her mother's familiar complaints in silence. However, for the first time in her life, she experienced the satisfaction that could derive from what, in the common cant, is known as "having the whip-hand" at last. Lady Catherine's fate was now in her daughter's power, a circumstance yet a stranger to the mother's suspicions. Anne felt a wholly new sensation of actual felicity, emanating from the certain knowledge of her mother's vulnerability. She did not see the letter which was despatched by Sir William to Lady Catherine a few days later, but was left in no doubt as to its success. She arrived home after an afternoon spent at the Pump Room to find Sir William comfortably seated beside her mother in the sitting room, Lady Catherine looking radiantly happy, and Sir William doing his best to appear so. Their own engagement could not yet be discussed, but Anne felt certain that, before the passage of many weeks, Sir William could successfully exchange the delusion of the mother for the hand of the daughter. In the interim, Anne rejoiced in the wisdom that her mother was soon to understand the unhappy alternative of either living as just another poor widow in greatly reduced circumstances amongst her acquaintance in Bath, or banished to the old, worn-out Dower Cottage (which it had never been thought necessary to repair), as just another poor widow at Hunsford.

CHAP. 22.

THE DARCYS WERE ALL in a great bustle, making ready to leave for the continent. Colonel Fitzwilliam remained some weeks more at Pemberley, assisting with their preparations and seeing his cousins off, and then spent a few weeks with his father and step-mother, before returning to the north. Without the steady pleasures of good conversation and the diversions of the family party at Pemberley, the colonel returned to his regiment in unusually low spirits. His pursuit of Mary Crawford had been conducted with such diffidence and respect for propriety that only the two principals—and then only because Colonel Fitzwilliam had at last resolved on the temerity of speech—knew that there was a courtship in progress. Accordingly, there was no danger of his being importuned by his fellow officers for his disappointed hopes to exasperate his melancholy. The weather was uncommonly mild, so there was hunting and exercise to contribute to his happiness, but it answered not. Remaining with his regiment only long enough to cause himself the inconvenience and expense of a long, cold journey, and seeing to his own comforts and provisioning, which he then immediately abandoned, the Colonel abruptly changed course and resolved on a stay at Tunbridge Wells to fill the days prior to his departure for the anticipated rendezvous at Geneva with the Darcys some weeks hence.

London lay in his road to Tunbridge, and the colonel resolved to pass the dreariest, most forsaken time of year in the city. He staid at the Hallendale's London house, thinking to share the company of his brother, but the Viscount was no-where to be seen; the colonel supposed that he—like everyone who had *anywhere* else they could be—was gone thither. The colonel had no inclination for wagering or other low pursuits, and so was denied the pleasure of frequenting even those thin assemblies at this season. He spent his days alternately walking along Oxford Street or Piccadilly, having coffee at Gunther's, or sitting in the Hallendale's library, thinking of what he would say, should anyone perchance walk in. Indeed, anyone who happened to look unawares at Colonel Fitzwilliam would have assumed that he was in town purposely to be lonely and ill-used. Satisfying even his own desire to feel himself miserable, he finally left for Tunbridge, but then only on the coldest, wettest day of the spring.

Taking a room at Mount Sion, Colonel Fitzwilliam resolved on visiting the coffee houses, assembly rooms, circulating library, tavern, and shops as a general antidote to his persistent depression of spirits. He saluted the ladies walking along the Pantiles under the colonnade in inclement weather, and through the lime avenue on bright days out to the country lanes, walking through the ancient farmsteads. He began to shape his days so as to take the waters in the morning, stroll in the afternoon, and attend a ball, concert, or some other entertainment in the evening. He purchased some small pieces of Tunbridge Ware: a glove box for Elizabeth with a beautifully inlaid flowering branch and butterfly, and a dressing box for Georgiana with a kitten curled up in a basket. A young, single man in a smart uniform of rank will always attract the fair sex, and Colonel Fitzwilliam was no exception. His ease of manner and congenial conversation added to his other attractions, and he was become quite popular within the space of a few days at Tunbridge. As a result, the Colonel was, in general, finding that his spirits, whilst not encouraged to the point of elation, were at least sufficiently recovered as to be called tolerably composed.

One dreary, wet afternoon, about a week following his arrival, as the Colonel was taking his customary stroll under the colonnade, he was startled from his thoughts by the press of an hand on his shoulder and an unexpected voice,

"Colonel Fitzwilliam!" cried Mary Crawford, "I am so relieved to find that it is you after all, and that I have not accosted a stranger with such fond familiarity."

"Mar...Miss Crawford," began the Colonel, trying to collect both his wits and his composure before having to finish the sentence. "What a surprise it is to see you here. I had imagined you in Norfolk these many weeks."

"Yes, we—my brother and I—are just come from town," she replied with a demure smile. "But, I see that I interrupt your walk and your thoughts. I hope you will forgive the intrusion, as it springs from the enthusiasm of friendship, and not from any design of disturbing your solitude."

"It does not follow, Miss Crawford," replied Colonel Fitzwilliam with just the hint of a bow, "that such obtrusion is unwelcome. How long have you been in Tunbridge, and what business brings the illustrious Crawfords hither?"

"Oh!" cried Mary, "We prefer Tunbridge to anything. It is so much more fashionable now than Bath, and so much less crowded than Brighton. How long do you stay, Colonel?"

"I am to stay on some few more days, until I travel to meet my cousins. We are to make a tour of Italy, and I leave this place to meet them in Geneva," he replied somewhat curtly.

"La! That is too bad, it is," she said, effecting a graceful manœuvre to take his arm. "Henry and I had planned on a much longer stay. I tire of town so quickly! I am far more at home in a respectable place such as this, full of innocent diversions, and the air so much more salubrious. After only a little time in town, I was quite frantic to leave, and as my brother is entirely susceptible to my whims and inconsistencies, I was able to persuade him to accompany me hither. Of a sudden, I determined that Tunbridge Wells should be quite the place to pass the last of the cold weather, and of course, I see that my feminine intuition was correct! Henry will be most eager to see you again. It is indeed a most fortuitous coincidence!"

Colonel Fitzwilliam thought, rather than felt, his discomfort at the familiar weight of Mary's arm on his; his reason revolted at the touch, but his heart did not. The lady did not allow him leisure to decide the contest, however, and continued speaking in her usual, engaging manner.

"A tour to Italy! I should like that above all things!" cried Mary. "Where do you go? Rome, Florence, Milan? Do you go as far south as Sardinia? Oh! How I envy you your journey!"

Colonel Fitzwilliam was yet master of himself to reply in a reserved tone, "Well, Miss Crawford, I wonder that you and your brother do not make such a journey. Now that Buonaparte is defeated, the country is quite safe, and I hear that the roads and inns are quite as comfortable as before."

"So we should! But, I find that I have not the heart to undertake it without someone who could act as a tutor—a learned guide. You, as one who has experienced such a wealth of study abroad, will afford your companions immeasurable delight with your knowledge and reflections. How I wish I could be of your party and share such excellent tutelage!"

"But surely your brother has travelled and may do quite as well," the Colonel replied tersely.

"Poor Henry, regrettably, came of age when it was not safe for the English to travel abroad. I am sure he would own himself as enthusiastic an interloper as myself. Pray, when do you leave?"

Whilst the Colonel was instinctively reluctant to share such a detail—for reasons he could not immediately elucidate—he could not help reply, "I must leave on Tuesday to be in Geneva at our appointed time."

"But Colonel Fitzwilliam, where *exactly* do you go? I am most eager for the particulars for, as I am not permitted to join you, I insist on travelling at this very moment through the description of the route you are to take, and your most knowledgeable understanding and excellent discernment in diversion."

"I am unlikely to merit such commendation; the Darcys are gone to Paris, as Mrs. Darcy and Miss Darcy have never travelled abroad. They will make some stay in Paris, before I am to meet them. We will spend some little time in Switzerland, but Italy is our main destination, and there we mean to make the greatest stay of our travels."

Miss Crawford was animated, indeed. "How delightful! I often amuse myself with planning where I should go, and what I should see, and what beautiful things I would buy. What will *you* buy?" She paused at this point, and looked up at Colonel Fitzwilliam through her fine, dark eyelashes. The Colonel, now lost in those eyes and, feeling his resolve waning apace in the familiar beauty of her face, began to look and sound much more like Colonel Fitzwilliam of Norfolk, all those months ago.

"I like the activity not," he rejoined with a defeated smile. "It has been labour enough to purchase a few trinkets for my family in the shops here." Certainly, the Colonel reasoned, it was a pleasure to speak with her again—Miss Crawford's conversation was invariably agreeable—besides, there were so few days remaining that all her charms could not surmount his resolution to keep his heart safe. He was not to be supposed in danger a second time; therefore, what harm could accrue from a little conversation between friends?

"I should enjoy hearing about these imaginary jaunts, Ma—Miss Crawford. Where should you visit first?" In another moment, she had nimbly taken his arm with both her hands, and in a playfully confidential tone continued, "Then indeed you shall. You must imagine, Colonel, that we have escaped the 'shores of this Greene and Pleasant Land,' and are embarking on a pleasure tour of a full six months' duration. We

will

will start, of course, with sailing from Dover to Calais, which would be quickly accomplished, as the conditions must be altogether favourable. Of course, I would not suffer the sea-sickness, for, as you know, I never tolerate even the smallest inconvenience to myself. The route from Calais to Paris, I would shorten entirely, for who wants to tarry in a land of dull rustics when there are to be experienced all the wonders and diversions of Paris? We shall arrive in the city and immediately secure the best rooms at the L'Hôtel Londres, where we will dine in beautiful *salons* on all variety of the best delicacies in France. Then, I should visit the most exclusive dressmakers, and immediately buy twenty gowns, each more beautiful than the last, and have my hair dressed in the latest French stile. We would promenade along Le Grand Boulevard, and laugh at all those not so fine as ourselves. And of course, I should buy a tiny French poodle-dog the colour of champaigne (I will call her 'Nonette'), and she would go everywhere with us in her diamond lead."

Colonel Fitzwilliam was—in spite of all reason and resolution to the contrary—finding himself once more captivated by her lively manner, and he encouraged her to continue. "And when we had tired of parading up and down Le Grand Boulevard, what should we see next?"

"Why, the opera, of course, Colonel Fitzwilliam. But—of course as savants—we would shun the Grand Opera and all its pretended superiority for the Opéra Comique. We would watch from a private box, and I should be greatly amused by the singing and dancing, but you would be quite bored and keep looking at your watch." The Colonel was dreadfully torn betwixt distrust and delight, but was irresistibly giving himself over to the latter, despite all his resolutions concerning her dark eyes, her uncommonly lovely face, and her enchanting figure.

"What!" cried Colonel Fitzwilliam, "Why should I be bored, Miss Crawford?" In this present state of mind, the Colonel was already but poorly equipped to imagine any cloud to the pleasures she was describing.

"Because, my dear Colonel, you have taken me to see Molière's *Les Femmes Savantes*, and as you do not believe in any such thing, you find the entire subject insupportable, and would not wish to credit the subject by appearing to enjoy the play, of course!"

"I have no such opinion, indeed!" protested Colonel Fitzwilliam, "Miss Crawford, you are just such an example that would convert even the most confirmed skeptic."

"For shame, Colonel!" cried Mary, "This is too much of flattery! You make me forget my itinerary—now, where were we?"

Miss Crawford's descriptions continued in so detailed and beguiling a fashion that Colonel Fitzwilliam could not help but imagine himself with her. She had such a talent for description—each imagined detour was full of intrigue and pleasure. In their walk, he travelled with her to Reims to taste the Champaigne, "for Champaigne is the only thing I could consent to drink in France"; and to Lyon, where they purchased the finest silks; to Poitou-Charentes to taste the finest cheeses; and to Marseilles, where they dined on *bouillabaisse* and dark red wine. Her knowledge of geography was excellent, and her enjoyment in her flights-of-fancy infectious.

At some point near Boulogne-sur-mer, Colonel Fitzwilliam tentatively suggested that her tastes were too expensive for his own fortune to supply, with the immediately result that Miss Crawford adjusted her ideas so as to reassure her captive: "The greatest pleasure for me is in the sense of sight, Colonel. In truth, I should like just a few pretty things, and then I should be content to spend only with the eye." The path was thus smoothed for the Colonel to consider that, with their combined fortunes, the fantasy was not wholly out of his reach. A few sentences further along in their journey, somewhere in the neighbourhood of Rouen, he was quite convinced that the plan was perfection itself, and only wanted a little time to encourage its probability and, thence, its fruition. Arm-in-arm, they strolled along the avenue until—upon having reached Orvieto—they found they had wandered so long that they were beyond their own knowledge, and were consequently astonished to realise the day was already grown quite dark.

"Oh, dear!" exclaimed Mary, "My brother will be quite shocked at my having been gone such a time! You must come in with me and take all of the burthen of blame for my prolonged absence, as he will never credit such an explanation from myself."

"With pleasure, Mar—I mean Miss Crawford. It is many months since I have had the pleasure of seeing your brother."

As the appointed day approached for Colonel Fitzwilliam's leave-taking, he was prevented from doing so by Mary's entreaties that he delay his departure by a few inconsequential days, so that they might all visit the ancient manor at Penshurst Place near-by. The old house was presently in a most fortunate state of rehabilitation, and Colonel Fitzwilliam and the Crawfords were able to view the Tapestry Room and the Long Gallery, full of royal and family portraits, and the State Dining room, which formed a part of the old mediæval manor-house. The next day, it was deemed insupportable that the Colonel could not grant his old friends some little extra time so as to allow them the pleasure

of

of a visit to Knole. Thus evolved his days; the Colonel's departure from Tunbridge was never so compelling as to disallow further alteration to his itinerary.

Tunbridge Wells was agreeably situated to encompass many interesting diversions, all of which afforded Mary Crawford innumerable opportunities to prevent the flight of her captive. In the next days, which stretched into weeks, Colonel Fitzwilliam, Mary, and sometimes Mr. Crawford went forth on long and short journeys to the various attractions in that neighbourhood of Kent, exploring down the shady lanes or along the mill-streams, eating a pic-nick on Rushmore Hill, visiting Hever and Sissinghurst, travelling through the Wealden towns of Cranbrook and Tenterden, and strolling out to the ruins of the old castle at Scotney. And so on it went—at the close of each day an insuperable summons for the pleasures of the next, invariably requiring an additional delay for the Colonel's departure to meet the Darcys. Instead of a week, Colonel Fitzwilliam tarried in Tunbridge for well over a month.

In the end, it was necessary to write thrice to the Darcys, announcing his delay. His letters were unusually brief and mentioned only that he had met up unexpectedly with a friend at Tunbridge, and would be obliged, out of civility, to delay his departure. Elizabeth and Mr. Darcy were much perplexed at what could detain Colonel Fitzwilliam for such an enormous time, but Georgiana, privy to the Colonel's flirtation with Mary Crawford before their meeting at Christmas, felt to a certainty that there was only one plausible motive which could account for his mysterious deferrals, but had no real evidence upon which to base her surmise. She was understandably loath to impute such a reason to his behaviour without any corroborating explanation, and so kept both her conjectures and her increasing misery of protracted disappointment to herself.

Colonel Fitzwilliam never reached Geneva, Milan, or even Calais. Indeed, his next journey took him in the opposite direction: to London.

CHAP. 23.

ONCE ALL THE ARRANGEMENTS for travel had been put in order and the last band-box, portmanteau, trunk, &c., had been secured in the carriages, the Darcys found themselves ready to step into the chaise that would transport them to Dover, and Georgiana felt her spirits improving. The excitement and anticipation that invariably accompanies the start of a long adventure gave her less time to dwell upon the Colonel's absence from the party and—as she believed he would be joining them after a few weeks—she began to give herself up to the novelty and pleasures of the present. After journeying across to Kympton on the first day, the party called in at the rectory, bidding *adieu* to Parson and Mrs. Overstowey and Mr. Bennet. Upon entering the small, comfortable sitting room at the parsonage, they discovered Parson Overstowey fast asleep in his large chair; Elizabeth surmised that this must be his most-accustomed pose. There was a brief bustle as Kitty called for tea, and the table was made ready.

"Hill! Please bring the tea directly! The Darcys are arrived! We will take our tea in the dining-room."

As the Darcy party removed their hats and travelling coats, Parson Overstowey roused himself to greet the Darcys, and made to leave a large volume aside as if he were reading, and not fast asleep.

"Mrs. and Miss Darcy, Mr. Darcy, how delightful to see you! I was just telling Kitty that I was afraid that you would not call in to take your leave, as it was grown so late. I am delighted to be within and able to wish that God-bless you and keep you, and God-speed you back to us in safety. Now, do you have all of your things?"

Elizabeth had a momentary vision of the coach-and-four with all of their possessions hanging from it: beds, windows, cabinets, carpets, pictures, and so forth, and almost managed to suppress a giggle. Mr. Darcy came to her rescue, thanking Kitty for her trouble about the tea, and reminding the party that there was little time for leisure, if they were to conclude the day's journey at a tolerable hour.

At last it was time for leave-taking, which was the occasion for many instructions, cautions, &c. On Kitty's part were recommendations as to the employment of her bonnet, and describing the presents she imagined would be no trouble at all, nearly all of which were repetitions of the conversation over the tea. Mr. Bennet's *adieu* to Elizabeth was longer and much more affecting, and as he took both of Elizabeth's hands and kissed her good-bye, she realised that they were actually going to be separated from home and friends for a long time. "What changes we may see when we return!" she thought. Mr. Bennet turned away from the party, resorting to the library for the purpose of cheering his spirits. Kitty settled back into her accustomed rôle of keeping house for her father and husband, and finding herself continually robbed of the pleasure of being unhappy by the dependable good humour of both. Parson Overstowey continued to wave and shout advice and good wishes from the lane well after the carriages were over the hill and out of view.

A stay at Kettering provided a convenient stopping-place for the first night. Although but a modest post-house, the Darcys assumed the customary perquisites of present-day travellers on an English road: pleasant inn-keepers, plenty of good-tasting, wholesome food, and clean apartments. What was expected as a matter of course was soon become a fool's paradise. However, for the present, the three journeyed comfortably onward into Hertfordshire, stopping at Longbourn, the seat now in the possession of Mr. and Mrs. Collins as, it being Sunday on the morrow, there was no travel. The Pemberley family seldom saw Mr. Collins and Mary, especially after their removal to Longbourn; the latter's income admitted of little travel, and their mutual inclination to remain within their accustomed circle did not encourage it. Mary did her best to make all feel welcome, and Elizabeth was both surprised and pleased at the energy with which she did the honours of her home.

Mr. Collins and his second wife suited each other exceedingly well; both had acquired a confidence and steadiness that had been wanting before their marriage. However, whilst Mr. Collins was less absurd and Mary more reasonable, making them extremely agreeable companions to one another in a constant intercourse seldom relieved by visitors to their family circle, the particularity of their views and habits had multiplied rather than mitigated the oddities of both. Mr. Collins could often be seen swaying beside his wife, eyes asquint close-up to the music-book as she played and sang, for in this case marriage had *not* led to a reduction in the activity, as Mary now had an uncritical audience whose delight in her display encouraged it often.

After supper, Georgiana, being equally sensitive to the shortcomings of Mary's performance and the joy she had in exhibition, was determined to decline Mrs. Collins's invitation to follow her own recital, and subsequently heard the triumph of Mr. Collins, who leaned down to his wife as she was closing the instrument to whisper, "You see, my love, she won't play after you, for she knows that her playing is not equal to yours." So saying, he turned to Georgiana and was so overtly obsequious to her and Mr. Darcy for the duration of the visit, that it was with little regret the Darcys took their leave the following Monday morning.

A few days' farther travel brought them into Kent; however, as Lady Catherine and Miss de Bourgh were abroad, they were able to avoid calling in at Rosings. Reaching Dover on the following evening, they obtained good rooms and a private parlour at Streiker's. Arrangements had been made for the party to embark across the channel on the following day. Unfortunately, the following morning they learnt that their vessel, the sloop *King George*, engaged in the mail-service between Dover and Calais, had been delayed in port due to an unfavourable wind, postponing their crossing for at least one day; there was no guarantee that to-morrow's wind would be any better, and so they were obliged to make themselves as comfortable as possible, and enjoy what diversion could be found in their surroundings.

"I am sorry to relate that we are unable to sail to-day. I have just left Mr. Flite's, where the horses and baggage are secured, and he went to the port on purpose this morning to determine if the ship would be sailing; most regrettably, it is not," said Mr. Darcy as he entered their rooms at the hôtel.

Elizabeth replied first, "That is inconvenient, indeed; however, the lack of wind for the sails also means a calm day for our walking abroad and seeing the town, at our leisure. Georgiana, would you like to walk out with me? Mr. Darcy?"

Georgiana welcomed the opportunity to walk after so many days riding in the carriage, and returned to her room to fetch her hat and shawl. Mr. Darcy, however, already sufficiently acquainted with the scant charms of Dover, declined in favour of inspecting the stabling of their horses and the safety of their baggage, then meeting with the captain of the *King George* to assure that their cabins and other

arrangements 163

arrangements were satisfactory. In the last of the afternoon sun, Georgiana and Elizabeth set out along the shoreline, looking at the sailing boats and watching the fishermen, in their trousers rolled up beyond their knees, catching shrimp with nets affixed to long poles. Both ladies remarked how cold the water must be at this time of year. The faces of the inhabitants of Dover were uniformly weathered and dark from exposure to the elements; Elizabeth conjectured that their knees must look remarkably similar to their hands and faces. Here and there, an horse-cart was visible far out into the shore, meeting the boats at low tide to carry their fish to market; fishermen and their wives were on the beach cleaning and mending their nets; and large sailing ships lay farther out into the harbour, awaiting the tide that would carry them in to the port.

The Darcy ladies had ample leisure to learn that Dover was a city without a single allurement that would tempt any stay longer than was necessary. Sprawling, ramshackle inns and taverns catered to all classes of travellers awaiting their turn to sail. Other than their own inn, there was no establishment sufficiently respectable and unquestioningly salubrious where Georgiana and Elizabeth could take their tea, so their walk was circumscribed to accomplish only the purpose of exercise. It was with considerable pleasure the next morning that the Darcys greeted the messenger who informed them that the *King George* was making ready to set sail, effecting their release; it was not unusual for travellers to have to wait a week at Dover for favourable sailing conditions.

The morning dawned heavy with clouds, and soon there was a steady, pelting rain. The inn was astir early with travellers collecting themselves and their belongings and going down to the pier. A number of open waggons were being laden with people and baggage; one particularly large woman was atop a comparatively small ladder actually being pushed in by the coachman! Dogs barked, a few couples embraced in a most visibly fond farewell, the land-lady standing in the door-way of the inn superintending the proceedings. In the waggon, a lady struggled with an umbrella to remain dry and protect her cloathing, the effect of which was entirely hindered by the success of the rain and the jostling of the other passengers in their efforts to reorder their cases, as more passengers attempted to push their way into the waggon. A man with a peg-leg wandered by, head bare, hat in hand, asking for alms; a woman selling pots shouted in all directions, attempting to keep the crowd of people and animals from treading on them; and, at the far end of the inn, a soldier embraced a young woman holding a basket of eggs, whilst another young lady in a night-dress was come out of a door, clearly in the intent of stopping the proceedings. The area where the ship moored was near pandemonium, with servants and every variety of traveller trying to get their cases on board—running here, pushing there, crying, laughing, shouting, cursing, all busy with making ready to leave. Despite the down-pour, friends who had come purposely to be in the way and wave their friends off to sea were ordered off by the bell, causing a renewed disorder, with fluttering hand-kerchiefs, outstretched hands, shouted instructions, commands, admonishments, and advice; a few gentle *adieus* and good wishes could occasionally be overheard. At last all of their baggage, carriages, and horses were loaded into the hold, and the family walked aboard. Elizabeth was vastly amused at the *tableaux* surrounding the departure of the ship, her spirits rising apace with the commotion and clamour.

By noon, the ship was underway and, with a fair wind, began its journey to Calais. At almost the same moment the anchor was aweighed, the rain ceased and the sun appeared. A fine, fresh breeze blew, which must have been especially welcome to those passengers without recourse to cabins, soon out on the deck drying themselves and their belongings. The storm, however, had produced a rollicking sea, forcing those who had the means to resort to their rooms below-deck, and others, to the railing. Mr. Darcy introduced his wife to the captain, who promised the Darcys a tour of the ship as soon as they were fully under sail. Having completed their walk with the captain, they returned an half-hour later below-deck to offer Georgiana whatever small comfort was in their power. After providing her sister with a cool hand-kerchief and giving Darcy their medicine-box, Lizzy returned to her own cabin and took out her new escritoire to begin her correspondence. As she had promised her Aunt and Uncle Gardiner that theirs would be the first letter written *en voyage*, she began her letter to London:

*March 13*th
The King George

DEAREST AUNT AND UNCLE GARDINER,

We are to sea at last and—as promised—the first letter to reach the English shores from your adventurous niece is destined for those to whom we owe so much of our present happiness. As I write this, the packet rolls and dips, keels and lists with an alarming turbulence, but for the present, my sea-legs have kept me aright and I confess that I am rather enjoying myself, although I never was in such a tumble on the road as the ship makes upon the waves. As is my habit, I indulge my own pleasure, and care not how I may be wounding your eyes as you attempt to decipher the scrawls and blots, which I charmingly blame on the sea.

I shall amuse myself by describing our ship, the *King George*. There is little else to occupy me, excepting the prospect of a ship's dinner, which, I fear, may warrant a whole letter in itself, and so you must both pay the penalty for my leisure and endure as lengthy and rambling a letter as I am pleased to send.

Much to the amusement of Mr. Darcy, I am become acquainted with the ship's Captain, a Captain Fanshawe, who—being a sensible man—favoured me with a tour of the *King George* at my particular request. The crew's quarters appear to be most desperately crowded and comfortless in the extreme—they live toward the eyes of the ship, whereas the passenger cabins (of which there are six) are in the stern. Made of matchwood and with little light, I have avoided mine, but poor Georgiana, who does not get on well with the rolling of the ship, is abed as I write this, with her dutiful brother to comfort her in my absence. The *salon*—by far the most commodious section of the ship, with the only comfortable seats and daylight streaming through its window—is my chosen anchorage at present, and because so many passengers are occupied with being ill in their cabins, it is wonderfully quiet for those of us who are lucky enough to escape such a disagreeable indisposition.

We have been to sea now for four hours, and the crew suppose, due to an unfavourable wind, we may be yet a few hours more before we reach our destination. For my part, I confess that I wish the journey vastly longer, but you know how fond of the unfamiliar I am and how little I consider the discomforts of others out of concern for my own pleasure. The delay and my paper allow me to display my now-extensive knowledge of travelling at sea.

The packet-commander is an extraordinary fellow, an handsome, reading man, and dressed in uniform similar to the officers of the Royal Navy. I hope I do not do him a disservice by claiming that it appears to be his first-mate who does all of the work that is to be done, whilst the captain takes the glory (as I write this, I am filled with a sudden horror that you must immediately bethink a mistress of a certain house in Derbyshire who is similarly fortunate in allowing a superbly capable sister to superintend all, whilst this mistress falsely assumes all credit for the excellent standard of house-keeping). The rest of the crew, excepting the bo'sun, who is somewhat sullen, are quite kind and

carry

carry out their duties in a commendable manner. I suppose this is not surprising when one considers the improvement in their circumstances and safety now the war is over, although Mr. Darcy did tell me that they are paid less in peace-time, so these are the lucky men who can bless their fortune as yet having a situation at-sea.

My dear friends, although I know I will be missing England, its comforts and sweet familiarity, the feeling of being on the open sea and on the edge of a great adventure is so exhilarating that I am sure I will not sleep a wink from Dover to Rome. Every morning, I consider my happiness and how little I have done to merit such an uncommonly disproportionate share of blessings; to-day more than ever, I thank you again and again for your wisdom in not going to the Lakes, and for your kindness which secured me the best of blessings; I am the happiest of women and the most fortunate of wives.

My husband beckons me to come to the relief of poor Georgiana. I seal this along with all of our love to you both and to the rest of your family, and an assurance that the absence of your indispensable selves is already much regretted.

Your loving and grateful niece,

ELIZABETH DARCY

Mr. Darcy had been reading *Chesterfield's Letters to his Son* aloud to Georgiana in her cabin. All of the passengers aboard were suffering the sea-sickness to some extent, but she was most discomposed, finding the sailing thoroughly unpleasant. The sachet of bay salts had failed to relieve her sickness, and her brother had next resorted to a draught of quince and lemon peel; she was happily now feeling almost up to the journey from her cabin to join the company in the saloon, where they were to be served their dinner. Elizabeth had thought it prudent not to mention the appalling cooking conditions of the galley, wisely preferring to keep her knowledge of the communal pot-boilers to herself. In any case, her descriptions were unnecessary, as they were all pleasantly surprised when their dinner arrived in a form quite palatable. Georgiana ate but little, and, after a few minutes, made her excuses and returned to her cabin to rest before their arrival in France.

Darcy asked Elizabeth if she would like to join him above for her first view of France; she assented with unalloyed joy as she took her husband's arm and bade him take her up onto the deck. Reaching the railing, her first impression was that they had been returned to Dover! Along the shore they saw men cleaning nets, fishing-boats laying at anchor, and horse-carts carrying in the day's catch. However, in the next instant she could see that the colour of the people's cloathes had changed: whereas the Dovermen uniformly wore light and dark-brown cloathing, with a bit of blue or red in their kerchiefs, the Frenchmen were chiefly dressed in bright reds and blues. Elizabeth could not immediately determine if the gay colours of their skirts and trousers made them appear more animated, or if their movements and countenances were actually more lively than were their English counter-parts.

The ship was forced to anchor offshore to await the tide, but within the space of two hours, they were once again firmly attached to the shore. With the most perilous part of the trip now behind them, Georgiana breathed a great sigh of relief, and more than once mentioned how happy she was to be again looking upon dry land. The ship had tied up along an enormous sea-wall; Elizabeth reckoned it must be taller again by half than the Cobb at Lyme Regis, and, unlike the Cobb, was a modern construction of hewn stone. Mr. Darcy explained to the ladies that they had been most fortunate in the height of the tide, as, had it been lower, all passengers and their goods must have been carried ashore in small boats. It was impossible to conjecture how their horses and carriages would have been so conveyed, but that, fortunately, was not necessary.

The ship, having reached the dock and tied up, the passengers were forced to wait to disembark whilst the French customs-men boarded and inspected its cargoes, animate and otherwise. Unlike the orderly English officers, the French agents were in various bits and pieces of uniform and rag-tag cloathing, most of which had not seen the effects of soap and water during the entirety of its existence. The men were like-wise unshaven, dirty, and gratuitously unpleasant. The gang-plank had barely been secured when the mob of customs-men hastened aboard; the scene was immediately one of complete confusion: every manner of bag, trunk, portmanteau, bundle, and parcel was strewn about the deck, no article secure from being torn open and having its contents disgorged and trampled. It was the habit of the inspectors of France to throw all of the baggage onto the landing and empty the contents of each trunk onto the ground; some portion of the contents would then be jumbled back into the case without regard to order or any *débris* that happened to be conveniently near-by through the unwelcome efforts of the porters, distinguished from the others assembled on the quay-side by the wearing of striped shirts, gathering at the dock for the purpose of assaulting their baggage. As soon as the items had been at least partially restored to their original container, these men

carried

carried the trunks away, up the stairs of the landing without the formality of having been asked, or taking any trouble to determine their ownership. The *dérangement* might have been considered farcical, but was prevented from being so out of concern for the uncertain fate of one's own belongings. The entire performance was carried on to the amusement of a large crowd of people on the top parts of the wall, who were alternately waving or shouting to anyone and everyone who happened to look up amidst the chaos on the landing.

The Bureau subjected their belongings to interminable inspections, making their exit from the port slow, indeed. Darcy was grateful for the advice he had received from Mr. Gardiner, that he carry sufficient letters of recommendation, as well as the obligatory passports and bills of health. His own expectation that his being a gentleman would prevent lengthy interrogation and inspection was soon proved to be entirely illusory. The Darcys' luggage that had been packed and stown with such care, was now ruthlessly and carelessly thrown onto the shore, and forced to expel its contents by rough and dirty hands. The two lady's maids were justifiably horrified at the devastation soon to result from such heedlessness, and, as soon as they could recover the use of their brains and limbs from the shock of such an iniquity, attempted to interfere with the progress of the agents. Georgiana's maid, Adéle, was soon shouting at the officers with such rapidity and vehemence that the general purport of her tirade could not be completely understood, even by Georgiana. During this altercation, Lizzy's maid was simultaneously shouting at the top of her voice at the men in English, and both women were variously and violently pointing at each other, the baggage, and the officers. The ladies were surprisingly effective, and managed to stop most of the cloathing and other valuables from being removed from their original positions. Elizabeth viewed the maids' audacity with some amusement, and a great deal of grateful appreciation, asking Mr. Darcy if he did not agree that their epithets and outraged gesticulations had intimidated the officers, with the result that the agents left off their depredations rather sooner than otherwise might have been the case.

CHAP. 24.

EXCEPTING THE CUSTOMS-MEN, the French were, as repute would have it, very polite; even the most humbly dressed was not without an astonishing grace of address and a becoming courtesy of manner. The second impression of the Darcys was to cover their faces with their handkerchiefs against the smell! The wind had been blowing away from the ship, and so it was not until they were landed and were in the shelter of the quay that they saw and *smelt* France. Darcy further observed, standing amidst their fellow-passengers crowded onto the tiny landing, that von Metternich had spoken the truth in his claim, "It is raining Englishmen" in France. Elizabeth laughed, suggesting as they were surrounded by so many English, that an *impromptu* rendition of "God Save the King" *en masse* before distributing themselves amongst their various paths through and out of Calais would not be *malapropos*.

The Calasians did not seem especially prosperous, but were courteous, active, and helpful. The women wore variously coloured cloathing, the coat always of a different shade than the skirt, and the younger women wore curious, tall white caps with a fall of linen to the shoulders at the back. Women of all ages had white shifts and aprons that were tolerably clean, and—without exception—all set off by long, heavy gold ear-rings and a very large cross. Elizabeth wondered if perhaps these pendulums were wedding-gifts, as the women seemed to be particularly proud of their size, the magnitude of which seemed to vary not with age, but by a slight superiority of dress. Some of the Calasians had wooden shoes in the manner of the Dutchmen, but many wore neither shoes nor stockings, in spite of being only early spring. The men were not as exceptionally dressed, and to a degree resembled the outward appearance of their English neighbours, different only in their preference for blue garments instead of brown ones, and the former's curious, striped round caps; but, oh! what a difference in their expressions! The French were so animated—laughing and talking all at once, as bright as their cloathing—so very different from the drab, reserved English stile of going about.

Mr. Darcy was the first to speak as they climbed up the steps to the street: "If there were any doubt as to the wisdom of bringing our own equipage, it should evaporate upon seeing the French coachmen—I have never seen such dirty, disheveled drivers! The harness is nothing but a collection of filthy rope, and seems incapable of safely attaching a wheel-barrow, much less a coach full of people *and* their baggage. The loriner would have but poor custom in France, apparently."

"What'n apperi'tion!" exclaimed Mr. Harmon. "Hoow c'n they git aloong wi' sech a team? T'ree abreast, wi' a cart-horse in t' mid'l, a cob on t' near-side, an't rag'd pony on't'other! The mid'l horse mun' have t' drag t' coach, and t'others as weell! An' t' drivver be a'wearin' t' hobnailed tall-boots fit fer drivin' nowt but a limber!"

"As if the horses were the worst of it," replied Mr. Darcy. "Look at that post-boy—that badge indicates the royal livery; it is a disgrace to all France! An English farmer would have turned out to better advantage! That filthy blue jacket would be more respectable were it clean and plain; the office of those under-sleeves and silver laces now appears only to accentuate the disparity between the pretense of the livery and these slovenly creatures. God hope they are more creditable drivers than their appearance would indicate!"

Mr. Harmon continued to abuse the post-boys' heavy, high boots, and thick, bobbed queues, lashing from side-to-side unimpeded by the rusty Japan hat topping it all to no apparent purpose, save adding to the caricature of the spectacle. At length, the Darcys' coachman was forced to abridge his patriotic comparisons as the diligence jumbled away, and his grooms announced that the horses had been put-to and were ready for his inspection.

Also differing from the smart English post-boys and the gleaming brass and leather of the carriage-horses, the Darcys found the *voiturins* exceedingly clumsy and queer-looking; the harness was chiefly of various kinds of ropes and cords, the collars looked like they had been made for elephants, and none had seen a brush or water for the duration of its existence. The guiding of the horses was accomplished by a postillion on the wheel horse, who held a varying assortment of these cords, shouted epithets, roared commands at the top of the lungs, all accompanied by

accompanied

the heavy boots with spurs, and an horn which seemed employed to no purpose save the amusement of his fellow *voiturins*. The man on the box lived only to crack the whip and shout, causing the horses to move in any direction save a straight line, dogs to bark, inhabitants to hasten to their doors, and such general confusion and noise that formed a concert far more irksome than agreeable. This was not the last instance that gave Mr. Darcy reason to hug himself in the choice of his own horses and servants.

Calais itself was small and pleasant, consisting of not above eight streets. Darcy determined, as there was no reason to tarry in Calais, that they would leave as soon as possible for Paris. At the recommendation of a fellow passenger on board the *King George*, Darcy had passed by Quillacq's and secured very acceptable lodgings at L'Hôtel d'Angleterre, more familiarly known to the residents as Dessin's. Elizabeth and Georgiana soon found themselves comfortably placed in the hôtel, which provided the travellers with the conveniences of a large court and garden, commodious baths, a small theatre, and a restaurant. The establishment was tolerably clean with excellent, comfortable furniture. The fare, however, was well above the average of the English way-side inns and the cost reasonable, even given such a difference in the quality of the supper, a pleasure the Darcys were to encounter frequently in France. Having the custom of all persons of rank passing through Calais, Dessin's provided the Darcy ladies with an opportunity to observe their fellow itinerants at that establishment. Elizabeth always approached her surveys with an uncommon enthusiasm, this day's especially so, as being her first in a foreign country. In the meantime, Darcy busied himself with seeing to the care of the horses, and assessing the condition of the carriages and their baggage. Only when he was satisfied with the arrangements for the morrow did he return to their lodging.

After dressing for dinner and removing to the dining room to meet Elizabeth and Georgiana, Darcy was approached by a smart-looking officer who introduced himself as Major Townsend, a friend of Colonel Fitzwilliam. Having done so, he was rewarded with an introduction to Elizabeth and Georgiana, the latter of whom he obviously admired. The Darcys were invited to dine with his company, which included a singular-looking older gentleman, a Mr. B——, of great notoriety, living amongst the hundreds who had fled England to avoid gaming debts, and was now resident at Dessin's through the generosity of his remaining friends. The evening, therefore, provided all the novelty and intrigue

that 173

that could reasonably be expected on the first night of an adventure, although Georgiana confided to Elizabeth at the end of the evening that the attentions of Major Townsend had made her feel quite uneasy.

"I know it is the fashion in France for ladies and gentlemen to dine out together, but I confess it makes me uncomfortable, for there is no escape—no possible relief—from an intercourse which may not be desirable to at least one of the parties. I do not possess that easy manner of speaking with strangers with which so many others are blessed, and you particularly, dearest Elizabeth. I should much rather dine with my family. From your smile, I see you are going to tell me I do not sufficiently appreciate these attentions and should welcome the admiration of a respectable Englishman, are you not?"

Elizabeth nodded her affirmation and laughed affectionately at her sister's distress. "You may not wish for the compliment, but I am afraid your complaint is not one likely to be met with much sympathy. Your disinclination for the attention, which—without wishing to speak an unkindness of the ladies of France—is apparently not so common in this country, and novelty will always arouse interest. Your blushes will only engage this particular officer's affections more securely, so you must gracefully, if not gratefully, accept that a pretty, modest Englishwoman will receive more attention than she may like, especially when she is so charming as not to seek it. Your being a little reserved is a general attraction—few men, I believe, wish for competition in speech, much preferring to listen to themselves." And so saying, she bade Georgiana good-night.

The practicalities of travel in Europe and seasonal difficulties in the hiring of post-horses dominated the conversation at dinner that first evening, with expert and novice travellers alike across the tables exchanging tales of perilous journeys, either undertaken themselves, or confidently retold. Mr. Darcy, therefore, determined that they must leave early the next morning in the hope of an easier journey. The family were travelling in the chaise-and-four, with servants and luggage in a second carriage of four post-horses and two out-riders, requiring at least four fresh horses at each post on the Paris road; it was, in consequence, desirable to get an early start for the day's travel. Early mornings, Elizabeth reflected to her husband as they dressed for breakfast, were but a small price to pay for the greater comforts of speed and safety.

In the morning, as they were making ready to get into their carriage, they noticed the Paris diligence which had stopt at their inn. Unlike

the

the light, graceful English mail coaches, the French equivalents were unwieldy, heavy machines capable of carrying only nine passengers. This singular equipage was drawn by five horses in an awkward and—as with the coach on the previous day—ugly collection of rope harness, and which, despite the additional horse, could travel no faster than a man's pace. The postillion wore a ridiculous glazed hat, a fur apron, and jack-boots that appeared to have been borrowed from a giant of children's fables. The Darcy carriages, despite being substantially larger than the diligence and carrying more weight, soon left the crawling, jumbling diligence behind, although the latter carriage had departed at least ten minutes prior to their own. Besides the lumbering diligences, the private carriages of the Belgians and French were queer contrivances, the former being little more than the size of a British pony-coach, making the passengers atop look like Gulliver in Lilliput, and the latter having such tiny front wheels as to appear to be constantly driving into the ground, instead of riding parallel with the roadway. In deference to the fairness of comparison, Georgiana noted that the Belgian equipage was proper and clean, and their drivers, who wore tall hats and great-coats, regarded the reins as the best method for directing the horses. In contrast, the more interesting attire of the French coachmen, as even those in livery appeared in coats of red, bright blue, or even yellow, caused Mr. Darcy to declare that the entire race were indistinguishable from British footmen, allowing, however, that the footmen were less exceptionally dressed.

South of Calais, the terrain was flat and uninteresting, leading Elizabeth to remark,

"Does this country not remind you of Wiltshire and Sussex, particularly the less-attractive areas? The houses in this part of France are certainly a contrast to the neat, well-kept cottages we passed *en route* to Dover, and the roads in this section are rutted and in a greater state of disrepair than the English highways, to my eye."

"I am not complimentary of the state of the road, to be sure," agreed Mr. Darcy. "The French preference for straight roads, cutting the way through fields and villages without any thought of going around them, not only cuts up the countryside with a most disagreeable result, but makes the road quite dull."

Passing through Marquise, the Darcys remarked on the unfinished tower there, erected by Buonaparte in commemoration of his anticipated victory over the English, and giving silent, grateful thanks to Providence for the narrow victory which had secured the end of this as well as all of the Emperour's other unfinished plans. At Hautboisson, Elizabeth began to despair of the remaining one hundred and sixty miles before they would reach Paris. Eventually, however, the scenery improved, becoming softer, as the carriage travelled up and around small hillocks, woodlands, and villages in an order almost resembling those of Somersetshire, with the exception of the crucifixes and painted statues of religious significance that dotted the roadsides and ornamented the towns of France.

"Mr. Darcy, do you notice anything especially different about the villages and fields of this area, from our own country?" asked Elizabeth, as they were going along.

Georgiana looked up from her book, attending to her brother's answer. "No, other than the dress of the commoners, which we have already described. What is your observation?"

"Merely that there are women to be *seen*. Here, we see women in the fields, in their gardens, about in the villages. In England, other than at harvest-time, women seem to be entirely locked away. These women must be healthier for the exercise and fresh air, as well as the pleasant effects of regular conversation with their neighbours upon their minds."

"In England," agreed Georgiana, "the women seem to be drawn away from country-work, instead almost preferring, it seems, the odours and noise of a manufactory. I wonder if the reason is pecuniary, or that Englishwomen simply chuse to remain in-doors; both surmises are equally unfortunate in their own way."

"In some of the southern counties, many of the female servants have left-off working in the dairy," continued Darcy, "believing that such heavy work is properly done by men. I agree, my dear," he said to Elizabeth, "that the country-women here—and, in Scotland, I would venture to add, despite the climate—have a glow and a freshness to their complexions that is generally lacking in England. We English may prefer to call such a browned appearance coarse, but there is certainly an animation and merriment to be seen in both sexes—and the children— which is against us."

"Yes, Husband, and I cannot credit a general appearance of pallor and the oppression of spirits naturally arising from being always within-doors as indicative of delicacy, as constitutes the common belief. How happy would England be, if the inclusive mirth and festivity of the harvest could be the rule in all months! This place is neither so charming nor as gay as our hay-fields in the harvest, but on average, I would venture that these women are happier—they certainly *seem* happy—to an uninformed observer such as myself."

The roads gradually improved, as the carriages drew closer to Paris, leading Mr. Darcy to note that travel in France, since his own tour thirty years before, had been materially improved through the construction of new roads, replacing the old by-ways with their rough and often steep terrain. The pretty woods on either side provided ample picturesque scenery, home as they were to a number of small huts built on wheels. Mr. Darcy stopt to enquire of a prosperous-looking peasant as to the purpose of the wheels under the constructions, which were inferior in size and condition to a dog's kennel in England. The good man replied that the shepherd's family followed their sheep-folds as they moved to their spring and summer pastures, the huts serving as their year-round accommodation! Elizabeth responded to her husband that the inhabitants were indeed fortunate that the area had not earth-quakes, lest they find themselves in pursuit of their houses, in addition to suffering every other inconvenience.

Post-houses were not as predictable as in England. The smallest, least prepossessing inn might as likely offer superior accommodations, excellent fare, and pleasant, active hosts as the more celebrated establishments of the cities. However, they all shared one disadvantage: at every stop, the travellers were escorted to the door of the inn by troops of ragged persons of all ages and sexes, all imploring *"Charité pour l'amour de Dieu!"* Not content with clamouring at the door of the post-house, these industrious mendicants would accordingly follow the carriage for a remarkable distance (despite many claims of lameness), and if the coach should ascend an hill, enabling these solicitors to catch it, they importuned most persistently and disagreeably until the traveller relented and produced some trifling payment. It appeared that they all operated under the dictum, "Never lose anything for want of asking." To complete the ensemble, even as the carriage was not yet stopt, the village *forgeron* would emerge from his dwelling and "discover" some loose or otherwise threatening portion of the carriage that necessitated its immediate repair. Fortunately for the Darcys, Mr. Harmon—with Georgiana's able assistance with the French language, fluently translating the strange pronunciation of the Normans—was in every way equal to the task of disputing the spurious claims of the blacksmiths, who returned to their sheds to sulk and await less capable prey.

At the French post-houses, the *aubergiste* would come forth in his dirty apron and greasy hands to welcome the travellers, entirely unlike the English inns, where travellers would be met by the inn-keeper, whose wife was usually at the hearth. There was also a marked distinction to the manner of speech of the servants; in England, the servants were quiet and universally reserved, whereas in France, it was considered polite to discourse with the guests, an injunction which the young Frenchwomen (usually the daughters of the inn-keeper) took to heart, conversing most readily and pleasantly with every class of their custom. Their conversation was intelligent and lively, with no hint of either impertinence or immodesty. In person, they were well-looking girls, gaily dressed, clean, and much given to a mirth which in no way impeded their unceasing politeness and attentions to the desires of their guests. When their guests did not need their service, the women would sit in a room next to the kitchen, employed with mending or other needle-work, chatting and laughing in a manner delightful to hear.

It took only a few days on the road for the Darcys to accustom themselves to the pace demanded by travel. The chaise was extremely comfortable, having been carefully designed and equipped for such a journey, and even with allowance for frequent stops along the way, they travelled quickly. By nightfall on the first day, they alighted at Boulogne where they rested at Parkers's Hôtel d'Angleterre. The town of Boulogne was very pretty, with crumbling, ancient city walls now overgrown by trees and vines. They had passed several elderly peasants walking along the road; to a man, they wore cocked hats and respectable suits of a dark-coloured cloth, very similar, noted Elizabeth, to the Sunday cloathes of the English villagers, so clean and proper was their appearance.

At their inn, the obliging *aubergiste* endeavored to demonstrate the extent of his desire to accommodate the habits of the English, serving the Darcys his own rendition of an English supper. Instead of the delightful meals they had thus-far enjoyed, this dinner was proved a disagreeable admixture of the worst of the cookery of both nations. All three stared at their bowls of melted butter afloat in rancid oil, which—for some unaccountable reason—was served to them in a tea-cup. This was followed by extraordinarily tough pieces of meat, which were denominated, by their beaming *chef de cuisine*, as veal cutlets. Despite being prodigiously hungry, the Darcys managed to eat little other than the bread—which, thankfully, was the true French bread— Mr. Darcy excusing their poor performance to the proprietor as the effects of indisposition due to travelling.

On the morrow, they made for Abbeville; a series of recent and well-publicised robberies by highwaymen caused Mr. Darcy to leave the ladies inside the chaise whilst he rode on the box with the coachman—

both men, the under-coachman driving the servants' coach, and all of the out-riders—with their pistols cocked and ready. Fortunately, the precaution was unnecessary, as they experienced no inconvenience of any kind on their journey through to Abbeville, excepting the now-familiar *ennui* arising from the arrow-straight roads and barren countryside.

"There is a part of me—the part we all try and sometimes fail to repress—Mr. Darcy," declared Elizabeth, as they cleared the troubled section of the route and reached the post-house, "that would rather enjoy being set-upon by highwaymen, just as in a novel. You, my brave husband, would heroically defend your terrified dependents and boldly challenge the perpetrators. Facing certain death in the process, you would somehow contrive to escape from their grasp, and disappear in a clatter of hooves and a whirlwind of dust; I rather fancy the idea that one of the miscreants would fall desperately in love with Georgiana, and would return our valuables in an apoplexy of remorse, keeping 'only the emerald ring she wore as a token of the love glimpsed but never possessed'." Georgiana interrupted this transporting vision to request that Elizabeth refrain from marrying her off to a felon, and Darcy stopt the recitation entirely by suggesting that his wife suspend the progress of the Gothic novel she was conjuring for their doubtful benefit, and write a much-overdue letter to her father and Kitty. The substitute letter was neither as interesting nor as compelling, but had the virtue of removing her husband and sister from the perils of Elizabeth's imagination.

Thickets obscured the many little villages and farmsteads inhabited by the rustics, and so in several particularly interesting spots, the Darcys removed from their carriage in order to better explore their surroundings. Elizabeth—fond of walking as she was—found great pleasure in these little deviations in their journey. The men of this area wore what appeared to be white night-caps and long smocks of indigo; Elizabeth surmised that the elderly men they had previously passed must have been dressed in the habit of the *Ancien Régime*, as was their long-custom, and that this unbecoming ensemble was the product of the *Nouveau*. They stopt at a post-house, named the Tête de Boeuf, and, whilst the horses were being changed, Elizabeth went inside to enquire for some refreshment against the dust. She wandered about, and seeing no-one at the door, entered the kitchen. A group of peasants were seated comfortably around a wood fire, awaiting their meal, which was being finished by a pretty, lively *paysanne*. As Elizabeth stood

watching 179

watching, she took the pot from the fire, and served them. The soup looked and smelt deliciously, and appeared to be a *ragoût* of vegetables, herbs, and the rinds of bread. It did not escape Elizabeth's sense of the absurd that, in England, it was the pride of every gentle family who could afford it to employ a Frenchman as their cook; in France, she would willingly compound for the talents of this simple young woman, in preference to any of the *aubergistes* they had as yet encountered.

Within the kitchen was seated an older woman, likely the proprietress, who regarded Elizabeth's entrance with some surprise, but apologised most civilly for the state of her kitchen. Unlike an English cottage kitchen, where the dishes and other utensils were kept upon the side-board or within the cupboard, here they were arranged everywhere about the room. Noticing that Elizabeth was looking at the crockery displayed in the kitchen, the *vieille dame* expressed her regret that the dishes were not as clean as they should be, but the flies made everything so dirty. Such an explanation was enough to inspire Elizabeth to quit the room without either refreshment or regret, and cheerfully rejoin her husband and sister in the carriage.

On the next morning, they passed through Samer where they stopt for breakfast. The owner of the post-house at Samer had particularly recommended they stop at another Tête de Boeuf in Montreuil. Elizabeth wondered aloud if only the cows had heads in France; or, if there were other animals possessed of that useful protuberance, why were there no inns of the name Tête de Chèvre, Tête de Cheval, or even Tête de Roi, instantly recalling the latter as a subject unfit for jest. The servant at the inn at Montreuil was *une demoiselle engageante*. Upon entering, the Darcys found themselves in a tidy ante-room where they were quickly served a very good tea by another neatly dressed *demoiselle*. They were informed that this latter young woman was the daughter of the proprietress, and the servant their *femme de chambre*. Both girls flew about the cottage, readying everything for their stay, not with only efficiency, but with cheer and a desire to please. They laughed and joked between themselves, including the Darcys in their banter with a becoming deference and a real joy at the questions asked by the their English guests. Mrs. Darcy asked the maid if she were married, and the young woman assumed a ridiculous countenance of tragedy, and said in a theatrical tone, "*Pas encore, Madame, mais j'espère encore qu'un bel Anglais possédante demandera ma main en mariage.*" The Darcys were delighted with the penchant of all classes of the French for good-natured *sens de la répartie*. Elizabeth remarked to her husband later that evening that an English servant who spoke thusly to her superiors would be considered impertinent and of no character, but that the French servants had a way of speaking familiarly with no hint of either disrespect or coarseness, opining that the latter method made intercourse so much more agreeable than the cold, artificial manners of their own countrymen. Mr. Darcy responded, "*À chacun son plaisir*," as he extinguished the light.

The country after Samer was become softer, with rolling hills of woods and grassy downs. Elizabeth remarked on the thinness of the trees, and their smallness. Georgiana replied that she understood the trees were always cut for fire-wood before they could attain their full height, as wood was preferred to all other combustibles, leading Darcy to remark about a "difference in their method." The way now passed from Montreuil to Nampont amidst seas of corn, wheat, oats, and other grasses. The *ramasseurs* used the wheat-stalks to plait little bouquets, which they threw into the carriage, begging a *sou* for their trouble. Their children began to sing and dance along-side their mothers. Georgiana was surprised to recognise the melody of a *quadrille*, to which the children were properly stepping; she could not imagine children of a similar status in England knowing anything of the kind, and remarked that the French must be born knowing how to dance.

"Yes, and do you notice how we frequently observe villagers in an *impromptu* dance? They dance in their every-day cloathes at the slightest provocation, taking up serving-maids, passers-by, anyone about, and beginning the quadrille. How much of our pleasure as a nation is suspended by preparation—rooms, time, dress—whilst these people seize upon every opportunity to be merry and happy in their place! It is no wonder they are more animated than ourselves—they make every moment an excuse for being so."

"Yes, but this does not decide anything. Are they merry because they dance, or do they dance because they are merry? It all seems so of a piece that we, as English, are not able to separate the cause from the effect," replied Georgiana.

"Spoken like a true Englishwoman!" laughed Elizabeth. "Whilst we sit about in the contemplation of this conundrum, they are dancing without regard to any theory of *why* it is they dance. For myself, I would much rather be merry than wise."

Meanwhile, Mr. Darcy was noticing the earliness of the crops, and told the ladies that their forwardness was due to the French practise of irrigating their fields.

"If it is such a benefit, why do not the English adopt such a method?" asked Georgiana. Darcy replied, "Two reasons: first, our island is generally blessed with the rain-fall needed for our cultivation, and our farmers know how to use the regular patterns of the weather to their advantage; the second is the cost of the labour to distribute water to the fields. The French seem to have overcome that deterrent by employing their women to assume the additional burthen of hauling the water to the fields, but I do not think such treatment of women in England would be countenanced, even by the lowest rank of farmer." They halted in Abbeville at another of the ubiquitous Tête de Boeuf that evening and— despite some information to the contrary—both the supper and the rooms of the inn were in every way satisfactory. The proprietress was an healthy-looking, handsome young mother with two small children. The little girls were remarkably pretty, with fine, clear dark skin, with glowing, rosy cheeks; their eyes were of an unusually deep blue, with long black lashes. The Darcy ladies complimented the woman on the beauty of her children, and were gratified to find that French parents responded to praise of their young in the universal way.

The town of Abbeville was not prosperous, and seemed to be fast falling into ruin; its peasantry were exceedingly poor, being only some little above misery. The dress differed to a surprising degree, being at so little distance from Calais, but the women of Abbeville wore dresses, not shifts, and, although they had the same wooden or leathern slippers and blue stockings, their hair was confined inside a turban, wrapt with a ribband of various colours. The only real similarity was the long ear-rings of the women, some more than a foot long! Mr. Darcy declared that these looked more like gravy-spoons than any other objects; Elizabeth questioned if such objects hanging from the head were not a threat to life and limb, it being impossible to turn around without their swinging out and away from the wearer with a dangerous velocity.

Abbeville's single attraction was its cathedral, a fine old building of striking architecture. The interior was—as is usual with churches of the Romish religion—filled with idols and other superstitious ornaments. Interestingly, it was described by Georgiana as having been built by the English when this part of France was under the dominion of the Kings of England. Two poor country women were kneeling in front of Our Saviour on the cross with an earnestness and piety not often seen in a Church of England. One of the women had a very small infant in her arms, and was beseeching the Virgin for its salvation. For all of its faults as a way of worship, its adherents obviously found it a source of

great

great comfort and consolation, more so, it seemed to the English, than the Protestants who must daily struggle to find solace in a faith not founded upon ritual and superstition.

They attended the theatre that evening, finding no people of rank at that place, only shop-keepers and officers of the Garde Nationale. The actors declaimed in a most singular stile, emoting with ridiculously exaggerated gesticulations and in extraordinary accents, which were very difficult to follow, a task made worse by the poses they and their faces adopted during their speech. The Darcys learnt that this was the usual form of a tragedy in France, the best houses of Paris included. By the end of the evening, Mr. Darcy's only remark was that he would never utter an unkind word about Mr. Kean or Mrs. Siddons again. Their inn, L'Hôtel de L'Europe, was very good. It had once been an handsome *château*, and there remained to it a lovely garden, formerly adjoining the convent that had given the city its name, the high walls already covered this early season by a profusion of blossoms delightful to see, and young grapes formed on the vines. The furnishments of their rooms were in a very superior stile, as were many of the better places in France, with chimney-pieces, thresholds, &c., made of marble, Mr. Darcy remarking that it must be very cheap and plentiful according to its frequent use.

As they left Abbeville, the scenery relapsed into the same flatness and lack of any interesting feature that could repay the tedium of passing through it. At the sides of the roads, there were many peasants employed in the making of ropes near-by large fields of hemp and flax. The country at last was become more verdant, and small plantations were spotted infrequently in the distance. The river Somme wound through a part of their way, and its course could be plainly delineated by the willows upon its banks, looking for all the world like parts of Berkshire along the Thames. The road-sides began to be ornamented with apple trees of the cider kind. These joys were not long in existence, as the road at Airaines grew straight and the country again barren, but the weather continued very kind—a pleasantly cool breeze blew under a bright sun. This day's travel had been particularly uninteresting, and all of the Darcys were impatient to quit this section of the road and arrive at their inn to supper and comfortable beds.

It became apparent that evening, however, that not all of the way-houses in France were as respectable or as clean as those they had thus-far encountered. The road dividing at Abbeville, Mr. Darcy had determined to take the westerly route passing through Granvilliers above Amiens, avoiding the much-praised cathedral that dominated the town, and ignoring the received wisdom that Granvillier's inns were best avoided. Georgiana and her brother shared an extraordinary avidity for history, and Mr. Darcy was especially eager to explore Caesar's Mount, which the Granvilliers road passed close-by. The entrenchments were discernable still, having been carefully preserved. However, their various *guides de voyages* were proved far too lenient on the deplorable state of the inns, unspeakably bad food, and disobliging manners the Darcys encountered at Granvilliers. So near to their arrival at Calais, the family had not expected such disagreeable accommodations, and after a dreadful dinner of stale bread, foul wine, and an anonymous cheese, they retired early to their beds—Elizabeth most thankful to have brought their own linens—all united in a wish to decamp at an early hour the next morning.

The scenery had hitherto been unexceptional, but the road from Abbeville to Granvilliers was lined with formerly abandoned monasteries and convents, which had been re-invented by Buonaparte as manufactories of diverse goods. A feeling of prosperity was discernable even in the poorest quarters, and it was clear that agriculture and industry were become more established than might otherwise have been the case. The closer the carriage advanced upon Paris, the more prosperous and ordered became the landscape. Darcy took pleasure in pointing out particular plants and fruits, and when he noticed a variety of especial interest, they stopt to enquire of a farmer of some cuttings, which were then carefully bundled in damp hessian, and stored in a lined case that Darcy had bespoken for the purpose. Vineyards appeared on the hills, the Cathedral of Beauvais could be seen rising above the woods in the distance, and here and there were seen some very fine houses in tolerable repair. A brief rain had fallen early in the morning, laying the dust somewhat, making their road yet more pleasant. Elizabeth was in fine spirits as the carriage approached Beauvais; looking at her husband and sister, she was again grateful for her many blessings and the present joy of travel.

CHAP. 25.

BEAUVAIS WAS SITUATED on the banks of the Therain, and notable, Georgiana related, for its having successfully rebuffed a siege in the year 1472, when a woman, Jeanne Hachette, commanded the women of the town against an invading army led by the Duke of Burgundy. The Duke's men were repelled by the ferocity of the towns-women, abandoning their enterprise and retreating into the hills. In homage to these brave souls every year, a procession of women from Beauvais paraded through the town, holding hay-forks, kitchen knives, and all manner of domestic weaponry. Despite such an heroic and feminine history, the town itself was deplorably dirty, and the imposition of a variety of disgusting odours was most unpleasant. Arriving early in the afternoon, and despite a near-inability to draw breath, the Darcys decided to walk about the town a little before continuing to their inn.

Georgiana had felt her spirits sink as she realised they had arrived at Beauvais on Saturday, and hence would not reach Paris for another four days. She was confused by the strength of her own impatience, and only after much reflection did she recognise both the malady and its cause. Not usually given to anxious sensibility, she found herself sitting forward on the chaise seat, every muscle in tension, and very disquiet in mind. Elizabeth asked if Georgiana were uncomfortable, and did she need a coverlet, or perhaps would she like to remove from the carriage and walk a little. Georgiana had not noticed any change in her own posture, but upon her sister's questioning, was immediately aware of the accuracy of Elizabeth's observation. Now even more anxious, in this instant, to minimise their concern over her perceived discomfort, Georgiana resorted to a small falsehood, and replied that she would be happy to have the coverlet and cushion, as she was wishing to rest. It was quite warm within the chaise, but, Georgiana reasoned, in the guise of sleep and the solitude it afforded, she could more quickly understand and dissuade herself from such an unreasonable agitation of spirits.

At length, Georgiana was able to acknowledge her restlessness and ascribe its origin as her impatience to reach Paris. Returning to her habitual course of musings, it was soon clear that she was grown fretful over her anticipation in meeting Colonel Fitzwilliam. Such agitation was unreasonable, she told herself; the Colonel had agreed to join them in Geneva. Hope, like many human conceptions, is bound less by the powers of the mind than the aspirations of the heart; a true comprehension of the subject would reveal that Georgiana had, since their arrival at Dover, never despaired of seeing Colonel Fitzwilliam around every corner, on every passing horse, at every post-inn, surprising them with his appearance days sooner than planned. The muted sentiments of her heart were now grown transiently optimistic of his forming a new species of affection for herself—away from Pemberley, away from the scenes of her childhood, Colonel Fitzwilliam would view her differently—not as brother or tutor, but with a new regard: the eyes of a lover. Paris, the city of endless charms and bewitching beauty, must have the intended effect, if such were possible anywhere. Her Utopia, however ardently desired, must be subdued; there was no reason, other than her own imagination, to cause such a perturbation of spirits. It was foolish—unreasonable. However, her fancy would obtrude, and an inexpressible need to be alone would not be overcome; Georgiana was forced to concede to her disquiet and ask if she might spend the morning with her correspondence, whilst Mr. and Mrs. Darcy went to church. Aware that Georgiana's spirits seemed unaccountably low, although without any understanding as to why, the couple could see no reason to disoblige her and, early the following morning, set off by themselves to attend the Romish services at the abbey, there being no Protestant church in that town.

"This fine tracery reminds me much of the Abbey at Bath," said Mr. Darcy to his wife, as they walked along the aisles of the church, following the service. "However, here there are almost entire walls of glass; this construction must be even later than that at Bath."

"It is exquisite. From the outside, it appears almost light enough to float upwards to Heaven, with only the delicate buttresses to anchor it to our own Earth," Elizabeth replied. "I am no connoisseur, but I could look at these tapestries for some time, and still, I believe, find new details to admire. The choir is incomparable, yet, I do not believe I have

seen

seen anything more beautiful than the windows. With the light shining through them, they appear more likely by the hand of God, than any hand of man."

Mr. Darcy read from the pages of their guide-book, describing the history of the building, its fires, failures, and present state of incompletion. Less admirable were the facts that the Cathedral had not been finished, and—as with much of what they had seen in France—was very dirty. Yet, in spite of the centuries of grime and decay, the strange proportions of the unfinished building, and the ever-present smells, the Cathedral was an enchanting place, even more so when seen through the early rays of the day. There were several peasants who staid at their prayers about the altar, where a guide informed the Darcys that these people were beseeching the patron saint of Beauvais, St. Pierre, for rain. Mr. Darcy asked her if she thought the saint would oblige them, and she looked her astonishment at such a question, and replied, "*Bien sûr, Monsieur! C'est pour cela qu'il est notre Saint!*"

Elizabeth and Darcy wandered through the abbey and its grounds, marvelling at the majestic sight of the royal tombs and their inscriptions. Buonaparte had repaired and restored the vaults, installing vast bronze gates to secure them, and erecting three enormous altars in the subterranean chapels, dedicated respectively to Clovis, Charlemagne, and the princes of the Capetian dynasty. One of the bronze gates originally placed in front of the vault that had been intended to receive his own family, had been subsequently replaced by a door of black marble. Elizabeth paused by the statue of the Duchess d'Angoulême, who forever knelt before the tomb of Louis XII, remarking to Darcy that she must surely be uncomfortable after all this time. He smilingly agreed and suggested that they stop at a pleasant-looking café they had passed *en route*, for a rest and some coffee.

Georgiana, meanwhile, whilst innocent in her intentions, was to commit what Lady Catherine would have considered to be an inexpiable breach of propriety for a lady in her position, as her first letter was to Mrs. Annesley at Pemberley:

21st March
Beauvais, France

DEAR MRS. ANNESLEY,

The pace of travel affords much leisure for correspondence, and I expect to surprise you by writing so soon after our departure. I am in hopes of hearing that you are well, and enjoying the relative peace and quiet of Pemberley in the absence of its master and mistresses. I miss Mademoiselle Blanche already, and, if possible, I would have smuggled my beautiful Blanche on board the *King George*, and am quite sure that she would be happily sitting on my lap as I write this, asking me to express her pity for the poor, thin *chats* here who wander the streets, crying for food. Please give her many kisses from me—I will send more next time I write to you—and tell her that she is much missed and that I imagine myself telling her about all of the sights we see.

We make excellent progress toward Paris, and we shall have our first glimpses of that famed city in a few more days' travel. The comfort of the carriage has made the journey a pleasant one. I must not forget to thank you for your kind thoughtfulness in sending along the seasickness remedies for, as you suspected, I succumbed almost immediately, and found great relief by your good medicaments.

I find I do not take to life on the road as readily as Elizabeth, who has, I think, never been happier. I grow less apprehensive by the day, and see and learn much as we journey. I wish you all joy in our absence, and ask that you look after yourselves and my beloved Blanche carefully until our return. I will write again upon our being settled at Paris.

Your grateful friend,

GEORGIANA DARCY

P.S. Pray do not forget the kisses for Mademoiselle. If I seem a little out of spirits, believe it to be only the natural effects of fatigue.

Georgiana then began the second letter, after taking a few turns around the room in an attempt to restore the composure of her mind.

21st March
Beauvais, France

DEAR COLONEL FITZWILLIAM,

I easily confess that we miss the company of our dearest friend a great deal, and you will blush to hear that you have often been the subject of many discussions since our departure. We all begin to despair of ever seeing you hither, but we make the best of travelling as a trio. My brother would claim the largest share of loss as his fate is to remain entirely in the company of women, but I, dearest friend, would dispute, even with my brother, for those doubtful laurels. As my French is but a little better than my brother's and sister's, I am required by our situation to speak a great deal, and I think you would be rather surprised to witness my conversations with our fellow travellers at dinner. I should not, however, write to give you false hopes of the success of your lessons, as it is vastly easier to merely translate the interesting speech of others, than to formulate such delights of thought on one's own.

I write to you from Beauvais, a place with an air of enchantment owing to the extraordinary Abbey church here. There is peacefulness, not a sadness, to be found, a sensation especially remarkable when one considers the horrible fate of this beautiful place of worship at the hands of Buonaparte and his adherents. My brother and Elizabeth have spent the day exploring the town and its surroundings, whilst I sit to correspond. I am afraid that the beautiful writing table my brother so thoughtfully installed in the chaise is unused by me, for I cannot help but feel the sea-sickness whilst reading or writing as we travel—even on dry land! I make a poor traveller, indeed, a deficiency made even more mortifying, as dear Elizabeth never appears to feel the slightest fatigue or other discomfort. Her enthusiasm for travel is a powerful blessing. I console myself with the reflection that having one's husband as a companion must be an infinite source of strength and contentment—I know it should be so with me.

I am sure Paris will be delightful, and I eagerly await the pleasure of our meeting together again in Geneva. I remain,

Your fond cousin,

GEORGIANA DARCY

Having successfully composed a letter that said everything and nothing at once, and sure of having concealed her heart sufficiently from its recipient, she carefully sealed both letters and gave them to the servant to post. As she began to dress for supper, a knock at her chamber door announced the return of her brother and Elizabeth. Mr. Darcy handed her a silver box, inside of which was the beautiful miniature of a white cat, framed within a golden locket. "Oh!" gasped a surprised and delighted Georgiana. "My dearest brother—Elizabeth—it is so like Mademoiselle Blanche—so beautiful! I hardly know how to thank you—I miss her so much—thank you—thank you!" Georgiana handed the chain to Elizabeth and asked her to help put it on, vowing to wear it until she was returned to Mademoiselle. Darcy and Elizabeth left to dress, allowing Georgiana a few minutes to compose herself.

Their inn did not answer, being ill-attended, inconvenient, and in every way disagreeable. There was even a difficulty to get tea, despite the habit of the inn-keeper and his servants of constantly opening the doors and banging them loudly as they went through their rooms.

Leaving Beauvais early the next day, and passing through Beaumont, they were rewarded by the sight of a countryside where the Seine first made its appearance; vineyards extended in all directions, and several fine *châteaux* were seen beyond the plantations, all increasing evidence of their approach to the environs of Paris at last. Elizabeth and her husband preferred to make a delay to see the abbey of St. Denis, in which were interred the remains of the kings and queens of France. Buonaparte had re-opened the church in 1805, hoping to atone for the damage inflicted by revolutionaries who had desecrated many of the tombs, and in 1815, the bodies of King Louis XVI and Marie Antoinette had been removed to the crypt. A whole day's stop was agreed to see the Abbey and explore its surroundings, before continuing on to La Ville-Lumière. The situation of St. Denis to Paris appeared exactly as Hammersmith was to London in former times: a jumble of poorly kept houses, filled with rough men, slatternly women, and untended, dirty children. Some of the men went about in a curious-looking, large, white night-cap, whilst others (who had business in Paris) preferred straw hats and short waistcoats. The lower orders were uniformly ragged, without stockings, and the condition of their horses, Mr. Darcy declared, was appalling. It was hard to imagine that this town, so close to the capital of the late Empire, could be so unprosperous and unprepossessing.

The most surprising conveyances, remarkable even to the ladies, were the stage-coaches that travelled back and forth from St. Denis to the city of Paris. These outlandish vehicles had three rows of seats, each holding two persons, inside a two-wheeled cart of extreme height, and disproportionately narrow width. Most curiously, there was only one horse in the shafts, and a second attached to the vehicle by means of a pole, much like the outrigger on a ship. In all events, the stage travelled tolerably quickly, certainly with greater speed than the clumsy, cumbersome diligences. These former *voitures* travelled only to a post on the outside of the gates of Paris as, most unaccountably, they were not permitted to drive through the streets of the city. Elizabeth remarked that it seemed very hard upon the traveller to be obliged to remove himself and his belongings to a series of carriages, just to get into the city. Mr. Darcy conjectured that the second horse running along-side the shafts made the conveyances at St. Denis likely too wide to pass through the crowded streets of Paris with safety. This explanation stood for the present, as no-one else had a more likely idea.

The next morning all was in readiness for their departure.

Georgiana felt a little more in spirits now that her letters had been despatched, and the travellers were come close-by their destination. The Darcys stepped into the chaise and embarked upon the road to Paris. Georgiana's hand could often be seen clasping her locket, and in one or two exchanged glances, husband and wife believed that they understood Georgiana's disquietude and *ennui*, rejoicing that the fortunate purchase of the miniature would provide a significant—if not entirely rational— source of comfort to her.

The six-mile road from St. Denis to Paris appeared almost one continued street. The carriages passed through the environs of the city, reaching the Porte Saint Martin just after ten o'clock. Georgiana related to Darcy and Elizabeth that Paris had been inhabited by upwards of eight hundred thousand souls previous to the dethronement of Louis XVI, and was since considerably diminished, its population now not exceeding three-quarters of that number. Paris was spared any appearance of abandonment, however, by the multitudes of visitors who now flocked to the city throughout the year, adding numbers in abundance. In early spring, the city was now fit to burst with a mixture of Parisians and pretenders to that distinguished title. The invention of a system to take away the waste from the city was instituted by Buonaparte, with the intention of a somewhat more salubrious air, and Mr. Darcy pointed out further improvements since his visit as a young man: the shops now being far more numerous, manufactories greatly improved, and new, elegant restaurants—seemingly on every corner—adding yet more credit to that city's reputation as a gourmand's paradise. There were theatres, coffee-houses, rooms for dancing, pleasure-gardens, and public baths.

These amenities did not improve the Darcys' first impressions of Paris. The Parisian customs-officers were extremely impertinent— to a point well beyond insolence—and importuned them at length, assiduously looking through their possessions and even the furniture of the carriages, to an even more preposterous extent than had the agents at Calais. This was all much to the vexation of Mr. Darcy, who could not readily imagine himself or his family suspicious candidates as conveyors of forbidden goods across the continent. The new French passports procured at Calais upon their arrival in France were circumspectly examined with a minuteness far exceeding that of their creation, and it was well into the afternoon before the family were at last reconciled with their belongings, which the customs-men had strewn about the carriages in total confusion. Having nothing left to disorder or no-one left to discommode, the family were pronounced safe to be allowed their freedom upon the streets of Paris.

The moment the carriages had quitted the customs office and moved out of the secured area of the *Bureau*, the two carriages were besieged with would-be valets and maid-servants, all eager to secure employment in such an obviously prosperous family. Darcy, who disliked being at the centre of any public spectacle, was visibly put out of countenance by the riotous clamour of the crowds, thrusting their reference papers through the windows, with some even climbing onto the carriage in order to promote their services.

"These carriage horses are worth twice their cost, for their only response to this madness is forbearance—any others of our stable must have surely have bolted by now, and we would have the blood of trampled Frenchmen on our hands!" He rose to close both windows of the coach, even in the warmth of the afternoon, "for they continue to obtrude upon our notice with an uncommon perseverance. As if this were the path to successful employment in the house of a gentleman!" Rapping his cane under the box, he declared, "We must drive on, and pray the servants are not similarly importuned."

If Mr. Darcy could have looked behind at this point, he would have seen the second carriage looking and sounding more like a rolling Tower of Babel than an English road coach carrying stolid, respectable English servants. All of the passengers in the servants' coach were leaning precariously out of the carriage in a state of high alarm, attempting to deter their French counter-parts with an astonishing admixture of English and unintelligible epithets in what they imagined to be the French language. The carriage was in some danger of being tumbled over in the *mêlée* as several aspirants attempted to board, and it was a considerable relief to the passengers when the area of the customs-house was behind them, the servants having escaped unharmed, but in a dreadful flutter of spirits. Mr. Darcy's valet was heard to exclaim that, for first time in his life, he *wished* for the company of Monsieur Jacques-Frédéric, the Darcy's cook, to deal with the "Frenchies!"

Having made their escape from the Porte Saint Martin, Mr. Darcy instructed the coachman to turn eastward, before proceeding down the Rue du Temple to avoid the crowds of foot-traffic through the parks that lay between the Rue St. Martin and the Rue St. Denis. The carriage continued the length of the Rue du Temple and thence along the Quay de la Grève, which ran along the Seine. They first passed the imposing *façade* of the Hôtel de Ville, where, but a few years before, hundreds of the country's surviving *élite* welcomed the return of Louis XVIII, in celebration of what they thought marked the end of years of horror and war, the Ile de la Cité, the vast form of the Notre Dame, and the enchanting Sainte-Chapelle. They drove westward, past the Conciergerie and Palais du Justice, after turning northward just before the magnificent *esplanade* of the Hôtel des Invalides. The *boulevards* of Paris were a constant bustle, busy with persons, animals, conveyances, and vendibles. Commerce appeared to be conducted from innumerable stalls, at which every article of necessity and diversion was sold, including books, cloathing, ironmongery, shoes, hats, fruits, vegetables, cheeses, poultry, and all manner of other victual. Elizabeth exclaimed at the custom of letting out seats, which were filled with respectable-looking persons by the score, all seated in a row, watching and being watched, and doing little else except exchanging a few words now and again. Itinerants were everywhere: blind-men, dwarfs walking with sticks and under hats that were nearly half their total height, ragged children begging for alms, and a man with a fantastical machine affixed to his back, from which he seemed to be vending a beverage of some sort. A woman bent under an enormous basket, from which she was selling melons to an officer; a man was strapped to a basket of equally large size from which sprang twigs and branches, apparently a wood-seller. A cheese-seller struggled under his wide yoke, a long, flat board as tall as the bearer and nearly as wide, along which were affixed several baskets, all filled with enormous cheeses. A washer-woman strolled unconcernedly through the throngs with an heavy burthen of linens, all wrapt in paper and tied with a ribband of some sort, balanced upon her head, miraculously avoiding a collision with a man harnessed to a large cart full of brooms, who had suddenly found *his* way thoroughly impeded by a menacing dog. Two pot-men could be seen amongst the crowd: one balanced what appeared to be an immense preserves pan upon his head, filled to over-flowing with at least a score of metal wares, a long row of progressively larger soup-pots hanging from one arm tied through with a cord, affixed to a range of other, larger pots carried in his hand; the other iron-monger of decidedly shabbier appearance, wearing an old, tattered frock-coat which had seen at least a score of years, carried only two enormous cauldrons slung by a rope about his neck. Amidst this scene of aspiring commerce trouped a group of girls, obviously from a *pension de jeunes demoiselles*, led from the front by a remarkably handsome young man dressed very smartly, with an hat and cane, and hurried along by a rear-guard in the form of an older lady whose years of this congenial employment had produced such an impassivity of countenance, as was incapable of any humour, good or ill. Swarming amidst the brigade of bonnets and muslins were the ubiquitous poodle-dogs, which the French considered indispensable.

A stand had been hastily assembled between two trees, surmounted by a string to which were clipped drawings; and a wild-looking man (the artist, Elizabeth supposed) was pointing to one for the benefit of a well-looking gentleman standing near. Another officer, wearing a cap with a tall plume, seemed to be inspecting the proceedings with an interest scarcely justified. There were jugglers, Merry-Andrews, mimes, musicians, acrobats, a sad supply of maimed soldiers from the Hôtel des Invalides, and, oddly enough, shoe-blacks advertising that there plied *English* blacking as some added inducement to custom. Bacon was vended by a woman carrying a charcoal fire by means of a leathern tray strapped from her shoulders; bakers in white *toques* and aprons hauled overflowing baskets quite similar to those of their northern neighbours; another wood-porter had faggots strapped to his back by means of an old board; an old cloathes-man dignified his humble calling—as the French will—with the appellation *Marchand d'Habits*; and patrols of solders in bicorns marched without apparent purpose or destination amidst innumerable stray dogs.

Water-carriers hauled water from the reservoirs and fountains to the houses; given the filth of the dwellings, it appeared that the substance must be very dear, indeed, although the cry of "*de l'eau*" was constantly heard. There were nuns in long, white caps, whose occupation was to visit the sick. An organ-grinder sang "Vive Henry Quatre," which, despite the dreadful character of his voice, was received by the French near-by with great energy and satisfaction. Adjacent to a very lofty and noble building obtruded the ragged, dirty stall of an old woman who mended stockings. The markets were distinguished by rows of large umbrellas, ten feet wide, shielding *poissardes* well-supplied with every variety of fruit, vegetable, fish, milk vended from open pails, and—to English eyes—a vast quantity of game. There were great numbers of dogs employed in pulling carts through the streets, donkeys laden with all manner of goods, exquisite equipages, drays pulled by miserable-looking horses, and amidst all of the clamor, dust, dirt, and general inconvenience, elegant ladies and gentlemen, officers of the *Chausseurs de la Garde Impériale* and the *Infanterie de Ligne* promenaded in their furs, spotless white breeches, and gleaming coats, the latter struggling to maintain their identities under a surfeit of medallions and gold braids. The city seemed to consist of an assembly of opposites: wealth and penury, magnificence and squalor, taste and filth.

VOL. II.

CHAP. 1.

THE FAMILY WERE TO STAY at the noted L'Hôtel de Londres. As they made their way through the labyrinth of small streets to L'Hôtel, Mr. Darcy commented that the Great Fire of London had the positive benefit of clearing away the mediæval footpaths through the centre of the city; there had been no such regularising opportunity for Paris to lay out its streets in a more efficient manner, other than the few stars, circles, ovals, and rectangles, which had seemingly been dropt into the middle of the old routes by Buonaparte. The bustle and noise that pervaded even this most fashionable neighbourhood of the city from all directions was overwhelming: hack-chaises careening through the streets, their drivers insensible of the throngs of vendors, buskers, beggars, travellers, animals, and exquisitely dressed Parisian ladies languorously waving to one another across the multitudes.

These scenes, with every imaginable insignificant variation, were in view for the two or three miles it took the Darcys to reach the centre of Paris from the gates of the customs-house. The streets were filthy and without pavements, narrow, and rendered nearly impassible through the habit of leaving their implements in the road whenever the workmen had been called away, intervals which appeared vastly more probable than any when the family saw someone using the tools. It was impossible to walk on any other streets than the main *boulevards*, due to the speeding cabs, drays, cabriolets, gigs, &c., all calling loudly, "*Gare!*" in lieu of minding the people walking ahead, the latter who had only the expedient of flattening themselves against the dirty walls, whilst the carriage passed a finger's-breadth from their persons.

The weather being fine, the odours emanating from the alley-ways were appalling. "I have read of the smells of Paris," said Georgiana after driving through the city for some minutes, "and was expecting even worse than what we met with at Beauvais, but it is not quite so overpowering as I expected, and yet I suppose we are not experiencing the city in the worst heats of summer." Elizabeth looked at her questioningly, and re-adjusted her hand-kerchief more firmly against her face.

The labyrinthine streets lined with merchants and buyers, all shouting to be heard over each other, and the noise of the iron wheels on the cobbled roads contributed to a din which all but took the breath away, and caused Elizabeth to wonder aloud how anyone could find such a continuous assault on his senses supportable. The society of cafés and display dominated Paris, and the chatter emanating from the thousands of those walking, driving, drinking, and dining along the *boulevards* and open shops mingled in a general cacophony that rendered the similar scenes of London ordered and sedate, in comparison. Darcy, who had visited this city of juxtapositions before, anticipated both the noise and the odours, but even the lenient Miss Darcy exclaimed at the great difference between a written account of the delights of the city and the city itself.

By this time, the exertion of managing a large chaise-and-four through the centre of Paris was wearying Mr. Harmon and his horses, and the under-coachman driving the servants' coach looked as if he were about to succumb at any moment, but was kept aright only by his indecision as to the agency of his infirmity, whether it be the noise, odours, throngs of people who were vying with the vehicles for their share of the street, the animals, hand-carts, the other drivers who seemed quite heedless of their own safety—and entirely regardless of what or who they were carrying, the sheer bombardment upon the sensibilities of a young man from rural England, or some ambitious combination thereof. The carriages clattered up the Rue Royale and thence, to everyone's relief, stopt before their hôtel.

As the horses slowed to a standstill before L'Hôtel de Londres, Elizabeth and Georgiana happened to look at one another and sighed with relief in unison. The Darcy party, at long last, walked out of their carriage, laughing at what they and their *entourage* must look like after weeks of travel, and the battles between the customs-men, themselves, and their baggage. Stopping just outside, Georgiana took Elizabeth's arm, remarking on the beautiful buildings.

"I have never seen the like of their construction; it is as though they have been conjured up out of the ground. And, Elizabeth—the dresses

❧   worn

worn by the ladies—I have never seen such lovely silks and so finely worn! Even my newest dresses seem plain in comparison! I believe that I may appear anywhere without trepidation. No-one will look twice at me, when there is so much beauty and finery to be seen in every direction. I believe that I may be safely invisible in Paris."

Instead of Elizabeth, Mr. Darcy replied, "I am aware that a male opinion in this case is neither requested nor required—which I fear is frequently the case. However, I feel it my duty as an husband and a brother to inform you that—before either or both of you are carried away by your raptures over the female fashionables of Paris—at least half the ladies *I* beheld on our drive through the city have quite ruined any natural beauty through the application of so much paint upon their faces, it is impossible to determine their features, and the other half are so obscured in finery they are become a flock, each one indistinguishable from the others. I cannot believe French men so different from myself in preferring a simple stile of dress that frames a natural beauty as opposed to overwhelming it, and any sensible man surely assumes this *camouflage* to be concealing some defect—or possibly many. Ladies often mistake fashion and expense for elegance; men, in general, have no idea of the cost of any costume, but the *effect* of the dress, in setting off the figure and countenance of a lady, her grace, and natural stile will always command more admiration than beauty, artful elegance, or adherence to any particular *mode*." Darcy held his hand out to help his wife and his sister safely down, and they felt all happiness walking into L'Hôtel, Georgiana on one arm of the tall and elegant Mr. Darcy, and Elizabeth on the other.

Georgiana's first action was to enquire of the concierge for any letters. Only those who have experienced the cleaving pangs of home-sickness can form any idea of the joy with which a person, far away from the fond and familiar sights of his life, hastily retires to the sanctuary of his own room to accomplish the initial perusal—to ensure that everyone and everything he holds most dear is safe and well—and then to indulge himself in countless, leisurely re-readings of the long-anticipated letters from those whose cares and existence are foremost in his thoughts upon the passing of every hour, and every new scene. Such moments of sublime felicity were not to comprise Georgiana's blessings, however, for upon her enquiry, there was neither to be found Colonel Fitzwilliam, nor even the far less-welcome pleasure of his letter. As she turned away from the tall dais of the concierge, she resolved to keep her disappointment to herself, and spare her brother and sister concern over

❧ her   3

her dispirits. The altruistic nature of her fortitude was, however, no guarantee of its success, and only with the most dogged determination did Georgiana feign interest and happiness in their amusements and occupations, when she would much rather have sought the solitude of her own apartment to indulge her disappointment.

The next two days were filled up with the compulsory occupations of all tourists' first experiences of Paris. Upon rising on the first full day in the city, Darcy was engaged in assisting Mr. Harmon to find sufficient accommodation for their horses and carriages for the length of their stay. In his absence, his wife and sister employed themselves in looking at the new fashions, walking past the shops of tailors, milliners, shoe-makers and hairdressers. Having little desire to make himself sufficiently fashionable to please the French, Darcy excused himself from the afternoon's occupations in order to pay a visit to the coachmaker in La Rue Beuve des Mathurins. Repairs were become necessary to the under-carriage of the coach, which, if left to its current state, might cause inconvenience on the onward journey over the Alps; accordingly, he left to assist Mr. Harmon in that errand, as the iron-monger was unlikely to speak English.

Walking along the *boulevard*, Elizabeth remarked, "I feel like one come from the provinces—I find the dearness of these items on display shocking! One would not think that the cost of things so similar would have such a difference in price. I do not believe that I require anything to such a degree that I could justify spending here what I would not spend in London."

"I cannot disagree, Elizabeth." replied Georgiana. "To be sure, I am as unable as you to understand what could produce such an increase of price. Perhaps it is just the fact that these goods are *from* Paris."

"And, I suppose I must agree, having no better explanation. However, unless one wishes to affix a large French flag, or perhaps a paper that says, 'Fabriqué à Paris,' upon one's bosom, such additional expenditure seems to return little for its having been made. It would not do for compensation that the bodice and nearly transparent skirts of the Parisian gowns announce themselves as such, as I do not think that the first impression of any Englishman or woman would be that the gown bespeaks someone who has been shopping in Paris—but Greece, rather."

"Elizabeth!"

"You may well reprove me, Georgiana, for being indelicate, but I am not *wearing* them, merely describing them! Have you any delicate way to explain the fashion of the ladies here?" Georgiana agreed that she had no inclination to attempt to portray the French gowns, as she could see no way to do so with propriety. At length, both Elizabeth and Georgiana decided that the new gowns they had brought from England would do very well, and so gave their custom on that day only to Mme. Milionotte, where they bespoke plain, thick boots lined with lambs' pelts for their journey over the Alps. Upon rejoining Mr. Darcy at the Hôtel for tea that afternoon, he found that his wife and sister had purchased only boots. "Well, ladies, I am the bearer of the bad news that you are obliged to repeat your errand on the morrow," said Darcy, removing his gloves and taking a seat at the little table in the smaller of the *salons*.

"Mr. Darcy, why should such a thing be necessary?" enquired Elizabeth. "I was anticipating the leisure for a later breakfast than we have been used to on the road, and that we may take some time to see the Musée du Louvre."

"I think you will be willing to change your views when I tell you that, upon arriving at our rooms this afternoon, I saw we had a card from the Duchess d' A—— for a ball, Tuesday next. I am sure this communication must happily over-throw all of your previous ideas about the requirement for new gowns."

Elizabeth replied that their new-made English gowns would do very well for the purpose, but Mr. Darcy suggested that she and Georgiana might feel more comfortable if they were not seen making their *début* dressed in any way that could be regarded as exceptional. Elizabeth was about to reply that she felt perfectly equal to the stares of the Parisians, but then, recollecting that Mr. Darcy's wife and sister should appear in a stile that would do credit to her husband, she made the reply, "I believe you are perfectly right, Mr. Darcy. Georgiana, we can begin to-morrow after a late breakfast. I do not think we had better put it off, as to-day is Wednesday, and so we have only a few days to get our things made up. Would this be agreeable to you, dear?" she asked Georgiana.

At tea, they marvelled at the great variety of comestibles of which the tea was composed. At supper that evening, the etiquette demanded they sample at least twenty different dishes. The Darcys retired that evening, well-supped and ready to retire into clean beds, grateful to be spared the jolting of the carriage for some days.

After a late breakfast, the ladies took leave of Mr. Darcy, and approached their task with some energy. The most enjoyable visits were those to Madame Leroy, the celebrated milliner, and Nourtier's, which housed the finest French figured silks and satins, and Florentine and Lyonnaise silks, from which the dress-makers created the most beautiful gowns. Both ladies admired the fashion for light colours that had accompanied the return of the Bourbons to the throne, but neither lady approved the suggested row upon row of trimmings, flounces, and hems adorned with fine silk braids, flowers, and other ornaments. Georgiana chose a *canzou* of a pale blue silk with a small ruffle and plait at the hem and sleeves in white tulle. Elizabeth chose a plain gown of a rose-colour satin with blonde lace, shewing Elizabeth's more petite form to advantage. The deletion of so much of the expensive trimmings and finery—as well as the insistence upon a somewhat more substantial bodice—did not suit the dressmakers, requiring Georgiana to be more *puissant* than usual. The dress-makers were at last prepared to admit that Parisian fashion, modified by an English aversion to superabundant decoration and *trop de décolleté*, looked very pretty upon these two English ladies; Georgiana and Elizabeth found that the French fashions pleased themselves as well.

The Darcy women next purchased delicate white cashmere scarves, whose popularity were due to the fact that they shewed a lady's shoulders so well, and planned to dress their hair simply with a few flowers. Their labours completed, Georgiana and Elizabeth met Mr. Darcy at tea, and then went for a walk in the Jardin des Tuileries. As it was yet cool of an evening, the Parisian women wore large muffs of fur, and boas knotted about the neck, as well as swan's down mittens and tippets. With the Darcys' visit so soon after the fall of Buonaparte, a distinction was soon evident between those ladies who yet preferred the sumptuous splendour that had characterised the fashion of the Empire, and those who favoured the simplicity of dress now fashionable amongst the younger ladies. Elizabeth reflected to herself that she and Georgiana might have spared themselves the effort and expense of new gowns for the ball, given the vast array of different stiles, materials, colours, and trimmings to be seen. However, it is not the most abhorrent of duties for a lady to bespeak a new gown, and certainly even less so when under the express instructions of her husband, so Elizabeth decided simply to be pleased.

Mr. Darcy may have been wholly insensible of the nuance of fashion, but the following morning, the many admiring glances the party received as he escorted Elizabeth and Georgiana along Le Grand Boulevard increased his natural pride; if he stood a little straighter, and took their arms a little more closely than usual, it may be safely imputed to the effects of the city's charms. This way was the favoured promenade of the affluent and opulent, and the only place in which

to

to declare oneself as being *arrivée*. Unaware of the considerable interest in their appearance, the Darcys continued down the *boulevard* in a most elegant, *blasé* manner: the fine, tall figure of Mr. Darcy— unmistakably the happiest result of family and wealth, that most potent and irresistible combination—and a fashionable lady on each arm, the trio moved on to luncheon at Tortoni's, newly resplendent in white and gold panelling. Here the difference between the fashionable sets in Paris became apparent, as half the men were occupied throughout the morning with business and shares, leaving the landed gentry to gather on the floor below to talk of hunting, horses, and sporting carts. A morning of observation of Paris society passes quickly, and in the afternoon Elizabeth and Darcy proposed to journey after dinner via Le Quai Voltaire to see the new steam-boat embarking upon its journey between Paris and Rouen, requiring a short boat trip out to the point where the steam-boat was anchored. As Georgiana's intentions had been to avoid boats entirely, owing to her dreadful experience of the channel crossing, she excused herself with fatigue and left them. Mr. Darcy delighted in the new, and had a keen interest in apparatus of any sort. He and his wife walked to Le Jardin Montagnes Russes at the end of Le Boulevard de Roule, where the *ton* of Paris shewed off their finery in a conspicuous promenade to the amusement of Elizabeth, whose practical English preference was for the warmth of the covered areas of the garden. This simple expedient marked them as visitors, as surely as did their speech. The transparent texture of many of the ladies' dresses, apparently designed so as to leave naught to the imagination of the beholder, gave Elizabeth some moments of confusion. Mr. Darcy was excessively diverted by the scanty garments, causing him to remark on the conundrum of such expensive, yet minimal, apparel.

That evening, the Darcys had an appointment at the Palais-Royal, the centre of luxury and pleasure in Paris, and the place for fashionable display. The time passed in the enjoyable occupation of watching the many interesting people who congregated there. Having yet no acquaintance in Paris, the family made little attempt to converse with the other guests, and settled down to dine at Véry's, in preference to Beauvilliers', the former having small tables seating two or three people, placed at sufficiently wide intervals along the walls to prevent the conversations of any neighbouring diners from being obtrusive. Most of the people present were standing or promenading about the wide aisle between the tables. Elizabeth noted the proportion of long gowns and gentlemen in evening dress. It was too late for the theatre or opera, so Elizabeth was forced to surmise that the recreation of dining was considered an entertainment by the fashionables of Paris; the large proportion walking and talking, as opposed to eating, certainly made it appear likely. Perhaps not, upon further thought: bicorns, tricorns, shakos, tall hats, no hats, and the occasional fez were worn by the men, and circlets, caps, turbans, veils, wigs, diadems, flora, fauna, day-bonnets, and nothing at all upon the heads of the women. There were short coats, long coats, frock-coats, tail-coats, and over-coats—and that was just the men's costume. Even the shoes in attendance seemed to be in utter confusion as to their purpose! Elizabeth abandoned her review with the satisfying supposition that it would be impossible to be dressed exceptionally amidst such an admixture of cloathing and stiles.

As soon as they had seated themselves, a smart waiter, attired in a snow-white apron with a knife and spoon stuck into his girdle to denote his status, presented Mr. Darcy with a bill of fare containing in excess of five hundred dishes! He bowed courteously, and made his way to the next group of English who were preparing to sit down. The Darcys gazed at the menu in bewilderment for some time before Elizabeth's appreciation for the absurd overcame her and she let out a laugh.

"If it were up to me to decipher this—*volume*, I would surely starve. I declare, even were I in England, a bill of fare this large would baffle me entirely. What are we to chuse, Mr. Darcy? How does one to decide in favour of one dish above an hundred others? Georgiana, do you have any ideas?"

Even Mr. Darcy looked a little overwhelmed. "I have the French, but not the patience, for a menu of this variety. We have a choice of soups, *fricassees, fricandeaus, ragoûts*, tame and wild fowl, omelettes, oysters, fish, roast beef and mutton, and frogs' thighs, and this on the first page. I believe we will eat much sooner if we consult the *maître d'hôtel* for assistance." In brisk and efficient French, Mr. Darcy established with the waiter those dishes that came most highly recommended, and ordered a moderate selection of foods and wine for the family. Despite the number of large parties taking their meal in the restaurant, the Darcy's table was almost immediately covered with a vast array of dishes, all of which were as delightful as the waiter had promised. Georgiana, quietly shewing that she had actually *read* the menu, assisted her brother and sister by explaining the contents and the method of preparation for each dish chosen. The Darcys retained enough of their national custom to refuse the usual serving of vegetables that invariably followed the *bonne bouche*, being both full and agreeing that the order of the service was very odd, indeed. When they had finished their coffee and were to quit the Palais Royal, Mr. Darcy stopt to give payment to the *limonadier* who was seated in state, elevated in an enclosure surrounded by exotic flowers and innumerable dishes, all filled with fruit and preserves.

"This seems more like tribute than a payment for dinner," laughed Elizabeth.

"Well, it is lovely, and we certainly could not have passed out without noticing where the establishment wishes us to pay," replied Georgiana.

Mr. Darcy closed the discussion of the great dais with a loud whisper, "I wonder what the King and Queen must do to compete with the throne of this *cashier*. We must all look *très obéissante* and perhaps we shall be permitted to pass."

In their walk back to the hôtel, all was well until Darcy was forced into the street by a speeding hack-chaise as they passed into La Rue de Richelieu, obliging a detour to the *décrotteur*—a most peculiar establishment where all classes of Parisian society could be seen with regularity getting their shoes cleaned—and Mr. Darcy's shoes, as well as his humour, were restored. Mr. Darcy made a trenchant comment to the effect that the streets were intentionally left unmended and unclean in order to preserve such an estimable occupation. The rest of the day passed without incident, and fatigued, but pleased, with Paris and their diversions of the day, the party returned to their lodgings for tea and to discuss their plans before retiring.

Elizabeth wrote to her father on the morrow, aware that almost a month had passed since they had parted,

Easter-day
Paris, France

DEAREST FATHER,

We are in Paris at last. We are well, and have managed to be shut up in the chaise for days all-together and yet preserve all of our original mutual regard and most of our good humour. Travel is become second-nature, and it seems very strange not to be jolting along, choaking on dust, and shouting over the noise of the chaise. We have survived not only the rigours of the sea-sickness, and the highway-men of Abbeville, but—what is more deserving of our collective gratitude—to see our safe delivery from the dirt and infestations of the post-houses of northern France. We were in agreement that they could not get by many degrees worse, before we must necessarily resort to the expedient of taking alternate turns sleeping with our own linens within the chaise. Fortunately, our hôtel in

Paris is quite clean, and we are very agreeably situated.

The Parisians have been, as they are reputed, very polite and courteous—more than that—they are universally urbane and well-spoken, even the lowest orders. I think you would be very amused by the attraction they evince for looking-glasses; their houses seem to be built of little other material than mirrors. I have noticed that the French *encryoable* is a completely different animal from our own English dandy: the first is an insolent, affected, fawning cox-comb, who believes it his vocation to charm every example of the fair sex upon the most insubstantial of pretenses; the second is an heartless, disdainful, conceited specimen, whose business of life is studied indifference and disapprobation of everything and everyone else. Whilst I cannot help laughing at the studied affectations of the Frenchmen, with their low bows and other obsequies, on the whole, I believe that I prefer them to the English variety: it is much more pleasant to be admired, than to admire an object incapable of any return.

The Parisian ladies are very voluble in company, and seem not at all reticent to put their ideas forward in company. They converse in society very willingly, and capably join in the discourse, even on more learned subjects. English ladies are usually content to be *imagined* intelligent through the simple expedient of remaining silent for fear of being thought forward or unfeminine. Here, the ladies assume their share of intelligence without scruple or hesitation, unafraid of possessing both wit and vivacity, and are not thought masculine for their temerity. The English insistence on feminine reserve and passivity produces, as one might expect, half of the pleasure as when both sexes are allowed to opine and dispute. Might I add that even the most *embonpoint* of ladies appear here *trop décolleté*; I wonder how they contrive to dance or even move about without losing their gowns! Georgiana made up for our excesses in the way of the bodice by going about *sans fioritures*: head, gown, or husband.

Upon the whole, I think that the most potent impression here is that all France is arranged for the advantage of the rich and the powerful. Negligible regard is given to the comfort of, or justice to, citizens of the lower stations: that this is the case is strikingly apparent upon entering Paris. Unlike London, which is well-lit at night, with clean, raised pavements on the sides of the main streets for the convenience and safety of foot-passengers—an effort which gives to the populace at-large evidence of the consideration of their government—Paris is but poorly and partially lit and, except for a few particular streets, is not

constructed

constructed with regard for the accommodation and protection of those who have not the means to travel by carriage. The less-affluent must find their way as best they are able, groping through the darkness, dashing behind pillars or fleeing into the door-ways of the shops to avoid being over-run by the carriages which are driven—it appears to me—so as to be as close to the passers-by and any other obstruction or obstacle as the driver pleases, with no apparent regard for the danger to life or property than the man in the moon. Similarly, the law leaves the middle and lower orders quite unprotected, exposed to the whims and insolence of the powerful who are, in France, generally speaking, above the law.

It is certainly true that the lower orders here are exceedingly well-spoken, very polite, and superior in appearance to the English inferior class; however, *"Un homme du peuple"* implies a want of education and manners, whilst *"Un homme comme il faut"* does not imply either sense or principle, but merely that the man is of high birth or high fashion, but potentially devoid of every quality of kindness, liberality, or honour that our "gentleman" comprehends. Yet, inexplicably, the same inconsideration produces a society of uniformly polished manners, a lively and informed people, and an astonishingly pleasant, easy familiarity betwixt masters and servants that would be insupportable in England.

Returning to the smaller (but no less illustrious) sphere of ourselves, despite having no acquaintance here, we have received many invitations to *soirées*, suppers, concerts, &c. So many, in fact, that we are in grave danger of being unable, in future, of entertaining ourselves. Fortunately, we are never able to accomplish quite all of what we intend, and so continue very well. We attended the morning service at the Protestant church here this morning, and will attend again in the evening as we do at-home. I must leave off now, to eat our cold supper before services, as the servants at the hôtel have this half-day off to attend the Catholick church.

Your loving and dutiful daughter,

ELIZABETH DARCY

CHAP. 2.

THE OBTAINING OF INTRODUCTIONS being a less formal practise in France than in England, it took little time for the Darcys to become acquainted with the most fashionable set, and before many days had passed, they had received invitations from some of the most highly connected families in Paris. *Cartes de visite* began arriving at their hôtel apace. Elizabeth remarked that the entry-table looked like an avalanche in the Alps, so covered was it in white cards and notes requesting their society.

Between five and eight o'clock each evening, it was the custom of Parisian society to visit one of the many elegant restaurants along the fashionable streets, the best of which were located on the wide *boulevards*, also the location of the best *salons*. Although early in the spring, oftentimes the weather was fine, and the Darcys would walk the broad avenues of the Champs Elysées or the Tuilleries, or along the wide pavements of the river, watching the fashionables of Paris promenade, sit, gossip, flirt, rendezvous, or otherwise engage in a thousand other frivolous occupations. From the heights of the house of Père de la Chaise, they viewed the exquisite architecture of Notre Dame and L'Hôtel des Invalides (although the gaudy supersufficiency of gilding quite spoilt the intended effect of grandeur). The Darcys enjoyed the Palais Royal and its beautiful fountain, the Jardins des Tuileries (unremarkable save their very fine orange trees in great pots), and the Jardin des Plantes (however inferior to Kew and the beasts at Exeter). The Louvre must be admitted as incomparable, even in its state of decaying splendour, and the length of the gallery itself was a thing of wonder. However, the idea of an avenue such as the Champs Elysées without a lawn was an anathema to English eyes, and Tivoli appeared to be but a dim reflection next to the brilliance of Vauxhall. The Darcys also drove out to the Bois de Boulogne, noting the surprising proportion of fashionable equestriennes in exquisite silk riding habits of all colours—cut remarkably along similar lines of the gentlemen's coats, but in much finer detail—with military-stile hats, and their hair in a long plait down the back; it was impossible to imagine a more gracefully refined, striking picture of humanity, calculated in every detail to shew off the form of both horse and rider to absolute perfection.

One of the first engagements they attended was an evening assembly at the *salon* of Madame Marency, a lady of fortune much-famed for her entertainments, residing in La Rue de Vaugirard, near the Palais du Luxemburg. The room, already occupied by upwards of thirty by the time the Darcys arrived, rivalled Versailles in its opulence. Mahogany walls were bordered with gold, figurines ornamented every corner, and the furniture was dressed in a red velvet that struggled for notice under its burthen of ornament—braids, tassels, festoons, and other *passamenterie*. As the Darcys were announced, a group of affected young men occupying a corner of the room panelled by enormous looking-glasses—which permitted frequent consultation of the appearance of their neck-cloths and the height of their hair—turned to bow. Having paid the Darcys the briefest of compliments, they returned to an animated conversation about the great men of French literature, a select group comprised of only one sex. Darcy raised his eyebrows as he heard one of them announce that Voltaire was infinitely superior to Shakespeare, and continued to find his way to the opposite side of the room, where he was soon in earnest conversation with an handsome gentleman.

"*Monseiur le Comte, c'est vous?*" asked Darcy, bowing to the gentleman.

"*Mais oui, moi-même,*" replied the Comte. "And you are the illustrious Mr. Darcy, I presume?" answered the Comte in perfect English. "I regret that you find me at this place, and amongst this insupportable crowd! However, having left her card, my mother and I were delighted to hear of your acceptance."

The Comte d'Estrouville was about the same age as Mr. Darcy—a little younger perhaps, but the years of terror had aged many of the French nobility beyond their true ages—respectably, but fashionably dressed in a dark coat and grey trousers, with light brown hair, and the complexion of a man who was often out-of-doors. He was a remarkably well-looking man, with intelligent, expressive eyes and a manner more akin to an Englishman in its openness and candour. Given the deference with which he was regarded by the other gentlemen and ladies surrounding him, he was obviously a man of some importance. The Comte and Mr. Darcy had been in correspondence for some time regarding the management of estates; this intercourse had been met with much mutual approbation, and both gentlemen shewed a genuine delight in the opportunity to further their acquaintance. Darcy liked him at once, finding his conversation to be both interesting and intelligent, a rarity, it seemed, in the drawing-rooms of Paris.

"I fear the task was easier than you perceive—you appeared to be the only man in the room speaking any sense," replied Darcy with a smile.

"Ah," replied the Comte in a tone of mock seriousness, "you English are always *très sérieux*, and do not know how to behave around people of such evident taste and refinement!" he continued, motioning with his head at the men by the looking-glasses. "I am sorry, in truth, to have you meet with such a collection of—er—how do you say *en anglais,* 'fops?' 'puppies?' You must have received a very bad idea of the men of Paris in just the time it took you to cross the room!"

Mr. Darcy bowed and gracefully replied, "Monsieur le Comte, do you not find that men are men everywhere? Were we all the same, it would be the ruination of all of the tailors, wig-makers, and perfumeries *dans le monde entier, non?* And, certainly no man of business could wish for such a catastrophe."

"Please, Monseiur d'Arcy, call me Estrouville, as I believe is the custom in your country, and I will call you Mr. Darcy, for the same reason."

"You are half correct, Estrouville, as I am sure you well know. Just 'Darcy' will do for me, thank you. Now, if we have finished with these interminable formalities, may we get to the subject of our last letters?"

"Darcy, you will be the death of our hostess and half of the good people in this room if we are perceived to be speaking here of farming, and I fear it will only be worse if we are heard to be discussing the uses of *steam* in that context. We will both be quickly relegated to the class of merchant-men, and no-one of any standing in the room will venture across a divide that my title and all of your consequence—nay, even, the charms of the two fair ladies who entered with you, but, to my deep disappointment, are as yet unknown to me—will surmount!"

"*C'est une faute énorme, et je vous prie de me pardonner,*" replied Darcy with a smile. "Pray, excuse my incivility—I will return in a moment with Mrs. and Miss Darcy, my wife and sister." Darcy bowed and walked to where Elizabeth and Georgiana were conversing with several older ladies, seated in the centre of the room on an enormous circular *banquette*.

Whilst Darcy had been engaged with the Comte, Elizabeth and Georgiana were noticed first by a group of older, comfortably plump, and exquisitely dressed gentlewomen who commanded the sofa. This group were far more welcoming of two handsome English ladies than the carefully posed *mademoiselles*, standing in exclusive arrangements about the edges of the room, their postures of studied indifference conveyed through the languid movement of their fans, and eyeing the Darcy ladies with thinly-veiled disapproval. Guiding Mrs. and Miss Darcy onto the largest sofa and motioning a footman for refreshment, the older ladies wasted no time in establishing the two ladies' identities and their histories. Shewing the best breeding of the group, the ranking lady rose and introduced herself as the dowager Comtesse d'Estrouville. She was a woman about the age of Elizabeth's father, and wore a simple cap of exquisite Brussels lace, a plain gown of dark lavender silk, and an impossibly delicate Kashimir shawl of an identical colour. She was yet a very fine woman, exceedingly handsome, and her features were rendered even more so by her warm, easy smile.

Upon learning that Georgiana was unmarried, the ladies fell into raptures, and any with sons were soon gesturing at the young men in the mirrored corners of the room to hasten thither to pay their compliments to Miss Darcy. Georgiana found herself in the midst of a sea of gallants, each eager to ascertain her tastes in reading, walking, music, and dancing, with many hints from their mothers, all of whom seemed to possess a remarkable ability for accurately attending two, or even three, conversations at once. Elizabeth noticed that Georgiana's blushes were progressively deeper shades of rose.

Georgiana was beginning to feel that she had quite enough of this particular exercise for one evening, and was saved from further exposure by Mr. Darcy's arrival to claim the ladies and perform the promised introductions. Elizabeth gracefully did the honours of presenting her husband to M. la Comtesse and her friends, and—at the same time—adroitly pulled Georgiana close between herself and Mr. Darcy; Georgiana's removal from the circle of gentlemen had the immediate effect of returning all of the young men to their previous occupation in the corners with the looking-glasses, whilst giving Georgiana a few moments' respite to regain her breath and her composure. This relative peace lasted only some few minutes when the Comte reappeared to claim an introduction to Mrs. and Miss Darcy, following the conclusion of which he then begged leave of his mother to introduce Mr. Darcy and the ladies.

"*Ah bien! Le voilà!* Guy—you are quite behind-handed! I have had the acquaintance of *les deux belles anglaises* for some time! For shame!" cried the dowager Comtesse in English, improved by a most charming accent. "You are not often so negligent! Mr. and Mrs. Darcy, Mademoiselle, pray excuse my son's faulty manners and do not judge the rest of us by his inattention to civilities." The look of affection that passed between the mother and son as he bent low to bow, smiling, and kiss her hands, let the Darcy family know that the raillery was in jest, and that this must form their usual pattern of intercourse. After some further nothings amongst themselves, the Comte, his mother, and the Darcy family said their *adieux* and left the room, but not before receiving enough invitations to supper to prevent their dining alone for at least a twelve-month.

"Despite your fine figure and consequence, Mr. Darcy," Elizabeth observed as they entered the coach to return to their apartments, "I believe we would not be half so popular if we were not accompanied by your sister who is—quite conveniently for us—both pretty *and* single. I declare, Georgiana, you are admired wherever we go; I wonder that it has not yet gone to your head, and that you do not pose about as do the French girls. If I had been so fortunate as to be the centre of such admiration, it surely would have turned *my* vanity! Sadly, before I married, I was of little consequence—being only tolerable-looking— and found myself slighted by other men, until your brother discovered his partiality for my eyes." Mr. Darcy, having been reminded of his early and long-disavowed assessment of Miss Elizabeth Bennet many times previous, gave his wife a smile that was a mixture of affection and forbearance, as he handed his sister in.

The following evening, the Darcys were offered seats in the d'Estrouville's box at the Paris opera, at L'Académie Royale de Musique. They arrived through streets filled with animated, elegant crowds to the *façade* of the opera house, overlooking the magnificent entrance to the Bibliothèque Nationale. Passing through the open gates and foyer, they entered the auditorium, which was so large as to provide seating for many thousands. The boxes behind the white balconies were a deep green, and the ceiling panels included designs of crowns, stars, and bees, which surrounded the central head of Apollo. Despite the increasing popularity of gas-light in England, the Paris opera was still lit by Argand lamps (most likely in deference to the fact that these items were of French invention), whose light could cast only a small distance, so that the usual pastime of examining the occupants of the other boxes was all but impossible. The stage, however, was well-lit, and from their box, the Darcys had a clear view of the orchestra beneath the stage. The renown of Kreutzer, the conductor, was such that Georgiana had especially wished to hear his orchestra, considered to be one of the finest in Europe. Tonight's performance was to be Glück's "Iphigénie" and included a fine *pas de ballet*.

The Darcys had been forewarned by the *concierge* that, in Paris, the sole purpose of attending the opera was to be seen, and not to regard the performance, but they were unprepared for the singular behaviour of the audience. They had arrived—they believed—unconscionably late to the box, but found themselves the only persons so placed, and their host and hostess were nowhere to be seen! Every seat had been reserved by the expedient of placing an hand-kerchief belonging to the occupant on the seat, who then determinedly spent until the last possible moment promenading up and down the lobby and corridors in an effort to display their *toilette* to best advantage. As the orchestra began, the patrons glided to their seats, completely ignoring all requests for silence, halloo'ing gaily to every acquaintance across the immense room. All but a few of the most important scenes of the opera were little attended-to, for the audience were far more occupied with the appearance of their *associés de conversation* than any other aspect of the performance.

The gentlemen were attired in long, light trousers, extremely tight-fitting tail-coats over satin or velvet waistcoats, and vastly ruffled shirts, accompanied by the requisite tall hat and ivory-topped cane. Other than the astonishing indiscretion in the cut of their cloathes—which formed such an exact adherence to the figure of its possessor that neither Elizabeth nor Georgiana could look about the room without blushing—the effect of their dress was exaggerated by all manner of cockades, orders, ribbands, and jewellery. Indeed, the secondary occupation of the gentlemen—other than the prevention of anyone near them hearing so much as a syllable or a note of the performance—was the putting on and taking off of their gloves, so as to attract all possible notice to their rings.

For the ladies, the plain fashions of *La Mode à la Grecque* had been swept away with the guillotine. The bodice seemed to have nearly ceased existence, and its office of covering the bosom entirely abandoned; the ladies' gowns were of such a revealing propensity that it was Mr. Darcy's turn to blush as he struggled against the competing claims of curiosity and propriety. The dresses were of the finest silks and satins, covered with ribbands, ruches, flowers, and pearls. The hair was similarly adorned and seemed to delight in competition with the elements of nature, effusing sprays of flowers, feathers, jewels, and almost every other device capable of being attached to the head. Bracelets, rings, brooches, necklaces and tiaras appeared in such profusion, that Elizabeth reckoned the jewellery of any one lady present would do herself for a month's engagements. And, if the noise and general din were not enough to discourage any but the most devoted of connoisseurs, the hats and head-dresses rendered the sight of the performance as impossible as was the hearing of the music. Darcy was disgusted, Elizabeth diverted, and Georgiana determined in the perversity of endeavouring to *hear* the music.

Georgiana, who had been looking forward to an evening of truly superior music, was put out of all patience by the behaviour of the Parisian opera-goers, and strove like Sisyphus to hear and see the performance. Elizabeth was not particularly fond of the opera, but for the sake of her sister's feelings, did not own her preference for the antics of the fashionable, hand-kerchief-wielding audience, rather than the action upon the stage. Mr. Darcy, soon wearying of either occupation, simply fell asleep.

During the course of another one of their evening engagements, Mr. Darcy was able to secure an introduction to a Mr. Sebastian Erard. This virtuoso was famed for the recent invention of a piano-forte that used a mechanism of an ingenious design, enabling the instrument to execute recent compositions of greatly increased complexity. For some time, Mr. Darcy had been looking for a replacement piano for Georgiana, whose own instrument was bought for her when a child. With this in mind, he made arrangements for the family to visit Mr. Erard at his establishment in La Rue du Mail, and to purchase a new piano-forte. Georgiana was delighted to make her choice from the latest instruments on display, but could not suppress a sadness which stole some pleasure from the moment, remembering Mademoiselle Blanche in her special place upon the old instrument, and missing *sa petite amie* so far away at Pemberley.

Elizabeth began to find herself fatigued by the late nights and stifling drawing-rooms that were an inevitability in Paris, and so arranged to take Georgiana to the beautiful and ancient Jardin des Plantes on a day when Mr. Darcy was engaged with the Comte. They made their way to the geological, mineralogical, and botanical galleries, which were warmed during the cold months by infusions of hot water drawn through pipes. Observing the many Parisians who wandered about the scenic gardens, Georgiana commented upon the numerous women who stood alone outside the café, looking eagerly up and down the promenade.

"They must be waiting for gentlemen, or they would not be standing about on the street alone. Do you think they are all mistresses? I have read that French men treat their mistresses better, and are more jealous of their mistresses' *affaires de cœur* than their wives'. It would seem a sad thing for marriage to be built upon such a notion, but it may be that even marriage is viewed differently here. Certainly, I could never be persuaded that a true union is possible with such a man as would look elsewhere for affection."

"You are rather severe upon the French gentlemen, Georgiana: I do not believe they are all so profligate as you suggest. Many of the married couples we have met seem quite as content as Mr. Darcy and myself, but perhaps I might be deceived. Things are not always as they appear—or, is it possible things *are* as they appear in this place, as you say?"

As she said this, she averted her eyes from the sight of a couple who embraced, at length and openly, before disappearing into the bronze pavillion, and wondered if, indeed, Georgiana's summary of French marriage might be more accurate than her own. Once again, Elizabeth found reason to rejoice in her good fortune in loving and securing the man who could contribute most to her own happiness in his character, constancy, and strength of mind. She attempted a momentary image of Mr. Darcy as a French man, but it would not do—there was no aligning his entirely English views of propriety and honour with the scene just recently before her.

CHAP. 3.

UNLIKE THE BENNET SISTERS, Georgiana had no compulsion to marry for want of independent means, and had no mother to convince her that the pursuit of an husband must be her chief occupation in single life. Her brother, who could yet see her only as a younger sister, despite her five-and-twenty years, never ventured upon the subject, having no inclination to hurry the day she should leave Pemberley. Elizabeth had sufficient delicacy and respect for the private nature of her sister to only *think* her comments about the prospect of one day Georgiana finding a suitor who might make her wish for a change. Free from the pressure of her family, Georgiana's own thoughts on the matter were simple: she loved a man whom every passing day seemed to put further out of her reach—his heart being engaged elsewhere. Her feelings could, therefore, never be declared, and she had neither the desire nor the necessity to marry without love. Despite Georgiana's quiet outward nature, there was nothing of compromise in her heart when it came to her own attachments, or of doubt to soften the pain of disappointment. If her present situation were allowed to continue indefinitely—and she had no idea that it could not—she could consign herself to an unmarried future with more complaisance than is generally felt by a woman at her time of life.

Two weeks after their arrival in Paris, the day dawned on which was to be the ball, held by the Duc de A——. As their evening diversions abroad had thus far taken the form of intimate dinners and *soirées* in the private *salons* of the city, the opportunity to attend a *soirée dansante*, where the French stile of dancing could be publicly displayed, was the cause of great excitement for Elizabeth and Georgiana. The discussion of the necessary dress and other minutiæ soon wearied Mr.

Darcy, so he betook himself to the Musée du Louvre to leave the ladies to their deliberations, but only after making his position clear as to the dispensability of a *bourse*, which he deemed was unnecessary if one's hair did not require it, and it certainly had no purpose in hanging about by itself on the collar. Elizabeth was amused at the various stiles she had seen, and had no reason to contradict her husband's distaste for a disembodied bow. The other necessary male articles of dress were already in the possession of Mr. Darcy, and so the ladies were left to their own devices and preferences. Perhaps, thought Elizabeth, the English notions of practicality were at general variance with the French predilection for fashion, which may well account for the universally acknowledged inability of the English to imitate successfully the elegance of the French. Recalling her husband's judgement of the *bourse*, and her own insistence on a serviceable bodice, Elizabeth felt that her theory was as likely true as any she had previously heard.

For Georgiana, the ball was more than simply another engagement. Her own reception in Parisian society had been gratifying, and over the course of this first week, she had begun to persuade herself that she needed to make a greater effort to recover her own spirits. She was, henceforth, determined to use the interval until Colonel Fitzwilliam was to join them to resist more earnestly the misgivings of her heart, and suffer her disappointed hopes with a more inured resignation, if she could not manage a more reasonable acceptance. The society of Paris would provide a balm to soothe her unhappiness, even if inadequate for a cure. At the least, her efforts would be amply recompensed in giving her brother and sister the happiness of believing herself amused and in good spirits. The night of the ball saw the *début* of the ladies' *robes de bal*. Elizabeth wore the necklet of pearls that had been a wedding-present from her husband, and both ladies wore only a few flowers in the hair— Georgiana a circlet of small white roses, and Lizzy two gardenias that the concierge had procured for her at Mr. Darcy's request. Elizabeth remarked to Georgiana, as they met at the completion of their *toilettes*,

"The French must regard us both as superlatively stupid, having nothing at all emanating from our heads; the profusion of fruit, feathers, or indeed entire branches of vegetation springing forth surely bespeaks a surplus of thoughts which cannot be contained entirely within the cranium. A few paltry blooms—and small ones at that!—can surely bespeak no excess of imagination, or even intelligence!" laughed Elizabeth gaily. "However, it is time to go, and I am sure that there is nothing to be done about it now. We might abuse the concierge for our want of proper adornment, but even I would scruple to put about such a falsehood, as he did get *exactly* what we asked. However, we need not fret: I noticed, other than our friend, the Comte, Mr. Darcy was much the tallest man we have seen, so we are safe, after all." Georgiana smiled at her brother, and they went down-stairs together to meet their coach.

As Georgiana stepped down from the carriage at the entrance to ——, the assembly room for the evening ball, she was greeted by a brace of handsomely liveried and attentive footmen. A large number of guests were mingling outside in the crisp evening air before their announcement, and thousands of candles and soft gas-lamps cast a flattering luminescence upon the beauty of the house and its impatient visitors. The overall effect was magical; accustomed as she was to the company of good society in England, there was, she felt, a splendour unique to Paris and an éclat about Parisians that defied imitation. The family drew a number of appreciative glances as they left their coach and made their way to the entrance, and those who had not yet seen the *famille de trois Anglais, sublimissimes et possédants* whispered and pointed, reminding Elizabeth of the night she first met Mr. Darcy, and the agitation the mere sight of him had created amongst the good people of Meryton.

Their arrival having been announced, they were free to wander through the halls and appreciate the atmosphere, the music, and the spectacle. The pale, billowing gowns of silks, satins, and lace, fine Kashimir scarves, and trimmings of every variety adorned the figures of the ladies in the room. Georgiana and Elizabeth's gowns were *complètement sans fioritures* compared with the prevalent *très orné* mode of dress. In contrast, Georgiana's tall, graceful form in her plain silk gown, locket, and some few roses dressed about her lovely, easy curls presented a most compelling example of natural beauty unopposed by a surfeit of contrivance. The immediate notice of the gentlemen and their approving glances at one another must have given those ladies who embraced the vogue for *Le Chapeau à L'Ancienne*—high coiffures sprouting yet higher plumage, and enormous evening bonnets overflowing with flowers, fruit, cockades, knots, and *aigrettes*—cause to feel somewhat *outré* by comparison. If the ballrooms of the next evening were somewhat less of a threat to the flora and fauna of France, it may be attributed to the enduring attraction of an imagination not overly sated by such a visual feast as was then on display.

There were a number of military-men at the ball, more than any of the Darcys would have assumed in peace-time. The French officers were easily recognised by their shockingly tight cloathes, in which, Elizabeth conjectured, it would be impossible to fight without soon becoming ragged and indecent. The Russians were easily distinguished by their ridiculous, long, bright-green frock coats that sported a kind of bustle at the back, and were tied about the waist with a gold scarf, concluding with a long tassel that Elizabeth thought would have been placed to better advantage restraining a curtain than a torso. The English officers were in their customary red or blue coats, and looked quite plain—but with more real elegance—when compared to the vast array of ornament on their Austrian, Prussian, or French counter-parts. The Prussians and Austrians were easily known by their enormous moustaches and dark countenances, which appeared so not much by any action of the complexion, but as the result of severe opinion and censorious thought. These three nations comprised the majority of the other foreigners present, with the exception of a few Swedes, Italians, and Americans. The Swedes were tall, handsome men, elegantly dressed in uniforms of blue and gold, all wearing a sash and order; the Italians were, as was to be expected, the most ornately dressed, but, thought Elizabeth, were more easily distinguished from their martial peers by their smiles, easy laughter, and energetic chivalry, directed toward everyone in some measure, but—as would be expected—especially toward the ladies. And, the Italians were certainly less prejudiced toward the younger ladies—bowing, complimenting, and kissing the hands of any woman within reach. The Americans, although there were no military representatives present, were also easily separated by their simple dress, entirely deprived of sashes, insignias, medals, or other badges (which, thought Elizabeth, seemed to be displayed in a profusion inversely proportionate to the merit of their wearer), and entirely unaffected speech and manners. Apart from silver epaulettes and buttons, the English officers appeared little different in their dress from the other gentlemen present, and their restrained courtesy would have pleased Elizabeth better had she not observed the open, engaging manners of the French, and the warm, unaffected sociability of the Italians. It was, she considered, an entirely foreign idea to the English consciousness, that manners and good-breeding could exist along-side—nay, be complemented by—an intercourse characterised by an active, familiar *expression* of interest in the thoughts, speech, and feelings of their fellow beings, entirely untainted by disrespect, impertinence, or impropriety.

A flutter of excitement passed through the far end of the room, the source of which, it soon became apparent, was the entrance of a gentleman of some importance. The noise and crush of the room prevented their seeing him or hearing his name. There were many gentlemen of pleasing figure and good-breeding; the popularity and charm of this *beau idéal* lay with his natural possession of the opposing and elusive blessings of an easy grace, united with a most attractive aristocratic mien. As he came toward them, the Darcys lost no time in recognising the Comte d'Estrouville. Despite his entering the room alone, within moments the Comte was assaulted by both courtiers and admiring, affected ladies, who used their fans and other accoutrements in an attempt to interest and excite in a manner that would never have been tolerated in English society. The Darcys quickly discovered that the Comte was a favourite in the best Parisian circles, and still, to the delight of that society, a single man. As soon as civility permitted disentangling himself from the multitudes wishing to be seen in his company, he stopt for a few minutes to converse with some of the card-players in the next room. Elizabeth stole a glance at Georgiana, whose cheeks had involuntarily coloured upon recognising the Comte. Georgiana quickly recollected herself and turned to look elsewhere in the room, missing, thereby, the smile that ensued when the Comte's eyes alighted upon herself. He walked as rapidly as was possible in a crowded ballroom toward the Darcy family, wishing to indulge his own preference for conversing with Georgiana and her family until the dancing began.

Owing to the pleasure that Mr. Darcy and the Comte each received in the similarity of their opinions, it took little time for the Comte and Mr. Darcy's family to move apart a little from the larger portion of the crowd. It was an inevitability that, as the orchestra made ready to signal the beginning of the dance, the Comte turned to Georgiana and, with a low bow, asked if he might be allowed the honour of the first two dances of the night. Georgiana, always uncomfortable in being noticed, was never more so than the moment when she realised that the eyes of the whole room would be upon her in a few moments; she knew not how she responded; in any case, the gallant Comte reacted as though she had the speech of Demosthenes, and led her into the middle of the room. Word spread quickly—as it will—around the entirety of the ballroom, that the Comte would dance his first with the tall English lady, who was so singularly dressed. The French gentlemen responded generally that they noticed only that she was very pretty, leaving their ladies, one supposes, less satisfied with the effect of their general censure than they would wish.

Their hosts' honoured guests of the ball were a noble Italian family who were staying in Paris for the spring, and who, being of a certain age, chose to observe rather than dance themselves. The Duc did not himself dance; therefore, upon their hosts declining to lead, the Comte had precedence amongst the company, with the result that he and Miss Darcy led the dance. This honour was a regular occurrence for the Comte, but an unwelcome additional embarrassment for Georgiana, who knew that all eyes would be upon herself and her partner. Her discomfort was heightened when the Comte requested from the orchestra, as a second selection, a waltz—a dance whose intimate nature continued to impede its general acceptance in English society—although, as with the general relations between men and women, pleasure invariably triumphed over propriety.

Georgiana was well-schooled in the art of dancing, and was always more comfortable in *doing* something for which her studies had given her confidence than in *speaking* the common-place nothings upon which good society depends. Her figure was the perfect counter-part to the Comte's, and she moved with an artless grace that pleased rather than captivated; the elegant figure and natural ease of the Comte's dancing kept perfectly the step and time of the dance, whilst expertly avoiding the crush of the other couples. The Comte, unlike the majority of Englishmen, danced with purpose and pleasure; the delight he took in the activity was transparent, and the earnestness with which he attended his partner was equally conspicuous. There was not an eye in the room that did not fix upon the couple as they circled the room. At first, the Comte made an effort to converse with his demure partner, observing the excellent similarity in Mr. Darcy's and his wife's stile of dancing, asking how long they planned to remain in Paris, whether she had enjoyed her visit thus far, and such-like, to which Georgiana responded but briefly. She was far too self-conscious to form any ideas beyond the *cliché*, and was so disinclined to any form of display to converse, when so publicly placed, with anything resembling ease. She could think of nothing to venture in reply, and the pair soon lapsed into silence, Georgiana feared that the Comte was, at that moment, thinking her especially uncivil. The silence grew, but Georgiana felt something quite unlike the awkwardness she expected, and glanced up, only to hastily look away again, for she found that the Comte was earnestly looking at her, his every expression bespeaking his pleasure in his choice. The directness of that look discomposed her, and, in her confusion and embarrassment, she misstepped so that the Comte had to gently guide her for the next few figures. To Georgiana's surprise, her error had not altered the Comte's smiles, other than perhaps to mark the happy complaisance more visible in his countenance.

The remainder of the dance was entirely conducted without further attempts at speech, the Comte being content to smile his communication, as Georgiana struggled to control the blush that threatened to expose her discomfort to the whole of the room. The Comte's obvious reluctance to relinquish his hold upon her hand as they quitted the floor could not pass unnoticed by the company, and young ladies across the room were soon appealing to their mothers and friends for sympathy. The Comte was entirely unaware of the horror he had created, for, to be sure, he had never looked at one of them more than another that evening, or any other. The Comte escorted Georgiana back to her brother, and, after respectfully bowing once more, he asked if he might have the pleasure of Mrs. Darcy's company, a request to which Darcy readily acquiesced. Elizabeth was led on out onto the floor, casting Georgiana a look of amused delight as she passed by, and causing her sister's blushes to reappear in force. The remainder of the ball passed without further incident; the Comte was unable to enjoy the pleasure of dancing with Georgiana again, and, at any rate, she was engaged for every dance before supper. He was prevented from sitting by her at dinner, doubtless through the machinations of the *duennas* of the Comte's various admirers. It was only as the Darcys made ready to depart, that the Comte was able to address them once more,

"I cannot in good faith attempt to persuade you to remain here any longer, for the ball will continue long past the hour when all people of sense have retired. It is also to be recommended that one leave early, for I can vouch with no little experience that the close of a ball is never as pleasant as its commencement. But, Mr. Darcy, we have had little time to talk, and there is much I wish to discuss regarding our respective occupations. Are you entirely engaged this next week?" Having quickly ascertained that they were by chance both to dine at the evening party of a mutual acquaintance the following night, the Comte was satisfied to leave them, but only after one long look at Georgiana, and, after making a low bow, kissing her proffered hand rather longer than expected.

Georgiana spoke little on the drive home, and would not be quizzed on her opinion of the Comte beyond an affirmation that he possessed "pleasing manners" and was "an attentive and accomplished dancer." The conversation between Elizabeth and her husband upon retiring to their own chambers was altogether more conclusive.

❧ I think   27

"I think, my dear, that I shall enjoy making a better acquaintance of the Comte. He is widely regarded as a rational, philosophical man, not averse to trying new methods. He has, I am sure, some excellent experience of fruit culture, which I shall be glad to learn of him. He struck me altogether as being very agreeable. Do you not agree?"

"Yes," replied Elizabeth, "it is impossible to find him otherwise: his manners are so pleasing and naturally open. He is much like Mr. Bingley in his ease of address, but with more *savoir faire* and an obvious—although not disagreeable—pride. I am delighted that you have improved your acquaintance of a gentleman whom you already esteem through reputation, and who is so very like yourself in his thinking. I would add, Husband, that this is not the only pleasing aspect of this association. The Comte was, as could easily be apprehended by the whole of the room, quite taken with Georgiana; the very artifice and officious attention of the French ladies appeared to disgust him. I am of the opinion that he values Georgiana for the artless simplicity of her character, and probably, to some degree, because she is so unlike *them.* I could discern nothing of *her* feelings at the ball, and she was silent on the subject on the way home. I confess that, impossibly high as my requirements are for anything that comes in the form of a lover to your sister, the Comte equals them in all respects. I can find no fault with him; he *seems* worthy of her, and she is certainly worthy of him." Mr. Darcy, who had been thinking much along the same lines, agreed wholeheartedly, and they retired, one dreaming of handsome plantations and the other of the pleasures of the evening.

Elizabeth was beginning to tire of the brilliance of Paris, but kept her feelings to herself out of deference to the pleasures of her husband and sister. Instead, she supported her spirits and passed her time with studying the variety of people to be met with in Paris. Elizabeth had long been an observer of the foolish and the whimsical, but Paris was a veritable microcosm of every example of fop, dandy, gallant, aesthete, scholar, *roué*, and gentleman—and that was only in the male line. There were despondent lovers, hoping to acquire the polish and charms of a foreign education so as to press a favourable end to their suits, or at least their *pursuits*; dowagers, escaping the tyranny of vengeful daughters-in-law, had decamped thither to make themselves happy and their tormenters miserable by their residence in the Fair City, with all of its imagined diversions; artists flocked to Paris in pursuit of their muse, who was, for some unimaginable reason, presumed to be of the French nationality; and learned ladies and gentlemen pursued each

other

other, hoping to illuminate their genius on these far shores. After what seemed an impossible effort, Elizabeth had at long last made Georgiana laugh when she proposed they amuse themselves classifying the Paris fair and the gallant in satirical solemnity, by dictating a letter to Mrs. Gardiner, describing their employments:

14th April
Paris

DEAR AUNT AND UNCLE GARDINER,

We remain in raptures over Paris, but are *délicieusement fatigués,* being *engagés* each day and evening in the *salons, opéra, théatre,* or some private entertainment, all in the same day. Our *mouchoirs* are become sorely worn, exhausted with the burthen of every night declaring our attentions and our intentions in some way or other to the gallant French *attentifs,* who seem to live or die, depending on our notice. Our voices are similarly depleted from the requirement of shouting across the largest rooms to people who are unknown to us, but who appear fashionable. We are received politely by the very reserved French, who hang about one in an intimate *degagée* manner. These *beaux* whisper their pretty speeches in a singular admixture of French, Italian, German, Mandarin, and Hindoo, relieved now and then with a little English; we are nearly overcome with the mortification of being proficient in only one language at a time. Daily we meet with such a variety of dress, despondency, and decorum, that it would amaze you to find it all in one city, small as Paris is. Our time is much in demand, so much so that we often sleep all day, emerging only at night to spare ourselves the exertion of remaining *dans nos lits,* as the most fashionable women have adopted the polite custom of receiving their visitors *en chambre* at all hours. The ladies here are particularly œconomical in their dress, exhibiting such commendable frugality as to forego covering the entirety of their charms, contriving to preserve a sum which, in turn, purchases such a forest of decoration for the head, that it is no wonder only a little money remains for the completion of their costume.

I should not neglect the men, who are similarly abstemious as to the cut of their cloathing, using their savings to purchase the most remarkably large looking-glasses you ever saw. We had planned to bring home several, but, alas, not even one would fit in our incommodious chaise. My own husband is so very disobliging that he refuses to flatter ourselves and our *chevaliers* through the simple expedient of imitation—notwithstanding that his *vêtements modestes* are *ganz outré,*

I assure you, *kein* quizzing-glass, a musical snuff-box, or—dare I speak it?—perfume; he further disobliges us by assuming the posture more appropriate to a footman, is clear in his speech (not a thingle thyllable will he lithp), and remains thus disagreeable for the entire evening. You can easily believe that we would not pass a single *minuto* in such company, except that his great height makes our own attitudes appear all the more gracefully *degagée.* In any case, you will not recognise us *auf wiedersehen,* we are become so *molto amélioré* by our travels.

Yours, &c.,

THE FAMILLE D'ARCY

CHAP. 4.

THE COMTE D'ESTROUVILLE had inherited his title and estates at an early age, and maintained both these and his head during the Terror by the simple expedient of remaining in the country throughout the turmoil and giving the appearance of being exactly what he was: a conscientious landowner providing food and cloth to the citizens of Paris. That he did so cheerfully—and at a substantial profit—did not, in the eyes of Buonaparte, lessen his value to the Republic. Thus, he returned to Paris at a youthful six-and-thirty, just as handsome, and even more rich. How much of this wise policy was due to his natural intelligence and sagacity, and how much to the similar mind of his lady mother was now not much to the purpose. That they had both escaped the horrible fate of so many of their family and friends was fortunate for themselves, and—thought the Darcys—for France.

Released from the voluntary exile of his country estates, the Comte re-entered Parisian society with éclat, and was soon regarded as one of the most admired gentlemen in Paris. This circumstance arose in some portion from his engaging manners, partly from his situation as to birth, figure, and fortune, and, at least as importantly, from his being yet a single man, who, the female subdivision of Parisian society averred in unison, must be in want of a wife. The elegant figure of the dowager Comtesse on his arm did not deter either matron or daughter in their attentions. Few, if any, evenings saw the Comte unengaged. Rather, he ate his suppers at the most fashionable *salons*, commonly seated at the right-hand of his hostess and across from some one or other of her eligible daughters. Such a situation in itself was not a surprise; the wonder was that after months of assiduous assault by the most charming women in Paris, he remained steadfastly single.

The constant stream of *cartes de viste* were invariably succeeded by invitations, as Paris recognised the consequence of the Darcy family, soon producing an intimacy with the Comte and his mother. Elizabeth observed the repeated *sorties* launched against the Comte's bachelorhood with interest and amusement. It did not escape Elizabeth's discernment that—more often than not—rather than attending to the fawnings of the legions of *jeunes femmes et leurs mères*, the Comte seemed to prefer the quiet, rational, unaffected conversation he found in Georgiana. They had not been many days in Paris before Elizabeth believed that Georgiana was more likely to captivate the amiable Comte than any or all of the single women of France.

The entertainments and engagements of Paris were relentless—indeed, it was doubtful whether some of the leading personages of society slept at all—and as the Darcys spent the afternoons and evenings at one entertainment after another, the brightness of Paris began to lose its lustre. Mr. Darcy, therefore, enquired of his wife one afternoon as to whether she might prefer to dine at their own residence, pleading an indisposition to the hostess of that evening's *soirée*.

"I would never wish to suspend your pleasure or that of my sister, but I own that I would be happy to spend a quiet evening in the company of my family," began Mr. Darcy one afternoon.

Elizabeth was delighted. "On the contrary, Mr. Darcy, I was unwilling to begin to suggest that we vary our routine of endless entertainments, *bons mots*, and interminable suppers, but I agree whole-heartedly that I long for a simple, comfortable evening with you and Georgiana, where we three can be as dull and stupid as we chuse. Shall I ask Georgiana what is her preference?"

"Yes, please, Elizabeth," replied Mr. Darcy, "and I am in such expectation of your success, that I rely upon the deception of your sending to the Marquise that we are sadly unable to attend this evening. If you like, I will be the culprit. You may say that you are sending your regrets, as your brute of an husband has barred the door and refuses to let either of the ladies pass."

"Oh, certainly! I will undertake the task at once for the simple pleasure of industriously circulating such a rumour. I am sure that will do quite nicely to set the tongues of Paris wagging even more violently in our direction than they do at present!" laughed Elizabeth. "Let me go to Georgiana directly." That evening, the Pemberley party enjoyed a quiet family evening alone: Darcy reading, Elizabeth writing some letters, and Georgiana at the piano-forte, until a footman knocked and announced, rather later in the evening than might be expected—even in Paris—a visitor. To the astonishment of all, the name given was the Comte d'Estrouville!

"Please forgive me the intrusion," began the Comte to Mr. Darcy, "but I was informed—it appears mistakenly—that your family were unwell, and I could not be easy until I had determined that none of your party were in need of such assistance as might be in my small power to give," he said, bowing first to Elizabeth, and then making a second bow expressly to Georgiana. "But," he continued, "it seems that I am entirely in error and, further, that I have intruded most egregiously on your peace this evening."

"My dear Comte," said Elizabeth, "it does not follow that such an intrusion is necessarily unwelcome. Pray, do sit with us, although I am sure we are quiet indeed, compared to the gay scenes you have just quitted in your kind solicitude for our comfort."

"Were I sure that an acceptance would not be an unpardonable imposition, I should like nothing more," replied the Comte to Elizabeth with a low bow. "You know enough of our society here to know that it is possible to spend the entirety of an evening in an elegant *salon*, with otherwise intelligent company, and exchange no more than ten words of sense or information in an hour altogether. Such an evening I have experienced this night. It is an uncommon pleasure to speak with friends who are so kind as to actually *listen*, and reply with information and new ideas, and whose eyes are not forever searching about the room for a more influential or agreeable object for their conversation. Mrs. Darcy, if you are sincere in your kind offer, I would accept your invitation with great pleasure."

During this exchange, Georgiana studiously examined her music-book. Elizabeth noticed her change in colour and quickly indicated to the Comte that he was to occupy a seat next to herself, sparing Georgiana the embarrassment of leaving her instrument and perforce joining the conversation. Even so, it was impossible for Georgiana to continue her playing, and she shortly rose and took a seat by her brother. At length, tea was brought in, and Georgiana naturally rose to assist Elizabeth in serving their guests. As she handed the Comte his cup, he took the dish in such a way as to momentarily touch her fingers, and, looking up at her, made a point to ask her how *she* found Paris society. Georgiana's blush of spontaneous confusion did nothing to lessen her attraction in lieu of the more knowing contrivances of the *demoiselles* assiduously courting the Comte. After some few syllables, he moved his hand to take the dish, releasing Georgiana with a smile that would have had the female half of Parisian society in a state of complete insensibility.

The Comte sat with them for some time, he and Mr. Darcy engaged in a discussion of plantations, machinery, and the management of estates, whilst Elizabeth took up some needle-work, occasionally joining the conversation; Georgiana took up her own work-basket, but beyond the few requirements of civility, spoke not at all. The remainder of the evening passed very pleasantly, and Elizabeth was grateful that the Comte provided some pleasure to her husband in the form of conversation on topics in which his usual companions could have little knowledge. Before leaving them, the Comte was particular upon the point of extending an invitation to the family. He was to return to his estate a little beyond Evry the following day, and he begged the company of the Darcys until his return to Paris some days later. He and Mr. Darcy would enjoy some sport in fishing and viewing the farms and plantations, whilst the Darcy ladies would wait upon his sister and mother, who were most desirous of the company of the Darcy ladies. For some days, the Comte had wanted to ask for the favour of a visit, but had not wished to put himself forward. He earnestly hoped the Darcys were now on sufficiently familiar terms for the family to accept his invitation. Mr. Darcy looked all pleasure at the proposal, and, turning to his wife, asked if she could answer for their being unengaged. Seeing her husband's enthusiasm for the scheme, Elizabeth answered that she did not believe there was any real impediment to their going, and she would send notes that evening to their hostesses, if that was the wish of her husband and sister. Georgiana made no objection, and upon the Comte's rising to take his leave of them all, he turned to Georgiana and repeated with what great pleasure he looked forward to seeing them on the morrow.

"Georgiana," began Elizabeth, as soon as they were alone, "you look as though you are not entirely in favour of a visit to the Comte's estate. If you do not wish it, we are not obliged to go; if you are at all uncomfortable, we may send word that we cannot come."

"Nay, Elizabeth, I am not averse to the idea, and in any case would never wish to suspend any plan which would bring you both such pleasure. My reservation arises only from a wish that the Comte would not be so particular in his attentions to me. Surely, he must be sensible that I do not encourage his regard. However, my disinclination is trifling, when compared to the satisfaction my brother would find in seeing Belle Aire. And, Elizabeth, you seem equally pleased with the prospect. I will gladly go, but resolve to be more guarded in my behaviour, such that I may not be—even unconsciously—guilty of encouraging his regard."

"Georgiana, I will not pretend that I cannot see his preference for you over any other of the women in whose company we have observed him," agreed Elizabeth. "Do you have other objections to his company?"

"No," replied Georgiana slowly, "but I would not wish to give rise to any expectations which would necessarily be disappointed. I am, on that account, somewhat uneasy as to whether it is wise to pass such a proportion of our time in his company. I would never knowingly be the cause of giving pain to anyone, if I could direct my behaviour in such a way as to prevent it."

Here, Mr. Darcy looked up from his paper and asked Georgiana, "I have not had the pleasure of attending to quite all of your conversation, but are you so sure, Georgiana, that you would not in the future find the Comte more agreeable than you do presently?"

Georgiana looked thunder-struck, and knew not how to reply. Her eyes flew immediately to Elizabeth.

Elizabeth was in an instant confusion as to how to respond without coming between brother and sister. After a moment's hesitation, she said quietly, "Georgiana, I do not claim to know the particular reasons why you are irrevocably decided against the Comte, but might venture to guess that you are prejudiced against the idea of returning his regard, as to do so would inevitably force you to choose between your home and your husband."

"Oh, yes!" cried Georgiana. "That is exactly the reason! Indeed, the Comte d'Estrouville is in no way to blame for my feelings; I know nothing ill of his character. On the contrary, he seems in every way a gentleman. However, I could never consent to such an unhappy arrangement as would require me to give up my home in England, whilst I had any power of preventing it. I have no wish to connect myself so far from home."

"Well, my dear," said Darcy, addressing Elizabeth after a moment's reflection, "again, your superior knowledge of such matters must decide what we are to do. In the light of Georgiana's feelings, do you think the acceptance of the invitation advisable? I own that my disappointment at the loss of some hours' fishing would be little counter-balance to such reflections of regret."

Elizabeth thought for some little time before replying, feeling like King Solomon in trying to please the two people she loved most.

"I think that it would be considered somewhat uncivil to decline the invitation, when we could never declare our reason for doing so, after having positively made the engagement. I would propose that we do go to-morrow, but that perhaps Mr. Darcy, when out of doors, could give the Comte such hints as to the nature of Georgiana's feelings as would put an end to any expectations. As you both well know, I always look at my proposals in the positive light of my own preferences. However, it does satisfy Georgiana's delicacy with respect to the feelings of the Comte, and we will remain the very picture of English civility as we attend his undoubtedly charming sister and the dowager at their beautiful estate. And, my dearest husband, you get to go fishing. As the one who is obliged to perform the disagreeable task of speaking with the Comte, does that seem an acceptable plan to you, Mr. Darcy?"

Darcy smiled and turned to Georgiana to ask if Elizabeth's proposal requited her uneasiness, and upon her quiet assent, took his leave to organise the carriages for the morrow.

As she slowly walked to her rooms in order to ask her maid to pack their things for the morrow's excursion to the Comte's estate, Georgiana reflected long upon the circumstance of the visit, for—even to this most diffident of ladies—there could be no mistake of the Comte's regard. Georgiana esteemed him greatly, and this evening she had observed her brother conversing with him so naturally and happily, that she was left in no doubt that her acceptance of an offer would bring much joy to her family. The Comte, with all of the virtues of an handsome and agreeable person—kindness, delicacy, birth, and fortune—had, she knew, all the requisites of the perfect husband. As she considered his character and amiable temperament, she recognised that, had her own heart been disengaged, her refusal might have spared her a few of many sleepless nights. Any such comparison was pointless, however, as her heart *was* engaged, and no army of such paragons, or even the loss of Colonel Fitzwilliam by his marriage to Mary Crawford, was ever going to make that heart available to another.

CHAP. 5.

THE ANTICIPATION FELT by her brother and sister in the chaise the next morning was so obvious that Georgiana's dread began to fade into a calmer equanimity, and the first sights of the *château* and its expanse of formal gardens, orchards, and open fields further improved her spirits to something approaching pleasure as the horses clattered up the winding drive. The French appeared to have no love of Mr. Repton; the *allée* wound through a delightful, thick wood and ended abruptly, framing the imposing front of the *château* most agreeably. The drive terminated in a circle, in the centre of which was a magnificent mosaic of roses, delineated with lavender. On either side of the lawns rose carefully trimmed yew and box, arranged with a symmetry and beauty that exactly complemented the *façade* of the house. Flanking either side of the entrance were deep borders, again arranged in the most enchanting designs, and beautifully wrought gates through which could be seen several terraces and their ornately contrived steps.

Here was an home as beloved as Pemberley, and its charm and prospect was as worthy of its master. The familiarity with which the Comte himself met their chaise, helping the ladies down and fondly introducing his younger half-sister, made his guests easy at once. His modesty and true gentility, as Elizabeth praised the exquisite exterior of the *château*, was evident as he hurried away the compliment, the house and gardens being the work of previous generations for which he could take no credit—securing him in even higher estimation, if such were possible. After the Comte's servants had shewn the Darcys to their chambers and all had rested a little from their journey, the party met in the drawing-room. The Comte lost no time in appropriating Mr. Darcy for the requisite gentlemen's tour of the plantation's piggeries, out-houses, kitchen garden with its conservatories, mushroom establishment, hot-beds, and the stables to admire the hunters and coach-horses, to which Mr. Darcy acquiesced with obvious pleasure. Elizabeth watched with delight as her husband left with the Comte—the two appeared to uncommon advantage together; Mr. Darcy's reserve all but disappeared, a rare circumstance when he was in the company of other than his family.

The Comte's pretty sister very civilly enquired if she might be permitted to take the ladies on a drive through the park whilst the gentlemen were making their tour. Elizabeth was eager to fix an opportunity to find out more about her brother in his absence, and, as Georgiana was equally anxious to avoid the Comte, both Darcy ladies accepted with alacrity. Amélie was not above seventeen, and shared her brother's good-natured and generous spirit, as well his genius for conversation—and this to a surprising degree for one so young and sequestered. She was not tall as was Georgiana, but had a very natural innocence to her countenance, a light, pleasing figure, and hair of a most beautiful light brown. To frame such natural attractions, she wore a plain muslin gown, with only a brown ribband below the bodice, the same colour as the fine shawl tied gracefully about her shoulders. She put on a straw bonnet made all over with white tulle, upon which were fastened a few white ostrich feathers on the outer brim and one under it, which had a most charming way of curling up behind her face. Elizabeth had never seen the like; never had borrowed feathers been placed to such an advantageous effect. At that moment, Elizabeth thought to herself, neither the finest silks nor gossamer lace could improve upon such a picture of perfect beauty and nature; no amendment could yield an effect so artless, yet so completely elegant. There was something special about a Frenchwoman's *toilette* that produced a result of enchanting taste and refinement, which every Englishwoman tried in vain to purchase—with widely varying degrees of success.

By the time the ladies in the Phaeton reached the wooded area of the park, it had become clear that *this mademoiselle* had no ulterior motive for her kindness; her intention was simply to shew the friends of her brother every possible civility. Georgiana and Elizabeth enjoyed her knowledgeable explanations of the history of the *château*, the number of gardeners employed to maintain the extensive grounds, the varieties of fish resident in the vast lake, the names of the trees, and the forms of the *parterres* and fountain which dominated both sides of the *château*. Feeling that they must soon reach the end of the sheer volume of numbers that formed the basis of the ground's description, Elizabeth attempted to steer the conversation toward her primary interest.

"You must be plagued with guests here. It is so beautiful, no one would ever wish to leave; do you frequently entertain friends of your brother?"

"Oh no! I was very surprised when my brother sent word that we were to expect company upon his return from Paris, for he never invites anyone to stay with us, although I am assured by all whose society he keeps, that he is a most popular gentleman in Paris, and is never in want of gay company there. I suppose that my brother prefers to keep those two spheres of his life apart, and so we see only family here at the *château*, and never his Parisian friends."

Upon Elizabeth exclaiming that she was even more highly honoured at such a distinction, Amélie replied,

"I must attribute the reason for the invitation to his high regard for Mr. Darcy. As I understand it, they have long shared a friendship over their common interests in farming and such-like, which, of course, are more easily discussed here than in the *salons* of Paris. And I am delighted that he has been able to secure Mr. Darcy's visit here, for it affords me such agreeable company of my own! And, of course, I must not fail to add my obligation to you for your gracious condescension in making your visit. Oh! And I am sure I must not forget to mention Mamma's pleasure in welcoming you to Belle Aire, as well. I hope that I have said things as I ought, as I rarely get to speak English here, although anyone in France able to afford the tutelage must surely learn."

Elizabeth privately thought that his sister had quite likely misplaced the direction of the Comte's intentions, but replied in eager agreement, and echoed Amélie's delight at the friendship between the two gentlemen, adding that the pleasure of both must provide an especial pleasure for men who perforce spent so much time at their own estates in the unrelieved company of women. Amélie shewed no less enthusiasm for her own good fortune, a compliment that had its intended effect of making her guests feel very welcome in their own right. Returned to the *château*, they were joined by the dowager Comtesse and sat down to tea.

The dowager Comtesse was something above sixty years, but had been generously spared the usual effects of time, as her face and figure were still decidedly lovely. She had beautiful, pale silver hair—and wore no cap to conceal it—and the sparkling light eyes of her daughter. Her dress was a lovely shade of lilac, and the delicate *fichu* would have been enchanting on a woman of any age, and set off her features to sublime advantage. She was, indeed, yet a very fine woman.

Elizabeth was seated opposite two handsome images, which she supposed to be the marriage-portraits of the late Comte and his young wife. The Comte wore a plain, dark coat with fine lace cuffs, and a long, richly embroidered waistcoat. Standing near a table, upon which was an open book—how like the late Mr. Darcy's portrait!—his attitude spoke of refinement and a cultivation of taste and mind. Unlike Mr. Darcy's father, *le Comte Père* had a slight but discernable smile. His young wife faced him in her golden frame, wearing a closed robe of brown taffeta, trimmed in ermine, with several layers of fine Brussels lace at the elbow. She was—unlike her husband—out-of-doors in a garden, carrying a small trug full of a flowering vine and some orchard fruits. How was it possible, thought Elizabeth, that there could be two such similar couples in all of Christendom as were the elder d'Estrouvilles and Darcys? Allowing for the greater taste for finery of the French, the parents were very alike, indeed. It was not so wonderful, she reflected, that the Comte and her own husband should, therefore, be so alike as well.

Amélie and Elizabeth were amused and delighted with each other, but Georgiana could not be comfortable, feeling that any familiarity on her side would lead the Comte into false hopes, and the others to assume an understanding, for, as her bother and the Comte returned from their walk, she could discern no evidence that the promised conversation between her brother and the Comte had transpired. At dinner Georgiana was most pointedly the object of the Comte's attention, a fact that did not in any way escape the notice of the dowager or her daughter, and clearly gave no rise in either to the slightest indication of disapprobation. The Comte had slyly contrived to have her seated to his right at dinner, and did so with such a subtle manœuvre that Georgiana was unawares until she was actually in her seat! Georgiana was uncomfortable enough, but the conversation was interesting and amusing to an uncommon degree at the dinner-table, and after the third or fourth course had been cleared away, she ventured a syllable or two of her own. She and Amélie played and sang after dinner. The Comte joined them at the end; in a beautiful baritone, he made a delightful third for "Trois Beaux Canards." As he walked her to the stairs shortly afterwards and handed her the light, Georgiana could find no reason to believe that the much wished-for conversation between the Comte and her brother had taken place, after the ladies had withdrawn following supper that evening. She was not mistaken, for a knock on her bedchamber door shortly after she had retired admitted Mr. Darcy.

"Georgiana, do I disturb you? May I come in?" Georgiana replied that she was only writing some letters, and that he was welcome. "I do remember that I agreed to speak to the Comte on your behalf, to inform him that there was no possibility of an attachment forming between you. I have not yet done so, as you may have since found your opinion alterable, and there might, after all, be a chance for his happiness. He speaks of you so properly, Georgiana, with such gentle hope and ardent admiration. I wonder whether there exists such another gentleman of equal taste, judgement, and intelligence. I see that your cheeks colour at this speech, but I must continue. If any possibility exists that you might, in time, grow to love him, I would ask that you permit me to stay my errand. You must sometime contemplate the possibility of finding someone worthy of your love and esteem. What is your wish? Do you release me to abandon my promise, at least for the present?"

"Perhaps you are right, Brother," she replied quietly, "but I cannot say with certainty that I *would* find happiness with the Comte, or he with me. I know, dearest Brother, that you believe yourself to be acting in my best interests, and that you would always wish my happiness in marriage, as in all else. For such a change, I would need to feel secure of such an unusual share of happiness to offer even partial recompense for quitting you and Elizabeth, and Pemberley. For no other reason, being settled so far from my home and everything I love would render such felicity impossible."

Darcy looked closely at his sister as she spoke these final words, trying to see any hesitation in them, but Georgiana met his gaze very earnestly,

"I understand that you might wish it otherwise, but I ask you, as one who stands in place of my father, to speak with the Comte as soon as you have occasion. I feel we are only compounding the evil by remaining here under false apprehensions. Certainly, Brother, the kindest thing we can do is depart."

Darcy asked if he might postpone the interview with the Comte until the day following the next so as appear less uncivil; they had agreed to stay some days, and such a precipitate departure must justly cause offense. Georgiana saw that he was perfectly right; she had no wish to be unkind to anyone, and such a delay could not be material. She was sanguine, also, that her brother had long wished to inspect the Comte's plantations; surely, it was selfish of her to put such an opportunity out of his power, now that they were actually at Belle Aire—he asked for so very little in the way of accommodating his own pleasures and was for-ever solicitous of her own comfort and happiness. In short, Georgiana could not refuse her brother such a trifling delay, and they parted with the agreement that he would speak as soon as he found the proper occasion.

As soon as Darcy left the room, Georgiana allowed herself to sink down onto the chair in front of the dressing table, staring at her own reflection and trying to keep herself from shaking. Her brother was doing what he saw as his duty, she reflected over and over again; he could not know how cruelly his words had wounded her, when he accused her as never having thought of love. At some length, she again could be mistress over the tumult in her heart and her head, and determined that no-one should perceive her dread of being in the Comte's presence, in his house, at his table, and worst of all, in his heart. She took no pleasure in his suit, and, even less—if such a thing were possible—in his certain disappointment. "Oh!" thought Georgiana. "Would to Heaven that I could wish myself back at Pemberley, in my own rooms with Mademoiselle Blanche, with my books and my music. How content I would be for-ever, and never wish to stir beyond the village!"

The following days at the *château* were much like the previous: the gentlemen rode out to view the Comte's plantations and farms, fished, and discoursed, and the ladies drove out in the Phaeton to view Belle Aire's large park, walked in the gardens, or staid within the *château*, talking and admiring. The last day, however, they were accompanied by the Countess, and were, therefore, obliged to take the Comte's barouche. With six horses, it was impossible to travel the paths winding through the park, so the Countess indicated to the coachman he was to make a route through the surrounding countryside. There, amidst vineyards and orchards, yellow-green seas of ripening grain, and cows grazing in deep pastures, the dowager Comtesse continually pointed out, with an obvious pride, the improvements made by father and son. The villages were well-kept and prosperous, and the cottages were in significantly better order than any others Elizabeth had seen *en route*. Everywhere there was evidence of the d'Estrouville family's liberality and sense, their pride as land-lords, and their ability as farmers. Never since leaving England had Elizabeth seen such industry and abundance. Indeed, she was put in mind of her own first view of Pemberley, and the awakening of appreciation for her future husband's abilities, his attention to the land, his deep regard for the families in his care.

Elizabeth's succeeding thought was less agreeable, but equally reasonable: it was quite probable the present tour had been expressly contrived by *la mère très invaluable* to shew Georgiana the extent of the Comte's estates and the wealth that derived from such a number of

large

large, prosperous farms. Obviously, the Comte's partiality to Georgiana had been communicated to the mother, if not the sister. Elizabeth was sorry that there were additional people who would now be involved in the coming disappointment. But, she reflected, the Comte had been somewhat precipitate in relating his intentions, and surely it must always be considered as possible that a woman will not return a man's regard, simply because he has formed such a preference in his own mind. As eligible and respectable as was the Comte, Georgiana's circumstances did not make it *necessary* for her to accept him, and certainly Georgiana should be free to determine and follow her own inclination. As highly as Elizabeth regarded the Comte, she valued more highly still Georgiana's independence of thought and action, and the hand of Providence that had made such an independence possible. She and Jane had been the beneficiaries of extraordinary fortune in securing the husbands of their choice, both Mr. Darcy and Mr. Bingley being honourable, liberal, and kind. Georgiana need not rely on the caprice of chance; nay, she was secure of a good home, a loving family, and the high regard of her relations. She could connect herself *if* and *where* she wished—no woman could ask for better blessings. Elizabeth was surprised by the strength of her own silent defence of Georgiana's privilege to determine her own future, especially in light of the exceptionally high esteem in which she—and her husband—held the Comte. Even if the Comte were the paragon they all believed, Elizabeth concluded, Georgiana's happiness had the first claims on herself and Mr. Darcy, and Georgiana had long reached an age at which she was right to direct in what manner she was to be happy.

When Georgiana walked into the dining room, slightly later than the rest of the party, the Comte perceived none of the dread that filled her heart; he noticed only her quiet grace and unaffected sweetness of manner. Amélie could not fail to notice the attention her brother paid to their guest, and the looks he sent in Georgiana's direction were so pronounced, that the rest of the party were forced to speak twice as much, and sound twice as lively to surmount the awkwardness of the evening. Georgiana herself said little, and concentrated on avoiding the Comte's gaze, an almost impossible task considering the frequency with which his eyes were upon her. After dinner, as Mr. Darcy made ready to withdraw from the table with the Comte, Georgiana saw her brother take the Comte's arm as they walked to the Comte's library. He turned, almost imperceptibly and gave her one last questioning look. Georgiana just sadly shook her head, and the gentlemen were gone.

The following morning brought no misgivings. Georgiana awoke with a strong sense of having acted rightly; her reconsideration of the events of the previous night left her in no doubt that she had acted in a manner that was both kind and just. She could never accept the offer of a man whom she did not love. Moreover—she had convinced herself—he could not truly love her; the period of time in which they were become acquainted amounted to little more than a fortnight. Infatuated he might be, but, indeed, he could know little of her character. He had been too precipitate—Georgiana's heart was not one to form an intimacy quickly, nor was it any more likely to soon release a strong attachment. The Comte d'Estrouville, who last night had been so sure of his esteem and love for a woman whom he hardly knew, was surely acting on impulse. He had been swept away himself by feeling it to be love, and his certainty that she would be similarly impetuous could not, in all likelihood, be avoided. Above all else, the well-worn comfort of loving Colonel Fitzwilliam and imagining the happiness of their life together was derived from the certainty that he *knew* her: over many years, he had watched her grow and *knew* her—nay, more: he had to a large measure, formed the woman from the girl. More even than her brother, he had guided her principles, praised her understanding, directed her reading, and applauded her singing and playing when there was no-one else to hear. He knew of her mistakes and triumphs, understood, and was the approver of her quiet habits; he had been the friend who had supported her spirits against loss and loneliness, giving her encouragement, sympathy, and purpose. In the light of day, Georgiana felt the singular peacefulness of mind that accompanies the consciousness of acting honourably, with a resolution as compassionate as it was firm.

The Comte's feelings upon waking, as may be imagined, were altogether of a different description. At long last, he had met a beautiful, intelligent, and gentle woman, whose family were equally engaging and unexceptional as to rank and fortune; his disappointment at having such sources of happiness put out of reach made it many minutes before he could sufficiently compose his mind and his features into a state that would allow him to meet the Darcys with equanimity. The Comte was a reasonable man, however, and his own feelings could not be cause for incivility to his guests. And, whilst he could not yet understand Georgiana's resistance, he could eventually put their separation in a philosophical light, and honour her for sparing his feelings and his pride by not allowing him to involve himself more deeply. Arriving at the breakfast table, he was surprised to find no-one to disturb his reflections. His sister was still out on her morning ride, and the Darcys, he was informed, were not yet come downstairs. Feeling slightly unjust at the sense of relief this information gave his mind, the Comte sat down with a cup of chocolate to wait for his guests.

Georgiana knocked on the door of the Darcys' apartment in order that she might go in to breakfast supported against any awkwardness in meeting the Comte alone. "All will soon be well, Georgiana," smiled Elizabeth. "This will all be over presently."

Darcy looked expressively at Georgiana, who again just shook her head. Darcy then addressed his wife and sister:

"I can well imagine the Comte's feelings at such a time, but I am equally sure of his behaviour as a gentleman. He will press us to stay and assure us that he is not resentful. However, I think it best that we take our leave as soon as all may be in readiness. Do you agree, Lizzy?" he asked, turning to his wife.

"Yes, of course. The Comte must be heartily wishing us all away with every moment."

Georgiana could only stammer out a quiet "Thank you," kissing her brother and sister, they went downstairs to breakfast and to ready their departure.

CHAP. 6.

IF THE DARCY FAMILY had apprehensions of the Comte's displeasure on the following morning, their fears were unnecessary. The Comte met them at breakfast perfectly composed, if not with his usual cheerful urbanity. Darcy received an handsome volume from the Comte upon their leave-taking, *Trait des Arbres Fruitiers*, an exquisitely coloured folio which, when opened, revealed plate after plate of the most wonderfully detailed depictions of every French variety of fruiting tree. The present of the book, thought Elizabeth, was indeed a representation of the Comte himself: cultivated, well-grown, bountiful, and in every way delightful. In deference to Georgiana's feelings, Elizabeth kept her *jeu de mots* to herself; it was just as well, she reflected, as Mr. Darcy might not find this particular example of her wit especially diverting. Having no firm idea of meeting the Comte, but in hopes that they might be able to view Belle Aire during the course of their stay in France, Mr. Darcy had thoughtfully carried along a set of the *Pomona Brittanica*. The Comte had very graciously and gratefully received the reciprocal volumes, and the gentlemen parted in firm friendship.

The Comtesse was not come down from her toilette, but Amélie was returned in time to wish them a pleasant journey. She seemed genuinely sorry to see them go; Elizabeth imagined that she had little other female society excepting her mother, and almost considered asking her to be of their party, at least as far as Geneva. However, in the reflection of the next moment, the requisite lady's maid and two footmen for the return journey would be very inconvenient to accommodate, and it would take some time for her to make ready. Elizabeth could also easily imagine that, in Amélie, Georgiana would be reminded of having occasioned the agreeable Comte distress, only serving to magnify her own. Elizabeth quickly resolved, with much practicality and not a little regret, to leave matters as they stood; within an hour, the Darcy party was down the *allée* and outside the elegant iron gates.

The first minutes of the drive that saw the Darcy family's departure from Belle Aire were characterised by an uneasy silence, and Elizabeth kept a tight hold of Georgiana's hand. In some little time, however, the awkwardness dissipated, and the travellers once again resumed their usual ease of conversation to some degree. Georgiana struggled to keep the appearance of happiness, although she now suffered under a double measure of distress.

"Indeed," Elizabeth reflected to herself as they passed out of Belle Aire, "it was all so very unaccountable how two men, separated by nationality, distance, and history, could be so similar in manners, taste, and even thought! I wonder if we will meet a Swiss Mr. Darcy? It seems more probable than an Italian example, but as I could not conceive of there being another such at all, it is certainly preferable to enter both countries without prejudice."

None of the party wished to return to Paris, all agreeing that its pleasures had been sufficiently tried. The Darcys had no wish to deride the magnificence of Paris, but, to the English, the city was also a magnification of extremes. Where a cravat was high in England, it positioned the head even farther from its shoulders in France. Side-whiskers and beards were becoming almost as verdant as those of the Kossacks; coats were higher and trousers tighter and thinner; bodices were lower and more tightly circumscribed about the bosom; dresses draped in a gauze diaphanous to the point of near-transparency. On the other hand, Paris was also a place of contradictions: a residence might have the most exquisite silk curtains and furniture, but the floor of the same was greasy and unswept; the most delicious food was served by filthy hands, and cooked in a room adjacent to a dung pile of months' accumulation. Where there was commerce, it had not the character of rational intercourse, but was a tumult of activity; the alternative to the disorder of daily business was a perverse and willful idleness. London had its poor, certainly, but it was not obvious to any of the English in France that the French peasantry were materially better off than had been their lot in the time of Marie Antoinette. And, as it was everywhere around them evident, where law ruled in England, France—and most particularly Paris—was governed by excess: of wealth, influence, display, and a disdainful disregard for the comfort of their fellow creatures, and certainly no concern for their censure. The

French seemed to live by only one creed: immoderation. To the English observer, such excess was the antithesis of good-breeding and set every rule of civility at variance; yet, there was no denying that the French were exquisite in their art, fashion, and architecture.

However, other things considered, it was the indescribable filth emanating from all directions, the wretched combination of odours, and the appalling condition of the streets of Paris that were to send the party in the direction most opposite. The alteration to their original plan led Mr. Darcy to express a desire to visit the vineyard of *Château d'Yquem*, below Bordeaux. This made for a lengthy deviation across the country, but Mr. Darcy was of the opinion that the delights of such a detour would well-compensate for the additional days of travel. At least two of the three travellers began to recover their humour and spirits in the prospect of testing the best examples of the French wine, and the wine-cellars were reputed as worth a visit in themselves. The guidebooks and Mr. Darcy's atlas were again consulted, and the family set off in the direction of Pouilly, fifteen posts distant, by the expedient of a detour southward.

This revised itinerary also permitted a visit to the region of Arcy below Auxerre. *Chesterfield's Letters* had brought Mr. Darcy strongly in mind of his late father, whose ancestry could be traced back to the French nobility of William the Conqueror's time. Darcy's father had traced his line as far back as the time of the Conquest, when a Norman knight, one Guillame d'Arecai, was granted a baronetcy and given a number of manors in the north of England for services to the new English king. Whilst several possibilities for the origination of the D'Arcy line existed in France, including Orsay near Versailles, and Arcy in Manche, the late Mr. Darcy had been firmly of the opinion that his family had originated in the Burgundy region of the Yonne. Darcy accordingly desired to visit the region of Champaigne, which was where, by repute, his family were originated. The late Mr. Darcy had, however, never visited the area, giving the change of plan an air of Walpole's serendipity.

"Every thinking man must have his portion of regrets," said Mr. Darcy, "but the one most affecting to my mind is that you never met my father. He was the kindest of fathers and the best of men. When I visited Europe as a young man, I was little interested in my ancestry, but now my situation and feelings are so wholly different, that I would very much like to honour my late father's memory by visiting the area and discovering such as remains of the Darcy history." Mr. Darcy, not

often 49

often given to sentimentality, looked at Elizabeth earnestly and asked if she had any disinclination to the change of route. She responded to the seriousness of his tone, "Mr. Darcy, I would be pleased and honoured for the opportunity to see the place of your family. Each time you and Georgiana speak of your father, it grieves me that I did not know him—and your mother, of whom you speak so respectfully. Such a visit would make France more than just a new country to me; it is the history of the two people I hold most dear."

In the opportunity to better see the countryside, the Darcys found their deviation from the usual tour route extremely pleasant. Leaving Belle Aire by the southerly roads leading out from Paris, the Darcys found them to be wide and smooth, some with even the convenience of paving in the centre. The latter had the effect of producing a disagreeable clatter of noise, but certainly made the job of the horses much easier, and the journey faster. They passed through the villages of Villejuif and Fromenteau, where the country was become especially delightful. Travelling along the Seine, and passing through pretty villages and by classically stiled broken columns marking the half-leagues along the road, they caught glimpses of fine *châteaux* amongst the vineyards on the hillsides, interspersed amongst the plantations. They stopt for the night at Essone, a village remarkable for nothing of note. The next day brought them through Chailly and to the dense forest of Fontainebleau, which was superbly lush and fine.

However, the verdant countryside also forced the Darcys to chuse between the unhappy alternatives of opening the carriage blinds to view the surroundings and breathe the fresh, cool forest air—simultaneously being devoured by the swarms of insects which ceaselessly surrounded the carriage—or closing the windows, depriving their senses, but sparing their skin. Elizabeth expressed her concern for poor Mr. Harmon, the under-coachman, and the footmen, all forced to endure the relentless plague of insects, whilst Georgiana replied that the horses were suffering as well, and they had neither great-coats nor livery to protect them. Mr. Darcy agreed, suggesting that they put the windows up, and unfasten them every now and again to see if the time or temperature had any effect on the inconvenience. Adding insult to injury, foregoing any attempt to sleep in the confines of the forest and the cloud of pests, they continued on, passing Fontainebleau, driving on until the light of day and their horses were become exhausted.

As there was no town of any significance on the road before Pont-sur-Yonne—yet another twenty miles distant—the Darcys were compelled to stop for the night at a dirty little village called Moret. The insects being no less numerous or voracious within than without, they collected their things before the first light and left as expeditiously as two large carriages full of people and their belongings could do.

Even at this hour, the women were already washing linen in the river, beating the cloathes with wooden mallets to clean them. They knelt along the stream on the large rocks that formed the shore, spreading their brightly coloured garments on the bank behind to dry in the sun. The costumes of the women working along the stream were otherwise unremarkable, except for being noticeably dirty. The effort spent in the washing seemed all but invisible on the cloathing of the washers.

In the distance, across the river, was a mill, with its grain-store rising above the mill-house and its weir. They passed by donkeys, so laden with rushes that only their faces and hooves could be seen. The pretty river of the Yonne was not enough to rescue the landscape to any degree of the picturesque; the land was again become flat and undistinguished by any pretty or interesting feature, and their road reverted, accordingly, to the detestable straightness that made them think fondly of the graceful, green roads of England. Even the vineyards were reduced to variations of sameness.

The one distinguishable feature of this country that caused some remark amongst the three was the gardens along both sides of the road, filled with every imaginable growing food, and unprotected from the travellers along the wayside by any form of enclosure. Elizabeth wondered aloud what would be the consequences attendant upon leaving comestibles in so unguarded a state in England, to which Georgiana replied,

"Would not you agree that this practice persists because the harvest of their neighbours is equally vulnerable?"

"But what of travellers? They must be as honourable as everyone living hereabouts, or the numbers of people we have seen passing along the road would deplete the gardens entirely, removing every edible thing the moment it was ready to be eaten."

Mr. Darcy concluded, "It must be their general understanding of the consequences of pilferage, and unwillingness to pay such a price as would be required by enclosures and vigilance. I would expect that there is some theft, but perhaps it is not so excessive as could not be regarded by them as a form of alms." No-one wished to oppose such a satisfactory conjecture, and the French of the Yonne were pronounced to be exemplars in their charity, if less than admirable in their exteriors.

They journeyed through Joigny and thence to Auxerre, where there was a fine cathedral and—by repute—a most excellent inn. Elizabeth was pleased to be staying at L'Hôtel du Leopard, which yielded some variety in animal, if no other amenity. The *aubergiste* was very particular to relate to the Darcys that Buonaparte had staid at his establishment on his road from Elba to Paris, although it was unclear to the English how this history should serve in any way as inducement for their custom. The inn, however, was as creditable as its reputation, being clean and well-attended. This blessing was felt in its entirety, the family grateful, indeed, to have left the infinity of insects behind them, and relieved to have a comfortable inn for their requisite halt of travel on the Sabbath.

Their first breakfast in Burgundy made ample recompense for all of the poor Les Boeufs, consisting in mounds of ripe fruits and melons, lovely fresh eggs and butter, and the French café, wonderfully strong and crowned with cream. Owing partly to its proximity to Arcy, and, to a greater degree than was enunciated, to the wisdom learnt through their experience of the varying degree of quality of French accommodations, they tarried some few days in Auxerre, making day-journeys to the small villages of Vermenton and Véselay, examining various church registers and any other ancient documents they could discover that might illuminate Mr. Darcy's ancestry, but to no avail. Mr. Darcy and his sister were disappointed, but not surprised at the dearth of records to have survived the vicissitudes of more than seven centuries. However, Mr. Darcy did remark, and the ladies agreed, that record-keeping in England was superior to the efforts of the French. Here, again, Georgiana was ready to excuse the French, saying that the English had been more fortunate in having a single monarchy since William the First, whereas the French had been subject to a more tumultuous history, including English and Austrian dominion, the several houses of the Capetians and Valois, the centuries-long struggles amongst the Ducs of Burgundy, Orléans, Bourbon, and Berry, and culminating in the most recent insult to the history of France.

"This valley of the Yonne appears remarkably like the English county of Surrey," said Elizabeth, "in this neighbourhood of large plantations of woods; however, I wonder that the trees are not so large as in England. Surely the climate is not to answer—it must be that the climate is much warmer than even Surrey."

Georgiana replied, reading from one of her travel-books, that the "trees of this area near-by Paris are cut, often so soon as their fifth summer, and, after being laid that autumn and cut into logs over the winter months, are sent thence to be consumed by the ubiquitous hearths of Paris."

"That plan is far from the optimum," opined Mr. Darcy. "Should they delay their depredations another few years, the tree will have doubled in weight, and there would be twice the amount of fuel, for only a little more delay. And, the succeeding planting will have a longer growth, so as to delay the subsequent harvest by the same half-period of time, again, as the initial harvest. I cannot see any advantage to this method; indeed, it appears—by my reckoning—to yield the least wood for proportionately the greater wait, and greatest use of labour in its harvest and preparation. There is some great mismanagement here, and I cannot fathom any reasonable explanation for their practise."

Pastures of sheep and goats were interspersed with forests. There appeared to be few cows, except for an occasional farmer's cow, and remarkably few pigs. Again, Mr. Darcy was not complimentary of the farms in the area: "All of the animals are in poor condition, especially given the grasses of the present season; the pigs particularly. With the French penchant for consuming the widest possible variety of victual, including"—he added with some disgust—"frogs, snails, and horses, I can only speculate that there is precious little remaining to sustain the swine to a more desirable size."

The *aubergiste* notwithstanding, the people in these parts were well-disposed to the Bourbon restoration. The Burgundians had little in the way of praise for the tumultuous days of Buonaparte, generally preferring peace and plenty, and not being overly concerned with the course of national events except as related to their own prosperity.

The landscape was now changed to open, ploughed fields, mainly corn. Other than a few women spinning on distaffs within their own doorways (which Elizabeth commented to Georgiana, she had never seen anyone use before, spinning wheels being ubiquitous throughout England), the area appeared almost uninhabited. The road was only occasionally shared by waggons, mostly pulled by oxen—yoked most curiously to the head—and sometimes by mules drawing a diligence. Passing the villages toward Bourges, the Darcys at last began to see more people, walking to or fro, or working in the fields. Some of the better-dressed peasants rose up in greeting as the carriages passed, and the gentlemen very courteously removed their caps as the ladies went by. Paradoxically, these same villages were also where the less-respectable attacked their carriages in droves—without the slightest proof of any delicacy or restraint—begging with a ferocity that was as relentless as it was disagreeable. The Darcys had been counselled by their inn-keeper to give nary a *sou* to these hordes, as doing so would only increase the violence and duration of their assault. At times, the clamour became so importunate that they were obliged to fasten-up the blinds of the chaise.

Elizabeth remarked, in large measure just to be saying something to distract them all from the discomfort and embarrassment caused by the indigents, "These cottages are done-up well enough, but I have not seen a single one which appears as neat or cheerful as the villagers' houses of the southern parts of England. There are no inviting paths, nor quaint cottages surrounded within pretty gates and borders, and here the weather must be much more congenial to gardening—certainly it is warmer here than it is even in southern England."

"Yes, Lizzy," Georgiana replied, "yet whilst I agree with the general observation, I venture to suggest that the French have the reciprocal advantage in being more concerned with people than with things. Their easy, sociable stile of sitting and talking whenever possible certainly does not lend itself to the exertions necessary for the establishment and maintenance of decoration, either permanently to their houses, or in the more transitory pleasures of a flower-garden."

"I can more easily forgive their preference for the pleasures of society above the labour a garden requires, than I am able to credit the general disrepair of the houses themselves. It would seem that a common attention to the condition of one's house is not an optional labour; it is necessary to prevent a rapid and total decline, not only to the house, but the comfort of its inhabitants. I agree that the open, easy manner of the French is very pleasant, but I would think a *little* effort in the way of repair would not require the extinction of leisure and amusement!"

Mr. Darcy was more concerned with the politics of the French people. Stopping at one of the posting-houses, he fell into conversation with a *voiturin*, who—despite the general views of his country-men—remained staunchly attached to the idea that Buonaparte would someday return. He indicated that he had carefully laid his green coat and insignia in a trunk, in the eventuality that the young son would return to reclaim France and the world. His adherence was perhaps more understandable in the history he related of having driven the returning Emperour in his flight back to Paris from Elba, and had been spoken to in the most courteous and respectful manner by Buonaparte himself!

Mr. Darcy was also surprised to see cows ploughing here, and remarked that is was very hard upon the beasts to have to bear and raise

their

their calves, provide milk, and work the fields. Elizabeth rejoined that there appeared to be no limit to the exertions the French required of *all* their females, human and otherwise. Other disagreeable observations followed: the cutlery was compared unfavourably with that of England; the plate deplorably dirty and unpolished; the china-ware deemed coarse and of a disgusting shape and clay; the carriages pronounced ugly, badly constructed, and inelegant; even the very locks upon the doors and their hinges did not escape a severe judgement. Viewed by more rational eyes, the Darcys were beginning to suffer—as yet unconsciously—from that ever-vigilant malaise of the traveller: home-sickness.

After a night at Sanserre, they stopt for a day at Bourges. The roads were quiet and the coach travelled quickly, taking them through the ancient towns of Châteauroux, Limoges, Perigueux, and St. Emilion; and before another a week of travel, they reached Bordeaux. Having been recommended to an inn by an English family they had met at Châteauroux, they took rooms at Le Marechal de Richelieu. The hôtel was clean and commodious, the servants efficient and courteous, and the dinners a superb selection of *releves, entrées* and *entremets,* for which the French were justly famous. The bill of fare, whilst not rivalling that of Véry's, included an astonishing assortment of *côte grillé, ragoût de veau, poulet rôti,* and *bouillabaisse,* followed by beautifully arranged selections of fresh seafood from the Bordeaux sea-coast. In France, it was considered essential that a selection of excellent wine accompany the supper, and here was the Darcys' only disappointment. Mr. Darcy was of the opinion that the wines from the Bordeaux region were previously vastly superior, and imputed their decline to the ravages of the Emperour, a surmise in which he was to be proved mistaken.

Bordeaux was, thought Elizabeth, one of the most handsome cities in France, complete with cathedral, quays, and Roman antiquities. Seated on the bank of the peaceful Garonne on a particularly mild day, Elizabeth took the opportunity to write an over-due letter to Jane, who, by now, must have welcomed her fifth child into the Bingley family.

14th May
Bordeaux, France

My dearest Jane,

I write without certain knowledge of how you are, but I am hopeful that the arrival of the newest Bingley was as easy and uneventful as in the past, and that you recover quickly with the kind assistance of Kitty and my father. My impatient desire to see my new niece or nephew must

remain

remain a future pleasure, for there are yet some months of travelling before I am able to dispute with you over the largest share of similarity in feature.

How I have wished for your sound advice and comfort these past few weeks! Although I have Georgiana's permission to pass on word of events concerning ourselves, I wish that you will keep this letter and its contents to yourself (excepting of course Mr. Bingley), for it is not my story to tell. Pray do not be alarmed; we are all of us well, and have escaped our latest scrape without any permanent disability.

We arrived without incident and settled in Paris at once. Parisian society was much to our taste, although the best of meat requires a change to maintain its savour. Having soon made some acquaintance in Paris, we spared no effort in behaving like proper Frenchmen with every night engaged: grand dinners, philosophical *soirées* and, of course, the balls. Georgiana and I charmingly assumed the onerous burthen of being even more amiable than we have done in England and, excepting time spent in the arduous task of procuring the necessities of gowns and the assorted finery so as to appear *a la Français*, we have done little else but stroll down the splendid avenues, and eat every imaginable delicacy in disgraceful quantities.

Our circle of acquaintance widened further at the event of a large private ball, and it was here that we were introduced to the dowager Comtesse d'Estrouville and her son, le Comte. The dowager is a lady of refinement and elegance, clever, well-read, lively, witty, and altogether engaging, although I would venture that her speech is apt to be too frank, and her character too ingenuous, for someone of her rank in English society. Her son has been a correspondent of my husband's for some time; the Comte is tall, well-formed, confident, and unassuming, an excellent sportsman and accomplished conversationalist, with an easy air and engaging manners. I need not tell you—for of course you will have guessed—that he was soon violently in love with Georgiana. A series of engagements brought us together, and the friendship between Mr. Darcy and himself led him to make us an invitation to his country estate of Belle Aire, some ways outside Paris. We generously accepted, of course, and spent a few days there with his sister, whilst Mr. Darcy and the Comte fished, and went over the plantations. It soon became clear that an offer was inevitable, despite such a little time passing since their first meeting—if our Comte has a failing, it is a propensity for celerity in both thought and action. I well remember Mrs. Gardiner's dictum that a man cannot find himself 'violently in love' after a short period of time—

that the phrase itself is become hackneyed and worthless—but violently in love the Comte believed himself to be. Mr. Darcy was charged with the unenviable task of pre-empting the Comte's addresses by speaking to him of Georgiana's certain refusal. We left the estate the next morning in a prodigious hurry, as I am sure you can easily believe.

I know your heart will be in agonies for the Comte, dear feeling creature that you are, but do not trouble yourself. There was no denying that his pride and feelings were hurt a great deal. He truly believed he loved her; we are all quite sure of that. But whilst a fortnight's acquaintance may be enough time for him to regret the loss of what might have been, his disappointment, I feel sure, will be got over in time, for he was likely more in love with the *idea* of love than the match itself. Georgiana worries herself a great deal over his disappointment, but begins to recover her spirits, for she knows she acted rightly and quickly to spare his feelings, but I do believe that she would willingly bear the Comte's resentment and the world's censure rather than marry where she does not love. I confess to being just a little disappointed, especially once we had been shewn 'round Belle Aire; it is a beautiful, bountiful country, and—as astonishing as it seems—a French version of Pemberley. Surely, it cannot be wrong to wish those we love all the blessings which we ourselves enjoy?

We are now come into the region of Auxerre, where we find yet more surfeits of food and varieties of wine. I wonder Buonaparte was able to march as far as St. Denis, let alone all over Europe, as fond as the French are of eating, drinking, and all manner of entertainments. As I said we might, we staid near to Arcy, exploring the area in search of any evidence of Mr. Darcy's family, but sadly were unable to discover anything.

By my husband's express desire, pray tell Mr. Bingley that we have written for an appointment at Château d'Yquem, an engagement that I believe Mr. Darcy is far more eager to keep than any we attended in Paris. By my own desire, pray do not mention the food or the wine to Kitty, for she will imagine nothing but our collective and immediate extinction.

We continue on to Switzerland after Lyon, and let us hope that we have learnt to be content to go on as we are, and encounter no love-lorn Marquis, grief-stricken Ducs, &c.

I send this with our sincerest hopes this finds you in health and happiness, and please give our love and good wishes to all.

Your affectionate sister,

ELIZABETH DARCY

Elizabeth was daily charmed by the manners of the French men, "They are always raising their hats to anyone met on the road, or giving some other expression of good-will. I am not nearly so complimentary about the affectionate way in which the French men greet one another," she continued. "To my English way of thinking, it seems excessively cordial the way the men embrace one another and kiss. However, this last peculiarity in habit is, however, not the greatest of my astonishments thus far along our road; Mr. Darcy, have you not observed the custom here-abouts of the farm labour being done entirely by women?" The country women were sowing, hoeing, bundling stalks, mowing the early crops, reaping, manuring, plowing, drawing carts, fetching water, tending to the livestock, and all like labour, which, in England, would have been done by men, with the exception of the universal employment at harvest of both sexes, children, the aged—all those able to lend their hands to the task.

"Whilst their women are labouring to provide for their entire subsistence," she continued, "the French men sit under the trees at the side of the field, idly smoking, drinking wine, and watching their women-folk at work. The old French expression of chivalry, '*Dieu, le Roi, les Dames*' seems entirely *malapropos*.

"Most unaccountably, the women seem very happy to be thus employed, singing and talking; as soon as they hear anyone on the road, they immediately leave off their labours, calling greetings and waving, and continuing to watch the carriages as long as they are in sight. The men take as little notice of what is passing along the road, as they do of the exertions of their women."

"I could more easily countenance such a reversal of labour, if the men were at some useful occupation, instead of lounging about under the trees. However, equally incongruous—to my notion of justice— is the mismanagement of men at the various tasks that normally fall to the lot of housemaids and chamber-maids: carelessly making up the beds, and doing what inconsequential cleaning is committed upon the premises. The men might be more effectively employed in the fields, and we might have clean rooms and properly made-up beds, were the situation reversed; having said as much—looking at the men sitting idly by—the result may be that the women undertake the labour within and without of doors, and the men do *nothing at all*," said Mr. Darcy.

"Indeed," began Elizabeth, "it seems very hard that the women should be subject to the drudgery of hard labour whilst the men sit near-by. The fields appear to be in good order and productive under the care

❦ of

of the women. Perhaps, Husband, women are not so incapable in the agricultural arts as is generally believed."

"I have far less difficulty, Lizzy, believing women capable of any occupation that does not depend upon simple, brute strength, than believing men—certainly the men we have observed in such an employment—capable of properly performing any task usually ascribed to the domestic sphere, such as the utility of the male sex as house-keepers. Under the latter arrangement, the rooms are invariably filthy, the beds and other furnishings untidy, and the men responsible for the dirt and disorder appear, universally, to have a 'live and let live' principle with respect to the armies of vermin in residence."

"To be sure," continued Elizabeth, "the condition of the rooms is positively at variance with any notion of real cleanliness and comfort. However, I would more willingly excuse their inattention to the plight of the rooms, were I spared the pointless intrusion by the *hommes de chambre*, who seem to regard it as their appointed duty to drift in and out of our rooms at all hours, to little or no effect but the discomfiture of those who are their guests."

Georgiana simply wished herself back in Derbyshire.

CHAP. 7.

THE DARCYS TRAVELLED to the southwest environs of Bordeaux, touring the seaside and the vineyards before turning eastward, passing through the *châteaux* of d'Yquem and de Roquetaillade, and the towns of Bergerac, Tulle, Vichy, and Lyon, stopping again at the latter for several days, before continuing onto Geneva. The descent into Bordeaux was magnificent: the river made a broad, wide bend, across which rose the spires of the cathedral. The Garonne was as wide again as the Thames, and the opposite bank of this splendid crescent was densely framed by woods, vineyards, and villas. Construction was begun for a bridge of immense length spanning this section of the river—which was later learnt to have been the result of a contest as to whether such a structure could even be devised, or if the Garonne would continue to flow unsurmounted, as it had for centuries innumerable. There were the beginnings of buildings very grand in scale along the Quai des Chartrons, and the Chapeau-Rouge was so complete as to justly deserve the appellation as the finest street in Europe, with its theatre and the exchange. Indeed, everything in Bordeaux was built on a grand scale: elegant promenades and imposing public buildings were regular sights throughout the city. The cathedral was a superb example of the Gothic, and was, as Abbeville, the construction of the English during the time they ruled the country.

The Darcys attended the theatre during their stay, and saw Mr. Talma in the rôle of Nero; Darcy remarked that his stile of acting was much akin Mr. Kean's, save perhaps the superior voice of Talma, which was shewn to greater effect in the soliloquies of the character. They took a voyage in the steam-boat to Pavillac to see the great confluence of the Dordogne and the Garonne. Georgiana read from her book that, many years previous, there had arisen a disputation between the partisans of each river to decide the appellation of the united stream; at last, the reasonable La Gironde was adopted, being the name of the region common to both rivers. Perhaps most surprisingly to all the Darcys, it was found to be nearly impossible to procure good-quality claret—and this in Bordeaux! Mr. Darcy discovered—to his extreme disappointment—that the produce of the vineyards was controulled by a few merchants, who found more profit in adulterating the local wines, augmenting the best with an inferior more cheaply had—this admixture judged sufficient for ready sale to the Russians and East Indiamen.

They took a southerly route from Bordeaux to Lyon, to view the Château d'Yquem and its famed vineyard, passing through Bergerac and thence to Mazères, Niversac, and Hautefort to see the lovely Château de Roquetaillade. The countryside about Lyon was become very lush, Mr. Darcy declaring the soil to be very rich, indeed, a fact confirmed by the number of very fine *châteaux* to be seen. They observed a variety of white cattle, again ploughing, but with a very peculiar veil of red hanging from their horns, over their ears and eyes, and concluding in a fringe of tassels. The *accoutrement*, upon enquiry, was said to protect them from the flies. This information led Mr. Darcy to remark that the cattle were better off than themselves, as they had no such deterrent against the continual swarms of biting flies and all other manner of irksome insects. His speech had the salutary effect, however, of reminding the ladies of their veils, which, along with their shawls, gave them some relief, if not universally extensible to quite everyone in the chaise, as Mr. Darcy selflessly declined the use of a bonnet.

"Brother," began Georgiana, "I wonder that no-one has resorted to the expedient of producing a veil to cover the windows. If we had such a contrivance, we could see out of the chaise nearly as well as with the blinds open, allow the breezes, but would be spared the influx of insects."

"Capital idea, Georgiana! Well done, indeed. I have seen blinds made of thin slats, which allow for some visibility, but this is far more preferable. I wonder if we could not find a coach-maker in Lyon or Geneva who could contrive such an inner frame for the veils?"

Mr. Darcy next enquired, "Are the veils permanently affixed to the bonnets? Or are they able to be safely removed?" Georgiana and Elizabeth quickly produced the veils from their bonnets, and Mr. Darcy proceeded to tuck the cloth around the window-frame. In a few minutes, the insects already inside the chaise had disappeared, and the family were as comfortable as if they had never left Derbyshire. Georgiana's "invention," as they called the window-veil, also had the advantage of disallowing some noticeable proportion of the dust.

"I suppose we must extend some sympathy to our veils," said Elizabeth, "but, as we have a choice of cleaning the window-veil or all of our cloathing, as well as the interior of the chaise, I think this vastly preferable. And, if I am not greatly mistaken, we will be able to find a more suitable article of cloth in Lyon, and may repossess our veils with no decrease in comfort."

Mr. Darcy continued to wonder as to why the window-veil had not been thought-of before, when at last his wife opined, "Mr. Darcy, if you had included *ladies* in your deliberations with the coach-maker, we may well have been spared all such inconvenience, assuming—of course—that dear, clever Georgiana were one of your counsellors!" Mr. Darcy was so perfectly satisfied by Elizabeth's explanation that he left off the subject entirely.

The children of Bordeaux were pretty, with plump, apricot-coloured cheeks on their round little faces, and ringlets hanging down about their shoulders, looking altogether healthy, well-tended, and happy. The women wore a very odd head-dress, consisting of a broad, dark beaver hat that looked to be about the size and shape of a soup-plate, under which was a white cap with a starched, tatted brim, and atop which were three long, black plaited ribbands, two framing the face, and one hanging behind. Elizabeth and Georgiana decided that the over-all visage was much more attractive than any description could render it, and Georgiana set to sketching the ensemble. The men wore enormous black hats, low and wide, adorned with a string of red and white baubles; dark blue jackets with waistcoats of various colours; linens shirt open very wide at the throat; and *sabots*, as had the other French peasants. The men and women of the fields were amongst the cleanest and most attractive the Darcys had yet seen; they appeared very content and industrious, and were markedly more civil toward the English than had been the lower citizens of Paris.

Lyon was a thriving city, and after Paris, the most prosperous town in France. The combination of industry and commerce had created a wealth that produced the finest theatre in France, and all of the luxuries of Paris. Looking similar to the city of Bath to the Darcys, in being constructed along the slopes of several prominent hills, Lyon was framed against vineyards, atop which were a number of castle-like constructions, with the Rhône travelling along the base of the hills quite grandly. Opposite was Buonaparte's Grande Place, surrounded by very tall, handsome houses, some of six or seven storeys. There was a great cathedral at Lyons, celebrated for its windows; the nuns walked about the streets in the usual black habits of the Catholick nuns in England, but with a very high wimple, covered about with a black veil, and very long beads, hanging down the length of their robes.

The Darcys hired a very odd type of vehicle, called a *carriole*, to take them to see the great confluence of the Rhône and the Saone, by repute one of the great wonders of Europe. Mr. Darcy exclaimed that the vehicle looked more like a wheeled bedstead than anything else: it had dirty, coarse Hessian curtains, and the seat, looking for all the world like a mattress for the bed, was hung on the inside, upon which the passengers sat back-to-back. This *ensemble* was made complete by a pair of horses greatly ornamented with ribbands and bells, and a coachman scarcely less so in nankeen breeches and polished gaiters, over a pair of unnecessarily yellow shoes. Such a journey would have been insupportable were the sight of the confluence less sublime, with its remarkable contrasts of colour continuing a great way before becoming so combined as to make the separate contribution of each indistinguishable. They were fortunate in that there had been a spring of good rain-fall, so that the two adjoining rivers were well-swollen, and the confluence long and wide.

The Darcys also attended the theatre, and saw a *tragédie*. The theatre was not at all clean, the seats were tatty and ragged—very surprising for such a prosperous city, and a city long-famed for its cloth manufacture—and the stage was the only area within, that had the benefit of candle-light. Despite these deficiencies, the performance was excellent, and the audience respectful and attentive. Mr. Darcy was surprised by the manners and conversation of the merchants and manufacturers, who attended the performance *en masse*, so very unlike those in England. As an Englishman, Darcy could not suppose there was any remarkable difference between the refinement and courtesy of the general populace of Lyon, and the courtiers of Paris or Versailles. He concluded his letter to Mr. Parker, having described the similarities and differences in their methods of farming, with the following:

As you know, with the depredations, first, of the Terror and then of Buonaparte, my own tour did not reach into France, and I went to Italy via a more easterly route through what was, at that time, Wurtemburg, Bavaria, the Tyrol, and the Venetian State; we plan to return to England via the reverse of that route. I add, Parker, as you

are

are such a *devotee* of the theatre, that the productions here in Lyon are generally believed to surpass those in London, and even Paris. The most remarkable difference here amongst the French is the attention paid the performance. Unlike our English audiences who go to the expense and trouble of securing seats merely for the sake of display and conversation, the French are most courteous and pay the actors and the production the highest compliments of silence and attention. I believe that, on the whole, despite the general French character of *joie de vivre,* young and old, scholars to the fashionable of both sexes, hasten to the serious theatre in preference to all other diversions. It is somewhat surprising to find that our far more reserved English society shews less respect for the tragedical subject, whilst the gay French sit in silent gravity, listening to long speeches that would have the English fast asleep, or leaving the place altogether. We English seem to require action on the stage—murder, mayhem, and general pandemonium— whilst the French are enthralled with sentimentality and fine language. The French have yet another advantage over us as regards their theatre: they have not such a great difference in the appearance and general refinement amongst the various classes, and therefore, characters of people of wealth and fashion are quite credible in those guises, whilst our poor players generally cannot belie they have but one farthing to share amongst themselves. One cannot conceive of meeting an English servant who could easily pass for a man of quality, but in France there are butlers and valets who are so polite, and possessed of such a refinement of manners and taste, that had they the proper *accoutrements,* they would be indistinguishable *de la chose vraie.*

Another remarkable aspect of the French is their closeness in conversation. They speak together in a proximity that would never be comfortable to our English notions. They speak in a loud, animated manner, and do not exhibit any of the reserve we would deem the hallmark of good-breeding. Yet, I do not find the French to be in any way more impertinent or disrespectful, simply more lively in their speech and address—my wife is quite taken with their spirit, but then Elizabeth by her own vivacity could well pass for a native here.

On the more serious subject of industry, I cannot help remarking that here is another marked dissimilarity. We English value industry, and regard the resources and time which are perforce expended in the defence of our country as a distraction—albeit a most necessary one—from the pursuit of industry. Commerce and industry are regarded by us as the most efficient means of improving the condition of the labouring class, and, as such, is conceived as a general good; the prosperity generated by improved methods in manufacturing and agriculture are employed for the advantage of *all* Englishmen. I believe that the rise of a Buonaparte was possible because of the French view that industry has no purpose other than the expedient of war. It seems hardly possible, but I cannot imagine that the lowest classes of France are materially better off than under the *Ancien Régime*; to-day they have neither bread nor cake, viz., I do not believe the present poverty and misery of the poor of France to be the consequence of the *fall* of the Empire. If misery and want did not rise with the accumulated riches and opulence of L'Emporeur, the condition of the French people certainly did not improve as a consequence. I do not mean to set myself up as a scholar, having read only the usual fare of the British school-boy, but from all that I have read and heard, if there exist conditions in England as I see in all but the most prosperous of cities in France, we would deserve the censure of the World.

We depart this day toward Geneva, where I look forward to the pleasure of sending you descriptions of their customs as regards above,
　　Yr. svt.,

Fitzwilliam Darcy

P.S. My wife notes that I have not sent our respects and compliments to Mrs. Parker, and so—by her express desire—do so, with my apologies.

Leaving Lyon, the Darcys decided to take the southerly route through Chambéry and Annecy, so as to avoid the steep Rhône valley to the north. The route was somewhat longer, but Mr. Darcy and Mr. Harmon reckoned that the extra distance would be more agreeable to the horses than the shorter, steeper road. Passing St. Laurent des Mures, groves of very fine chestnuts, walnuts, and all manner of fruit trees appeared, as the land changed from flat fields to gentle hills and woods. Mr. Darcy was very favourably impressed by the local custom of plaiting the grape-vines through the fruit trees, forming a kind of festoon from tree to tree. Mr. Darcy opined that this plan was not only most judicious in its use of the land, but that the task of picking the fruit from the trees and the vines might be combined, to the great advantage of saving labour. They stopt for lunch and to bait the horses in Bourgoins, where they met a German family travelling toward Lyon. In conversing with them, Georgiana learnt that the French and Savoyards had been latterly spoilt by the legions of free-spending English, with the consequence that the inns on the road to

Chambéry and Montmeillant had adopted a most dishonourable custom of over-charging *les milords anglais*. Georgiana was advised to assume the nationality of a German in order to avoid the inconvenience. As if to prove a point already conceded, they found themselves shamefully over-charged for a quite modest repast.

"Husband," said Elizabeth as they resumed their road, "the country hereabouts is lush and rambling. Do not you think it much like the south-western parts of England we have visited? Georgiana, dearest?" The villages, amongst great plantations of mulberry trees, were populated by local women sitting on their door-steps with their distaffs, working silk and flax, all talking and laughing together as they laboured. "The inhabitants seem healthy enough, in the main parts, but do you notice those very large tumours some have about the throat?"

"The malady you see is evidence of the *goître*, Elizabeth, and is most regrettably associated with a great increase in idiocy in the local inhabitants, both being blamed upon the waters that serve this area," said Georgiana, shewing Elizabeth a drawing in one of her travel-books, which illustrated the head of a woman with an enormous bump the size of a large apple protruding from her throat.

"As if this unfortunate distinction were not enough," cried Elizabeth, motioning to a woman on horse-back who was at that moment passing by their carriage, "that peasant woman is riding *astride*! Such an odd appearance this custom gives to the silhouettes of these women *and* their skirts; how very unbecoming an appearance!"

Mr. Darcy admitted the sense of the arrangement. "However much I willingly agree with your strictures on silhouette, I am sure it is a *safer* method than the absurd practise of riding side-saddle, to the detriment of the ladies' spines as well as those of their horses. Usually the fashion will follow the royal lead, and so I will recall the portrait of none other than Marie Antoinette, entirely clad in a suit of armour—no less— sitting astride a charger."

"There is much about poor Queen Marie Antoinette's conduct that would not bear close scrutiny, and correspondingly many *habits* that a woman might not, with propriety, emulate," rejoined his wife, with a smile. Despite the custom amongst the French women, neither Elizabeth nor Georgiana could conceive how such a posture could be bearable, and must preclude all comfort, in addition to all modesty. Elizabeth had attempted to envision the elegant Parisian *mademoiselles* astride, but could get no further in her own imagination than Jane's graceful figure in her habit on the white mare she had ridden on that decisive visit to

Netherfield some ten years before. *À chacun son goût,* indeed!

After Beauvoisin, they were detained by the customs-men, as they were now entering the Savoy, and were become subject to the laws of the King of Sardinia. Gratefully, the Sardinians were more inclined to be reasonable toward a party of gentle-persons making a tour of pleasure through the King's dominions, and merely questioned Mr. Darcy briefly, peered into the chaise and coach, walking around all sides, taking note of their baggage—actions that Mr. Darcy claimed were merely a feint to give the appearance of *inspecting* to their superiors, who remained diligently within the customs-house.

The weather had turned fully into spring during their travel southward, and the houses and villas began to assume a more Italian appearance. Mr. Darcy noted with approval that, in these steep fields, mules were used to the plough, instead of cows. The cattle now deviated from the all-white cattle of the Charolais, appearing in every shade between black and white, all grazing amidst good pasturage, or standing contentedly by the gates awaiting milking-time. Woods began to overtake tilled fields as the countryside was become increasingly mountainous. The road continued increasingly steep until they reached the summit at Eschelles, a small village that looked as though it would be at any minute swallowed-up by the surrounding mountains. There, it was customary to add two horses to the larger carriages, but none were at liberty, and so an ox was added to each of the carriages before continuing through the mountains. Mr. Darcy and Mr. Harmon were content with the arrangement, noting that, whilst the horse was faster than the ox, and that their carriages were considerably lighter—even under their great burthens of baggage—than were the French coaches, one ox did more work than a pair of horses. Both praised the tempers of the great English horses as being of a nature to endure being yoked with oxen, if necessary, whilst the lighter carriage horses would have reacted violently to the cattle in such close proximity; Elizabeth opining that it was a natural effect of the great conceit of the blood-horses, and the mortification they would feel if seen harnessed to cows. Mr. Darcy and Mr. Harmon re-inspected the under-carriages and made sure that the footmen were alert to drop the drag-irons in a moment, whenever they were wanted.

The road was very good, demonstrating another side of Buonaparte's genius, but the terrain would not admit of a moment's inattention to prevent catastrophe. Just after passing the border, the family came upon an accident which had just then occurred: an heavy coach had been proceeding down one of the steep declinations, when the tattered ropes had suddenly broken, causing a wheel-horse to fall, and the two leaders to scramble to freedom. The carriage had been stopt by the fallen horse, which, surprisingly, seemed to have escaped with only minor injury. By the time the Darcys' carriages had pulled up, one of the postillions was returning up the road with the wayward horses. Mr. Harmon (assisted by Mr. Darcy) asked if they needed any harness-pieces. To Mr. Darcy's surprise, and the utter indignation of Mr. Harmon, the coachman of the other carriage thanked them for their offer, but replied that this was a customary occurrence, and he had plenty of rope with which to make another knot!

At regular intervals the ruined skeletons of all manner of carriages could be seen, having fallen off of the road-side, some with their shafts pointed directly at the powerful current of the Rhône, causing Georgiana to reflect with sadness as she imagined the fate of the horses which had been bound to the shafts. Gratefully, the Darcys reached Chambéry without further incident. Chambéry was the capital of the Savoy and the former residence of Rousseau, where it was still possible to see where he lived so openly and disgracefully with his mistress, M. de Varennes. As they arrived at the ancient capital, it became clear why there was a business in over-charging the English visitors, for at that place joined the roads to Torino, Marseille, and Geneva. It seemed the very crossroads of England, so many English were there, going to one place or another, coming, staying, eating, shopping, and every other activity possible in such a confined place. Their inn was unsatisfactory, and upon entering their rooms for the night, Elizabeth made a comment to the effect that, by this point in their journey, a clean inn was certainly more remarkable than otherwise. They were all become so inured to the French stile of house-keeping, that there was certainly no advantage in dwelling upon so common-place an inconvenience.

Mr. Darcy planned to stay at Chambéry two nights, resting the horses before the final ascents to Geneva, so as to arrive at the latter by Saturday night, as the following day's travel would be necessarily suspended in honour of the Sabbath. That evening, Mr. Darcy discussed the idea of making a short diversion, in order to take in the Grand Chartreuse, a detour southward of about twenty miles. Mr. Harmon had determined it to be exactly *three*-and-twenty miles, and that the road was far more inclined than any they had yet travelled, necessitating at least four days to view the great monastery and its grounds. Mr. Harmon then suggested, if Mr. Darcy were decided upon the detour, he reckoned it made more sense "for the horses" to continue into Grenoble, and thence to Torino. This put the detour out of reach for the present journey, and the three were necessarily to be content with the views afforded by Georgiana's guide-books. In lieu of flying about the tops of the mountains of the Savoy, the Darcys enjoyed a pleasant day of walking about the ancient capital, viewing the path of the Leysse through the town, the cathedral, or the *château* of the Ducs of the Savoy, and its enchanting Ste. Chappelle.

The road along this area was become very shaded and pleasant through the planting of mulberry trees along both sides of the road, and, Mr. Darcy noticed with pleasure, groves of great chestnut trees. Many of the peasant women were seated within their door-ways, employed in spinning silks or working flax for sale to the manufactories in Lyon. There were no men to be seen, either within the doors, in the forests, or out amongst the fields, leading Elizabeth to comment that the men must have staid abed, so as not to disturb the work of their women.

That very afternoon, the Darcys were to experience a small example of the terrors attending upon travellers through those great mountains, as, of a sudden, the postillion riding at the front of the Darcy's chaise disappeared! Mr. Harmon had not fully apprehended what had happened, and had not yet brought the team to an halt, when the postillion's face, *sans chapeau et sans coleur*, suddenly appeared in the window of the chaise! By the time Mr. Harmon had stopt the horses and recovered the postillion from the ladder of the chaise, Georgiana and Elizabeth had regained their breath, and Mr. Darcy was become fully awake and was out of the chaise in an effort to ascertain what had occasioned such an unexpected event. The postillion had apparently fallen asleep—having been constantly employed for the last several days, with only a few hours' rest—and tumbled off, leading Mr. Darcy to remark that the man's method was likely the only way to fall, what with the quiet and steady nature of the draught horses; in the common case, it would have been the *horse* looking inside the carriage. Mr. Harmon assured Mr. Darcy that he would inspect the *voiturins* more carefully in future, and question the inn-keepers more carefully as to the histories of the men before engaging any of them. Unfortunately, as Mr. Harmon spoke no French, it was impossible for him to interrogate anyone, and so Mr. Darcy assumed the blame himself for the present near-catastrophe, and the burthen for avoiding any such *contretemps* in future.

Along their road, they chanced upon a team of very disagreeable mules, urged on to the heights of the fury and violent actions possible within and without the traces, rearing and kicking out in all directions, at the command of their driver, who was alternately shouting and abusing the animals at every step with his whip. After getting safely past the team and the careening waggon, Elizabeth remarked, "I declare myself unable to assign the greater portion of blame amongst that last equipage: the mules who seem to be busy with little else than being awkward, or the driver who seemed as misdirected as his animals."

Georgiana instantly rose to defence of the mules, commenting that a teamster was not fit to drive any beast, if he could not do so quietly, safely, and gently—an opinion to which her brother readily assented: "We are very fortunate in Harmon; he is as careful of the horses as any man. He sees not only to their safe use, but to their health and care—their minds as well as their bodies. Woe betide any of his grooms who are seen being neglectful or otherwise cruel to the beasts. Harmon has brought along the under-coachman very admirably; he is somewhat young for such responsibility, but he is as gentle in his ways as Harmon, and drives the servants' coach very admirably."

"My Dear Mr. Darcy!" agreed Elizabeth, "just think of our sufferings had we been in the hands of the *voiturins* we have seen goading their horses along with an handful of frayed ropes, ceaseless epithets, and their merciless whips! I would never have consented to leave Calais in such a manner as do the French, hazarding their very life and limbs to such commotion. Not to mention," she smiled, "the *inelegance* of their appearance. I am grateful to Mr. Harmon, certainly, but more indebted to you, dear Husband, for all of the diligence and care taken in planning our journey, and the wisdom of your arrangement of horses, carriages, coachmen, and, of course, travelling companions."

The Darcys' journey, excepting the incidents mentioned above, was tolerably pleasant until reaching Switzerland. There, they found post-horses in such scarce supply that they were compelled to hire draught horses taken straight from the fields from the Swiss *voiturins* at an exorbitant cost, and even at those prices, they were often obliged to wait hours for fresh horses to arrive. There was another change: the English and French post-boys rode only between adjacent post-houses, whilst the Swiss *voiturins* preferred to remain with their employers for any distance, and any number of days, requiring that the Darcys feed and house them with their other servants, an additional burthen of expense beyond the already extortionate fees. Mr. Harmon's dissatisfaction with the *voiturins* had other points of confirmation, all of which he enumerated so continually, one listening might have assumed his own

position

position to be in jeopardy from the foreign post-boys, an idea extremely unlikely to have entered the thoughts of his master.

It was Mr. Darcy who called attention to the immediate change in the dress of the inhabitants as they crossed from France into Switzerland, "almost as if opposite sides of the same mountain demanded an opposition of costume." It was with some relief that the Darcys found themselves in Geneva where they, their servants, and their horses could rest before undertaking the road over the Italian Alps. The Darcy family—as planned—reached Geneva late on Saturday afternoon, descending from the mountain to the rocky banks of the river. There was an uncommonly beautiful sunset over the Jura mountains, and several boats on the lake. The vessels were a type of barge, but entirely unlike the English variety: these boats had pointed bows, two forward masts with sails criss-crossed in a most peculiar fashion, six oarsmen rowing whilst standing erect aforeships in front of the cargoes of barrels, and a tillerman at the rear. Mr. Darcy wondered at the curious construction of the vessel, and Georgiana promised him a drawing of the *barques* of Lac Léman, their *voiturins* called them; as Mr. Darcy said it was impossible to describe them in any language he knew.

As they entered their hôtel, they were met by an interminable parade of exiting English, prompting Elizabeth to remark that she felt like a small fish attempting to swim upstream against a strong current. Speaking with a few of the gentlemen, Mr. Darcy understood that these throngs of their countrymen were being turned away, as this hôtel, and *every* other in the city, were full! Enquiring as to what event was precipitating this influx, one gentleman replied in a very tired tone, "Did the gentleman not know that there were above 30,000 English now abroad in Europe? It should not be surprising to expect a considerable portion of them in Geneva, looking for accommodation." As Mr. Darcy always took the precaution of sending ahead for their reception, the *hôtelier* of Les Balances was very gracious, and the Darcys were shewn to a suite of excellent rooms at once, the largest apartment overlooking an expansive view of the Rhône. After sitting down to a very agreeable late supper, everyone was happy to retire. The rooms, although less ornate and somewhat less spacious than those they had recently taken in Paris, were vastly cleaner, and the hôtel in every way better ordered than had been the accommodations in France.

As it was Sunday on the morrow, there was no travelling, and worship at the English church. After such a scarcity of Protestant churches in France, the Darcys were grateful to attend familiar services.

To

To their pleasure, the service was well-conducted, and the singing very good. In the afternoon, the family and some of the senior servants went to the Oratory. Elizabeth noticed Mr. Darcy and Mr. Harmon fast asleep, likely due to their having walked about the town since service; she saw also—with disgust—that it was the custom of the French and Swiss men to expectorate everywhere and frequently, an habit she could not wish to be more generally prevalent.

There was a cold collation for dinner, and, following tea, the evening was spent chiefly in correspondence. Elizabeth Darcy wrote her father a long letter on her impressions of the peoples and places they had seen:

Sunday
Hôtel Les Balances, Geneva

DEAR FATHER,

It is the Sabbath-day and so our self-permitted intrusion into the privacy of our neighbours is temporarily suspended. We have, as you see above, reached Geneva. It is a relief to come into Switzerland where the inns are clean and the habits more akin to ours: general industry and tranquility, after the noise and inattention to house-keeping of the French. The hôtel here is well-appointed, not in the sumptuous stile of the Parisian hôtels, but, happily, much cleaner and quieter. The food here is plentiful and wholesome—not up to the justly acclaimed standards of the French, much to my own relief, as were it in the French stile, I would have had to order all new cloathes, being no longer able to cover myself decently with those I now have. Mr. Darcy is also enjoying the relief from the dinners of seven or more courses, each comprised of more than a dozen different dishes, from which one is obliged out of courtesy to take something. The French seem to stand in greater fear of their cooks than even the English, and to slight even the plainest *ragoût*, is an offence of the gravest iniquity.

In contrast, the Swiss are not only uniformly industrious, but seem cheerful, religious, and respectable. The appearance of the wealthy is not so distinguished from even the labouring class, the former having no very great taste for luxury and finery, and the latter so well-employed as to be above want. This blessing of universal prosperity is, I believe, the result of education being widely available here—to both sexes— being the burthen of the state (which our own England would do well to emulate); and, wealth is also not restricted to the male line, an antiquated practise from which our own family has suffered. The Swiss shew an elegance and simplicity of taste which contrasts very favourably with that of other nations where opulence is only surmounted by an even greater excess of the same, but I suppose that if the latter were less objectionable, it would be, in consequence, less desireable.

You will be interested to know that we have been to Ferney and seen the house in which Voltaire resided, it being but a small distance from the centre of the city. The *château* is not imposing, but very handsome. It is scrupulously maintained by the Genevans exactly as when the great man himself occupied it. Voltaire had a very eclectic taste, and there are likenesses of those men he particularly admired adorning the walls, in a profusion and variety which would astonish you: Milton (despite Rousseau's very severe comments upon the *Paradise Lost*), Newton, Corneille, Helvetius, &c., and Washington and Franklin! I cannot account for the absence of Paine and Lafayette in such a pantheon. In addition to the house, the gardens are quite large, and are open to the citizens of Geneva. This prospect from the eminence on which the *château* stands not only commands a view of Geneva, but the Jura Alps, Lake Geneva (which is here called by the French and Swiss Lac Léman), and Mont Blanc, and so is quite popular with both citizens and travellers. There is a large theatre, seating upwards of 700, in this place where his plays were performed. I do not recollect any place in England where we have preserved such a scene in honour of a man of letters, much to our own discredit.

To-morrow, we are to visit some places where watches and music-boxes are made, and the following day, we have been very obligingly invited to the home of an English gentleman for dinner, he suspecting, I suppose, that we have not had our share of tough mutton and boiled beef since leaving England. We are all in hopes of fish.

Assuming we survive the rigours of sight-seeing and eating far more than is good for us, we plan to visit Byron's Villa Diodati, as well as the *château* of the pitiable Empress Josephine, Prégny-la-Tour. Mr. Darcy and I have contrived to surprise Georgiana with a visit to Coppet, an act for which we shall receive too much of gratitude for the sake of our own pleasure.

My husband has been busy collecting some very large books for the library at Pemberley; may they be as interesting as they are heavy. The scenery is sublime, and I would be well content to remain here, excepting for the love I bear you and Jane, and the rest of my dear family, and the distaste I have for giving myself such trouble as to become tolerably proficient in the French language. Your esteemed selves and my beloved Pemberley require me to learn nothing, a study already mastered with considerably less inconvenience to myself.

Please give our love to Kitty and Parson Overstowey, and assure the former that we eat nothing excepting a few leaves and a very little thin broth, and that only every other week.

Your loving daughter,

ELIZABETH DARCY

The following day, the concierge at their hôtel had arranged for a tour at a watchmakers', where persons of all ages and both sexes were busily employed. The Darcys concluded the afternoon by exploring about the town. The shops were very good, and the Genevois more generally reserved than the French, but very clean, elegant, and urbane. They drove out to La Jonction, where the azure waters of the Rhône meet the River Arve somewhat west of the city; it was a most curious sight as the waters from each flow side-by-side for some distance without mixing, the former of a bright blue, and the latter of a grayish colour, and of a greater contrast than were the waters of the Gironde. There was a great appearance of rain, and, still a bit fatigued, the Darcys returned to the hôtel at an hour earlier than usual, took supper, and retired, being engaged to dine away from the city in the village of Annemasse the following day. This proved fortunate, as early in the evening a violent storm broke out. The vivid and frequent lightening produced extraordinarily long peals of thunder that echoed off the surrounding mountains, making a frightful noise. In the morning, the air of the lake was very pure, and the towns opposite Geneva along the vast lake could be seen, although more than twelve leagues away.

CHAP. 8.

THEIR DAYS IN THE ENVIRONS of Geneva were spent in day-travels to the other principal sights of Lake Geneva: Lausanne, Thonon-les-Bains, Yvoire, Evian, &c. Georgiana made use of her sketch-book, and Mr. Darcy noted the various trees, geological wonders, the types of birds and fish to be seen, whilst Elizabeth assisted Georgiana by pointing out the various peculiar costumes of the natives and their habitations. The lofty mountaintops encircling Geneva were dense with forests of pines, beech, oak, hickory and other valuable woods. The meadows lower down contained lush pasturage and great sweeping vineyards; across the lake, the snow-capped peaks of Mount Blanc and the Rhône alps provided a background of almost unimaginable beauty for reminiscences of *Julie*, which Mr. Darcy read to the ladies in the evenings.

One morning during their stay in Geneva, Elizabeth found Georgiana reading whilst waiting for herself and Mr. Darcy to come down to breakfast. "You are reading *Corinne* again, Georgiana?" cried Elizabeth. "How many times you must have read that book! I did not know you had brought it with you. I am sure you know that Madame de Staël's *château* is close by—should you like to visit?"

Georgiana, who had, in fact, brought the novel in hopes of seeing Coppet, the late novelist's home, was delighted. "I would like very much to see it, if such a plan were agreeable to you. Several of her works are housed at the library here, and I have been reading about her during our stay here. Might we go to-morrow, if the weather is fine?" Darcy could not hide his pleasure at Georgiana's eagerness for the plan, and immediately set about making arrangements for the family to travel up to Coppet by boat early the next day, stopping only to remark that Georgiana desired to go, indeed, if she were urging another journey aboard-ship.

"That is certainly true, Brother," answered Georgiana, "The very recollection of the voyage to Calais is sufficient to produce an apprehension of the sea-sickness. However, I believe the lake to be much calmer than the Channel, and so willingly—*temporarily*—forsake the shore in favour of a visit to Coppet."

For this day, Georgiana appropriated the office of guide wholly to herself. As they sailed to the village, she related a brief history for the benefit of her brother and sister. The Château de Coppet was purchased and improved by de Staël's father, Jacques Necker, who had the prescience to purchase a safe haven in the wake of the long years of upheavals in France. Following his daughter's public denunciations of the Emperour, Buonaparte—unsurprisingly—exiled Madame de Staël in retaliation. Living at her father's estate at Coppet until her death, she entertained the leading intellects of the day. Since that time, pilgrimages to her home were become *de rigueur*, and the Darcys found that many of their fellow passengers on board were similarly bound for the *château*.

In Coppet, a closely packed mediæval village, a short walk up the hill brought them to a fairly modern *château* of rose colour, decorated and furnished in the fashion of Louis XVI. Walking through the large courtyard, Georgiana imagined herself as the heroine Corinne, cast aside by her one true love. She walked slowly through the rooms of the house, leaving Elizabeth and Darcy outside to admire the views of Lake Geneva and the snow-covered Alps, explore the stables, and inspect the wine-press. Walking through the north end of the courtyard, she found herself in the portrait room, where she spent many minutes examining the faces of de Staël's two husbands, looking for an aspect of cruelty in the first, and of gentleness in the second. A portrait of Madame de Staël as a child caught her attention, the little girl sitting stiffly on a small chair, with her powdered hair piled high upon her head. The portraitist had captured her in a pose of conversation, and the child's earnest, serious face reminded Georgiana of herself.

Continuing up to the writer's bedroom, was startled by at the sight of the magnificent carved, lacquered bed, swathed with Lyon silk, which had been a marriage gift from de Staël's second husband. The rest of the house was full of exotic treasures brought back from the Far East by her father's French India Company vessels. However, it was the portrait of the authoress as a child—a lone, stiff little figure—that engaged Georgiana, looking always for a resemblance to herself, returning to the portrait each time she would pass through the room.

Georgiana was reminded of Byron's lines immortalizing both the authoress and the lake beside which she spent her last days, reciting the sonnet to herself before the portrait:

> Rousseau—Voltaire—our Gibbons—and de Staël—
> Léman! these names are worthy of thy shore,
> Thy shore of names like these! wert thou no more,
> Their memory thy remembrance would recall:
> To them thy banks were lovely as to all,
> But they have made them lovelier, for the lore
> Of mighty minds doth hallow in the core
> Of human hearts the ruin of a wall
> Where dwelt the wise and wondrous; but by *thee*
> How much more, Lake of Beauty! do we feel,
> In sweetly gliding o'er thy crystal sea,
> The wild glow of that not ungentle zeal.
> Which of the heirs of immortality
> Is proud, and makes the breath of glory real!

It was late by the time the family were returned to the boat and their rooms at Geneva. All were ready to retire after an hasty supper, but the two letters pressed into Georgiana's hands by the concierge were to put sleep far out of reach. The first letter, dated the fourth of May, was from Colonel Fitzwilliam and addressed to the Darcys; Georgiana assumed all rights of possession-in-fact, and read it immediately upon reaching her apartment. Upon opening the packet, she found that there was another note folded within. In the letter sent to them generally, the Colonel wrote to inform the family that he would be again slightly delayed in his journey to meet them at Geneva, but thought he might see them in Milan, or, if not thence, Venice. Carefully she removed the wafer from the smaller paper and read the note addressed to herself:

4th May
Tunbridge Wells

DEAREST GEORGIANA,

I have not been entirely candid with my cousin and Elizabeth as to the reason for the postponement of our rendezvous, but I did not wish to make my circumstances known until I am secure in my object. I can have no secrets from you. You, who know my heart better than anyone, will surely have surmised that I have been detained for love. Your sagacity, I am sure, will have led you to believe that I am become re-acquainted with Miss Crawford. She was come to Tunbridge with her brother to escape London (you see how greatly we share our opinions!); we met here by the action of Providence. Georgiana, you know that excessive praise is not my custom, but she is an angel! I do not believe that any woman alive can equal—let alone surpass—the manifold attractions she naturally possesses—and in such a singular admixture of incompatible blessings! She is at once elegant in her figure, lovely in her countenance, with a fine, soft complexion that sets off her exquisitely dark and lively eyes. She has a most innocent air, which complements rather than competes with a very natural vivacity. She is artless and clever, composed and impetuous, and possesses a very delightful wit, rendered uncommonly agreeable by a happy and original mode of expression. She has read much; her mind is informed, and, whilst subtle, exhibits a profundity and breadth of ideas to supply hours of interesting and diverting conversation. Added to all of this, she has a charming voice, sings with a delightful natural taste, and plays upon the harp with exquisite grace. I never met with such a woman before; I believe that she has no equal amongst mortals. I am very much in love. And, dearest cousin, the wonder of it all is that she now appears to wish for the same happy event that I despaired of all those months ago! She has left that set which so clouded her own preferences and caused me such disappointment; I mean to secure her against returning to them by asking for her hand. I ask your prayers for my success, Georgiana, and am hopeful that I may bring her to Pemberley to meet you upon our return to England.

Your fond cousin,

GEORGE FITZWILLIAM

Under the increasing misery of every sentence, Georgiana sank lower into her seat, grateful that she was spared the trial of being observed during such distress. Hands trembling, Georgiana laid the wretched paper to one side, and took up the other, which was addressed in the careful hand of Mrs. Annesley. The letter was brief and, if possible, contained even more dreadful news than had the letter previous:

30th April
Pemberley, Derbyshire

DEAR MISS DARCY,

I thank you for your last letter, and all the good wishes that were sent with it. I will not trespass on your patience; I write of news that will give you nothing but pain, and for this I am most grieved upon my errand. My dearest Georgiana, it is my sad duty to tell you that your beloved Mademoiselle Blanche was carried off this evening. We all did our best for the dear little creature, but you see, she would not eat, and though Cook and I tried every way we could and offered her every delicacy, in the end she did not seem to want to go on. I can comfort you only with the assurance that your dear little Blanche died peacefully in her sleep. I wish to Heaven that I had not been burthened with the relation of such dreadful news to you, for I know how you loved her. We will get a kitten just as soon as you get home, although I know you will say that Blanche can never be replaced in your heart. I am so very sorry, dearest Georgiana. May God bless you and sustain you in your grief.

I eagerly await your return, and that of Mr. & Mrs. Darcy, and remain your devoted friend,

Isobel Annesley

Georgiana felt that this was, indeed, her darkest hour. Sitting alone, she reread the hateful letters containing the news of the certainties of the two inevitabilities she dreaded most in the world, and tried to collect her thoughts; tears succeeded the brief effort, which, perversely, produced only the most painful recollections of Pemberley, Blanche, Colonel Fitzwilliam, her old pony, her piano-forte—in short, every idea most likely to increase her wretchedness was immediately before her, and she knew not whether she wept most for the loss of that which represented the past, or for that which presaged the emptiness of the future.

As may be expected, Georgiana managed little sleep that night, and awoke the next morning to see the two letters open on the table beside her bed, extinguishing a momentary hope that the news in the letters had been the product of a most dreadful dream. Noting from the height of the sun that she had slept beyond her usual hour, she hastened down to breakfast, taking the letters with her. Upon joining Elizabeth and Darcy downstairs, she passed two letters to her brother without a word, grateful for the point of honour which required she keep the Colonel's second letter to herself. Never was she more thankful for the kindness of the brother and sister who understood her so well, for neither of them attempted to comfort her beyond a look, and, for some time left her to compose herself before beginning the discussion of the unexpected news. Darcy and Elizabeth could have no idea that Colonel Fitzwilliam's delay in meeting them could have affected her so entirely, and, therefore, assumed that the blame for her pale, tear-stained face must be the loss of Mademoiselle Blanche. Nevertheless, they treated both subjects with the utmost compassion for Georgiana's misery, and their united dismay at her sorrow knew no bounds.

"Poor, dear Georgiana, and poor little Blanche. We must try to find solace in the reflection that kind Mrs. Reynolds and dear Mrs. Annesley will have neglected nothing to secure the little cat's comfort. Blanche was a brave old thing, but we could not have taken her with us on our travels—and surely she must have been more comfortable at home—in spite of your absence from it. I am sorry you were not there to say goodbye to her, dearest, for she has been a true companion and friend to you these many years. I entreat you to remember that she knew how much you loved her, and is surely at peace now. In time, you will wish for another kitten, although such an idea is inconceivable at present." Elizabeth pressed her sister's hand, and took up Colonel Fitzwilliam's letter to the family, to read it once again.

"I have an idea that the reason for Colonel Fitzwilliam's continual delay in journeying out to meet us must be his attentions to a woman. Colonel Fitzwilliam sounds so content, we must view the circumstances for his good fortune with happiness, even if it means we are to be denied the pleasure of his company for some additional days."

"If my cousin is content at Tunbridge Wells," replied Mr. Darcy, "then I wish him very happy, although I hope he will bestir himself to meet us in Milan, as he promises us. I have never seen him in love before, but he is, in general, very rational in his method. If George has formed an attachment, as your feminine intuition suggests, I do not doubt that he will have made himself an excellent match, as he has always been a good judge of character. You are right, Lizzy; we must deal with our disappointment, that he does not come to join us, as best we can, and make ready to question him at length about the reasons for his unpardonable delay, when we are finally together again." With this last, he looked across at Georgiana, and easily perceiving her increasing distress, gently suggested that she retire to rest for a few hours more, after which time he would go with her to the library. Georgiana nodded her assent, and excused herself from the breakfast table.

"Would to Heaven that anything could be done to relieve such unhappiness!" exclaimed Darcy, as he watched his sister leave the room. "I will be back in time for lunch, Elizabeth, as I must undertake some matters of business this morning. If we are to quit Geneva this week— as I think we should; a change of scene must be preferable after this unhappy episode—it is necessary to hurry my business here."

In truth, it was not business, but pleasure, which was to occupy

Mr. Darcy's morning. In their walks around the city, Elizabeth had admired *en passant* some jewellery that was displayed in a window of one of the *joaillières*; fixing their departure date made his errand consequently more urgent. Darcy had decided on an ornament for the hair that he was sure would suit her taste for small, fine pieces, and selected one that had the additional benefit of its being able to be fitted up as a brooch. He chose a pair of diamond ear pendants that would look well with the other, were it stationed on the head or on the bosom. Elizabeth wore little ornament, but Darcy knew that she admired fine things; he further reasoned that he had never purchased a proper wedding-present for her—the pearls had been his mother's—and was pleased with the results of such an unusual employment.

As he completed his errands, he passed by the shop window of Rojard's, and admired the small size and elegance of the new pocket-watches on display. Pausing outside the shop window for a moment before entering, his attention was caught by an assistant demonstrating a mouse automaton, finely covered in rows of pearls, much to the delight of a gentleman and lady within. The animal was perfection, from its golden nose to its woven tail. The movement was extremely life-like, all four feet scurrying, and the little head moving up and down as if it were inspecting the ground. As he watched, the mouse suddenly stopt in its tracks, and performed twice a *volte-face* before scurrying off in the opposite direction. It was a master-piece of precision and artistry, and Darcy had never seen the like. Entering the shop, he quietly waited by the door whilst the assistant enquired whether the couple meant to purchase the automaton. When the assistant named the sum, the gentleman laughed his dissent, and, donning his hat and taking his lady by the arm, he bade Mr. Darcy and the assistant a good day.

The assistant recognised the tall Englishman at once, for Mr. Darcy had visited the shop on a previous day to enquire of some of the jewellery. "Mr. Darcy! It is indeed a pleasure to remake your acquaintance again. Please, sir, if you are pleased, we must rewind the automaton, for you miss the beginning of his trick." By the time the machine had finished its display, Darcy had determined that the mouse was the very thing to amuse his sister after the loss of her Blanche, reflecting that the mechanism was more than worth its price, if it might allay Georgiana's sadness. The clerk presented the automaton to Mr. Darcy in a beautifully inscribed silver case in the shape of a cupboard and drawer. Well-satisfied with the result of these exertions, he walked directly back to the hôtel in the happy anticipation of the pleasure the gifts would bring his wife and sister.

Elizabeth had a surprise of her own, however, as the previous day she had also called in at Monsieur Rojard's. The late Mr. Darcy had given his son his own pocket-watch shortly before his death. The watch was a very old and valuable piece, but it was not accurate; in addition, it was much larger and heavier than the modern time-pieces that were now extraordinarily precise, and of a much smaller and more elegant form. The old watch was English-made and in an heavy, engraved silver case, with a highly ornate face and hands. Elizabeth wanted a replacement that would not be seen as an imitator of the old watch, but rather one in accord with all of her husband's ideas on the value of innovation and progress. She and Georgiana had viewed and rejected a vast array of watches and clocks: some that were automatons, some that had jewels to their case and faces, some that played music, some that shewed the phases of the moon, one that had a gentleman pushing a lady on a swing as it ticked, some contrived so as to shew the entirety of the mechanism inside, and those that were in the shapes of balls, urns, musical instruments, and many other ingenious and diverting inventions. Monsieur Rojard, himself, had come from his offices to shew her a pocket-watch of the most recent design, and which was the picture of elegant simplicity: it was of the highest-quality gold, oval in shape, with a plain white dial, a set of English numbers, and very fine black hands. Monsieur Rojard explained to Mrs. Darcy that there was not a time-piece made that was more accurate for such a small size, and averred that her husband would be delighted with the precision and mechanics of the article, above all of the others on display. She requested that he inscribe the watch-back as from herself, with the date and "Geneva." She arranged with the proprietor that the parcel be delivered to their hôtel later that day, Elizabeth wishing to choose exactly when she might present the gift.

Mr. Darcy forced Elizabeth's hand on the morrow, however, by producing the boxes for herself and Georgiana at breakfast, and was to reap a fitting reward for his effrontery, as Elizabeth must necessarily answer his volley with that of her own. Upon receiving the watch from his wife, his look bespoke a deep and tender attachment, and a recognition of the thoughtfulness evinced by the gift, which had—among others— the happy effect of rendering words superfluous. Unused as he was to accepting the generosity of others, it was Darcy's fate that he must learn to express not only his admiration *for* his wife, but also his gratitude *to* her, possibly even beyond what he felt he deserved.

CHAP. 9.

THE GENERAL SPIRITS of the Darcy family having been somewhat
restored, it might be assumed that the family were able to enjoy their
last hours in Geneva without further upset, but two pieces of bad news
being invariably succeeded by a third, this last found its way to the
family through delivery of a letter to Mr. Darcy, addressed in the
generously proportioned hand of Lady Catherine de Bourgh. Both
Mrs. and Miss Darcy attended to the letter, which the recipient read
aloud for their benefit, and to their collective astonishment.

7th May
Grand Parade, Bath

DEAR FITZWILLIAM,

You may receive my news with some surprise, having presupposed,
no doubt, that my tender feelings for Sir Lewis would prevent any second
attachment, but your assumptions are mistaken, for upon your return
to our country, married I will be, and happily so. Our recent residence
in Bath was occasioned, of course, for no benefit of my own, but rather
to provide a scene of more diversion for your cousin, Anne. Imagine
my surprise to find that I, myself, was the object of a gentleman of our
acquaintance. I am renowned for the natural modesty of my character,
but the ardency of the intentions of the gentleman in question being
quite unmistakable, an attachment has been formed, and Sir William
Elliot and I intend to announce our engagement without delay.

I write to you not only because I know you would wish the earliest
knowledge of my happiness, and so to avail yourself of the opportunity
to wish your aunt joy, but also to impart to you some advice, for I find
that my intended is in the happy position of possessing many friends in

the world of business, and a most advantageous investment opportunity has been presented to me. Sir William informs me that you are under quite a misapprehension in your notion that the coal-gas is the most advantageous for lighting. The errors of this notion have been made apparent to me during my own particular researches of these past weeks. I am, sadly, bound to the strictest secrecy, and can tell you no more at present, but suffice to say that I am in expectation of a large return. Please send my fondest regards to your sister.

With great affection, I sign myself—for perhaps the last time,

LADY CATHERINE DE BOURGH

A silence descended over the table as each of the Darcys attempted to make some sense of the letter's contents. Mr. Darcy was the first to attempt a response.

"This news gives me cause for concern, indeed. My aunt does not communicate any details about the scheme or the gentleman she is to marry, but if the speculative is an alternative to the coal-gas, she is unlikely to receive any return from her investment—profit or otherwise. I shall write to her at once and attempt to dissuade her from taking any further part in the idea. Her decision to marry is beyond my influence, and so in her personal fortune I must wish her happy." Though he could not in general abide folly in others, Darcy felt certain that someone had imposed most dreadfully upon his aunt, and Elizabeth was surprised to feel that her own reaction was something closer to pity than diversion, even though her own existence had been omitted from the letter entirely.

"I believe I have heard of the name Sir William Elliot once before, but I do not remember the particulars." Elizabeth tried to recollect the memory, but could only remember its origin. "He was mentioned, I am sure, by Anne Wentworth. Sir William is, I believe, a relation of hers, for her elder sister, whom we did not meet, is unmarried and is a Miss Elliot. Shall I write to Mrs. Wentworth about Sir William? I am almost certain that she spoke of him with disapprobation from some cause or another, but did not inform me as to the reasons for her opinion—or perhaps I do not recollect. We are friends enough that I am sure she will not consider my enquiry as impertinent. I shall write the letter at once, if you wish, and we may safely rely upon the veracity of her response."

Mr. and Mrs. Darcy both engaged in the important business of letter-writing, the morning passed quickly, and it was soon time for the family to make ready for their onward journey over the Alps. Mr.

Darcy made use of some of the time spent waiting for their baggage to be secured and horses made ready to write to the Bingleys.

8th June
Geneva, Switzerland

DEAR CHARLES AND JANE,

As you did me the honour of particularly mentioning that an occasional letter by my hand would be agreeable, I am in hopes that you will accept my letter in lieu of Elizabeth's this week. We were delighted to receive your letter upon our reaching Geneva, and are thankful for the blessings of a safe delivery, and that your little girl does well. Georgiana desires me to say that she is honoured to be named her god-mother, and that she would be gratified, indeed, to make over her own christening gown, if you would be so good as to instruct Mrs. Reynolds to remove it from the chest in her apartment and have it made ready. We plan to be home sometime in late October, and would certainly wish to be there with you and Bingley, but we also understand delay in such matters is undesirable.

I cannot do better than give some account of our experiences of Switzerland, and our chief occupations whilst we resided here. It took four long days of travel to reach Geneva from Lyon. Not surprisingly, the travelling becomes slower and more difficult as one approaches the Alps, but Georgiana and Elizabeth continue to enjoy the journey, and we find the long days amply recompensed by the extraordinary beauty of the countryside. We came into Geneva from the direction of the south and west, and had our first view of the city with its unusual cathedral— the home church of Calvin—and many large and substantial structures silhouetted against the sunset over the Jura Mountains. The situation of this city is beyond comparison, close-on the narrowest section of the lake which bears its name (to the English, or Lac Léman to the French and Swiss). The whole country is an Arcadia, centreed by the large, clear lake, surrounded on all sides by hills of vineyards and the various ranges of the Alpen mountains and the glaciers of the Savoy, Mont Blanc rising in the distance, much like an immense coronet. I have never seen any town or city more sensibly situated, comfortable and sheltered amidst the two rivers of the Rhône and the Arve, which meet at the city; a large and bountiful lake provides both sustenance and the convenience of travelling by boat to all of the areas surrounding it, and is bordered nearly about its circumference with handsome orchards and vineyards. After being come recently from the thoroughly unpleasant crowded streets and unwholesome airs of Paris, we have been agreeably surprised by the Swiss streets, which are clean, well-lit, well-ordered, and well-paved.

Our first days at Geneva were occupied in locating our warmer coats, for the climate of Switzerland is a great deal colder than France, at least at this time of year. In 1789, the frost was so severe that the lake was frozen over entirely, and the Duke of Kent passed over it in a coach-and-six, accounts of which we have had to endure several times in just the first three days of our stay, it being a favourite history of the English amongst the good residents of Geneva.

The public library here is extraordinary in that it possesses, amongst its many thousand volumes, a considerable collection of manuscripts, including many curious and rare copies. It is our particular delight to spend some part of each day there. Our recent English discoveries in electricity and fixed air are held in the highest esteem here in Geneva, and, due to the work of Priestly and Watt, the English continue to gain great credit in this city of learning. Of course, the names of Voltaire and Saussure are heard wherever one goes here, and we have paid our respects as aspiring savants with pilgrimages to their respective *châteaux*.

There is a great deal of pleasant society in Geneva to be met with, and many have welcomed us most affably. Those who have an establishment in the city issue such general invitations, that we regularly meet to take in the papers, and enjoy walking and discussing the events of the world in the gardens. The Swiss are knowledgeable and urbane, and both sexes discourse on the most learned subjects. The women are very well-read, and not at all reluctant to engage in discussions, with great interest, along-side the men—much the same as the women of France, but with a more congenial and reasonable stile of address. The calm orderliness of the city and the modesty and industry of the Genevans is a marked contrast to France, and the atmosphere of tolerance amongst the Swiss—of ideas, of dress, of education, of everything—enables me to understand why men such as Shelley and Byron sought the liberality of its society. We have not met them, although exiled writers are plentiful here, and tales of their irregularities of behaviour provide an endless source of conversation for the respectable Swiss. It is doubtful that our own family will be adjudged to have acquitted ourselves creditably against such standards of eccentricity of which we are daily reminded, and I fear that the Darcy family will be remembered for saying only things very dull, indeed, as measured against such exemplars of the creative genius.

Bingley, I will congratulate myself heartily on the choice of horses and the carriages. The coach and chaise have proven very comfortable and commodious against all manner of poor road, and the horses have gone most admirably through the least expected of situations without moving off an hair's-breath from straight. The harness we have seen! English fishermen have better rope than that which binds the French horse and coach—such a bundle of knots and irregularity of construction you cannot imagine. The wonder is that anything or anybody gets down the road in one piece. Harmon remains in continual indignation over the state of the French equipage, and we have been here nearly a week. I secured a few days of capital fishing in France, and hope to be able to get in a few more days' sport ere we return, but will defer my raptures until I have more leisure for writing.

I have been reminded thrice by the desire of my wife and sister to send their love and many kisses to baby Georgiana. I will only add, God bless you,

FITZWILLIAM DARCY

The Darcys left Geneva in early June, the earliest date to promise safe passage over the Alps. They decided to take the southern route to Martigny, stopping first at Les Bégues to dine, and arriving that evening at St. Martin at the Hôtel Mont Blanc, so-called because it afforded travellers a perfect view of the Monarch of Mountains. The Darcys encountered some of the travelling families they had met in Geneva; at supper, the conversation was all of travels and travails of the Simplon. The scenery in all directions was magnificent: high mountains capped with eternal snow, deep ravines where the melted snow dashed downward from high gorges with a terrific roar, and streams of water appearing from no-where through rocks, offering a cool and refreshing drink to the traveller. The Genevan territory extended only a few miles farther on that road, but, whilst within Switzerland, the countryside continued similarly prosperous, industrious, well-cultivated, and well-ordered. Having passed through the hamlet of Chêne, and crossed the bridge, the Darcys entered the Savoy; their immediate impression was that there could not be two adjacent countries less alike on the entirety of the earth! The sensation of surprise was universal upon beholding the poverty and miserable conditions of the Savoyards. The country was comprised at first of high mountains, cloathed with a dense forest forming one side of the Valley of the Arve. With the exception of a few crop-fields and some handful of poor vineyards, the entire landscape was comprised entirely of wilderness. A small number of Savoyards were seen with their narrow ox-carts, employed mending the road in a dilatory fashion.

Along the route, the Darcys saw numerous picturesque ruins of castles, adding to the grandeur of the mountains and the sparkling Arve. They stopt the first night in Les Bégues, the capital of Fancigny, that was presently—following the Congress of Vienna—a duchy subject to the crown of Sardinia. The Arve flowed through the centre of the town, situated amongst a succession of mountains capped with snow. The hills above the town were well-settled with cottages, and the road through Les Bégues lay under a canopy of stately old trees. Such pleasant initial scenes were succeeded by a sight far less agreeable, as the village of Les Bégues was dominated by the sight of a large prison with its high towers vigilant above the surrounding vicinity and all who passed-by. As if in defiance of this scene of melancholy, an inn was near-by the tower, where several tables of rustics in their large-brimmed straw hats and light trousers, and a few soldiers in their tall shakos and plumes, accompanying the only ladies present—save the serving-maid—were gaily drinking and cheering one another with tumblers of wine. In truth, thought Elizabeth, the men looked as healthy and strong as they should, even with the great quantity of *à votre santés* drunk in just the time it took to pass by.

Resuming the road to Cluse, the towns became more prosperous-looking and picturesque: in the distance, children, youths, and maidens tended herds of goats and sheep wearing tinkling bells; comfortable cottages dotted the hill-sides below the pastures; and a most luxuriant canopy of trees shaded the road. The village of Cluse lay in a small valley at the base of immense, snow-capped peaks, which over-shadowed the Arve and the road. The river rushing through the small valley was very noisome, and it was apparent to the travellers that to be trapped in such a place in an heavy rain would be most alarming, indeed, and brought to Darcy's mind King Lear's "whereso'ere you are, that bide the pelting of this pitiless storm." Moving quickly on, the superstitious nature of the cottagers was evident in the numberless crosses and images of saints displayed in niches carved into the rock along the road-sides, all the way to Sallenche. How very different from the urbane and rational Genevans! The Vale of Sallenche was of nearly indescribable beauty: a panorama of a wide valley of fields, through which meandered the glistening Arve, amidst villages, spires, and plantations, all within a circlet of enormous crags, many topped with gleaming ice, and culminating at the far end with the imposing majesty of Mount Blanc.

Reaching St. Martin, which—to a very general relief—had an unusually fine inn, they were well looked-after by the land-lord and his wife and daughters, the latter of whom placed an hearty hot supper and a bottle of excellent wine before the tired and hungry travellers.

In the morning light, the Darcys could see the face of Mont Blanc from their inn, covered in its glacial blanket, and the Arve winding before it, and under the graceful bridge of St. Martin, a wonderfully contrived structure of a single span. Mr. Darcy remarked to the ladies that such a sight was a great restorative to improper pride; surely there was no better illustration of one's own insignificance. Georgiana and her brother had settled into the comfortable routine of Mr. Darcy directing what she was to sketch, to be reviewed at the day's conclusion as to determine which views qualified for a more permanent representation; Elizabeth made short notes for inclusion in her correspondence.

The three left St. Martin early, continuing on to St. Gervais-les-Bains to view the famed cascade; they found the water hot and stinking of sulphur. None of the Darcy party felt sufficiently ill to drink of it. *En route*, they passed numerous queer waggons called a *charabanc* in those parts, a sort of dray with numerous forward-facing seats and no cover; the noise and clatter on the stones roused considerable sympathy for the unfortunate occupants who must nearly be shaken to pieces and stone-deaf by the end of the day. Mont Blanc continued to dominate the scenery as the Darcys travelled along the base of the mountain, occasionally hidden by a bend in the road, bursting suddenly back into view with a blinding whiteness in the rays of the sun.

Arriving at Chammouni in the early afternoon, the party decided to rest themselves and their horses for two days. Georgiana had been feeling increasingly unwell, and even Mr. Darcy was in depressed spirits from the effects of the arduous journey. The town was sufficiently commodious to boast of two inns; having chosen the Hôtel de Londres, the family were startled at daybreak the following morning by the unceasing roar of the close-by mill. However, the view commanded by the hôtel was magnificent, including a view of Mont Blanc's two glaciers, one at each side. As Georgiana's maid was quite ill the next morning, Mr. and Mrs. Darcy concluded that this was the most hospitable place to rest until all were ready to continue, and fortuitous in offering an healthy diversion in the exploration of such magnificent surroundings. Indeed, immediately following breakfast, Georgiana left the Darcys and other travellers, pleading indisposition.

"Husband," began Elizabeth that evening after they had left the others, "Georgiana is not such a great walker as we, but does it not strike you that she is declining to accompany us, retiring early, and such-like more frequently since we departed Geneva?"

"Yes, Lizzy, it does. I have been noticing it with concern. I would think she is saddened by the loss of Blanche, but her indisposition seems to *increase* as we pass the days, and not otherwise, as I would expect."

"I agree, and cannot fathom why she will recover her spirits—such as when you presented the little mouse, or when you are directing her sketching—only to resume her dejection, and to an ever-increasing degree. I have always believed pleasure an antidote to low spirits, but in this case, it seems entirely otherwise! It would be hard, indeed, were this to be the general case."

"One fears to do too much, as well as not enough. I wonder if we are aggravating some malaise by pretending to understand her need for solitude, without even the slightest idea of the cause. This is a most wretched conundrum, and one entirely beyond my powers to apprehend. You are better at these puzzles of the mind than I, Lizzy; surely you must have some notion."

"Of all people, I am grieved to disappoint *you*, Mr. Darcy. My only recommendation—and it does my own understanding no extraordinary credit—is that we observe more closely these spells of melancholy and try to draw from them what conclusion we are able." Mr. Darcy agreed that an increased vigilance was the wisest course for the present.

Elizabeth and her husband were to spend the next day ascending Montanvert to see the Mer de Glace. Having arranged to begin early in the day, the guides met them at the entrance to the hôtel, carrying long spiked poles, and sufficient provisions for the day. Mules carried the party to the foot of the mountains, where they began to ascend, after crossing a river and passing a few scattered farmsteads. The mules picked their way along the narrow pass, strewn with fallen rocks, fallen trees, and fallen snow in the form of a small avalanche. Eventually, the road became impassable even for the dexterous mules, and the party and their guides continued on foot. The scene of the avalanche was horrible: large trees were uprooted, and many bent to the ground, stript of their branches. The falling rock precipitated by the cascading snow was awesome in its power; within memory of their guide, entire villages had disappeared beneath moving seas of snow and rock, despite the crosses and processions established to arrest the power of the glacier. Such scenes required great composure to pass without alarm, and the precipice was frightful, more so with the certain knowledge that one mis-step would send the unfortunate into the chasm, never to be seen again. Several small avalanches were heard throughout the day, initially mistaken for thunder, so loud was the roar of falling ice and rock. It was necessary to stop and rest frequently, and these brief respites were usually attended by children bringing milk and strawberries and other fruits in a charming manner for purchase by the walkers. At length, when Elizabeth was ready to believe that she would never see the end of their ascent, the Mer de Glace appeared: an immense sheet of solid ice enclosed by mountains of stupendous proportion. Tall trees framed the scene, the shafts of dark green contrasting with the intense whiteness of the glacier. This sea of ice was eighteen leagues in length and surmounted by yet another frozen sea and two more glaciers, descending all the way to the plains beyond. The only respite against the interminable whiteness and frozen stone was an oasis: an island consisting of a large rock protruded from its surrounding sea of ice, upon which had grown up a garden every year—miraculously, thought Elizabeth—and in the current season was blooming profusely with wild-flowers.

At this summit was a small, rustic dwelling kept by a peasant who sold refreshments, as well as curious stones and mountain plants to the collector. There was an album, contained in the dwelling, into which had been inscribed a few lines of verse by no less a personage than the Empress Josephine, describing her sensations upon reaching the Mer de Glace:

> *Ah! je sens qu'au millieu de ces grandes phénomènes*
> *De ces tableaux touchans, de ces terribles scènes*
> *Tout élève l'espirit, tout occupe les yeux;*
> *Le coeur seul, un moment, se repose en ces lieux.*

The quatrain was dated 1810, and had been removed by some industrious soul some years previous, doubtless a detestable collector of autographs, but the registrar had retained the lines within his memory, and had faithfully recopied them into a later page. Elizabeth was moved less by the words than a somber reflection of the sad last days of the Empress, and silently wished that her isolated, remaining years had been relieved by many pleasurable memories of the journey hither. After a few minutes, the glare of the glacier became painful to the eye, and the Darcys requested that they begin to make their descent. *En route* homeward, the guides pointed to seemingly barren mountains that, upon closer inspection, proved to be covered with a thin, short grass and other plants, serving the villagers as summer pastures. Mr. Darcy expressed the idea that some of the Derbyshire sheep should have been brought along to witness the meagre diet of their brethren hereabouts, and be more grateful (and fat) as a consequence. The descent was very toilsome, so it was with weary gratitude and relief that Elizabeth and her husband espied their waiting mules.

CHAP. 10.

THE FOLLOWING DAY was Sunday, and, therefore, the Darcys took their rest in Chammouni. The day was inclement and—necessarily in these mountains—designated as a day of rest, regardless of one's religious habits. Other than attending a service in the morning, Elizabeth was most ready to remain quietly within, being somewhat knocked-up by the previous day's walk, using the hours of leisure to write her letters.

13th June
Chammouni, Switzerland

DEAR AUNT AND UNCLE GARDINER,

We are to rest here in Chammouni for some days whilst Adèle recovers from indisposition, and to own the truth, we are all grateful for the excuse to rest as well. My husband and I are quite dull to-day from a very long walk yesterday to a sea of glacial ice quite high up in the mountains, the justly famed Mer de Glace. I am done with scenes of snow and ice, and quite happily anticipate leaving it all behind in the next day or two in search of warmer climes.

To begin, we have received some astonishing news from Bath. I do not know if I am at liberty to relate it, as it concerns Lady Catherine, but if Mr. Gardiner were to write to my husband, I am sure he would tell you all.

We are also very grateful for Jane's easy delivery, and Georgiana is delighted to be named as her god-mother—so pleased is she, that her pride may eclipse that of the parents. And, as there are now five little Bingleys, perhaps Jane might generously consent to be somewhat less fond as a mother, so that her aunt may claim the greater share of admiration for her tiny fingers and toes.

To-day we were fortunate that a clergyman of the Church of

England in Dorsetshire, travelling for the health of himself and his family, was also resident in our hôtel. A room was obtained for his reading of Church prayers for the benefit of those of us preferring Protestant service. We later learnt that our land-lord was roundly abused by the village priest for allowing such a service to occur in his establishment. In order to repay the land-lord for his kindness, some of our fellow residents later attended the Romish mass at the Catholick Church, and were much interested with the performance of the service, and the simple and rustic appearance of the congregation. I am hopeful that their penance procured the good land-lord's pardon. However, I understand from some of our fellow travellers that, in Heidelberg, there is the same church used for both Protestant and Romish services, so the Priest taking such offense is truly unaccountable, especially as they all the same speak the German language in their daily lives. We are to visit Heidelberg on our return journey, and then I may be able to give you a better explanation of this strange etiquette.

The houses here are of a wholly different construction from those we have previously seen, being all quite similarly constructed of broad, gently sloping gables and roofs, the latter of which are covered with slates of enormous size, I suppose to preserve them from the power of the winds which blow through the valley. A gallery with a rail is to be seen on one end, where the wood-store is located. The upper section of the building forms a store-room for fodder and provisions, and for small fowl. The lower part is usually divided, one half of which is used by the family, and the other for the livestock. The villagers are also different from their Valasian neighbours to a surprising degree in their dress: the women wear a short jacket of blue with white sleeves, petticoats of various colours, and caps that are topped by round, straw hats with a shallow crown. Shoes and stockings are seen, but do not appear to be regarded by the inhabitants as a necessity—which I do not understand at all, it being often very cold here, and always one walks with sharp stones under-foot. On Sundays and days of religious festival, all wear stockings—I have heard of the custom of covering the head in honour of Our Lord, but I never heard that the feet were similarly offending. The complexions of the rustics are generally brown, and many in these parts are afflicted with throats swollen from the goître, which is apparently very common, for which the water is blamed. The cottagers are industrious and clean in their dress and persons, but the houses and churches are often quite dirty.

We also met with a group of Swiss soldiers, returning from the border, I imagine—or I should say groups, as they were rather straggling than

marching

marching. In appearance or in dress, being cloathed in rag-tag bits and pieces of no particular uniform, they bear no comparison to our smart and manly English men-at-arms. Here the men are one and all trained to arms in their youth, and, in defence of their own country, I am sure are as brave as any in Europe. This country is unusual in that, although all Swissmen have required military service each year, the defenses of the country rest with a relatively small army of mercenaries. Looking about me, however, the mountains of Switzerland are certainly its most formidable army.

As with many of the villages in Switzerland, at Chaummouni we are surrounded by valleys of immense glacial seas of ice, of an astonishing thickness and extent. Fearful chasms and yawning gaps are everywhere to be seen and crossed in passing. Looking down into the depths of these gulfs reveals ice of the most beautiful and variegated colours—no uniformity of blue or white, as one would expect, but a veritable rainbow of colours arising in response to the light of day.

The inhabitants here are a curious set; their occupation is chiefly in the raising of goats. I cannot conjecture why any person would willingly live in such an inhospitable environment, but they seem quite content and industrious; the men hunt the chamois and other animals, from which the women make up their food and cloathing, and also serve as guides to travellers over the mountains and passes because of their great familiarity with the terrain. Our guide related a story to us that perhaps most aptly describes the danger in these mountains: he had been driven by an avalanche the depth of fifty feet down one of these valleys, and after some difficulty was safely drawn up and alive to tell the tale. It seems that any noise or incident on the mountain is enough to set in motion one of these horrifying waves of rock, ice, and snow; you may imagine that we are all much quieter than would otherwise be thought possible.

We leave perhaps to-morrow or the next day, depending on the severity of our various complaints, the weather, &c., for Martigny, and thence to into Italy. As I reread this, I am minded to assure you that we really are well—there is no serious illness, just a little fatigue from the rigours of travel on these mountain roads. And, pray do not mention the above to Kitty or my father—Father will worry, and Kitty, whose constitution resembles that of my poor mother, is so much guided by her nerves, that I fear the very thought of our being anywhere near such imagined peril might carry her off at once.

We send our love and best wishes to all of the Gardiners, large and small,

ELIZABETH DARCY

Georgiana related the history of Martigny, which they reached the day following their departure from Chammouni, noting that five hundred years before, an avalanche had caused the Dranse to flood the valley, destroying all of the bridges between St. Maurice and Bagnes; before inundating the town of Martigny, it completely washed away the surrounding fields and villages within a few hours. The bridge, an unprepossessing wooden structure whose northern side was marked by a large wooden cross, looked more like a scene from a story-book, so small was the thin, rickety construction compared with the size and violence of the river plunging below. Mr. Harmon declared he would not venture a goat over that bridge, and indicated strongly to Mr. Darcy that he certainly *hoped* the route took them nowhere near such a fright. Fortunately, their road lay parallel to the river, hence there being no need for either goat or adventure. There were stone bridges both before and after the wooden one—the sight of which brought relief to everyone, not merely Mr. Harmon—and their very construction, connecting the sheer cliffs above the torrent, was a marvel.

The valley beyond Martigny was rich and, the climate being much hotter than the surrounding area, produced a very strong wine, and the honey collected in the area was esteemed as the finest in all Switzerland. In general, however, the indolence of the Valaisans was apparent in the shabby appearance of the villages, unlike the tidy groups of cottages seen previously amongst the Swiss. Martigny was only otherwise notable as the location of the monastery of the monks who attend the Hospice of the Great St. Bernard, as well as that of the Simplon, where the Darcys planned a stop to see the old building and refresh themselves before continuing on their road to Italy.

The days being grown longer, the Darcys planned two long days in crossing from Martigny to Brieg, a distance of almost twenty leagues. They were very desirous of reaching Italy, and were glad to reach Martigny. Leaving early the next day, they stopt at the convent of the Hospice of the Great St. Bernard and the Simplon. The monks were of the order of St. Augustin, and regarded it as their duty to give hospitality to all who pass that way; in the winter months, they ventured out into the roads with large dogs especially trained to find lost travellers who might otherwise perish in the snow and freezing winds. The monastery was situated at the highest habitable point in Europe, about 8,000 feet above the level of the sea. The approach to it in the last hour was steep, slow, and difficult. The buildings were not visible until—when no more than a few hundred yards away—the road made a turn, and the small plain upon which were the monastery and its chapel immediately came into view. Upon the Darcy's approaching, one of the celebrated dogs began braying. The dog was extraordinarily large, and of a white and brown colour. The monks retold stories to the Darcys of the great courage and sagacity of the dogs, having been saved themselves by the dogs' presentiments of danger, leading their masters by a different route, and later learnt that their planned path had been destroyed by the seas of sliding snow.

East of Martigny, the town of Sion was fronted by a dense forest, and silhouetted against glacier-topped mountains. The town surrounded two hillocks, upon each of which sat the ruins of a castle, with a third between the two. The village was beautiful, and of greater interest than any since leaving Geneva, so the Darcys decided to make the journey into three days, rather than the expected two, exploring the scenery near-by Sion. The houses of the ancient town were almost all painted in white, making a pretty contrast to the fertile green plain of the Rhône, winding through the valley. The Darcys visited the town's cathedral that—quite surprisingly—contained a Roman inscription in honour of the Caesar Augustus, another appeared in the Episcopal palace, and others were seen about the town. They ascended the hill to the castle of Tourbillion to see a panorama of the Upper and Lower Valais, shewing all of the gradations in climate from the frozen ice fields of the mountains to the fertile valley fields; as with Martigny, the climate in Sion was as warm and productive as any in Europe.

The following days' journeys were over similar terrain within the Valais, as they drove through the villages of Chalais, Sierre, Leuch, Visp and thence into Brieg. The Valaisians produced excellent wine, and the mountains above furnished rich pasturage to the cattle, sheep, and goats, which were tended by the children. Passing through to Brieg, the Darcys noticed that the German language was grown more common in the Upper Valais, such that as they progressed, it became necessary that Georgiana conduct their business, she being the only proficient amongst them in that tongue.

The Darcys agreed—with some mortification—that the road was becoming merely a succession of wonders: mountains, valleys, cascades, rivers, snow, ice, and the occasional avalanche, all of which were grown increasingly indistinguishable from the others of their kind already encountered. However, if rationally considered, such a sentiment follows quite reasonably from travelling in the same country many days together; such a numbness of the senses was followed by the humbling thought that one's powers of observation had more similarity to those of the generality of travellers than could be agreeable.

Brieg was a pretty town seated at the base of the Simplon, with two large churches and a castle silhouetted against the great pass through the mountains. The Rhône wandered through the valley, there joined by a smaller river called the Saltine, descending from the mountains of the Simplon. Cottages were dotted about the hills, interspersed with plantations, *allées*, and pastures.

"The very buildings hereabouts seem to be made of gold!" exclaimed Elizabeth. "It makes them appear even more grand, and is certainly very beautiful in the sun, but how is this done?"

"The chief buildings in Brieg are well-built in a wonderful glistening stone that the natives called *giltstein*," read Georgiana, "which glows brightly in the few hours when the sun rises above the mountains and shines into the valley below. I believe we call it 'Fools' Gold' in England, Elizabeth. Brieg suffered horribly in its attempt to resist Buonaparte at the end of the last century," Georgiana continued, as they everywhere noticed evidence of the destruction perpetrated upon the town by the French. "The climate is so mild in this valley, that not only are very superior wines produced, but saffron as well!"

"I am very surprised to find the local climate can be so different from the surrounding areas as to permit such Mediterranean cultivation. I cannot account for it, other than to speculate that the mountains are arranged in such a way as to shield the valley from the winter winds and snows," Mr. Darcy replied.

"On the whole, however, the beauty of the surrounding countryside, its location near the new road, the warm and sheltered climate, and the commerce that passes through town over the Simplon, must necessarily restore the area in time," opined Mr. Darcy. "Buonaparte's new road over the Simplon is regarded as his greatest and most lasting achievement. Even his greatest detractors have been forced to acknowledge the art and genius with which the new road traverses the great canyons, spans seas of ice, is carved through wide galleries from solid rock through the highest mountains, and ties Italy firmly to the rest of Europe. I read that the road cost above one million pounds, but the most astonishing feat of all, to my understanding, is that the work is the result of collabouration between French and Italian engineers—I had not imagined the two peoples unable to agree on so much as the *measurement* to be used—metres, toise, French leagues, feet, or miles, Italian leagues, Roman miles, or *stadia*, the geometric mile—and here is an entire passage over the Alps!"

Georgiana continued from her book, reading "Since ancient times, there has been a path over the Simplon, traversable only by foot or mule. In the seventeenth century, a man named Baron von Stockalper laid out money to improve the road to a width of three yards, affording easier commerce between the low countries and the rest of Europe. Since that time, however, the road had fallen into such disrepair that Buonaparte found it again fit only for feet and mules. The martial significance of the road has diminished, while increasing to a far greater extent the commerce and pleasure-travel afforded by the wide, gently rising and falling highway."

All of the Darcys were struck by the audacity that had been turned, by Buonaparte, into the modern, safe highway they now travelled, and many times was the thought, "Thank Heaven I was not required to use the previous road!"

The longest day of travel was thirteen hours in duration, involving a journey from Brieg over the Simplon to Domo d'Ossola, a distance of over fourteen leagues. The military road, finished in 1805 at the joint expense of France and Italy under Buonaparte's direction, was such an extraordinary feat of engineering that the ascension of the carriage was barely perceptible. The road, cut through rocks and bridging precipices, boldly defied every obstruction, although some parts of the route were desolate in the extreme, and the sharp descents on the side of the road opposite the mountain-side served to remind the travellers of the perils entailed in the journey through these mountains. None of the family had expected to find so much beauty and sights of such admirable grandeur on this part of their road. The highway itself was consistently five-and-twenty Paris feet wide, and some fifty bridges joined the mountains to form a safe passage. Travelling along it, the Darcys could readily believe why it was universally regarded as the eighth wonder of the world.

Beginning at Glis, near-by Brieg, the Simplon passed over a bridge on the Saltine through villages, forests, and tremendous precipices to the first of the numerous galleries, often a league or longer in length. The passageway was extremely flat and good, with a substantial railing protecting any side where the ground fell away; and where the road had been cut deep into the mountain-side, a thick stone wall had been constructed with openings along its base, allowing water to pass through that otherwise would have flooded the road. A short distance past the bridge of Ganther dwelt the inspector of the road, who gave the travellers greeting and refreshment. The Darcys stopt for a few minutes to take advantage of the respite, whilst Georgiana hastily sketched the handsome, white stone bridge that spanned the Saltine and led to the second gallery.

Resuming their road, the Darcys passed over alarming chasms, marvellous bridge-works, enormous seas of glacial ice, and powerful cataracts falling from great heights of gorges cut into the mountains above. The glaciers, Georgiana explained, were called Tavernetto; to one side was the glacier of the Ganther, and the other stretched toward Italy. The streams formed from the melting ice produced a seemingly infinite number of cascades. The Gallery of the Glaciers could be viewed by looking back along the great road through the mountain, appearing for all the world as though Titans had carved the passageway through the very centre of the immense monument of rock, over which flowed the many cascades. The Darcys were awed by the genius that had envisioned such a feat, much less contrived its construction.

The highest part of the Simplon Pass was marked by a mile-stone indicating the summit, immediately below which was the ancient hospital to the right, and, on the left, the foundation works for the new hospital of the convent of St. Bernard. The whole distance over the pass from Glis to Simplon was a mere eight leagues and was, thanks to Buonaparte, now easily traversed in two days by the largest and heaviest of waggons and coaches. The Simplon itself proved to be a flat plain of barren rock, relieved only by the perpetual ice that covered the higher mountains farther on, and the peak of Rosboden. In this place, the new monastery was being constructed. The new hospital was to be large, and rents had been assigned from some Italian lands for the purpose of providing for its maintenance.

"I praise the love of God that inspires these men to live in such a desert," said Mr. Darcy, "and to willingly remain in this inimical climate during the unrelieved months of darkest, dreary winter. Even now, in the height of summer, we are surrounded by seas of ice and buffetted by strong winds—and uncomfortably cold!"

"Yes," agreed Elizabeth, "and to do so knowing that, whilst everything in their sight is buried in snow, day after day, with only the violent winds to shift the view, for many months of the year, the valley below is warm and alive with trees and flowers."

"Praise of such self-deprivation and piousness seems almost a profanity," continued Darcy. "So meagre are our thanks to such men who devote their lives to the preservation and consolation of the

miserable

miserable traveller who loses his way. I hope this new building relieves their privations to a significant degree"; Georgiana added the great dogs of St. Bernard to this panegyric, and they returned to their carriage after taking tea at the convent, but not before Mr. Darcy had pressed a generous note into the hands of the monk who bade them farewell.

Just beyond Simplon, and down the south face, Domo d'Ossola was a farther six leagues. The new road on this face of the pass was even more remarkable. As they reached the edge of the plateau, which lay nearly a mile above the sea, the valley was become more contracted, and the road began to descend. Here and there, flowers appeared with the season, but the scene was yet mostly one of ice, and a sublime blue-whiteness in every direction. In a short space of time, the village of Simplon appeared, with its several square towers perfectly silhouetted against the ice fields of Rosboden. At the bottom of a wilderness surrounded by high mountains, the village saw no sun for the greater part of the year, and, in consequence, the winters were long and cold; indeed, here of a twelve-month, eight were in winter. The inhabitants seemed cheerful, in contrast to their surroundings, and were comfortably situated: in the summer they raised sheep and tended the valley pastures, and in the winter, the men assisted with the transport of goods over the pass and clearing the road of the rock, trees, and snow which perpetually reburied it—much to their profit. However, the villagers were forced to purchase every necessity, and the brevity of the summer was not conducive to growing any food, not even potatoes. Georgiana told how the snows in winter frequently reached to the second floor of the houses in this place, and even in the midst of winter, there were no fewer than two hundred carts a day passing through the village, so important was this road to commerce.

The place-names became an increasing confusion of Germanic and Italian, with some French added in for good measure. The Darcys planned to take their midday meal at an inn just before Gunt, as it was named in the German language, but more commonly known in Italy as Gondo. The town was reached via the Gallery of Algaby through the granite chasms of the Krumbach, and into the dark Valley of Gondo, so-called because the sun does not penetrate to the valley floor but a few weeks of the year. The gallery was one of the longest on Buonaparte's road, and had been carved out of pure granite rock. Near-by the gallery was a building designed to protect travellers overtaken by severe weather, and to serve as quarters for those employed in clearing the road. Georgiana continued her description: "Before the present road was constructed, when the only mode of conveyance for goods was upon the backs of horses and mules, several hundreds of those animals, when suddenly overtaken by dangerous weather, might be detained at the inn at Gondo for many days." Excepting for occasional details that she read from her guide-book, Georgiana was entirely silent, and it seemed beyond the abilities of either Elizabeth or her husband to draw her into longer discourse.

The inn was a very old and queer place of seven or eight storeys, and had been built by the same Herr Stockalper for the convenience of merchants carrying cargoes over the pass. The old inn was clean and comfortable in the Swiss way, and the Darcys could well imagine the relief it had afforded the multitudes of weary travellers over the centuries, where it remained the only accommodation on the Italian side of the Simplon. They began again early the following morning, the new road winding now along the bank of the Doveria. Just past Gondo was a bridge of particularly ingenious construction, spanning the chasm into which fell a cascade of a remarkable brilliance. The glitter in the spray of the waterfall was owing to the stream issuing from the gorge at Zwischbergen, where there was a gold mine. Georgiana described the glittering rock as pyrite—not gold—originally contained within the granite, but liberated from the stone by the force of the water. Beyond Gondo, a small chapel marked the extent of the Valais, and, remarkably, the German language. Their carriages next passed through the Grand Gallery, which, like its neighbour, had been hewn through solid granite. Georgiana described it as, whilst less than seven hundred feet long, having taken a full eighteen months to complete, men labouring night and day. At the end of this gallery was the simple inscription, "Ære Italo."

At the termination of the Grand Gallery appeared a short bridge, spanning a roaring torrent issuing from the mountain rivulets above. It was inconceivable by what ingenuity the Italian engineers had contrived to erect the bridge over such a violent rush of water. Just over the bridge lay Isella, where the family were again stopt and their belongings scattered and searched, this time by the beneficence of the Italian officials. The Darcys and their servants were become so inured to the regular searches and questions, that they not only replied politely to the impertinent questions, but the servants assisted the customs-men in their inspection, as it proved to limit the disorder caused by their searches. They next crossed the enormous ravine of the Yselles to Divedro, which, in spite of the genius of Napoleon and his engineers, yet remained impassable after heavy rains and storms because of the risk of falling stones.

Travelling under more galleries carved into the mountains, past terrific wildernesses and desolation, and over bridges of wonderful ingenuity which gave passage over the most frightful ravines and cascades with ease, the Darcys at length reached the tall, handsome bridge of Crevola, traversing the Doveria, whence in one place can be seen the barren peaks and torrents of the Gondo valley, and in the opposite direction, the soft meadows and shady groves of the valley of Ossola.

CHAP. 11.

THE BRIDGE AT CREVOLA was said to be nearly one hundred feet tall, with two piers of twenty yards' width, and linked the Simplon with Gries, the other grand passage over the Alps to the Valais. The dress of the inhabitants of Crevola, whilst unremarkable in itself, was in such contrast to the residents of Domo d'Ossola, just one league away, that the Darcys could not help but comment.

"I have observed that the Crevolans of both sexes wore very coarse woolen cloathes, always of a brown or deep red colour, with thick, red stockings, whilst the dress of the residents of Domo is both varied and more elegant," said Elizabeth.

"And art adorns even the smallest of buildings," agreed Darcy, "even though this is but a small place. To my mind, this is the first truly Italian scene, though we have been travelling in Italy a good while. The border of Italy having been drawn and re-drawn so many times, there appears no improvement to its haphazardness, at least if one is to look at the inhabitants of the Simplon."

"Domo was a fortified town at the base of Monte Domo, at the upper end of the valley of Ossola." As they were descending from Crevola, Georgiana continued, "Domo probably gets its name from its being the first church in the Ossola Valley. In ancient times, Domo was a fief of the Bishop of Novarra, who built the castle seen now as a ruin. It was then subject to Milan, then Sardinia; at the end of the last century, it was reunited with Milan by Buonaparte as the Cisapline Republic, and, as we know, was returned to Austria in 1815 at the Congress of Vienna, along with Lombardy."

The town of Domo was prosperous and busy. The ancient convent of the Jesuits was of black and white marble. The whole of the place was planted with vines, growing on stone trellises, and a pergola similarly covered led to the river, beyond which were lush pastures being grazed by cattle. An hill a small distance from the centre of town was of the name Calvary, and the distance from Domo to it was lined with picturesque, round chapels, each housing a life-sized figure from the life of Jesus, at which the pious knelt to pray.

As they descended into Domo, the towns-people pointed and repeatedly cried, "Eccolo! Inglese! Inglese!" The Darcys staid at a small inn at Domo, where the food was remarkably fresh and good, especially so after the days spent in the mountains where victuals had been perforce more scarce and usually of poor quality. That evening, they enquired of some fellow travellers how the Italians knew they were English by the sight of their equipage. An older gentleman by the name of Ponti answered,

"In Italy, it is considered the height of impropriety for a woman to be seated on the outside of a carriage. Doing so shocks their notions of the deference and courtesy due to women—notwithstanding any consideration of rank. It is only the English who suffer their domestics to endure the pleasures of fresh air and the companionship of her fellow-servants on the box, as opposed to being seated within, sweltering and choaking in crowded proximity to everyone else inside, with whom she could not converse with propriety." The other guests were content to make the usual charges against the English, those of pride and *hauteur*. Elizabeth could not gainsay even such a universality as that supposed, given the friendliness and courtesy with which they generally had been received; in her reflections on the reserve and self-restraint that denoted good-breeding and civility in England, such formality could easily, she thought, be translated into arrogance and pretention by a people who regarded an easy familiarity, warmth of expression, and openness of manners to be indicative of courtesy.

Leaving Domo on the morrow, the Darcys passed through Villa d'Ossola, and thence through Ponte Mazzone and Manangione, where the road reached the wide, level valley, and thence through Orvanasco, Gravelona, and Feriolo, crossed the great bridge of Baveno, with its view of the lovely Madre Islands, and into Stresa, on the shore of Lake Maggiore. After one night's stay at Stresa, Elizabeth and Darcy left Georgiana, who wished to remain there to rest, and embarked upon a boat trip across Lake Maggiore to stay the night on Isola Bella, before they rejoined Georgiana and their carriages at Sesto-Calende. Isola Bella was the site of a palace and chapel built by the Counts of

Borromeo, now partially in ruins; on the southern part lay a grove of citron and orange-trees, figs and peaches surrounded by myrtle, jessamin, and roses of all colours. The Darcys learnt that, as the island was not protected from the strong winter winds, as were the other Madre Islands, the Borromeos went to the extraordinary expense each year to cover the vegetation on the island with thick, interfitting planks to protect the delicate plantings. The Darcys settled in at the only such habitation on the island, the curiously named Dolphin Inn. Before supper—which was served quite late, even later than the European practise—they circumnavigated the island, viewing the walls of the castle, atop which sat many marble statues, obelisks, and urns of exotic plants. An immense unicorn, the emblem of the Borromeo family, topped the castle. Rain-water, carefully collected from the terraces and stored in a reservoir beneath the gardens, was then distributed to fountains and *jets d'eau*. The view from the upper-most terrace was magnificent, giving a panorama of the lake and all of the surrounding mountains as far as the glaciers of the Simplon.

The Darcys rose tolerably early, and took a barque along the western shores of Lake Maggiore past Stresa, Arono, and Dormelletto, to Sesto Calende, where the Tessino leaves Lake Maggiore. Arriving at Sesto Calende, the Darcys met their carriages and Georgiana and continued on, as Milan was yet beyond the reach of a day's journey by carriage. They noted that the Simplon Road did not end at Simplon, or even Domo, but the wide, flat road, bridges, aqueducts, railings and other works of Buonaparte's effort appeared all the way to Milan. Sesto was succeeded by the plains of Lombardy, a flat expanse cultivated with immense swaths of corn and other grains, interspersed here and there with grape-vines and mulberry trees. Somma claimed to be the city where Hannibal defeated Scipio. In one of the gardens that surround that city was said to be a cypress tree of enormous girth, but the Darcys agreed that they would suspend the pleasure of seeing another tree— even a very large one—in favour of reaching their inn at an earlier hour. They stopt the night at Cerro Maggiore which, despite its grand name, afforded only one inn, poorly kept, and deplorably dirty.

Whilst *en route* to Milan, Georgiana valiantly struggled to keep up the appearance of composure, if not actual felicity. She was thankful to have her guide-books with her, and so could fill the hours rumbling along the final stage of the Via Sempione, relating the very bloody history of Milan, which had been besieged, sacked, and destroyed with an astonishing frequency. More recently, she concluded, in the past century alone, the city had been the possession of Spain, Germany, Austria, France, two states of Italy, and was again now a subject of Austria. Elizabeth wondered aloud how the Milanese could keep themselves in writing-paper with such frequent alteration of address, but perhaps the industry of the printers was a portion of the apparent prosperity they now beheld. Mr. Darcy smiled at this *bon mot*, but Elizabeth might have been speaking to herself, for all of the response she drew from Georgiana. At length, Georgiana recollected herself enough to inform them that present-day Milan had a population of about one hundred and fifty thousand souls.

Driving into the city, their route took them past the terminus of the Simplon, Buonaparte's Triumphal Arch, sadly unfinished. The end of the Simplon as it approached Milan was very grand. The main road, passing through the great gates into Milan, was at least as wide as Piccadilly, with wide pavements on each side for the benefit of those walking. Unlike Paris, Milan was a warren of small, irregular streets, with few avenues of any size, and many streets so small that they could but barely accommodate a coach-and-four. Mr. Harmon was greatly vexed at the manœuvres required to get close to their hôtel. The streets were a riot of carts, waggons, persons crossing everywhere, with no regard as to whether their way was clear, men standing in the street, shouting at one another, at passers-by, and even at persons at windows above the street. The noise and odours of the city were unlike any other of their knowledge, and made streets of Paris look like an oasis of well-regulated tranquility by comparison. They, at last, arrived at the Albergo della Gran-Bretagne, where they were to pass several days, and saw their baggage removed into the hôtel, and their horses and carriages disposed of safely in a mews near-by. Before they could settle into their rooms, it was necessary for Mr. Darcy to agree the price of their stay. As disagreeable as it was to the sensibilities of the English, Darcy had been advised that making a previous bargain was the only method of securing himself and his family against the greater evil of a dispute upon departure.

Milan was the last-intended meeting place of the Darcys with Colonel Fitzwilliam, but upon their arrival, a letter awaited Mr. Darcy, again full of apologies and explaining that the Colonel was delayed again a mere few days, but he would be sure to meet them at Venice. Georgiana, not having an idea previously of such an effect being possible, her heart now sank even further and she grew proportionately more silent and melancholy. She knew not how she could support herself well enough to

appear

appear composed, and was unable to make any excuse for her obvious indisposition upon their arrival, other than she had the head-ache and would be glad to lie down. She later sent word that she did not care for supper, and would rather rest until the morrow.

It was said that the music and theatre of Milan eclipsed even that of Paris. The three, of course, attended La Scala and La Canobiana, where the spring season of performances was in its final weeks, and as a consequence were exceptionally fine. There were numerous other modern theatres, including a remarkable recent construction, Il Teatro Carcano, built entirely of wood inside, said to have very superior sound, and the latest, Il Teatro Rè, built purposely for the staging of comedies. However, Il Teatro Filodrammatico, designed by Antolini, was notable not only for its exceptional plan which forbade the customary private boxes (in the interest of requiring the would-be box-holders to attend to the performance!), but also its practise to provide nearly one thousand seats *gratis* to the citizens of Milan—and that the company was comprised entirely of amateur players. It seemed to the Darcys to be the last bastion remaining of the days of the Repubblica; they were not at all surprised to learn that its informal appellation was, "Il patriotico." There was a theatre of marionettes—of almost human size—that performed all of the action of the piece with a naturalness that almost led one to believe that they were real people, so especially well did the voices from behind match the action of the puppets. Mr. Darcy remarked in a very droll manner that the puppets acted like men, whilst in the play of the previous evening, the men had acted like puppets.

During the day, they visited the principal sights: the Duomo, a construction entirely of white marble taken from Lago Maggiore, which had been, unaccountably. chosen by Buonaparte to stand as the exception to his policy of desecration of the vast cathedrals—including those of France—to such a great degree that the Duomo had actually been *completed* by the Emperour only some few years before his defeat. The exterior had been adorned with a great quantity of gilding, and countless statues, reliefs, and other ornaments, all executed in marble of the purest white. However, the interior, with its legions of marble columns, was its real ornament. The inside of the Duomo was cavernous. The crypt, supported by columns of silver and variously coloured marbles, contained numerous ancient scenes on ivory in-set with jewels, and a great sarcophagus of silver and gold—through which the corpse was visible! A prefect was called to shew them the tomb, which was revealed by opening a sliding door. Visible within the glass coffin was the blackened body of St. Borromeo in his mitre and what remained of his vestments; an innumerable array of jewelry, precious stones, and gold surrounded the body entirely. The Darcys said what was proper and exited the church.

"It is not my place to decide any theological question," began Georgiana when they had quitted the gloom of the Duomo's interior, "but such a display approaches too nearly to idolatry for my comfort. I am sure he was a very good and a great man, but he was a *man*; such reverence and display seem—to my view—to promote the worship of the man more than the God who made the man, and the Saviour who redeemed him. And, surely, all of that wealth that surrounds the saint could be better used in feeding and cloathing the poor, relieving the worst of their wants. Such wealth and veneration appears—in my own view—to be more a distraction from faith, than a corporeal justification for it."

"But remember," answered Mr. Darcy, "that to a Catholick adherent, the Pope is God's representative here on earth. It was Pope Paul V who conferred Borromeo's divinity."

Georgiana was not usually wont to reply to such a definitive conclusion, especially one received as the wisdom of her brother, but she answered his explanation with a firmness that Elizabeth had never before witnessed: "Yes, Brother, but he was a *man*, chosen by men. Whether or not the choice of these men is acceptable and consistent with the will of God is a matter for each to determine according to his faith. *My* faith dictates that such a sumptuary display and reverence for any *man* is offensive to God, and from everything I have read about the life of Charles Borromeo, I would venture his agreement." Mr. Darcy was both too surprised and too satisfied by her answer to rejoin.

The Darcys visited the ancient Church of St. Ambrose and saw its mosaics; Santa Maria della Grazie and Leonardo's "The Last Supper," which existed in a most deplorable state of decay; the Palazzo Reale and its grand Sala Cariatidi; various *piazzas* and *casas*; the square of the ancient Castle of Milan, which is all that remained; the Great Hospital; the Ambrosian Library and the Brera Gallery. The family frequented the shops—selling every conceivable luxury, and seeming to vie with one another for the most opulent interior—walked along the Giardino Publico, La Rena, or the *esplanade* of the Castle, and took refreshment in one of the numerous and elegant coffee-houses.

They visited the great mint, where the money was coined from large bricks of silver into the finished pieces. It was a wonder of machinery,

being

being entirely water-driven, including the immense coin-stamp which, they were told, could mint 1,500 pieces of coin every hour! The coins were verified by weighing each on a balance that was so precisely constructed as to indicate a difference of one eight-hundredth of a grain. The coins, designed by Buonaparte, were perfect: appealing in their design, easy to distinguish, and of sufficient size as to present no impediment to use by the old, the young, or the blind. The Darcys were again grown weary of such a satiety of the senses, that the three were become nearly unable to distinguish one example of wonder from the next. However, the avocation of the traveller does not admit of such defeat, and they valiantly continued their inspections and educations with an increasingly forced enthusiasm.

On Sunday, there being no Protestant church, the Darcys sat for service at two of the Romish places of worship, before retiring to their own rooms for private devotion. At each church, an old priest, carrying a staff with a pouch at the end, pointed this rod at the face of each parishioner in turn, and, shaking the stick in a most offensive manner, demanded a donation for the services! The Darcys were torn betwixt amusement and offense, and even Mr. Darcy could not quickly formulate any response to such treatment; after the first such episode, they concluded that a small token would be sufficient to acquit both conscience and civility with credit.

Milan, despite being an handsome city, had the air of being somehow incomplete. This impression was settled more firmly in their minds ever since the Darcys had driven through the triumphal arch. The exterior of the magnificent Cathedral—one of the largest churches in Italy—like-wise remained in a state of progress, and despite the beauty and scale boasted by the city's other fine buildings, including many theatres, libraries, and colleges, they felt a sense of disappointment with the city. The decay and dirt that over-spread the monuments of Milan detracted from their magnificence; it seemed to the English that the surfeit of antiquities and monuments had made them invisible to the Milanese, who seemed to care not at all for their condition.

On the last day of their residence in Milan, the family were finishing their letters and other small occupations, when the under-butler requested to speak with Mr. Darcy urgently; the steward's boy was nowhere to be found! Mr. Darcy immediately thought of despatching Mr. Harmon in search of the boy, but then recollected that not one of their servants spoke Italian; Georgiana's French maid, Adèle, might be intelligible to the Italians, but was more likely to get lost herself than

assist   113

assist anyone else in being found. Consequently, Darcy determined to go himself, and asked Georgiana if she would accompany Mr. Harmon so that they could expand their search in a shorter period of time. He found her in her apartment, looking vacantly out of the window with a book on her lap; but, upon his application, she was very willing to assist. In the space of two hours, the boy returned alone, relating that he had lost his way in walking about the town; it had grown dark, and he was unable to remember the name of the hôtel. He had been walking about for over an hour, not knowing which was the right way back again, was become bewildered, and could see no familiar-looking landmark to guide his path home. He had tried speaking with innumerable passers-by, who alternately stared or laughed at his language and pointed at him. He had then found himself the object of a small crowd, entirely surrounded by Milanese, making great sport of his distress. He was grown very frightened; when, at length, an older gentleman had approached asking, in English, if the boy needed assistance. Strangely, he had been walking within a few streets of the hôtel all along. Mr. Darcy returned sometime thereafter, having had no success, just ahead of Mr. Harmon and Miss Darcy—all very pleased to see the young man safe and returned to them. Without further incident, the party met their horses and baggage the next morning, and continued on the north-east post road to Caravaggio *en route* to Venice.

CHAP. 12.

THE DARCYS PASSED THROUGH a rich agricultural district, dotted with pretty villas and gardens, in the environs of Caseina de Pecchi, Gorgonzola, Caravaggio, Chiari, and Brescia. The roads were become dusty and very hot, and so the cool area of Lago Gardia and their rooms at Desenzano were a welcome relief. That evening, there were several showers, which abated the heats of the following day, and helped to lay a portion of the dust. Enclosed by the Southern Alps, the area around the lake was a vast expanse of vineyards of very old vines, some of which had been trained as arbours over the roads of the country, forming a long arcade that shielded the carriages from the worst of the sun. The Darcys were by now grown used to the strong sun, brown fields, and dust of Italy. Their memories of pictures of sun-drenched villas covered in flowering vines were of no assistance in the reality of the heat, glare, and dirt which comprised the day-time hours of their travel. However, the land was very productive, and the food served at the posting-inns was very fresh and delightful in every way, especially a dish the Italians called *pasta*, a type of boiled, unleavened dough that was fashioned into every imaginable shape and size, and eaten amidst a *ragoût* of tomatoes and other vegetables, or in a rich cream gravy. The Italians were like-wise fond of a great variety of sausages, again of nearly every conceivable geometry, which were also very savoury. The Darcys adopted the Italian habit of taking their mid-day meal in baskets made up by the inn-keeper, and composed of these sausages, some fruit, the wonderful Italian bread, and a bottle or two of the local wine; these comestibles made for a jolly pic-nick along the road, and did not require the party to suspend the meal until they were come to an inn.

Along the road to Verona, fruits appeared in abundance: grapes, figs, pomegranates, and orchards of apples, pears, mulberries, nuts, olives, &c., easily and cheaply procured. Verona was an ancient city, with numerous arches and an enormous marble amphitheatre in unusually good condition, all of Roman construction. The Darcys arrived just after midday, in time to see the Cathedral, with its wonderful paintings, and the Theatro Nuovo, with its portico designed by Palladio, a native of that city. Elizabeth and her husband took a short walk beyond the ancient gates of the city, the Porta del Borsari, to see the crenellations and towers of the city walls framed by the blue Alps behind, the sparkling waters of the Adige, and the four bridges that connected the city to the handsome villas and their gardens, plantations of shade trees, and dark cypress which dotted the near hillsides. Such a fine prospect painted in the last rays of sunlight provided a welcome palliative for the ills of noise, jostling, and general tedium of travel.

Their enjoyment of Verona was suspended most abruptly when, returning to their *pensione*, the Darcys met an old gentleman coming from the opposite direction whence they had just come, visibly distressed in his mind, as well as his person, and the contents of his chaise in great disarray. Mr. Darcy assisted the spare, elderly man down from the seat, and learnt that he was just come from Vicenza and had been set-upon by a troupe of *banditti*, armed with pistols and knives. He was a physician from Geneva, and had been at Padua to attend some scientifical lectures there, when, on his road home, he had been beaten and robbed. The masked *banditti* had forced the postillion to dismount; they then secured his neck with ropes under one of the wheels of the carriage to prevent his assisting his master. The largest highway-man had then proceeded to attack the gentle doctor, whilst his associates threw everything out of the chaise, including its seats and carpets, taking anything and everything of value. The old man was spared only after shewing them where anything of value had been stored; consequently, he had been robbed of all of his cloathes, save what he was wearing, and had been deprived of his watch, his money, his boots, and even his hat and gloves. The *banditti* had apparently mistaken him for a personage of greater fortune; thus, the doctor counted himself extremely lucky to have escaped with his life, so enraged were the highway-men at finding that his valuables fell greatly short of their expectations. Mr. Darcy attended him into the hôtel, and saw that the doctor was well-treated and comfortable, before returning to Elizabeth and Georgiana.

In consequence of the poor doctor's misfortune, Mr. Darcy secured the services of two Austrian mounted soldiers to ride with their carriage, and,

❧   leaving

leaving Verona early the next morning with their baskets full of foods for eating *en route*, he planned for only a brief stop at mid-day, arriving at Vicenza that evening. Despite their early departure and the many trees adjoining the road, the drive was hot, dirty, and seemingly interminable. The entire length of the road from Verona to Vicenza was lined with mulberry vines, to which various fruits and flowers had been anchored; Elizabeth remarked that such Arcadian surroundings seemed at great variance with the necessity of travelling with armed guards. Arriving late, and taking an hasty supper, the Darcys tarried some little time in the morning to see Vicenza, before setting off for Padua, a less arduous distance than the previous day's journey by one-third. Their guards were to leave them at Padua, asserting that the road to Venice was unquestionably safe.

Still in the country of the great Palladio, Vicenza had other works by the master, including six of its renowned palazzi, and the modern—for its time—Teatro Olimpico. The Darcys elected to visit the town only briefly that morning, using the remaining hours of leisure to admire Palladio's own house just south of the city. They passed the grand Villa Valmarana on their way to the Rotonda, with its sweeping gardens, but it was not yet open for the day, so early were they gone out of Vicenza, and so the paintings of Tiepolo missed seeing the Darcy party on their road to Padua.

As with the greatest proportion of the paragons of human ingenuity to be seen in Italy, objects which—at a little distance—seemed delightful and sound, upon closer inspection revealed marks of inattention and decay. The Rotonda Capra was situated at the foot of Monte Berico, and like the other works of the architect at Verona and Vicenza, the square house with its round saloon was in a sad state. Despite the ruination of the building, the genius of its conception was yet apparent; equally so was the wisdom of Lord Burlington who constructed a copy at Chiswick, the latter of which was in far better repair, and so more easily admired. The four sides were ascended on wide stairs, surmounted by porches delineated by Corinthian pillars. The saloon had exquisite proportions, and the effect of the whole presented a magnificent form when viewed from any direction. Darcy was thorough in his admiration; Elizabeth thought it interesting, but did not think that it was likely to have been very comfortable as an *home*—unlike dear Pemberley—and Georgiana was content to approve everything said by either, but her commendations seemed little more than absence of mind.

The day was unrelentingly hot, with the consequence that the dust and dirt on the road were even worse than the previous days', although the punishment was of shorter duration. Their travelling cloathes were now a uniform light brown, as were the contents of anything not tightly sealed, despite having taken the precaution to wrap the trunks and portmanteaux affixed to the outside of the carriages in tarpaulins made for the purpose. It was inconceivable what magnitude of dust would afflict the insides of the trunks thrown unprotected into the basket of the public coaches!

The Darcys arrived in Padua at an hour sufficiently early to afford them a short rest before supper. Georgiana appeared downstairs with her brother and Elizabeth, but seeing the dining room had but one large table, declared herself unequal to dining *en famille* with the other guests at the inn, owing to fatigue, and asked that a tray be brought up. Elizabeth was spared the burthen of making Georgiana's excuses, as she really *did* look very tired and somewhat unwell. Elizabeth felt her sister's absence more than usual, as the conversation around the dinner-table that evening was unusually interesting and pleasant. Everyone around the table had some story or anecdote to relate, but one in particular was sufficiently amusing that Elizabeth resolved to listen especially closely in order that she might relate it to Georgiana on the morrow:

"My family is now just come from Venice, where we received a most peculiar treatment from the keeper of a *pensione* in that city. Some years before, the Emperour and two of his brothers had lodged at the same inn as we were then presently. The inn-keeper was so vain of this instance, that no other subject could interest him. He entertained us with interminable particulars regarding these illustrious guests, it being an impossibility that he forget these trifles, so constantly had they been repeated. At length, it was necessary that I interrupt this succession of nothings to enquire what we could have for our supper. He answered that we should take our meal in the *very same* room in which His Imperial Majesty had dined. Wherefore, I repeated my question, to which he replied that he did not believe there to be three more affable princes in all of Christendom. I answered this by stating that I hoped supper would be soon upon the table, whereupon he told me with the utmost assurance, that the Archduke was fond of *fricassee*, but that the Emperour preferred a capon, plain-roasted. At this last, I was grown impatient, and said that my family and I would be much obliged if he would send in the supper as expeditiously as may be. The good man finally walked to the doorway of the kitchen, but before disappearing through it, he turned about once more to declare that his Majesty had eaten no more than any other man, yet he had paid like a king!"

"Did you at last get your supper?" enquired Elizabeth.

"That we did, in something above an hour hence, at which time I cared not what was placed before me, so hungry was I become in that long interval," he replied, "but the good man then requested that we 'please to disregard and be pleased' at the small quantity of food and how poorly it was dressed, as it was impossible to conjure satisfactory food from the very air!"

The country between Vicenza and Padua was flat, and despite the lack of rain in the present season, some low parts were wet and fen-like. Crossing the Brenta on the Via Vicenza into the Via Savaronola and through the ancient ramparts of the heavily fortified city, it required no extraordinary stretch of belief to accept the assertion that Padua was northern Italy's oldest city. Georgiana read aloud from an history of Padua: the city has used the port of Noventa Padovana since ancient times. In the thirteenth century, the first of the canals joining the port with Padua was constructed, creating a waterway between Padua and Venice. Portions of the walls around the city were still visible, with mediæval sections leading to the ancient Carmine Church, and the earliest sections within those, surrounding the old town centre, palaces and University. The Darcys did not find Padua an handsome city, excepting its University, as designed by Palladio. The most striking building in the city was the enormous Palazzo della Municipalita, built in the twelfth century to form one side of the market-place. There were wonderful ancient frescoes, but in a desperate state, despite having been repainted within memory. The Palazzo's vast roof, unsupported by visible pillars, was said to be the largest in the world.

In the leisure before supper, Mr. and Mrs. Darcy walked about the town by themselves, and took coffee in one of the many pleasant coffee-houses near the Duomo. Later, Georgiana felt well enough that evening to join them for dinner; she ate but little, and Elizabeth's better knowledge of her sister allowed her to discern that this briefest of civilities required a great effort. When she did labour to animate herself, it appeared she did so more for the purpose of relieving her family's apprehensions than finding some reprieve from her own.

Writing to Jane that evening, Elizabeth gave vent to the frustrations of this portion of their route:

DEAREST JANE,

I must warn you from the outset, that I am hot, tired, and cross. Our journey to-day has been a long one, about eight leagues, but blessedly shorter than that of yesterday. The dust has been appalling, and is everywhere: on our cloathes, in our eyes, and over as well as inside every item we have within or without. It is very warm here—warmer than I can ever remember. The summer is just yet beginning; I have no wish to know better what the inhabitants of Italy must suffer in the odious heats of late July and August.

I should stop my general pattern of incivility here and pause long enough in the recitation of my own complaints to hope that yours are tolerably minor, and that you are all nicely cold. Colonel Fitzwilliam did not meet us in Milan, as planned—or as I should say—planned for the second or third time to meet us somewhere or other, only to find his letter—instead of his person—at place such-and-such, apologising for his further delay. It is very strange.

I do not wish to alarm you, but Mr. Darcy and I are both quite anxious over Georgiana's health and spirits. She becomes quieter and more unsettled with each day, and loses weight and colour. Beyond that, I have little to relate. I have given many hints to her, by which I hoped to encourage her confidence, but have had no success. Instead, she reads to us from her collection of travellers' books and tries to hide her unhappiness from our notice. She is quite looking forward to Venice and is rereading *Udolpho* by night and day, so I hope our arrival there in a few days will answer for a general improvement to her spirits. I would usually make some pun on "mysterious" here, in conjunction with having mentioned Mrs. Radcliffe, but Georgiana's indisposition has attended her too long, and her spirits are, in general, so depressed, that the subject does not lend itself even to my ready wit; I must, therefore, resume my own complaints, which will, I hope, prove more useful.

I suppose I should next remark on the grandeur of the scenery or the wondrous works of man we have seen, but I cannot. Nature I will allow to be praised to whatever extent you please, but the works of our fellow-man are more apt to find censure in my assessments. The great monuments, paintings, buildings, &c., are surely very beautiful, and many rise to magnificence. However, everything we have seen in Italy is—to a great degree—in a such state of dirt or decay that, oft-times, all beauty and awe are left entirely behind. One is seldom able to form a very complete understanding of these master-pieces because of their deplorable condition. I do not wish to seem to congratulate ourselves at the expense of others, but I declare the British Museum at Montague House is in far better order than anything I have seen since leaving Geneva. It is not very wonderful that it should be so: the general dirty state of the houses and inns is evident, as well as the very populous state of the vermin; fleas and insects of every shape and colour are become our inseparable companions, clinging to us with an avidity akin to love. They rise with us in the mornings, secure themselves about our cloathing and belongings, travel with us all the day, and retire with us at night. I wish I could give you a better account of their faithful servitude, but I am afraid that we are all of us so querulous as to declare such generous attentions in every way disgusting. I impute their legions to the fact that men are generally employed here as chamber-maids, a most unnatural situation. What is more, what the English would regard as the common water-closet is generally hereabouts unknown, and the odours, in consequence, defy any polite power to describe. I realise that these are not the accustomary panegyrics of the traveller, but I will have no reserve from you, dearest Jane, even though you must, by now, be heartily wishing for it.

Thankfully we are to arrive to-morrow at Venice. I will not write again until I find myself in a more generous humour.

Your loving sister,

Elizabeth Darcy

In the shade of the acute disappointment occasioned by having reached Milan, only to find Colonel Fitzwilliam's continued truancy, the scenes thenceforth were unlikely to yield consolation for the increasing pain of his absence, and Georgiana had been predictably miserable. Neither wishing to be a source of anxiety to her family, nor having any inclination herself for the heroic ambition of existing in a state of perpetual torment, she learnt instead to anticipate the pleasures of Venice. She found sympathy in contemplating the dark tones of that city, which coincided with the temper of her thoughts: gloomy, apprehensive, alien. She knew Radcliffe's descriptions of Venice well enough to fancy herself already there; passing through Padua, she abandoned Emily hardly long enough to acknowledge its fine cathedral, claimed to have been designed by the great Michael-Angelo himself.

From near-by Mestre, which the Darcys reached the next afternoon, and where they would leave their carriages, Venice was only five miles away by water. Not wishing to suspend any pleasure of Georgiana's, the family travelled directly across that evening, rather than staying ashore that night. Like Emily's first view in *The Mysteries of Udolpho*, as Venice appeared, the sun sank in the west, colouring the waves into a blanket of saffron and the marble colonnades of St. Mark's in a golden haze. To Georgiana, the city seemed to be ascending out of the sea, apace with the rising moon. In Venice, one could look in any direction and see the dark outlines of palaces, churches, and other magnificent buildings. Georgiana felt that all of the prose and poetry about Venice was insufficient to do it justice; it was necessary for one to experience such foreign sensations in order to appreciate its singular mystery and charm.

C H A P . 1 3 .

GEORGIANA'S RELIEF IN ARRIVING there had the additional compensation of her retaining little expectation of meeting the Colonel in Venice, and, hence, sparing herself some portion of additional disappointment. Having settled themselves at the Albergo dell' Europa near the Rialto, the Darcys walked about near their hôtel, first making their way to St. Mark's Square. The family admired the Basilica and the Doge's Palace, imagining the final passage of the criminals across the bridge latterly immortalised as "The Bridge of Sighs" by Lord Byron, connecting the interrogation rooms at the Palace to the prisons. The Square of St. Mark was several hundred feet on a side, enclosed by a colonnade surrounding the whole extent, enclosing beautiful shops, cafes, &c., on three sides, with the Cathedral of St. Mark, the Doge's Palace, and the Campanile Tower—where Galileo had recorded the movement of the stars—on the fourth. The square was well-lit and had altogether a most magnificent appearance. In the centre, a military band played festive marches and charming Italian airs.

The first day's outing necessarily encompassed a visit to St. Mark's church. The building itself was constructed principally of Grecian materials, and the effect of the innumerable columns, pillars, galleries, balustrades, and cupolas gave the church an almost Mohemmetan appearance. The dark, heavy interior was over-sated with such an encumbrance of colour, gilded decoration, and mosaic that its effect acted contrary to whatever architecture was evident. Applying to one of the procurators to see the famous treasure, therein they saw pillars, said to be from Solomon's temple at Jerusalem, a fragment of the Virgin Mary's veil and a lock of her hair, the knife used by the Saviour at His last supper, and a vast quantity of other relics, all said to be of saints and martyrs. There were jewels and vessels of precious metals, but perhaps the most remarkable single item was a painting of the Virgin, said to be by St. Luke. The picture was very plain, especially in contrast to the sumptuousness of its neighbours. Darcy recalled a witticism that had been written of this picture: "I have known many very good painters who would have made bad saints; and here is an instance of an excellent saint who was but an indifferent painter."

They hurried over to the Ducal Palace, as it had started to rain. The palace was an immense edifice created entirely in marble, and, once inside, they saw that the walls were all-over ornamented with works by the Italian masters. In addition to the residence of the Doge, there were chambers for the senate and other departments of the Venetian government. The exterior was of a most unpleasing design, especially in the country that had produced the genius of Palladio: massive walls resting on a filigree of slender frets, arabesques, arcs, and circles. The corners of the building had been cut away to give room for spiralled columns, which would have been placed to better effect almost anywhere else. The over-all impression was that the building appeared eternally on the verge of collapse, so slender were the supports for the massive, high walls.

The Darcys' immediate impression of the Venetians was that they were a lively and imaginative people, extremely fond of public amusements—especially of the comedic variety—and yet very attached to the real enjoyments of life: family, food, and pleasant society. Despite the surfeit of ornamentation that everywhere appeared, the Venetians themselves seemed to have little regard for vanity or ostentation in their persons. The lower orders appeared remarkably sober, obliging, and kind. They were a tall, attractive people, less given to corpulence than many others.

"I was under a continual misapprehension that we would see no-one but those hiding behind a mask," said Elizabeth, as they were walking about the city one evening, "and that all of the women were hid behind bars, chained under lock and key. Instead, women in Venice go about with a remarkable degree of freedom, unusual even for London or Paris. Moreover, a mask is no-where to be seen! Georgiana, what do your books have to say on these matters?"

Georgiana briefly replied that masks had disappeared with the French governance, as had, presumably, the practise of securing women within the house.

Mr. Darcy replied that he believed the whole mystery of the mask to be one largely of fiction. "When I was here previously, the mask was become an innocent affectation, conceived in antiquity as the general method for hiding the identities of murderers and thieves. The anonymous evils once commonly perpetrated via the *stiletto* had even then been long-remedied. Indeed, so long ago as to be within even *my* memory, a mask was at that time only used by such gentlemen who wished to go abroad without the encumbrance of wearing full dress. A mask stuck up in the hat and a great black cape, was regarded as acceptable dress for any appearance in Venetian society. In the last years before the French occupation, I believe that masks were regarded as a quaint affectation of older gentlemen who *wished* for a reputation of intrigue, but who would more likely prefer a warm seat by the fire to the most beautiful woman in Venice."

The following morning, the three went to see the Royal Academy of Arts, where were collected a great number of the most extraordinary pictures and statues, as large and as natural as life. The Accademia had been moved to its present location by Buonaparte, and the pictures seemed to be an unrelated jumble attached to the walls of the old Scuola. As everywhere in Italy, the works of the great masters–Veronese, Tintoretto, Titian, Tiepolo, Bassano—suffered evidence of unarrested decay, some to a disgraceful degree. In some places, the roof had failed its office; in others, the soot and general city soil rendered the figures in the paintings indistinguishable from one another; in yet others, the painted-in repairs seemed to be at variance with their object. Mr. Darcy supposed that the Venetians must be blinded by the surfeit of art around themselves, unable to see the state of decay. Elizabeth was heartily glad not to be a connoisseur, as a true proficient in the arts must be dismayed beyond recovery by the shocking condition of the statuary, paintings, and even the buildings that housed them. Georgiana wandered about without appearing entirely aware of her surroundings, and when called upon for an opinion by her brother or sister, would start, and either ask for a repetition of the question, or beg their indulgence, as she had not been quite attending. Upon leaving the Accademia, the weather that had been exceedingly fine since the morning, underwent a remarkable change; the rain descended in torrents. The three hastened to the hôtel, preventing their further commentary as connoisseurs for the remainder of the day.

That evening, they attended a comedy by the Venetian Goldoni, *The Mistress of the Inn*, which was highly diverting, and all the more enjoyable as the libretto in the soft dialect of the Venetians was able to be heard by all in attendance. Considering the modest number of its inhabitants, Venice boasted an extraordinary quantity of playhouses, there being above eight, including the opera-houses. Admittance to these productions cost so little, that those filling the rear of the pit included footmen, labourers, and gondoliers, all in the cloathing they had worn during the day. The interiors of the houses were very plain and dark, especially compared to the brilliancy of those of London or Paris. They Darcys learnt that the boxes were purposefully kept dark, so that the inhabitants could *not* be distinguished—the very reverse of Paris! The performance on the stage, however, was so well illuminated, that every eye could see the acting in every corner thereupon with ease. The theatre curtain never rose earlier than 10 o'clock and, as it soon became apparent to the family, people of rank never appeared before midnight. That rule applied particularly to ladies, unless the performance were a *première*, when punctuality was demanded.

The Darcys also attended opera and its accompanying *balleto*, but could not admire the performance as they had in Paris and Geneva. The Italians were principally acrobats who set the movements to music, as opposed to an intentional combination of the two arts. Despite this, it was apparent that the Venetians were, as with their English counterparts, partial to the dance. Much of the opera had gone unattended by the audience, but the instant the dancers appeared, all conversation was universally suspended, and all attention fixed upon the stage. They attended the premier performance of Rossini's *Eduardo e Cristina* at the Teatro San Benedetto. The interior could not compare with the grandeur of La Fenice, but the production was quite enjoyable, nonetheless; and, as with the theatres in Geneva and Milan, was attended-to diligently by the Venetian audience, especially when compared with their Parisian equivalents, much to Georgiana's satisfaction.

La Serenissima was justly characterised as a city of ambiguous extremes, and beneath the piety of the congregations in the churches and the Apolline beauty of the exteriors, the city also harboured a prospering underworld of licentiousness and libertinism. Georgiana saw enough—viewed through the lens of decay in the externalities—to discern, much to her disappointment, a scene of degradation, both of the moral and the physical, that could excite but little admiration. Try as she might, she could not leave her prejudice aside, and view Italy inherently with the eyes of the Italians. As she spent more time in Italy, this tension increased rather than otherwise, and Georgiana found she could not resist comparing everything to the familiar scenes and

employments

employments of home. Georgiana believed herself suffering under an ever-increasing burthen of that common malady—homesickness. She was not afraid of those sensations—such uneasiness was too common-place and too reasonable to require remedy. However, to speak of her distress was unthinkable, for fear of sounding ungrateful; she kept these feelings to herself, only daring to allude in the most tentative of ways to her yearning for England in the letter that she wrote to the Hallendales a few days after their arrival in Venice.

It was most painfully clear to Georgiana that Colonel Fitzwilliam was not to meet them in Venice, or anywhere—that he was again under the spell of Miss Crawford no longer admitted of a doubt. Georgiana pined for release, for a general deliverance from the fatigue, the requisite raptures, but mostly from the unending exertions to appear happy. When, by some grateful chance, they bent their steps northward, her heart felt an irrational joy at knowing they were even *looking* in the direction of home. Adding to her misery was the certainty that her brother and sister were as yet vastly enjoying the novelties and entertainments; hence, she could form no certainty of the day that would end their travels, and secure her release. Each day found her heart heavier and her spirits less supportable; it required all of her strength and resolution to affect a plausible cheerfulness, and she knew not even when she would find herself at last on the road to home.

Although neither Mr. or Mrs. Darcy would have admitted such for worlds—even to one another, in deference to the pleasure of the others—it was not only Georgiana who was beginning to tire of the road. They had not spent a week in the water city of La Serenissima, when they began to feel that Venice, for all its magnificence, was strangely devoid of amity, and the present ruination of anything that remained of past grandeur was oppressive. To the English, it was unsettling to find that the dirt and decay had attached itself for so long, it was become a feature of the place. The Darcys were of the true English stamp; that is to say, general preservers from—rather than spectators to—such decay as was everywhere around them. And, to see such treasures the victims of neglect and the ravages of time! Soil covered not only the exteriors and streets but also every surface within, and seemed to be carried on the very air of the city. The buildings appeared to be hastening on their way into the sea, and the glorious paintings and frescoes fading away from the ingress of water and dirty air. Added to this disappointment, their hôtel was unpleasant, and the owner singularly indisposed to answer their requests for attention to their apartments. *Enthousiasme pour le voyage* was become more difficult with each passing day.

It was, therefore, a singularly fitting destination for Colonel Fitzwilliam's last letter, written to inform the Darcys of the tragedy that had befallen the Hallendale family, and appealing for their immediate return.

10th June
London

Dear Darcy,

If I felt less, perhaps I might write more, but, as it is, this letter will be brief, and contain none of the niceties that might be reasonably expected. My brother, the Viscount, is dead—murdered—and—if such is possible—this wretched event is made yet more tragic by the scandalous nature of its circumstances. I have no wish to intrude upon the sensibilities of the dear ladies who are with you, Darcy, and know you will spare them whatever you can. I will not take the time to write of the particulars of the discovery of my brother's corpse, excepting the fact that he was chanced upon by an early morning watchman, in a poor and obscure part of London. More than this must wait for an investigation in Bow Street, which Mr. Gardiner has undertaken to institute even as I write this.

My father and mother are now hastening to London. I await them, having been myself the first member of the family to receive the news, upon which I immediately departed from Tunbridge. I depend upon your knowledge of my dear father to convince you of the depths of his despair when confronted by the iniquity of his eldest son. The only balm for my worst fears for his health is the knowledge that he is comforted by the best of women, and could, therefore, not be in kinder or more capable hands.

If my brother's demise were to be the only issue of significance in this circumstance, t'were bad enough, but I think you may guess that the cause of his death must necessarily uncover further calumny and defamation of his character. The revelations of the investigation might well mean the ruination of my family.

I cannot deny, Darcy, that it would be both the greatest kindness and the greatest sacrifice, if you would return as early as your pleasure and that of your dear companions will permit. I know that my lack of scruple in begging your swift return is asking a great deal of my friends. My family are all very desirous of your assistance. I know not what I write. Be assured that I remain your most devoted, and obliged,

George Fitzwilliam

"Heaven preserve us! How can your poor uncle endure this dreadful misfortune? It is everyway horrible," responded Elizabeth, with tears in her eyes. "Mr. Darcy, I know not what to say. The Hallendale family is entirely undeserving of anything of this kind. That the Viscount's sense of decency and honour should admit of doubt is shocking indeed, and surely must not reflect the truth of the matter."

Darcy could well imagine the underlying history of the Viscount's debts of honour and other proofs of his dissipation, but he had no idea that such knowledge would help the ladies to comprehend the event more clearly. He looked impenetrably grave for several minutes, and Elizabeth and Georgiana knew enough of his character to understand that he was in earnest contemplation of the best plan for their return to England, and what, if anything, could be done, before he could himself arrive, to be of service to the Hallendales. Darcy replied in the affirmative, and said only,

"As your Uncle Gardiner is already involved in the business, we may take some comfort in the knowledge that whatever is possible is already being done in the way of securing the assistance of those most able to discover the truth surrounding this heinous crime, and how best to effect redress. You must know that there can be little hope of remediation for such an act that would render it less painful, or even more acceptable. We are best to prepare ourselves for the worst and return to London in the safest, most expeditious manner possible."

"I think it advisable that we remain together through the return to Geneva. The passage over the mountains is certainly improved over what it was, but it is no journey for two women to undertake in the care of servants. You may remain in Geneva for some days until you are rested, and then recommence your journey back through Paris. I will leave you at Geneva and return to London on horse-back, if you are able to travel further by yourselves."

Georgiana and Elizabeth were quick to assure Mr. Darcy of their ready approbation, and to declare themselves quite able to see themselves, their servants, and their belongings back to England. Hastily dividing the business to be done, all was soon settled for their imminent return. As Mr. Darcy left to see to the carriages, find his coachman, and issue instructions for their departure, the women turned to supervising the hurried packing, and making all ready to be put into the trunks, which would soon arrive for lading. Georgiana took the opportunity of her maid's being gone to see about the baggage, and asked Elizabeth quietly,

"Elizabeth, I cannot but wonder about this turn of events. It seems that my brother is concealing something from us, but what could be worse than what we know already? And, what can Colonel Fitzwilliam mean about its being 'scandalous?' Does not murder necessarily involve scandal to the greatest extent possible?"

Elizabeth could well guess that Mr. Darcy had, in reading between the lines of Colonel Fitzwilliam's letter, a good idea of the circumstances surrounding the death of the Viscount, if not the actual perpetrators. Elizabeth had not the information of her husband, but did understand, from Lady Sarah—and others—that the Viscount had been lately living in what could only be called a stile of dissipation and, quite probably, depravity. However, judging as her husband must have done, it was useless to conjecture and possibly add further insult to the enormity of an already unthinkable injury. She, therefore, replied after the few moments these thoughts required, saying quietly,

"Georgiana, we must not worry ourselves in what can only be most painful speculations and useless alarm. We must keep our own spirits up and comfort ourselves in a manner so as to occasion Mr. Darcy the least apprehension in leaving us, as he must, and get ourselves, our servants, horses, and belongings to London—alone—safely—in the most rational and capable manner."

"Oh! Elizabeth, I know you are right—my greatest fear is for Colonel Fitzwilliam: he not only has to bear the loss of his brother—his only brother; support the spirits of his father, who is in uncertain health; manage the affairs of the law; and such other burthens as I cannot even imagine—but must do so without either my brother or myself there to support his spirits and ease his suffering under such a blow!"

Elizabeth could not quite see the matter as did Georgiana, but imputed Georgiana's disproportionate concern for her cousin as the result of the shock of the news, and her own great confidence in Lady Sarah's management of her husband.

"Georgiana, you must not forget that the Colonel is a grown man who has seen worse than this. Remember that he has been in battle, commanding dozens—nay, hundreds of men—fearlessly and honourably. It does him no service to give way to this borrowing of trouble, which must only serve to further aggrieve those already afflicted; were he to know of your distress, it would only add further to his cares, not sustain him in these dreadful hours."

Georgiana looked stricken by Elizabeth's last words, and heartily did the latter wish them unsaid, as Georgiana sank into the chair and began sobbing with all her heart.

"Oh, dearest Georgiana, whatever can be the cause of such wretchedness?" said Elizabeth kneeling next to her chair and taking Georgiana's hands into her own. "Pray, dearest, do not believe that my words are from an unfeeling heart. I am grieved—more—I am suffering, as is Mr. Darcy and anyone who knows the Hallendales must be at this time. Dearest, dearest, please tell me what is the matter."

Georgiana would only shake her head and continue sobbing in a most distressing manner. Mr. Darcy came in shortly thereafter, and silently gestured to Elizabeth as to the meaning of such utter misery. Elizabeth could only look her perplexity, and indicate that she could not understand Georgiana's disconsolate reaction to the news any more than could her husband. In a few moments, Mr. Darcy came back to his sister with a cool hand-kerchief and, kneeling by her, entreated that she dry her eyes and tell him what he could do to offer consolation to such distress. Georgiana now realised that she had involved her brother in exactly the way Elizabeth had counselled against, with the result that her tears only increased. Darcy continued to kneel by her, and attempt to comprehend the misery of her feelings.

At length, Georgiana was able to bring herself to speak, and then, only in syllables that were broken between the sobs, said, "D-dearest brother, p-pray do not mind me. I am f-fine. I am j-just overc-come. It has b-been d-dreadful... B-blanche... M-miss"—here Georgiana checked herself sharply—"m-m-my aunt d-de Bourgh, and..n-now this. I am s-s-so s-sorry," and saying this much, rose and ran into her room.

It was Elizabeth who first spoke following this scene, and asked her husband, "Mr. Darcy, do you understand what she meant by 'miss'? Is there some source of affliction about which we are unawares? I would only surmise, that she was in unaccountably low spirits *before* the news of poor Blanche."

"I confess I do not understand it myself, Lizzy. It is wholly unlike Georgiana to give way to such a display of any kind, and although the present circumstance is in every way afflicting, I cannot see that the latest news should result in such profound despair. I cannot believe that she was attached to Dunfield in any way—she hardly knew him—that is why George and not he was appointed as guardian. If it had been George, *I* would have been thus aggrieved, but William— Dunfield—I know this will sound abominably cruel, but we may as well prepare ourselves for his history—his life has been so much given to selfishness and dissipation, that I do not expect anyone but a parent could reasonably lament his loss.

"Mr. Darcy!" exclaimed Elizabeth. "I cannot ever remember you using expressions so uncommonly strong—what can be your meaning? I confess myself now doubly bewildered, between your violence of speech, and Georgiana's violence of feeling!"

"I did not wish to add to your distress when I know what you must be feeling at returning to England without my protection, but I believe we will find that Dunfield's death was not surprising, in the present circumstance. I will not say more, as I do not *know* more, but can only surmise what such a stile of living can comprehend as a means to this most deplorable end. Pray, Elizabeth, be satisfied for the present, and I am sure that we will both have better information when we are returned to England; if Fitzwilliam is incapable himself of discovering the truth of this wretched matter, remember that Mr. Gardiner is there and will be as diligent and careful as anyone could wish."

Elizabeth, whilst unused to a lack of confidence in her reason as the present discussion suggested, also had such a complete trust in her husband's judgement, that she resolved against further questions, and replied, "I understand, Husband. I will go to Georgiana and see to her maid and to her preparations. I am sure all will be well. She has not had a chance to grieve properly for Blanche—and this news is come upon all of us so suddenly, and is so shocking, indeed, as it must be to one of Georgiana's tender feelings and gentle views of the world in general; I am sure she had not imagined such an evil possible. It is to this last that I impute such a disproportionate and unreasonable reaction."

"I am sure you are right, my dearest Elizabeth," he said taking her hands and kissing them. "I will see to our account here and the other arrangements that must be completed before we may depart Venice." And, turning quietly, he was gone from the room.

CHAP. 14.

IT TOOK ONLY ONE FULL DAY for the Darcys to settle their affairs in Venice, make arrangements for the return journey, and depart by boat for the mainland. Finding that travel over the Alps in the warmer months afforded them an easier passage via the more direct route, they retraced their steps to just beyond Brescia. Then—yielding to the advice of their hosts in Desenzano—they avoided Milan and went through Como, to the north of the lake, and thence westward at Bellinzona, rejoining their original way at Domo d'Ossola, a detour requiring almost two additional days, as the roads had not been improved on that route. At last, they were out of Italy, and thence across to Lake Geneva. Arriving at Gample late in the evening, they found that there were no beds available at the solitary post-house, and in addition to this misery, the Darcys were forced to wait an additional hour for fresh horses. By the time the horses were arrived, it was become thoroughly dark, being a cloudy night and a crescent moon. Mr. Harmon, in speaking with some of the other coachmen at the post-house, learnt that a portion of the road was fallen down between Gampel and Sierre, destroying the wall along the side nearest the precipice, and making the passage difficult to traverse safely, even in the light of day.

By the hour they were back on the road, it was nearly ten, and the carriages had a further eight miles to go before they could reach the next posting house. The inn at Gample had been dark, unkempt, and uninviting, but the alternative was considerably worse. However, there was no choice before them but to continue on the road, trusting the memory of the post-horses, and the wits of the very capable Mr. Harmon. The carriages arrived in Sierre after midnight, necessitating the additional exertion of awakening the inn-keepers. Despite having been driven from their bed, and requiring them to provide something in the way of dinner for the travellers and their servants, the *aubergiste* and his wife were obliging and pleasant. In less time than anyone would have thought possible, the Darcys were fed a cold, but very satisfactory, supper, and found themselves abed in surprisingly clean rooms, the linens fresh-washed, and the furniture scrubbed and commodious. Having travelled farther than expected the previous night, in the morning the family and their party slept somewhat later than usual, and had an easy journey from Sierre, through Sion, and thence to Martigny.

At Martigny, they again departed from their prior route, turning sharply north toward Villeneuve. On this route, they passed over the famous waterfall of Pissevache and the bridge of St. Maurice, a single span over-arching the narrow valley with its ancient castle atop a promontory, and dividing the Vaud from the Valais. The waterfall had been one of the most sublime in Europe until an enterprising miller had built a mill directly beneath the fall, breaking away the picturesque projection of rock so as to unify the course of the stream, to the benefit of his wheel. The mill no longer existed, and the view of the Pissevache, as rendered in the older drawings, shewed a greater fall of water as it ran over the amputated projection; still, it was a very remarkable torrent.

Georgiana now read from her guide-books just to provide some relief for the time that must necessarily pass until their arrival back in London. She read aloud that the torrent of La Salenche fell from more than 700 feet. The spray from the cascade produced an halo of rainbows in the sun, and the noise could be heard for several miles, were the wind in the right direction. St. Maurice had been the Roman Agaunum, the place to which they conveyed their dead from all over the adjacent countryside for interment; the pavement of the church at St. Maurice had been constructed from the sepulchral stones of the ancient graves. The very bridge they were crossing over had been built in the time of the Roman Cæsars. The mountains at that point were as high as 18,000 feet above the sea. Above the town lived a blind hermit who walked the steep slope to the village and back every day. She read everything and anything in an effort to distract all of their thoughts from what lay ahead at the conclusion of what had begun as a trip of pleasure. No-one wanted to be on the road; they were all three desperately wishing to be delivered from the fatigues of the wearisome, joyless return journey, yet dreading each moment that they were come closer to its unalterable, wretched conclusion.

Passing through the valley, the Darcys rolled past Monthey,

❧   stopping

stopping for the night at Bex, as it was reputed as being one of the very best inns in the world; the Darcys were most agreeably confirmed in that opinion, and Elizabeth and her husband agreed that—under different circumstances—both the inn and its surrounding scenery was worthy of a longer visit. They continued on the next day through Aigle, Le Rhône, and Roche, before reaching Villeneuve.

This was their last night together as a family, until they were to be re-united in London; Mr. Darcy and his valet would leave them at Lausanne the following day and continue on to London, whilst they drove on the short distance to Geneva. Mr. Darcy had written ahead to secure the arrangements necessary for Elizabeth and Georgiana to travel onwards, accompanied by the servants and both carriages, stop for some few days' rest in Geneva, and then continue on to Paris. Travelling as expeditiously as possible, the heavy coaches had already required two full weeks to reach Lausanne. Using post-horses, Darcy might be able to travel upwards of fifty miles a day or more on horse-back, if the weather were agreeable, and could continue through the night on the diligence, as compared with thirty—or fewer—miles, encumbered by the two carriages, their servants, and their baggage. Rising very early, he bade a succinct, but affecting, farewell to his wife and sister, and rode swiftly away.

Lausanne was much like Bath, built upon several hills. The town overlooking the lake was very clean, with pretty flowers adorning the houses and gardens of the area; Elizabeth thought she would have been very content to remain here some days, had the return journey allowed. As Elizabeth and Georgiana left their inn, they watched the sun rise over Mont Blanc. Taking breakfast at *La Couronne* in Rolle, a neat little village on the shore of Lake Geneva, the two ladies were pleased with the well-ordered inn, which proved to be possessed of a very satisfactory kitchen. They continued on to Nyon, and thence into Geneva. Mrs. and Miss Darcy, although apprehensive of the prospect of onward travel without Mr. Darcy, were nonetheless grateful for the small respite from the previous two weeks' arduous pace of travel, spending two days in Geneva before, like Mr. Darcy, they bent their steps homeward.

"How differently I imagined our return to England!" began Elizabeth to Georgiana, sitting in their rooms on the first night that found them again in Geneva. "I had anticipated our triumphant approach into Dover in joyous company, our entire party (including Mr. Darcy and Colonel Fitzwilliam), following our planned peregrinations up through Innsbruck. We will miss Bologna, Florence, Rome and Naples, the Rhine, Strassbourg, Luxemborg, Brussels, Antwerp, Bruges—even the names sound elegant!—and, of course, the happiest prospect of our jolly arrival back at Pemberley. I expected the Hallendales, Bingleys, and all of the little Bingleys would be at Derbyshire, ready to receive us home from our Grand Tour. How altered is my vision now!" Elizabeth tried in vain to interest Georgiana in lamenting their roads not travelled, but could get on no further than an abstracted "Oh, yes. It is so very sad." It was thoroughly unaccountable; Georgiana had an avidity for geographical subjects for as long as Elizabeth had known her. Now, it was as though she had no idea of any place beyond their sitting-room in an hôtel!

Georgiana, whose imagination had like-wise furnished her expectations with a markedly contrary scene of the conclusion of their travels, remained unintentionally silent. Her dismay at the turn of events, resulting in unimaginable heartache for her aunt and uncle, must see her returned to the frequent—daily—company of Colonel Fitzwilliam. How could she ever have foreseen that *his* presence would be the cause of such misery! She believed he must surely by now have come to an understanding with Miss Crawford, as only an event of such import could have been the reason for the Colonel's prolonged stay at Tunbridge Wells; surely if he were *already* married, he must have mentioned it in his letter. The very idea weighed like a great stone upon her; it formed the thinking of every minute of every hour. Elizabeth's frequent regrets that the Colonel had been prevented from joining their party were a sustained trial, and Georgiana's attempts to steer the conversation away from the circumstances in London were bound to failure, as being both the cause of Elizabeth's separation from her husband, and the motive for their altered and comfortless journey home.

In his ardent desire to ensure the safe travel of the two most dear to himself, Darcy had written to the Comte, begging his assistance to the Darcy ladies from Paris to Calais, and onto the packet bound for Dover. He paused in his rapid pace only long enough to stop at Paris to deliver his note to the Comte's mother, who was at that time resident at the Paris house in advance of her son's arrival in the course of the next few days. His assurance to the dowager Comtesse of the urgency of the case was rendered unnecessary by the dirty state of his cloathing and the obvious anxiety of his mind. Avowing his great obligation to and esteem for her son, Darcy gratefully entrusted the letter into her care, and immediately withdrew to continue on his way. Consequently, by the time Elizabeth and Georgiana entered into Dijon, they were in receipt of a letter from the Comte, explaining that he would meet them upon their arrival into Paris, provide accommodations for them at his own house, and assist them with every possible detail necessary to ready themselves and their belongings for the return voyage to England.

Elizabeth received the letter with some fretfulness at the thought that Georgiana must necessarily meet in daily intercourse with a gentleman, to whose hopes she had so recently given disappointment, but upon shewing the letter to Georgiana, she was surprised that her sister appeared to approve the plan, and, even more unexpectedly, did not seem at all unwilling to be soon and frequently in his company!

"I believe that the friendship of the Comte is far more genuine than any other we have had the good fortune to secure in the course of our visit to Paris. I have never for a minute doubted the sincerity of his regard for *all* of us. He will, I know, be eager to render this service to my brother, in honour of their mutual regard—it has nothing to do with me. I am confident that the Comte will treat us with every courtesy and unremitting kindness, as is his way, despite the unfortunate circumstances of our parting. Time will have removed the pain of our last encounter, and I do not believe he can now care for me in any other way than as a friend, and esteem me as the sister of a man he respects and admires. I do not at all feel unequal to our meeting."

Elizabeth, relieved by Georgiana's expressions of her own good sense and unwavering belief in the kindness of others, considered that her sister was probably correct in all but her conviction that the Comte would no longer be in love. She not dare voice her secret half-hope that Miss Darcy might, upon meeting again with the gallant and amiable Comte, re-examine her heart and find a place in it for that gentleman. Elizabeth reflected that her own esteem and love for the man who was become her husband had been the product of a twelve-month's revelation of Mr. Darcy's character and history. However, in the present case, there was no misconstruction of character or prejudice to require such an interval necessary for the rectification of an hasty and erroneous judgement. There was no indication that the Comte's honour, family, or disposition had any blemish to impede happiness in marriage. On the other hand, mused Elizabeth, if they had all misunderstood the Comte's character, and consequently found themselves similarly deceived, then the effect of their error would be a most happy one indeed, preserving a most beloved sister from certain misery *and* the pain of separation from all her friends and family. On balance, however, Elizabeth was content to rely on her husband's excellent judgement and the hope that

Georgiana might, in time, alter her opinion; in this case—as it very nearly always did—his impeccable understanding exactly coincided with her own.

The Darcy ladies traced a route back to Paris in as straight a line as possible, stopping no-where longer than one night. Although only late August, the climate was cold, dark, and disagreeable. More than once did Elizabeth imagine that they could magically find themselves at Park Place or—what was better, Pemberley—seated in front of a good fire by their own warm hearth. They quitted Geneva, heading directly northward for Dijon, thence to Troyes, west to Montereau-Fault-Yonne, and finally passing within five miles of Belle Aire on their way back into the city, and driving through the gates at the Porte d'Ivry. Mrs. Darcy's hopes were unfortunately misplaced, for, upon their arrival in Paris, the Comte had been the very picture of courtesy, and more than once looked at Georgiana with an admiration that would have stopt the hearts of the entire female population of Paris; Georgiana responded to his attentions with a steady, innocent friendship. The Comte saw the Darcy ladies safely to his own house for the duration of their stay in Paris, placing their comforts under the kind and capable hand of the dowager Comtesse; took them to dinner and any other amusements that Paris might provide for their pleasure; harried merchants who were not immediately forthcoming with their commissions; bade his servants unpack and clean their belongings and then repack their cases, loading them onto freshly polished coaches; fed and rested their servants and horses; and, lastly, arranged for his own coachman and servants to accompany them all the way to Calais, assuring their own safe passage and the simultaneous arrival of their belongings in the hands of only their English-speaking servants.

The last morning of their stay in Paris brought the delivery of a much-anticipated letter. Elizabeth had written to her friend, Anne Wentworth, during their first stay at Geneva, but the reply having been directed so ill, the letter had only reached its recipient in Paris many weeks later. Elizabeth read the letter out loud to Georgiana, dismay increasing with every paragraph.

28th June
Wentworth House, Shropshire

DEAR MRS. DARCY,

I received your letter this morning, and, without delay, determined to respond to your enquiry in as full a manner as I am able. The

circumstances

circumstances which you relate are as familiar as they are despicable, and I must urge you to act immediately upon the information that I shall send by return of post, to ensure the safe-keeping of your aunt's fortune, as well as her heart. I only wish I had been more general in my exposure of his true character, for I might have spoken a word and prevented this whole affair from ever arising. This letter will serve as poor recompense for my previous error of judgement, indeed.

Your recollection that Sir William Elliot is my cousin is entirely correct, although I was not myself acquainted with him until five years ago, following an accidental meeting at Lyme. Sir William (at that time he was only Mr. William Elliot) subsequently decided to renew an association with my esteemed father, to whom, I was later to learn, he had previously behaved with a most deceitful and scandalous disrespect. If I may speak frankly, Mrs. Darcy, Sir William pursued me with an ardency that was as unexpected as it was unwelcome. I found him to be all that appeared respectable and honourable, yet I remained in question as to his real character, partly due to his sudden change of opinion regarding my family, whom he had previously been content to ignore entirely, and also from my own observations. I will only add my gratitude to Providence that both preserved me from his suit, and fulfilled my long attachment to the man who was become my husband, Captain Wentworth, with whom you were acquainted when we met at Bath.

It was only when an old friend, Mrs. Smith, enlightened me as to the particulars of William Elliot's past, incorrectly suspecting me of intending a most regrettable alliance with Mr. Elliot, that I learnt the truth about my cousin. I regret to tell you that he is both artful and unprincipled in his every dealing. His conduct in his marriage was disgraceful, and he spent the fortune of his first wife with no restraint, and even less regard for her happiness. In his effort to prevent my father from marrying again—and consequently producing an heir, which would, of course, have spoilt his chance to inherit—he began an illicit affair with the very woman who threatened an intimacy with my father! To my knowledge, he still keeps his mistress, Mrs. Clay, to this day. On the melancholy event of my father passing on, Sir William inherited his title and Kellynch, our family estate. I suspect his funds are low, and can only surmise that his overtures toward your unsuspecting aunt, a woman older than himself, can best be explained by his requiring her fortune.

Further, despite maintaining a façade of respectability, my cousin preserves a sizeable acquaintance of dubious integrity, at the centre of which is one Colonel Wallis. I know of no particulars, but believe them both to be involved in any number of unscrupulous schemes. It is in this light that you must see your aunt's danger. I am too well aware how a sensible woman may be imposed upon by the arts of one of Sir William's stamp; suspicion would not be in a lady's nature, and she could have no means of readily discovering his character. Dear Mrs. Darcy, you must surely believe I had not an idea that any friend of yours might ever find herself in the unfortunate circumstance of knowing that such a person in the world as Sir William Elliot exists, much less innocently forming a connection with my cousin, or I would have related the whole history to you at once. Forgive the candour of this letter, and please write to assure me that your aunt is safe; or if there is anything Captain Wentworth or I can do to redress this grievous mistake, for I fear that your aunt faces ruination.

Yours &c., &c.,

ANNE WENTWORTH

The extremity of Lady Catherine's case being established beyond a doubt by the particulars of Anne's letter, Elizabeth had no recourse but that of waiting, for she knew that Darcy had, by this time, arrived at London, and a letter would reach him no more quickly than could herself. Elizabeth carefully laid the letter by. The two women packed up their things in a sombre mood, and prepared for their departure to Calais.

CHAP. 15.

MR. GARDINER, Elizabeth Darcy's uncle, had been known to the Hallendales since the Darcys' marriage. He always conducted himself with such propriety and integrity, that the Hallendales came to look upon him almost as their agent in London, so often did he act for them on matters of business, getting some agreement or another properly drawn-up, or arranging pecuniary details, even though his business was in quite a different line. Immediately upon Colonel Fitzwilliam making the circumstance of Viscount Dunfield's murder known to him, Mr. Gardiner approached one of his acquaintances in Bow Street, and instituted the proper investigatory pursuits. That Lord Hallendale should undertake such a task was not to be contemplated; Colonel Fitzwilliam was suffering under his own grief, and was too sensible of the affliction of his mother and father to be of any real use. The Colonel, in any case, was required to assist his parents with the sad details of burial and locating whatever remaining effects could be found; at any rate, he must be in Derbyshire to see to the estate in Her Ladyship's absence. Accordingly, after learning what was known of the matter from Lady Hallendale and her step-son, Mr. Gardiner sought out the most senior of the Bow Street constables and set the case before him.

Lord and Lady Hallendale had been in town for more than two months by the time Mr. Darcy arrived in London. Darcy tarried at his London house only long enough to change his cloathes, and then quitted it immediately in search of Mr. Gardiner, after calling at the Hallendale residence with his condolences, and those of his wife and sister. He found his uncle weary and despondent. Lady Hallendale was suffering under the same great strain of the double blow of death and scandal, but, as she was the more habitually useful, she had the dubious blessing of the details of the inquest as well as the daily matters of the estate to distract her from such painful scenes. Lord Hallendale was so thoroughly undone as to be incapable of any action; in Darcy's absence, it had remained, then, for Lady Hallendale and Mr. Gardiner to direct the discovery of any details of the murder, answer the questions of the inquest, and attempt the salvage of whatever was possible of respectability of the Viscount's memory, which was little, indeed.

Stopping but briefly to see his uncle and aunt, Darcy imparted whatever words were possible in the present circumstance of such affliction that might offer even momentary relief. Upon Lady Hallendale's enquiry, Darcy assured them that his wife and sister were being well looked-after, and communicated to them briefly that which had passed between Georgiana and the Comte, merely to be saying anything at such a time that might yield a diversion from the main course of their unhappy thoughts. He spoke much of the Comte's good character, and hinted that he was not entirely unhopeful that, as Georgiana and Elizabeth were going to be in the Comte's company for a number of days, Georgiana might yet have a change of heart.

He was preparing to leave the Hallendales to meet Mr. Gardiner, when of a sudden, Lady Hallendale announced that she would accompany him—she had not spoken with Mr. Gardiner for several days and wished to hear what he knew of recent information. Mr. Darcy assured her that he would obtain the details of what had been discovered in his own absence, and return to them on his way home. Lady Hallendale was adamant she would go with him, and, asking the house-keeper to look in on His Lordship whilst she was gone away for a short time, took up her hat, and allowed Darcy to hand her into the chaise.

Mr. Darcy and his aunt met Mr. Gardiner in his office. After greeting his guests and seeing to their seats, he asked his clerk to bring in refreshments. He looked tired and care-worn. Lady Hallendale begged him to start at the beginning, so that Darcy was correctly and completely informed on the details of what was known.

"I am grieved, but the news from Bow Street is uniformly shocking and of the worst kind. The runners have discovered the details of the murder and, what is more appalling, the motive for it: warning to serve as example. The Viscount's body was found in the squalor of Whitechapel in Rosemary Lane near Tower Hill, which—I doubt you have reason to know—is beyond the regular patrols of the constabulary. The outer garments had all been stript, and it was evident by the attitude of the body that Dunfield had been deceased for some time before being abandoned in the lane. In the course of the investigation, an informer came upon a resident of Tower Hill who claimed to have heard the sound of an heavy carriage early in the morning of the death. The rain had washed away any signs of carriage wheels, but the corpse, the corroborating evidence of the witness, and the lack of any sign of a struggle suggest strongly that the body had been transferred by carriage to the location where it was subsequently discovered. As I had not been acquainted with the Viscount, perforce Colonel Fitzwilliam undertook the sombre task of providing the positive identification to the coroner."

He paused to let Mr. Darcy recover his breath and to ask any questions; upon hearing none, Mr. Gardiner continued the sad history:

"Dunfield, being a peer and gentleman of fashion, was a well-recognised figure throughout the best gaming clubs of London. In the weeks before his death, Dunfield's habit had been daily playing at Hazard, often from the evening of the previous day, into the following afternoon. He lost prodigious sums. Logically, the runners' initial enquiries had begun at the gentlemen's clubs of which Lord Dunfield might have been a regular member. The detectives consulted the gambling books at White's, Brooks's, Boodle's, and the numerous other gaming establishments frequented by the gentry in Pall Mall, and found the Viscount's recorded wagers of increasingly desperate amounts. Darcy—again, I am truly distressed at what I must next relate—enquiry into the Jerusalem Room at Brooks's and other such venues of vice revealed that the Viscount had been in debt to the Jewish money-lenders for no less than one hundred thousand pounds!"

Here, Mr. Darcy gasped, but did not interrupt Mr. Gardiner: "The Viscount had not been seen at any of the better clubs for a little over a week before his death; approximately the date at which the money-lenders began to refuse him additional credit. Most dreadfully for Dunfield, and all of your family, these details—and others of a similarly shocking nature—were corroborated by the clubs' proprietors, and were generally known at the time of the Viscount's murder."

Mr. Gardiner asked Darcy if he wished to hear the findings of those employed in the discovery of what could be known of the events surrounding the murder. Mr. Darcy gave a sad and barely perceptible nod of his head. Mr. Gardiner continued, "Darcy, this much has been established: the runners bent the course of their enquiries toward the less creditable gaming establishments, located in King Street, as well as the more remote environs out of the reach of the regular London constabulary. A gentleman answering to a general description of the

Viscount had been seen at various of the lower gaming dens in the days prior to his death, nearly all of which are believed to belong to the infamous William Crockford."

Here, Mr. Darcy looked up and asked Mr. Gardiner if he should know the name of William Crockford, as he did not.

"Darcy, would to Heaven that you did not need to know it *now*. The maleficent Mr. Crockford is known in London police circles as 'The Shark.' Crockford is reputed to be a man of a deceptively torpid countenance, but one who is possessed of an uncommon intelligence and implacable determination, both of which he has used to great effect in the creation of a vast criminal network of assorted felons, whose debts have placed themselves under his service. His considerable fortune— estimated to be several hundred thousands of pounds, as conjectured by the Bow Street officer-in-charge—has been amassed through clever exploitation of unlucky gentlemen gamesters, regrettably, just such as was the Viscount. Crockford has been implicated in the ruination of numerous gentlemen through various dishonest gaming practises, but the association is of such a secretive kind, that no records exist which could conclusively tie Crockford to any specific misdeeds. It was possible for the officers to establish, however, that Dunfield had recently borrowed substantial sums from several of Crockford's money-lenders. The officer and I conjecture that this perilous act was a vain attempt to win enough at the lower establishments in order to redeem the debts of honour previously contracted. Crockford being better at his game than his victim, Dunfield had lost the entirety of the borrowed sums in the low gambling houses within the week prior to his death."

In an attitude Mr. Gardiner had never before witnessed, his nephew sat in the chair with his head bowed, and supported on his hands in a most abject manner. "I do not deny that this history is almost too dreadful to be credited as the truth, especially as it concerns one so closely connected with an ancient and respectable family. I entirely understand, Darcy, if you do not wish me to continue." Darcy only raised an hand and silently motioned for Mr. Gardiner to proceed.

"There are yet doubtless a number of undiscoverable debts to these money-lenders, who operate within the extremely lax system of credit in the less reputable establishments, but the discovery of those debts—and to whom they were owed—is rendered virtually impossible by the extra-legal nature of the establishments themselves. The officers have searched the usual districts where such wagering takes place in an attempt to discover the Viscount's movements, speaking with their informants in the districts of Whitechapel and Spitalfields, Houndsditch and Ledenhall, Pettycoat Lane, St. Giles, and especially the darker neighbourhoods of Drury Lane and Covent Garden. These latter areas, being just removed from the regularly patrolled streets, are where the money-lenders ply their despicable trade. The regulars chanced to discover a brown gentleman's glove in a dirty, unlit side-street off Drury Lane, only a mile from the Viscount's residence in Pall Mall. The glove, having been dropt—by the perpetrators who removed the Viscount's cloathing, it is assumed—at the side of the street and disfigured by mud and rain, had not been earlier discovered. A cipher was set into the glove, along with a Viscount's coronet, which the Colonel has subsequently confirmed as belonging to his brother. Upon closer investigation in the immediate area of the discovery, traces of blood were found, and, as the alley-way is close by, the mud adjacent to the buildings still bore the signs of having recently been disturbed by three sets of shoes, and indentations apparently made by a falling body matching Dunfield's height and weight. The runners conclude that the Viscount was murdered in the alley and transported thence to Whitechapel."

"They have also discovered witnesses who saw Dunfield returning to the Hallendales' London residence late on the evening before the discovery of his body. He was observed by the servants to be hastily packing a large valise and setting off in the direction of Piccadilly. Before you ask—no, the bag and its contents have not yet been found. Colonel Fitzwilliam was much against any idea that his brother would have contemplated such a disgraceful breech of honour as quitting the country in order to avoid his debts; we had not mentioned anything about this discovery to the Hallendales—I am truly sorry, Your Ladyship—until there were enough circumstantial details to corroborate the conjecture. That this was most probably the case was evidenced by the valise, as well as the fair-certainty of the Bow Street superior, that Crockford had Dunfield murdered, as he suspected him of flight, and further—in consideration of his being a well-known personage— that his murder would serve as a particularly effective example to those remaining in debt to Crockford, signalling to them that, one way or another, Crockford meant to collect."

At length, Darcy recovered somewhat and enquired why Dunfield would have been murdered for his debts, instead of pressing his father to pay.

"It is customary—if also repugnant—that gentlemen sometimes resort to duelling in order to settle debts of honour," explained Mr.

Gardiner. "The gentlemen creditors of your cousin would happily have turned to this expedient, or more probably to your uncle for payment, had they the opportunity. However, Darcy, by the end, it was believed that your uncle's estate *in its entirety* was worth only a fraction of such a sum as was owing, so the money-lenders would have demanded satisfaction from Dunfield directly. When he could not pay, he was forced to borrow at even higher interest. Sadly, but also unwisely, instead of paying off at least some of the debts of honour and redeeming some of his personal credit, he chose to use this money in a final, unsuccessful, attempt to recover his previous losses. At that juncture, it was clear to someone of Crockford's stamp that the double debt was irrecoverable; and—as the most profitable recompense remaining—the murder of a man of Dunfield's status would surely give notice to *all* his debtors—high and low—that they should not contract a debt they could never repay, or hope to escape through flight."

Not usually obtuse in matters of deduction, Darcy questioned Mr. Gardiner, "Surely there is *some* doubt that this was a murder, as you have described it?"

Mr. Gardiner had hoped to spare Darcy the worst of the report and was genuinely distressed to recount the horrifying conclusion of the Bow Street superior's report. Looking first to Lady Hallendale for her permission to continue, she responded by looking disconsolately at her nephew, and gave her quiet consent.

"Darcy, a common murderer would have killed the Viscount and either left the body in the alley-way, or, more readily, have disposed of it in the Thames. That the body was vandalised and left for discovery in Whitechapel is compelling evidence, in my view, that the murderer was interested in neither robbery nor revenge. This base act was an announcement, an exhibition meant to secure protection against future losses."

Darcy only nodded vacantly and, at length, responded, "Then, we are all to receive this cold comfort: Crockford, or whoever has committed this iniquitous act, cannot come forward to claim payment from my uncle Hallendale, because his doing so would identify himself as a murderer."

"Yes, Darcy," replied Mr. Gardiner quietly. "I have seen the books at White's, and the last entries by the Viscount's name are marked, 'Unpaid.' There is no-one who will come forward to collect from your uncle, of that we can all be certain."

The agonizing particulars of the Viscount's final days, and his moral ruin, were administered further proof when a pawn shop in Dean Street was discovered to possess the Viscount's watch-fob and chain, which, as they had been given to him by Lord Hallendale's father, were amongst his most treasured possessions. Mr. Gardiner had generously redeemed the articles, presenting them to Colonel Fitzwilliam in memory of his brother, a small consolation and fitting conclusion to the end of a life at once so promising, and ultimately so wasted.

However, the sordid picture of the Viscount's last days was not yet complete: he was found to have been living away from the Hallendales' London house in an effort to conceal his movements and his whereabouts—living with a woman! The woman was believed to have been introduced to Dunfield some months before by a Mr. Tom Bertram of Northamptonshire, the heir to a baronetcy. She was, it was presumed by the Bow Street superior, Bertram's former mistress. At some point previous, Mr. Bertram had contracted a serious illness and was despaired of for many weeks, the recovery from which had led to the renunciation of all of his former habits of dissipation, including his liaison with the lady. She had then, it appeared, transferred her hopes, if not her affections, to Bertram's former friend and ally in their joint profligacy, Viscount Dunfield. She had gone so far as to shelter Dunfield until he had either wearied of her, or—if it were possible to construct a creditable story in such circumstances—may actually have broken off the affair in a noble, if futile, attempt to save her from being implicated in his own certain ruination. He had given the lady her *congé* in the last days of his attendance at White's, a circumstance related to the officer by several of the Viscount's former associates. The lady was no longer at her London residence, nor could she be found at her brother's Northamptonshire estate. No successful effort had been made to trace her further until, to his horror, Colonel Fitzwilliam found himself giving the Bow Street regular information on the last-known whereabouts of Miss Mary Crawford.

As the sad business came to its inevitable conclusion, Colonel Fitzwilliam had ample leisure, imposed by the necessity of his remaining near his father, to observe the close and steady friendship that existed between Lord and Lady Hallendale. He could not but be conscious of the double blessing in his father's choice of such a wife: she not only soothed his fears, supported his spirits, and encouraged his hope, but directed the servants, met the visitors (oh, could they but be spared from the condolences of the curious and the fraudulent civilities of the uninvolved!), saw to their daily needs and comforts, responded to the most pressing of the correspondence, and a thousand other details, large and small. Without such careful attention, the confusion and anguish of those first weeks must have been infinitely worse. Colonel Fitzwilliam watched her as if in a dream, aware that he had never fully appreciated the manifold trivialities and unending stream of importunate matters of business that comprised the substance of her days. He saw also, with fresh pain, the helplessness of his father in the present calamity. His father had never heeded the present, and in his thorough preoccupation with his own studies, had failed to enact any scheme to secure his estate for his heirs. Although he inherited an estate dreadfully encumbered, he had done nothing himself to secure it from ruin; that credit must be owing entirely to his wife. The simple fact was that the Hallendale estates were more valuable than was generally believed—much more valuable. Colonel Fitzwilliam—now Viscount Dunfield—had the clarity of mind to comprehend that, had the efforts of his step-mother been more generally known, his brother's life might have been spared, only to the certain destruction of the entirety of the Hallendale estates, beyond even Lady Hallendale's abilities for its recovery. He was thankful— beyond thankful—that the wisdom of Providence had spared his father such an analysis, and had further put the decision between two such wretched alternatives beyond the power of any mortal.

The obvious blessings of such a wife—intelligent, active, determined, devoted to her husband—had the not very wonderful effect on the Colonel, who, for the first time, powerfully felt and understood the value of such a companion. In the midst of these melancholy reflections, Colonel Fitzwilliam kept returning to an image in his mind—an image of capability and comfort—but of whom? It was certainly not Mary Crawford—whose image was now one of disgrace and repugnance. He struggled in vain to recollect the countenance of just such another of his acquaintance, but his memory would yield neither the who, nor the where. In the lassitude and despondency of the hours attending his father, Fitzwilliam returned to Georgiana's letters as a means of simple employment and escape from the distress everywhere around him, written through the course of the Darcys' journey. In this more leisurely reperusal, he was at once struck forcibly by a new understanding of the words which spoke of the open simplicity of her heart; he now saw—in every line—her joy in the expectation of his arrival, her dependence upon his approbation, her ready compliance with all his opinions—in short, he saw with unmistakable clarity that Georgiana must be in love with himself!

Another

Another equally satisfying image quickly succeeded the first very flattering conclusion—so foreign to a man of Fitzwilliam's modesty: it was, in fact, Georgiana Darcy who reminded him of Lady Hallendale. Georgiana's nature and accomplishments, strength of mind, and integrity of character were such as would support the blessings of a marriage equal that of which he was now daily a witness. She had further claims on his esteem: her steady friendship of many years, and the generous and loving nature behind that friendship; the artlessness of her speech, and the kindness in her actions; her quiet attention to those she loved, and the reciprocal care of the love given to her in return—in short, she was everything he could wish for in a wife, and she was—at least had been—in love with himself! He had wasted that love on someone wholly unworthy of either love or esteem. How heartily did Colonel Fitzwilliam regret his replies to those precious letters! How ardently he wished unwritten those pages full of contemptible praise for another!

In this second reading, he saw with shame and horror the pain written between the lines of her replies to his letters, which had been full of little else than the virtues of Mary Crawford. How blind he had been! Equally blind to deception and to merit! The lucidity with which Colonel Fitzwilliam now realised the frailties of his own judgement would have overwhelmed a less modest man. The small blessing it was, the Colonel was not obliged to add the mortification of self-delusion to his present unhappiness.

A third image of *much* less appealing nature would obtrude: Georgiana's ignorance of the place she held in his heart, and the agonising probability that she had, by this very hour, already accepted the eligible Comte. His reperusal had also allowed him to understand that Georgiana had very reasonably concluded that Mary Crawford was to be—or had *already* been—confirmed as his choice. The Colonel could now add to his present state of affliction, the additional trial of realising that he had foolishly placed himself in the rôle of a distant and insecure lover. This deplorable state of affairs had occurred, perversely, at the time when every possible objection to a marriage between himself and his cousin had been nullified: whilst the Hallendale estates were not so grand as Pemberley, thanks to his step-mother's endeavours, his estates were now respectable and of such considerable value that there could be no mean imputation he had chosen Georgiana for her fortune; in addition, Georgiana, of all the women in the Kingdom, was fit to be a countess—by birth, person, manners, understanding, accomplishment, and temper—in short, everything! And, the consummate blessing was his reflection that, at least within the last two months, he was convinced that she had been in love with himself.

His reflections now took another turn. He contemplated his long pursuit of Mary Crawford, who, seen now with impartial eyes, was in every respect Georgiana's inferior. It was true that Mary was uncommonly pretty and could exert herself to have the most engaging of manners in company, but Georgiana was just as lovely to look at, and in a less calculated, more natural way. Georgiana did not have Mary's gift of speech, but was that not a blessing, when balanced with the more private pursuits of marriage? It was inconceivable to Colonel Fitzwilliam that a woman such as Mary Crawford would be content within the confines of the daily amicability he observed in Lord and Lady Hallendales' intercourse. His father and step-mother inhabited a sphere of their own fond creation; a universe exactly filled by two, complete and content. Such a picture would not—could not—accommodate the noise and display of a Mary Crawford; but the soft, approving eyes of Georgiana made a vision of another union—equally blessed—a most compelling picture, and one which the repentant Colonel now desired with all his heart.

What could be done to relieve such effusions of love and tenderness? Nothing! Georgiana must now be daily in the Comte's company. From Darcy's picture, the Comte had at least equal claims as himself, and— added to Colonel Fitzwilliam's now-complete wretchedness—the Comte had never committed such folly as to squander the opportunity for such a prize as Georgiana. The Colonel reasoned that he had not only wasted the chance for the prize, but overlooked for a period of—quite probably— years the fortune that Providence had placed before his own eyes! No, the Comte had recognised her virtues, and manfully endeavoured immediately to acquire such a treasure for his own. For all he might otherwise have wished to despise his opponent, Colonel Fitzwilliam was forced to honour the Comte for his choice, and his celerity in attempting to secure her.

There was nothing to be done for a period of at least a week— probably longer—except to wait and pray to a beneficent Providence for his own happy deliverance. A patience for inactivity was not his virtue by nature or by choice, but wait he must, and through his own willing, deluded design, which, for Colonel George Fitzwilliam—an active man and a military man—was a most severe penance, indeed. His only employments in such an urgent interval were counting the

days

days until Georgiana could reasonably be expected back in London, and enumerating the ways and days of his own folly.

His pain was increased in the most mortifying of ways, when a letter, written by Georgiana to the Hallendales and sent from Venice, eventually found its way to the family in London, having been misdirected and delayed. The letter, evidently posted before the Darcys had received news of the Viscount's death, was full of Georgiana's thoughts of himself: her eager anticipation of his arrival, her dependence on his promises, and the now-apparent portion of her own happiness that was comprised in her affection for himself and his family. In the wake of such pure and almost giddy joy, the afflicted Colonel also discerned Georgiana's obvious pleasure in the Comte's company, for the last lines of her letter were full of her anticipation of their return to Paris and its pleasures.

18th July
Venice, Italy

DEAR AUNT AND UNCLE HALLENDALE,

We read your latest letter with such delight, and are very happy to hear that all the family are well, for we have heard little of late from Colonel Fitzwilliam. We are still in expectation of his arrival, although he has been delayed considerably at Tunbridge Wells, to our great disappointment, for we miss the pleasure of his company and conversation daily. I have your latest letter beside me now, and the good wishes and kind words make me long for the comforts of home and my friends more than ever.

Venice is such a place of dreams that I wake up each morning fearing it will have disappeared, and I will be left sinking into the sea in its wake. We arrived some days ago, at dusk, and my first sight of the Water City was as enchanting as in my imagination. Yet, after some time here, it is also strangely confining; in Venice one goes about everywhere by gondola, concealed by the cloth-lined shutter—forced to return to the sea. I will admit only to my dear aunt and uncle that I am lately feeling a little tired of life in Italy, for the society seems strangely unvaried, and the Venetians rather more distant than the inhabitants of Paris, by whom we were made welcome, indeed, particularly by the most gracious attentions of the Comte and his family.

Titian's "Assumption" is as glorious as its many descriptions imply, and I believe I will visit the Tintoretti collection in The Accademia delle belle Arti again during the course of our stay here. Of course,

St. Mark's is splendid, and the beauties of the Doge's Palace are incomparable. Rialto Bridge is full to capacity with little market stalls, and gondoliers enjoying the mid-afternoon sun from their seats on its steps. For art and beauty I want for nothing, but I miss the comforts of Paris, nonetheless, and I cannot help reflecting that no city in Italy compares with the many splendid diversions and comforts we enjoyed during our stay in France's capital. I know I should not say so, but I cannot like Italy as much as perhaps I should, as it is so very dirty. Paris is not clean, but the dirt there is of a more modern character; the grime that covers everything in Venice is so ancient, that I am ashamed to say that I cannot venerate it for all its antiquity. It is also somewhat tiresome to be obliged to travel everywhere by boat. Elizabeth and I are more accustomed to walking, and I feel myself strangely fatigued through want of exercise. Paris, of course, is a lovely city for walking.

Please send our kindest regards to the Viscount, whom we look forward to seeing upon our return, to compare our experiences abroad with his. And if you should happen to see the Colonel, please let him know that we await his arrival with much expectation, for there can be nothing that compares with the pleasures of meeting old friends. We sincerely miss you all, and I remain,

Your fond niece,

GEORGIANA DARCY

As he read and re-read those lines, envious even of the pen she held in her hand, the poor Colonel could little know that, for fear of sounding ungrateful, Georgiana dared not write of her ardent longing for home—that even the barest, most forsaken foot-hold of rock in England would seem an Eden. She had, instead, substituted Paris as the object of her desire, imputing that any praise of that city would be unexceptional, yet still remain within the strictest compass of the truth—Paris was indubitably closer to England than was Venice. The probable presence of the Comte in Paris had not entered her thoughts at all; she simply saw the city as the final delay before her return to England, and imagined herself there engaged in the happy pursuits of readying everything for their final departure homewards. In the eyes of the tormented Colonel, however, Georgiana's eagerness to return to the "diversions and comforts" offered by France's capital was tantamount to a declaration of love for its chief gallant—the Comte d'Estrouville—and, thus, the letter intensified, rather than alleviated, his growing apprehensions of the distance and the days that yet divided himself from Georgiana.

CHAP. 16.

INSTEAD OF A LETTER, as expected, about a week after Mr. Darcy was returned to London, a dishevelled and distracted Lady Catherine made her own appearance at an extraordinarily late hour, just as Darcy was finishing some letters of business and preparing to retire. Looking up as she was announced, he immediately noticed her pallor and unkempt appearance. She had all of the outward aspects of having dressed hurriedly and, extraordinarily for Lady Catherine, with no concern whatsoever for her manner of dress.

"Good God, Madam!" cried Darcy as he stood. "What is the matter?"

Her story was as breathlessly delivered as it was impossible to immediately credit.

"My daughter..." was all she could get out; sinking into a chair, she covered her face in her hands and sobbed.

Allowing Lady Catherine a minute to compose herself, Darcy rang for the servant to bring a glass of strong wine. At length, after taking the better share of the wine, she was recovered enough to speak. Darcy, by now convinced that a dreadful accident had befallen her daughter, had moved a chair near to hers and waited.

"My...my daughter," began Lady Catherine trying to speak between the choking of tears, "...Anne...has left me...gone off...Sir William"; and having succeeded in finishing the entire thought, she resumed weeping without seeming to notice him further.

After some time, she again became mistress enough of herself to continue, and related to him the events of the previous day:

"As you know, Fitzwilliam, I believed Sir William to be a man of substance and honour. In both qualities, I have been most unhappily deceived. I was persuaded by his behaviour to myself to believe him in love, and waiting for the opportunity to make me an offer of marriage." Lady Catherine paused to use her hand-kerchief and wipe her eyes.

Sitting straight up and staring ahead, she responded, desperately attempting to keep both her voice and her person steady, "Above three months ago, Sir William and I had a most dreadful misunderstanding. Upon his requesting to speak with me privately, I mistakenly assumed him to be making *me* an offer. To my mortification, he was asking for my blessing and the hand of my daughter!"

Still wringing her hand-kerchief, she continued, "We agreed that it had been a most grievous error on both our parts, and that the best course of action was for us each to go on as if nothing of the kind had happened, and that was how it se-e-emed." Again, Lady Catherine burst into tears and required some minutes' time in which to compose herself, before continuing: "Indeed, he sent me a letter taking all the blame for the misadventure upon himself, and begging to be restored to our family circle. We *did* go on as before, but yesterday, when I arrived home in the afternoon, I found this letter on the table."

She removed a much-folded and damp packet of writing-paper from her reticule and handed it to Darcy to read. Turning away slightly in her chair, she was the very picture of misery.

Darcy could not immediately fathom what had occasioned such distress, but the first line of the letter immediately relieved his suspense.

31st August
Bath

Madam,

By the time you read this, your daughter and I will have left for Gretna Green. Any attempt to follow us and prevent our marriage is foolish; she comes with me as a willing woman above the age of consent. She is aware of the deception you have long maintained regarding your late husband's will. Neither of us regrets to inform you that you are no longer welcome at Rosings or the London residence, although as per your marriage articles, your daughter graciously conveys the use of the old Dower Cottage for your life-time. As you are aware, there are no rents that accrue to that property, as per the bequest of Sir Lewis.

In all happiness, I remain,

Sir William Elliot

When he finished reading, he returned it to Lady Catherine. "Is it true, what he says concerning Sir Lewis's will?" asked Darcy.

"Yes—all of it."

"And you withheld the substance of the legacy from Anne?"

"Yes. All of it."

"Lady Catherine!" expostulated Darcy, "That is tantamount to theft! Whatever could motivate such a disgraceful deceit?"

Lady Catherine looked, if such could be possible, even more wretched than before. She quietly replied, "I was afraid of what my daughter would do if she knew. I had no recourse against the will; I had already tried without success to find a way to have it annulled. The solicitor told me that the will was drawn up in such a way as to prevent my assuming authority over my daughter's fortune, even if she were incapacitated, or if she had deceased prior to her one-and-twentieth year. Any trusteeship would have passed to you and George. My husband was very thorough."

"What about the duty of the trustees, when the will was read? Was there no-one else present to inform Anne, in default of your effort?"

"My husband overlooked one particular, which allowed me to hope that I could succeed in retaining controul of the Rosings property until Anne married; at that point it would not be material, as she would naturally have connected herself well—to *you*, as your mother and I had planned—and the bequest of her father's estate would not be in question until she deceased. Old Haggerston was named by Sir Lewis as executor. Only he and his clerk were present when the will was read—you and George were named only as successor trustees, and were away at school. Haggerston was the only impediment until such time as the two of you had attained your majority. I easily convinced him that I was delighted with the terms of the will (having my own independent fortune), and that I would inform you and George by my letter. Anne was too young and delicate to be burthened with such matters, and I assured him that I, as her mother, was most able to choose the proper time to relate its contents. Mr. Haggerston left off his business shortly thereafter, and his clerk was in no position to dictate my duties to me. I heard that another man purchased his concern, but, fortunately, amidst the other matters Mr. Haggerston left to his successor, this one minor transaction was likely to be overlooked."

At last, Darcy spoke and broke the dreadful silence that had arisen since the end of Lady Catherine's last speech. "I am sorry, Madam; there is little I can say or do to either console or encourage you in such circumstances. I assume that Anne has notified the servants that you are not to be received at your—the house here in town?"

"She is her father's daughter. She has been so thorough as to have her solicitor affix a bill to the door, indicating that I am not to be allowed onto the premises."

"In that case, I welcome you to *my* house for as long as you desire," he said rising from his chair.

Lady Catherine did not move, but looked even yet more distressed. Darcy was himself quite tired, and weary of the seemingly unending succession of calamitous events: "Is there something else, Madam, that is troubling you?"

Lady Catherine took a large folio of papers from the valise she carried and handed them to Darcy.

"This is all I have in the world, Fitzwilliam. When I gave Sir William my money, he gave me these papers. I wanted to have you look at them, but he told me that secrecy was of paramount importance, and that we had to act immediately."

"Good Lord!" cried Darcy, sinking back into his chair. "How much did you give him?"

"The £7,000, which is all of my jointure," she replied in a voice so low as to be nearly inaudible.

Darcy took the papers and quickly leafed through them. In a few minutes he replied, "Lady Catherine, I am not hopeful, but I am also no proficient in matters of philosophical science such as these. I have an acquaintance, who I believe has not yet left town, and who may be able to give us some advice on the value of such a scheme. I recommend that we rest ourselves now, in order that we will be better able to think and act with clarity on the morrow. Good night. I am extremely sorry for your present distress." Making his bow, he left for his chamber.

The house-keeper came in directly and shewed Lady Catherine upstairs to an unused apartment. For the first time did the seriousness of her situation manifest itself clearly in her mind: she truly *was* a guest, and, as such, dependent upon the kindness of others for her every comfort. This was not the last of many long, sleepless nights for the widow of Sir Lewis de Bourgh.

Darcy was downstairs, and had despatched a note to Mr. Parker before Lady Catherine made her appearance in the breakfast-room. Mr. Parker bounded in mid-morning, cheerful as ever, and full of curiosity as to the identity of the mysterious "complication" that could have resulted "in such an early summons, and on a Saturday, too! You must have a very high opinion of yourself, Darcy, indeed! To ask a man to leave his..."

He was taking off his hat and coat, and handing them to the butler, when he noticed the countenances of Mr. Darcy and an older woman sitting next to him in the drawing-room. He paused mid-sentence and said,

"I am afraid I have come at a bad moment. We are just this day leaving for our seat in Sussex," he said, bowing to Lady Catherine. "I am not sure why I am here, but I came as quickly as I could after receiving your message."

Darcy looked impenetrably grave, and handed the folio packet to him with the briefest of explanations: "Lady Catherine, may I present to you Mr. Sidney Parker. Mr. Parker and I are partners in some speculations of a not dissimilar nature to the one in which you are invested. I have asked him here to give us his opinion on the merits of the scheme from a mechanical and scientifical perspective. He is eminently qualified to make such an evaluation; I am not."

Darcy and his aunt waited silently for Mr. Parker to speak. When he did, after looking through the papers for only one or two minutes, and shuffling back and forth between several sheets of complicated diagrams, he continued to look at the papers and cried,

"This is madness! For God's sake, Darcy, tell me that you have not ventured any or all of your considerable fortune with this madman... this charlatan!"

"No, Parker, I have not, but my aunt, Lady Catherine, has become significantly involved in the venture. In fact, Lady Catherine has invested the entirety of her ready fortune in this scheme. Do I take it by your last pronouncement that you are not sanguine of its success?"

"Success! I could not so much as imagine the possibility, if you told me that the creator of this apparatus were the great Watt himself!"

Recollecting Lady Catherine and pausing to adjust the flow of his ideas to be of a more civil nature, or at least more comprehensible to Lady Catherine, he continued in a slower and milder tone:

"Madam, I have no idea how this gentleman has imposed upon you, but I give you my most steadfast assurance that this scheme is wholly impractical from the point of view of œconomy, or even common sense."

"But, the drawings...," began Lady Catherine, "I have seen the steam-lights myself, in the foundry at Telford. They produced a strange, but quite agreeable blue light..."

"That they would, Madam," replied Mr. Parker. "You say that you saw these installed in a foundry?"

"Yes, near Telford. I travelled thither myself to inspect the apparatus and view it in operation. A Mr. Wainwright's foundry—Mr. Roberts had installed his steam-lights in Mr. Wainwright's foundry." Lady Catherine looked deathly pale, and appeared in some confusion of mind. Darcy suggested that she might be more comfortable if she were to rest, and leave the discussion to himself and Mr. Parker, but Lady Catherine would remain to hear what Mr. Parker had to say.

"A foundry, Madam," he said, nodding to Lady Catherine, and turning to Darcy, "Sir, is quite a noisy place, is it not?" Lady Catherine agreed, and added that the factory was heard well before it could be seen.

"And these steam-lights, how large were they?"

Lady Catherine indicated, "The light-globes were about the size of a band-box, only, of course, of a spherical proportion."

"Did Mr. Roberts tell you how much each of the steam-lights cost to produce?" asked Mr. Parker in a disgusted tone.

"No, it was not discussed."

Darcy was growing impatient, and at length broke in abruptly: "Parker, what are you getting at? Say what you have to say, for pity's sake, and do not keep us in suspense in this manner!"

"I understand your impatience, Darcy, and I apologise. I was trying to fathom how a sensible person could have been induced to invest in such a speculation, but you are right—that is nothing now," replied Mr. Parker. "This apparatus is simply not practical for several reasons: the prospectus indicates that water is abundant and that it is much safer to transport via a system of pipes than the coal-gas. The first is certainly true, but, I assure you, steam under high pressure is as explosive and as deadly as any gas. Second, the system of steam-pipes would have to be provided, just as the system of gas-pipes has been installed in the better parts of London. It would be pure folly to make a second set of excavations and a duplicate system of piping simply for a different method of lighting. However, neither of those considerations is decisive, in my view, and would be surmountable if the steam-light were likely to prove advantageous in the long-term. From the view-point of the venture, owing to the complexity of the turbine and static generating mechanism, the cost of each steam-light so far exceeds that of a simple gas-infuser, it is impossible that so complex a device could ever be produced so cheaply as to be a serious rival to gas-light. A second consideration is that the gas-light has no moving parts that eventually tire and require replacement; the steam-light has *many*. Then, there is the *noise*. This could never be used even on the busiest street. The din produced by even one device must be appalling! You would not hear it in a foundry over the general din, but I assure you most heartily, that such an apparatus would be intolerable anywhere *but* such a place as a foundry." Mr. Parker paused.

Lady Catherine was not yet entirely without hope and asked, "But Mr. Roberts said steam-light was the best possible method in any factory where there was open fire, due to the combustive nature of the coal-gas. And he further indicated that the steam-light would be most œconomical where there was already a steam supply, such as exists in many places of manufacture already in England."

Mr. Parker smiled and said, "Those are both true statements, Madam, taken one at a time. However, as a defence of the mechanism, it will not do. First, the gas is contained in a system of iron pipes and, hence, is less combustible than, say, the wooden floor of the factory, or worse, the particles of dust that arise in any place where things are *made*, and can spontaneously combust at any time. As to the œconomy of an existing steam-supply at-hand; whilst true, the noise of the steam-light would surmount any such savings. It is impossible to move the turbine farther off, so as to partition the source of the noise from the work-floor, as it is the turbine that generates the static electrical charge that produces the light. Mr. Robert's steam-light is, in my opinion, going no further than Mr. Wainwright's factory, and probably only thither as Mr. Wainwright has got the lights free of expense to himself, and cares not for the insupportable noise—Mr. Wainwright is very probably stone-deaf himself at this point from working in such a place as a foundry over any period of time."

It remained for Darcy to conclude, "Then you do not feel that there is any point in pressing Mr. Roberts as to his intentions for the steam-light."

"No more than I feel Uxbridge's leg will be seen walking to Whitehall, Darcy, I am sorry to say. My good lady and I send our compliments to Mrs. Darcy, as well as our regrets for missing the pleasure of seeing her before our quitting town—and I depend upon seeing you next at Richmond in September, Darcy." He bowed to Lady Catherine and took his leave.

CHAP. 17.

THE FOLLOWING MONDAY, Mr. Darcy left early to meet with the Hallendales' solicitor and Mr. Gardiner at the Hallendales' London residence. Mr. Gardiner had asked to speak with Mr. Darcy urgently on a matter of some delicacy. To Darcy's surprise, he was greeted by Lady Hallendale, whose attendance had been particularly desired by Mr. Gardiner, and he found them both seated at the table upon which were spread what appeared to be several sheets of new-drawn estate plans for the Hallendale properties. The solicitor was unable to be present, but Mr. Gardiner assured Mr. Darcy that the three persons in the room were the most necessary for what he intended to impart.

"Darcy, I have no wish to over-step my bounds as a friend, or be impertinent, but I seek your advice as to the best plan for the welfare of the Hallendale estates. In the past days, I have reviewed my ideas with Lady Hallendale," he said, making a bow in the direction of Her Ladyship, "and I have secured her consent for all I now venture to propose to you." Mr. Darcy assured him that Mr. Gardiner's advice was always not only welcome, but received with gratitude. And so, after they were all seated around the library-table in the study, Mr. Gardiner continued.

"Lord Hallendale is most dreadfully distressed with the recent unhappy events, even though he is aware of only a small part of the whole. Lady Hallendale has been away from the business of the estate for nearly three months now, and, at any rate, is wholly occupied—as she properly must be—in attending His Lordship and trying to divert him from such unhappy scenes as are before us. And, Darcy, here is my concern—and please stop me before I offend you—Colonel Fitzwilliam—Viscount Dunfield—is a good man and a capable soldier, but he has no education in the management of a large property. The Hallendale estates are now nearly entirely recovered—nay, profitable—owing to the extraordinary diligence and care of Her Ladyship." He bowed again to Lady Sarah before continuing, "However, Her Ladyship will never, I fear, be able to reassume such an amount of work as well as care for her husband. It is imprudent to depend upon the Viscount's ability to assume such a complexity of duties in a time sufficiently short so as not to re-endanger the estates. Please believe, Darcy, I have no wish to discredit your cousin, but to lay before you the risks that the Hallendale properties may suffer—have already suffered—in the months that Her Ladyship has been away."

Mr. Darcy looked expressly at his aunt for her concurrence, and was satisfied. "Gardiner, far from resenting your advice, I am honoured with your confidence, and most appreciative of your concern for my family. I see in your expression that this concern is only a part of the topic here, am I correct?"

Mr. Gardiner smiled and agreed. "You know me too well, Darcy, for my ideas to be received with the éclat they so justly deserve. But, let us return to the business at-hand, and this is what especially concerns yourself. With Her Ladyship's approbation, I have been looking for an agent to supervise the running of the Hallendale properties. These are the first of a new set of plans drawn up by the firm of Kent & Pearce—I am confident you have heard of him, thorough as you are; Charles Kent is the son of Nathanial Kent—he has just begun on the Home Farm," said Mr. Gardiner, pointing to the sheets. "Lady Hallendale and I agreed that a new survey was required, especially as the encumbrances are now cleared, so the land may be re-apportioned more rationally, a task far more easily done on a table than in the fields."

Mr. Darcy replied, "I am very familiar with Mr. Kent, Senior—his book is my bible at Pemberley. I doubt there is one man in England who has done more or better work to improve land management. Let us return to your discussion. You have found a suitable steward? I have no reason to form any view against such a plan, but fail to see why I am concerned."

"If you would but let me finish, Darcy," he continued with a smile, "I have questioned a Mr. Adams, who was late in the employ of the Earl of W——. Where is—here is his letter—he writes well, do not you agree?" said Mr. Gardiner, briefly waving the papers in Darcy's direction. "As you see by the letter, he entered the Earl's service as a foot-boy at an early age, having been educated at a foundation school. During the twenty years he has been with the Earl, he has successively

🌿

served as a groom, footman, valet, butler, and house-steward in one of the first establishments in the land. The Earl's properties have lately become so—encumbered—as to make Mr. Adams' place redundant. In addition, Mr. Adams is seeking a position not only with a future," again nodding in the direction of Her Ladyship, "but with an increased portion of over-sight; he is an ambitious man and seeks to better himself and the situation of his family. Without wishing to seem overly warm in the man's praise, he is a keen woodsman and very enthusiastic about just such experimentation as you favour. He has read much, and seems in every way most qualified as a land-agent, or, in a few years' time, as an estate steward."

"Yes, yes, Gardiner, please come to your point. I would like to arrive home in time for supper, this day," Darcy rejoined, smiling.

"Well, here is the issue of delicacy: Mr. Adams comes with a Mrs. Adams. She, too, is from the Earl's estate, having begun as—here we are—a maid-of-all-work, and then serving as house-maid, laundry-maid, under-cook, under house-keeper, and lady's maid, before finally being named as house-keeper at this same place, where she has occupied an unusual position of trust for above ten years; my source was most emphatic on that point. Here is my thought, Darcy: your Mrs. Reynolds must be nearing the age when she would naturally wish for a diminution of responsibility. I propose that you secure Mr. and Mrs. Adams for Pemberley, replacing the good Mrs. Reynolds, and allowing your Mr. Bakewell to assume the responsibilities as agent for the Hallendale estates. Bakewell is well able to relieve Her Ladyship of the vast majority of her cares, allowing her to devote her days to the care of her husband; their current house-steward would return to his proper sphere, in addition to acting as bailiff. Thus, the Hallendale estates are prevented from returning to an almost certain decline; and Her Ladyship is allowed a well-earned retirement from the demands of daily business."

"Thank you for my share of the favour, Gardiner, but I am not convinced that I wish to part with Bakewell. What about the decline of *my* estates?"

"Look, Darcy, Adams is a younger man than is Bakewell, and will be able to serve you and Pemberley for the future. Bakewell is very close-by, and can educate Mr. Adams when he needs help in discharging his new duties. Mrs. Reynolds can similarly see to Mrs. Adams, not to mention Georgiana. Surely you recognise that Georgiana is the proverbial 'key' here—besides your esteemed self, of course?"

"You were speaking sense until the last statements regarding my sister. What has Georgiana to do with the Hallendale estates?" asked Darcy in an impatient tone.

"Darcy, I do not think—and, again, remember your pledge to stop me *before* I have offended you—I do not believe you to be aware of the significant rôle Georgiana plays in the running of *your* household. She has had a most excellent model and guide in Lady Hallendale (bowing to Her Ladyship), and has been a most attentive pupil. For these ten years past—and probably more—she has been assuming a steadily greater share of your burthens, as well as assisting Mrs. Reynolds as she nears the age where she is increasingly less able to properly see to the extents of such an house as Pemberley. Who do you think has been seeing to those letters of business, receipts, provisioning, and such-like? If you dislike believing this as the truth, upon your return home, go to the house-keeper's office and see for yourself what has accumulated in—not *your* absence, but Georgiana's. You can refer to Her Ladyship, if you prefer not to credit what I say. And, by-the-bye, I have this sheaf of papers which have arrived from the house-steward at Hallendale House. Would you be so good as to take them to Georgiana to review, and see to the urgent matters upon her arrival? I hesitate to leave them to Lady Hallendale under the present circumstance," he said, again bowing to Her Ladyship, and paused, with a gesture indicating that he had finished his speech.

Darcy saw little point in referring to Lady Hallendale for corroboration, as, had she disagreed, she was there to say so. For the next half-minute, Darcy looked as though he were beginning to find Mr. Gardiner's comments impertinent or, at a minimum, officious. Another half-minute's reflection convinced him of the reasonability of Mr. Gardiner's plan—in its main points—and he was soon able to credit Mr. Gardiner's assertions *in toto*, and had only to wonder at his own lack of perspicacity concerning the value of his sister as an help-mate, and the present burthens of his aunt. Numerous hints from his own wife on exactly those points came instantly to his mind, and he was momentarily overcome with some remorse and not a little self-reproach. Recollecting himself, he rose, nodding and smiling, and shook Mr. Gardiner's hand. "Well done, Gardiner, as always. You are right in every detail. I am ashamed that I was blind as to both the extent of Georgiana's part here, and the proper view of what must now be before my Aunt Hallendale. I readily concede Bakewell—and more—if you like. Are there any more of my household that you care to appropriate for the general benefit— my wife, perhaps?"

Both gentlemen laughed and breathed more easily than they had for many minutes. Mr. Gardiner looked at Lady Hallendale and continued, "Whilst you are in such a generous humour, I will importune you further—yes, there is one more thing, Darcy."

Darcy replied, "As long as it is *not* Elizabeth, please consider it as yours or as done, as you decide."

"No, no—it is not my niece that is here concerned," said Mr. Gardiner with a smile and a shake of his head. Recollecting the seriousness of the subject, he continued, "This concerns the new Viscount. Assuming you entirely consent to the Bakewell-Adams exchange, I think it wise that George travel into Derbyshire to meet with Adams and Bakewell without delay. This arrangement will give him a chance to feel absolutely in-charge, to properly know the extent of his own responsibilities, and, moreover, feel that the plan is by his own design. Above all of this, I believe it imperative that we give him a change of scene for a week or so—he is looking remarkably ill—which puts an additional burthen on Lady Hallendale, out of concern for both father *and* son. To my way of thinking, his absence for a few days will produce an effect of a generally salutary nature."

"As you wish, Gardiner. I again express my gratitude for the concern and care you have always taken for my family, and, again, I thank you. Now, may I return to what is left of my own establishment?" he said, still retaining his light-hearted tone as he moved toward the door, bowing to Lady Hallendale.

"Fitzwilliam," said Her Ladyship quietly, "I am very obliged and very grateful. I regret that it is impossible, under the present circumstances, to acquaint His Lordship with the particulars of your kindness and generosity. There is one favour *I* would ask of you."

"Yes, Aunt, whatever I can do is both my duty and my pleasure."

"Both Mr. Gardiner and I feel that you are the best person to speak with George—the Viscount. He respects you not only as he always has—as a brother—but also as a land-owner—as an improver. We all know it to be impossible that His Lordship undertake such a task, and I believe that George would much prefer to take direction from you on this subject, than myself or Mr. Gardiner. I do not scruple to trespass even more on your kindness as, in addition, if you were to offer him the benefit of your very capable assistance, it would add—I am sure— greatly to the confidence which is needed to undertake these many new responsibilities so immediately. Even more importantly, Fitzwilliam, I think that you—if anyone—can convince him to leave his father for a

few

few days—tell him that, now you are come, he is needed in Derbyshire. Dear Georgiana will be here before many days and can assist me. Will you undertake this errand, or do I ask too much?"

"Very willingly, Aunt Hallendale. I cannot promise success, but I will do what I am able, to induce him to act as you wish. Gardiner, anything *else* you require?" Darcy asked with a smile, and a bow to his aunt.

"No, Darcy. We have done. I leave you to attend to your dinner. Pray, remember Mrs. Gardiner and myself to your wife and sister, and beg they will visit us as soon as they are come home."

CHAP. 18.

Mrs. and Miss Darcy arrived at the door of the London residence at Park Lane late in the evening on the ninth of September. Georgiana had, by this time, been so long over-wrought as to be in a state of complete exhaustion, and so excused herself and went to her own apartments immediately upon receiving her brother's assurances that the Hallendale family were as well as could be expected at such a time, and that Lord Hallendale's health had not been injured. As soon as she had left the room, Mr. Darcy commented on her pale complexion, and her being remarkably thinner than when he had last seen her.

"Is my sister unwell? I have rarely seen her so distressed, certainly not since that deplorable—well, that is nothing now to the point. Was there some mischance on the road home, Elizabeth? I am shocked by her appearance!"

Elizabeth tried to reassure her husband, but had no ready explanation. "I am afraid I do not know. I have, several times, attempted to educe what troubles her, but delicacy prevented my pressing her further—or worse, compounding her misery through ignorance. I can offer only surmises: without a doubt, Georgiana has found the relentless pace of travel a severe trial. Our brief stay in Paris was so taken up with the safe transport of our belongings and planning our onward journey, that I fear it was no respite at all for her. And, although the Comte was the very picture of courtesy, and an immeasurable source of comfort to us in your absence, it was to be expected that she would find the experience of seeing him again unsettling, after their awkward parting. Our journey from Geneva to Dijon was fraught indeed with her anticipation of their reunion—although, I hasten to add, she insisted she had no further apprehension on that score. With her increasing anxiousness, and a corresponding depression of spirits, it does not require a great sagacity to comprehend that *something* grievous troubles her; possibly Georgiana found her sensibilities completely overset by her expectations of the meeting. In opposition to this idea, since our meeting with the Comte, and receiving his disinterested and generous assistance, she has been a little quieter, but this change has produced a sombre effect—instead of relief to a troubled mind—the closer we were come to home. It is beyond my power to explain why she should be *less* happy to be coming hither. In retrospect, her unhappiness grew worse as we travelled *away* from home, and still further to increasing misery as we travelled *en route* homeward. I am mortified to admit to you, Husband, that I am able to produce only these pitiful conundrums and conjectures. I know with a certainty that she is suffering under a dreadful affliction, and one that has not been relieved by our return home. But, as she will not venture what troubles her, I cannot honourably demand to hear what she does not wish to tell."

"There is no possibility, then, of an union between the Comte and herself? I had considered that a second meeting might convince her of his worth. I do not comprehend her continued rejection of his suit, and he has since written to me, assuring me of your safe return to Paris, giving not a few hints in the letter than his wishes remain unchanged. Is it impossible to surmise that her distress is a realisation that she *did* love him, and wishes herself back in Paris?"

"She does not love him, Husband." Elizabeth was gentle, but firm, upon this point. "Although she esteems him greatly and sees a great deal of her brother—whom she adores—in his person and his address, she continues to view him only as your friend, and I believe no amount of time would change her mind on this matter. She was, of course, grateful for the care and assistance—as was I—he provided in your absence."

"I am only sorry that I was forced to leave you. If you could but know with what pain I rode away from the two whom it was my bounden duty to protect, and thinking that I was, in a most dishonourable manner, foreswearing my most sacred oath. Thank God you are both safe and home! I am further aggrieved to admit that my early return to London has accomplished little, for the situation is quite beyond hope." And with his customary œconomy of speech, Darcy informed Elizabeth of the particulars of the events surrounding the death of Viscount Dunfield and the results of the subsequent enquiry.

Elizabeth was aghast at the depravity of the circumstances, and

asked

asked question after question, until she was of a sudden struck by the recollection of another matter of import, and produced the letter from her pocket-book sent in reply by Anne Wentworth regarding Sir William. "The letter was poorly directed, and missed us at Venice. I only received it upon our return to Paris. I fear it is too late for the warning she gives to have any benefit, but it is imperative that you read it, for Sir William's character is base, indeed, and surely endangers Lady Catherine's fortune."

Gravely, Darcy took the letter. "I am afraid, Elizabeth, that the contents of the letter may be easily conjectured. Any warning will have come too late to be of use. I have been with Lady Catherine these few days—or rather, I should say *she* has been with *me*, in London; her situation is, I am sorry to report, almost surely beyond remedy. She has invested the entire sum of her jointure in an ill-conceived scheme recommended to her by this scoundrel, Elliot, who has since deserted her. Anne de Bourgh, it seems, is to marry the man herself. Lady Catherine's independent fortune is almost certainly lost, for the investment is worthless, and there was nothing that Gardiner or I could do by the time she appealed to us."

Elizabeth was wholly unprepared for the news concerning Anne de Bourgh, and enquired further into the particulars.

"Lady Catherine was informed of Anne's elopement and her own disappointment by the expedient of a brief note from Elliot, saying that they were gone off to Scotland. Anne gave notice to her mother that she was now no longer welcome at the de Bourgh town-house or at Rosings. However much I am loath to say it—if the truth is as we comprehend it—they must suffer together for the iniquity of such a scheme. Gardiner has been indispensable, assisting in the matters of Lady Catherine and the circumstances of the Viscount's death. I have given many a grateful thanks to Providence for the happy chance some years ago that brought you into Derbyshire, and secured me the friendship of the good Mr. Gardiner in the bargain. There is, I believe, no better man in England."

"How can Lady Catherine thus be turned out? What can Anne mean by such a statement? Where is your Aunt de Bourgh now?" gasped Elizabeth without even pausing for his replies.

Darcy related a shortened version of Lady Catherine's late history, sparing his wife the information concerning Lady Catherine's malfeasance in the matter of her late husband's will, and concluding with the answer, "Lady Catherine is residing here, visiting solicitor after solicitor, in the vain hope that she will find someone to contradict

Mr. Parker's assessment of the worthlessness of her shares. You will find her much altered when you next meet. We shall have to see what we can do for her, for Anne obviously intends to occupy Rosings herself upon her return from Scotland, and Lady Catherine shall have nothing but the old dower house." Elizabeth could not believe how far her aunt had fallen for the sake of an infatuation—and at her age! Unable to fully comprehend the succession of extraordinary events which had occurred in the comparatively little time they had been away, she made her way to bed, but not before extracting from Mr. Darcy a solemn promise that he would not make abandoning her on the road a regular practise.

Georgiana staid in her apartment the whole of the day following their return, asking for a tray to be brought up, and that she not be disturbed. When Mr. Darcy enquired after her that evening, Elizabeth again conjectured that she was not yet fully rested from their journey. The next day, Georgiana came down and met Elizabeth at breakfast. She sat silently, taking only a cup of tea whilst Elizabeth briefly acquainted her with the details surrounding the Viscount's death and the extinction of Lady Catherine's home and fortune, without dwelling on those details which must be doubly painful to one so immediately concerned. She had expected Georgiana to be much moved by her accounts, but she appeared strangely unaffected, and reacted not at all beyond a few bland platitudes. Elizabeth found such behaviour astonishing, especially in light of Georgiana's own compassionate nature, but could see no opportunity for questions. As an alternative to conversation as a restorative to Georgiana's dejection, Elizabeth proposed that they take a morning walk to Hyde Park Corner to see what changes to London their four months' absence had brought.

"And then I suppose we must stay at home, as Colonel Fitzwilliam—or as I should now address him, Viscount Dunfield—is to have returned last night from Derbyshire, and I am in hopes of a visit from the Hallendales. I long to see them; four months is a long time to be parted from friends, especially friends who have so undeservedly suffered such misfortune."

Georgiana was uncommonly hasty and warm in her refusal. "I beg you will not take offence, dear sister, but I would much rather be alone this morning. I find a great need to collect my thoughts. Pray, do not think me ungrateful—I am only in need of some time to reflect and compose my mind now that we are come home. So much has changed—or may have changed—or might change. I will walk now and see the new buildings as you suggest. Please be so kind as to make my excuses to

the

the Hallendales—or whoever else should come—please say anything and nothing, except the truth that I am unable to suffer company at present. Thank you for your unexampled kindness and patience—this must seem very strange and uncivil—I am sorry, Elizabeth—thank you."

"Georgiana, I am willing to do as you ask—and more—but are you quite sure? Will you not take Adéle? It will look peculiar if you are entirely alone, but it is early, and you would not venture imprudently. If you prefer this morning to walk alone, I will most willingly oblige you, but I would never wish to leave you, if you are in any way distressed or unwell. Should not you rest here until you feel stronger?"

But Georgiana was adamant, and upon rapidly collecting a parasol and her reticule, she left the house, stopping only a moment to reassure Elizabeth that she would not be long. Elizabeth could only conclude that Georgiana was in need of respite from the constant companionship of their travels, and wished to take the first opportunity to be by herself and do what she wished, without the hindrance of the consultation and compromise demanded of the last few months. Deciding she would not walk by herself, she settled down to correct her visiting-book, and begin her morning correspondence.

Elizabeth had not yet finished the first of her letters, being addressed to the Bingleys, when the sound of the bell alerted her to the arrival of a visitor, shortly to be followed by a commotion across the hall as the butler ushered her guest into the drawing-room. The hour was yet early; Elizabeth had yet not prepared herself for guests, and she considered whoever it was to be rather forward in calling at a residence at that early hour of the morning. Shrugging off her irritation, and checking her appearance in the looking-glass, to note with satisfaction that this morning at least her appearance—if not her good humour— was ready for company, despite the early hour, she walked out of the parlour and into the drawing-room. She was greeted with the most welcome sight of Colonel Fitzwilliam, who stood to attention upon her entering the room, and made his way toward her with rapid movement.

"Mrs. Darcy—Elizabeth! It is an uncommon pleasure to see you again. I am told by the servant that Mr. Darcy left early and remains abroad for much of the morning—It is indeed a pleasure to see you!—I am sorry I call at such an early hour—to be sure, it must be most unexpected, but I hope not entirely unwelcome, for we have been apart for such a time—such a pleasure to see you!"

Colonel Fitzwilliam was almost wild in his speech, his dress dishevelled—the customary light breeches were of a distressed brown colour, stockings loose, waistcoat misbuttoned, and the sleeves tucked up under the cuffs of his coat, the epaulette of which was struggling in vain to keep pace with its shoulder and was, consequently, trailing behind, across the back. His cravat was apparently unwilling to add to the confusion and was missing entirely. Moreover, Colonel Fitzwilliam was continually glancing toward the door. Elizabeth decided it best to impute his careless dress and singular behaviour to the natural disorder of mind that the recent events must produce. Upon her pointedly calm enquiry after the health of the Hallendale family, the Colonel replied,

"Our family keeps well as may be—Darcy has been a most necessary assistant to us these past—past weeks. I mean, I wonder what might have happened—or not—or—without his being—It is delightful to see you, Elizabeth—Mrs. Darcy, truly."

Elizabeth listened with some consternation to this strange salutation, which was most out of character in its repetitions and deviations. What on earth could have happened to provoke such unaccountable behaviour in Colonel Fitzwilliam? Really, amongst the extraordinary actions of the Colonel, Georgiana, Anne de Bourgh, Lady Catherine, and the Viscount, Elizabeth was beginning to feel positively incapable of adjudging if she herself were destined for Bedlam, or was it—alternatively—that nearly all her family would soon be found thither?

"It is like-wise a delight to see you, dear Colonel Fitzwilliam—Viscount. You have been much in our thoughts these past weeks, and we are all most anxious to be of service to your family."

"Pray, call me what you have always called me—I cannot bear to hear that title, as it most painfully brings my brother to mind. Please forsake the etiquette out of your kind compassion for my feelings. You know not how much I depend upon your kindness, Elizabeth, and the kindness of *all* your family."

"Of course, Colonel. Who could oppose such a plea? But won't you sit down? I would like to hear all your news, good or otherwise, for the sake of both relieving your mind and answering my own questions. Would you like some coffee?"

The Colonel waved away the offer of refreshment, as Elizabeth sat down upon the settee, inviting her cousin to take the chair opposite. Fitzwilliam made to sit, but resolved immediately to receive at once the information that would make him either the happiest of mortals, or the most miserable, and so asked Elizabeth about their journey from Geneva. Elizabeth was expansive in her praise of the Comte.

"We were met at Créteil by the Comte himself, and were never out of his care until we boarded at Calais. He assumed all of the burthens for the collection and packing of our things upon himself and his servants. In retrospect, I do not know how we could have managed it—French tradesmen can be so awkward about concluding any business, once they have received their payment. But the Comte is a most determined gentleman—he reminds me exceedingly of Mr. Darcy in that and other ways—and saw to everything. He certainly left nothing for us to do, although we are not nearly so incapable as to require such assiduous attention. And, as you know, Georgiana can converse like a true Frenchwoman, she is so proficient."

"Did he travel to Calais with you?" asked Colonel Fitzwilliam.

"No, he left us in Paris, but sent his coachman, servants and a waggon with us. God bless him for doing so—our servants were so completely undone by the loud and wild manners of the French, that it did not signify that they understood nothing of the language—they seemed to be waiting every moment for the guillotine to appear! They were all but useless, and could not be depended upon to complete even the most routine of their duties to ready us for sailing."

"I wonder he did not come to Calais...," began the Colonel.

Here Elizabeth was in some confusion as to how much of the history of the Comte and Georgiana she ought to relate, when she could not help but say, "I do not know. I never considered that he would travel so far with us. At any rate, I believe that doing so was impossible out of consideration for Georgiana's feelings."

"I know not how to understand such concern. Surely his presence must have been a source of comfort to you both?"

"Yes and no, Colonel. I am unsure of how much of this history my husband has imparted to you, but ever since that dreadful morning at Belle Aire, Georgiana has been under a severe oppression of spirits. Unaccustomed as she is to giving disappointment, she has been suffering since, and it is no wonder that being constantly in the presence of the Comte would only serve to amplify such feelings of agitation. You must know also, by this time, that her little Mademoiselle Blanche is no more—poor Georgiana!—I had not considered until this moment, that being in this house without her Blanche would be yet another severe trial. And then when you did not come to us, I own she appeared disappointed out of all proportion by your delays. It all must have been too much for her to bear in such a little time, and such disagreeable events were surely compounded by the usual fatigues of travel."

Elizabeth continued, "Nothing we have suggested seems to be of any use against such suffering. Indeed, we have tried everything in our power to relieve her despondency, but our efforts are all for naught; in fact, her misery seems only to increase. It is in every way unaccountable, and I have no good news to give you. She is pale, and grows thinner each day. Poor Mr. Darcy is sadly grieved, and has this additional weight to his other concerns for your family's recent misfortunes."

"Pray, I have not the advantage of knowing this history—whose disappointment?"

"Oh! I apologise—I thought my husband must surely have mentioned this. The Comte was very close, we believed, to making Georgiana an offer, and Georgiana was adamant in her certain refusal. We all thought it best that Mr. Darcy speak with him privately, and give him to understand that his suit was in vain. We left his estate almost immediately thereafter, and did not see him again until we were returned to Paris."

In a sudden motion the Colonel stood and turned toward Elizabeth again, and asked the question that had been plaguing him. "Is Miss Darcy not here? I believed she would be here, with you—at home—this morning. I have come so early with the express desire of seeing h—you both. Is she resting? Am I to return in an hour?"

The same question having been addressed to her in so many different forms at once, Elizabeth was momentarily at a loss. "Georgiana is gone for a walk. She left not an hour or so ago, but she did not say what time she would return. May I offer you some refreshment, Colonel Fitzwilliam? Would you like to wait for her return?"

"Where was she going?" Colonel Fitzwilliam cried, waving away Elizabeth's offer, and stood over her, expectant of her answer, taking up his hat.

"I-I am sorry, but I only know that she is gone and that she left in the direction of Piccadilly," Elizabeth replied, momentarily unsettled by the Colonel's impetuous manner and unaccountable incivility.

"I am sorry, Elizabeth—Mrs. Darcy—but I must leave immediately. I know that I should explain my behaviour, but I beg your pardon—beg your leave to do so later—forgive me—forgive me." Colonel Fitzwilliam bowed rapidly, and in an instant was out of the room and out of the house.

"This is a season of wonders!" Elizabeth Darcy exclaimed as she watched the Colonel stride in haste—nay, run—down the street, from the vantage-point of the drawing-room window. "I cannot, for the life of me, imagine what extraordinary caprice or eccentricity we are to

witness

witness next from our nearest friends and relations. In spite of my self-proclaimed sagacity in such matters, at present the only conclusion that may be drawn with certainty is that I hardly know anyone, anymore. Perhaps Mr. Gardiner will be seen riding an hippopotamus down Rotten Row—or, Heaven forbid!—Mr. Darcy will be caught bathing in the Serpentine!" In some confusion of mind, Elizabeth walked back to her bureau to finish her letter to Jane, and then turned away to find another employment. "It will not do to attempt to describe the recent events to Jane—I must first be able to decipher them myself!"

In the next moment, her attention turned away from the latest sequence of surprises, Elizabeth saw with complete clarity what had been before her eyes for months. Upon Darcy's return, she acquainted him with the fact of the Colonel's visit, but not its purpose, and bade him remain at home for his cousin's return. Elizabeth regarded it a fair certainty, that the Colonel would return to Park Lane accompanied by Georgiana, both miraculously improved.

C H A P . 1 9 .

ELIZABETH COULD NEVER HAVE reckoned that Georgiana's rapid departure from the house was the result of her inability, in her present state of mind, to endure the visit from Colonel Fitzwilliam and Miss Crawford that must surely be expected of the morning. The Colonel, in the pain of the loss and public disgrace of his brother, would, Georgiana reasoned, surely have become closer than ever to the object of his affections. The thought of someone other than herself providing those words of comfort was inexpressibly painful, and she simply did not possess the strength to wish them joy when she was herself most abjectly miserable. It was not that Georgiana did not wish the best blessings in life for her cousin—she did, generously, and with all her heart—it was simply that she must now comprehend how far removed from those blessings she, herself, would be, and indurate her mind— and to whatever extent possible, her heart—to the prospect of such an unmeditated future. She knew that she did not wish to marry the Comte—or anyone else—as recompense for her disappointment. However, that assurance provided only a small portion of relief to her misery, as such a reflection served only to define what she did *not* want. It was now attendant upon herself to examine such that remained of her many blessings, and to fix on those most necessary to the recovery of her own happiness, now that Colonel Fitzwilliam—the Viscount—was lost to her for-ever. This was a great deal to consider and decide during the course of one walk of a morning, but Georgiana was firm in her resolution, that she have her thoughts arranged before she could meet the Viscount and his intended with equanimity.

She walked the length of Park Lane, along Mount Street to Berkeley Square. It was early enough in the day to go into Bond Street, and she walked into some of the shops therein without any consciousness of her actions, simply as the day was fine and their doors were open. She continued down into Piccadilly and along the broad street, noting that there were buildings in progress everywhere. Just before Piccadilly, Georgiana noticed the Burlington Arcade. As it was necessary to occupy some hours until she could be sure that the Colonel's visit would be concluded, and he and his lady gone, she decided to bend her steps thither as the Arcade was sure to be extremely busy and, hence, would prevent her being seen by anyone. Three arches led to a single walkway lined with shops, displaying jewellery, beautiful writing papers, perfumes, watches, porcelains, silver, and other lovely things. Georgiana thought that, in truth, Paris had nothing more than did her own London.

Standing to attention outside the establishments were Lord Cavendish's Beadles, guarding the length of the building, ensuring that the atmosphere of calm and elegance was not disturbed. Georgiana wandered slowly up the walkway, seeing everything and nothing, and occasionally stepping inside one of the shops just to be doing something. She had visited the Arcade with no intention of buying anything, but upon seeing a pretty shawl that she thought Elizabeth would like, she entered the shop, and engaged herself for some time in the comforting occupation of purchasing a pretty gift for her sister, especially having just quitted her with such unjustifiable incivility. Having done this, she was entirely at a loss as to how to pass the morning before going home, so she decided to take a dish of tea, and, afterwards, look to find some present for Jane.

Any enforced occupation, no matter how agreeable, is rendered arduous by its necessity, and Georgiana despaired of finding enough to do in the interval that must necessarily pass to secure her safety. She reflected, with some envy, on Elizabeth's ability to occupy herself in the observation of her fellow creatures, and imagine the crowd as a kind of pantomime, finding sufficient amusement in the actions of those around her as to make such periods of inactivity pleasant. This thought was immediately succeeded by her recollection of the Colonel's own dislike of shopping, and Georgiana was, at that moment, much in similar antipathy. At length, she purchased a book, and sat down on a bench to read—at last!—an occupation for her mind that would help the time to pass quickly and not disagreeably. The book, however, did not answer, and she spent her time alternately turning the pages without seeing the words, and looking about. Glancing at her watch, she saw that the hour had come when she might take some tea; Fortnum's was likely to be filled with the *haut ton*, and Georgiana had no wish to be seen.

Walking up Piccadilly, she was roused from her thoughts by the small, choking sobs of a child. Looking about, she saw no-one leading a toddler or holding an infant. She was just past the gates of St. James, when she heard the sound again, and turning back against the crush of people walking up to Regent Street, looked down to see a very ragged, dirty little girl standing by a sack, crying miserably. In a moment, Georgiana had interposed herself squarely between the child and the crowds roughly pushing past her, and took her hands.

"Oh, dear. My name is Georgiana. What is your name, little one?" she asked softly. The girl stopt her sobs briefly enough to reply, "B-b-Betsey V-vale, ma'am," and then resumed sobbing with all her heart.

Georgiana kept a firm hold of the little hands lest Betsey take fright and run into the crowd, and asked, "Whatever can be the matter, Betsey, for such unhappiness?" Georgiana managed to infer from what she could hear between Betsey's gasps, that her father was going to drown the sack of kittens.

She had taken the sack whilst he was asleep, and was going to find some kind person to take them, as, if she returned with them, "Not-not on'y will P-p-papa drown the kit-kit'ns, bu-but he-he w-w-will b-be ang-ang'g-g-ry 'n d-d-drown Tabby, t-t-oo," and her broken sobs increased even more desperately, if that were possible.

"N'if h-he ff-f-ine's ou-out, I-I-I w-wil' g-g-g't a wh-wh-whip-p-p-'n—" the sad relation of which sent her back into sobbing so hard, Georgiana feared for her very breath.

Georgiana bent down and opened the sack. Inside were three very small kittens, mewling piteously, but their tiny cries could not be heard over Betsey's choking tears and the crowds in the street. "Betsey, can you tell me where you live?"

"B-be-be'ind, n' up-up-s-stairs," pointing to the backs of the garrets of Jermyn Street. Betsey, being thoroughly fagged, out of breath, and out of tears, had stopt crying for the present. Georgiana imagined the squalor and the noise rising upon noise, the disorder, and the brutality—brutality to whip a child!

"I think we can see to the kittens safely," said Georgiana. "I will take the sack, whilst you take me to your house to collect Tabby and see your Mamma."

"What will you d-do wif' T-Tabby, ma'am?" she cried with a remarkable terror and suspicion for one so young. Georgiana could only just imagine what kind of life would raise a child to such fear and distrust. Betsey had shewn a remarkable independence of spirit and courage to defy such parents! And, with such unflinching determination did she anticipate the punishment sure to come!

"We will return her kittens to her, as they are far too young to leave their mamma, and then we will ask *your* mamma if you, and Tabby, and all of her kittens can come with me to my house. Would you like that?"

"W-Where is y'r house, ma'am?" she asked, much mollified by Georgiana's answer.

"Not far, Betsey, from your house," and picking up the dirty sack carefully, and cradling it in her shawl, she kept Betsey's tiny hand firmly in her own. They walked along slowly to Jermyn Street, as quickly as Betsey's little legs would allow, to the tenements above the gaming houses. Betsey well knew where she lived; Georgiana could only wonder how many times this child had been left with no-one to mind her, roaming the streets of London. As she led Georgiana timidly up the many narrow, filthy, rickety stairs, a thin, dirty cat came running up and calling loudly to the kittens in the sack, trying desperately to use her paws to drag it down. Georgiana set the sack on the soiled floor of the landing and handed Tabby gently inside. There was an immediate cessation of all sounds from the sack, as the kittens were reunited with their mother.

Georgiana tied the top of the sack securely, and taking Betsey's hand, entered a door that was open. There appeared to be no-one inside.

"Where is your mamma, Betsey?"

"She goes away to meet th' gen'mum."

"What about your papa?"

"He p'b-bly stil' 'sleep. He won' wake up un'les Mamma com' home wif' his sup'r."

"Please go and wake your papa, Betsey." These words produced such a terror in the child that Georgiana immediately recalled them.

"I have a much better idea, Betsey. Will you go out to the landing and hold the top of the sack very tightly, if Tabby tries to get out."

"She won' wan' to get out 'cause she loves her kit'ns."

Kneeling by the child in the stairwell, Georgiana took her little hands again and looked into her tear-streaked face and the swollen eyes, now even more distorted with anticipation of her father's wrath at being awakened. "You are to stay here, Betsey, and do not make any sound, do you promise? We must all be very quiet, and I will return before you say to yourself, 'Tabby has three kittens' twenty times. Can you count to twenty?"

Betsey looked down at the ground, shook her matted curls, and whispered, "No ma'am," and in an instant was cowering down next to the sack, covering her head with her arms!

Georgiana's indignation at the child's terrified response gave her whatever small dose of resolution might have been wanting before that moment, and, softly replacing the feather-like arms down by her sides, Georgiana said quietly, "That is much the better. We will just say, 'Tabby has three kittens' until I return; will you do that? Remember, Betsey, you must be very quiet and stay right here, no matter what you hear. When I return, we will take Tabby and her family, and go to my house. Do you understand?"

Betsey nodded almost imperceptibly, but seemed to sense that Georgiana meant no harm to her or the cats. If Betsey was not a mindful child, left the kittens, and appeared in the room with her father, Georgiana had no idea of what cruelty the man would be capable, and could bear no such conjectures. She turned to Betsey a last time and said, "You must be very quiet and stay right here with the kittens and Tabby. Will you do as I ask?"

Seeing a more hopeful affirmative, Georgiana took a deep breath, stood up very straight, and walked into the squalid, cramped, and windowless garret; the only light came through the cracks along the ceiling and between the tiles of the roof. Georgiana had many times visited the tenants of Pemberley, but their tiny cottages seemed palaces of order and cleanliness, compared with the room in which she was now standing. The odour inside made it nearly impossible for her to draw breath, but when Georgiana recollected what depravity, privation, and violence comprised Betsey's hours, those images had the immediate effect of bringing her own resolution more sharply before her.

The father was found in a small closet to one side, and the smell of spirits allowed no doubt as to his condition. Georgiana stood over the man, who was audibly fast asleep in his unwashed, unmended shirt and trousers. It required several prods with the point of her boot to rouse him. When he was at last disturbed, he rose shouting and swearing for his wife, and threatening everyone within hearing, if he were not immediately brought food and drink. Georgiana waited for the disgraceful tirade to subside, and then addressed him:

"Mr. Vale, please wake up. I am come to take Betsey away. Here is ten pounds. I believe that is a fair exchange, do you agree?"

Mr. Vale seemed wholly unconscious that there was another person in the room until he heard the phrase "ten pounds." He shook off what remained of his stupor and asked with many oaths who she was and why she was in "his house," "his castle," and continued some minutes to declaim loudly and insensibly about "the rights of an Englishman." Hearing no change of discourse for several repetitions of the like, and fearing that Betsey would not be long able to bear the shouts of her father and remain where she was, she drew herself up, standing as tall as she could in the tiny garret, and talking in a voice with such force and authority as would have amazed all her acquaintance, Georgiana repeated loudly,

"Mr. Vale, here is ten pounds. I am come to take Betsey away. If you do not agree right *now*, and sit up and take this note, I will take Betsey, and you shall not have the ten pounds. Do you understand me, Mr. Vale?"

At that, Mr. Vale sat up sharply and grabbed for the note. He was in no condition to act more quickly than could Georgiana, who pulled her hand holding the note back sharply and, looking at him with a stern and steady look, said, "This is the last time I shall ask you, Mr. Vale. Do you agree that I may take Betsey away?"

Mr. Vale's countenance changed in the space of a second from wrath to an appalling self-pity. He said, "Ma'am if you please, let me have that, and another one f'me poor wife fer bread."

Georgiana simply stood over him and repeated her question very loudly, "Do you agree, Mr. Vale?" In the space of time it took him to look at her tall, white figure, Georgiana reflected that he must think her an Amazon, and, she answered herself, "and I have every intention that he should."

He grasped again for the hand holding the note, and she looked at him with a countenance that no longer tried to hide the scorn and, indeed, the anger she felt for such as he who would live off of his wife, and terrify his own child. This anger was closely followed with some relief: "Thank God, there is no evidence that there are other children in this place!"

In another moment, his face changed again; he dropt his hand and said simply, "Take her. That's right, take her. Now, give me the *tenner!*"

Georgiana handed him the note, and, as she was walking back to the landing, placed a second one on the table under a grubby bowl, with the intention that his wife might find it before her husband. Mr. Vale was in no condition to follow her, and was obviously again asleep before she reached the door. She bent to wrap the dirty sack in her shawl, and, asking Betsey if she wished to come to her house to stay with Tabby and her kittens, she received a whispered, but unequivocal, "Yes'm." Georgiana was rewarded with an astonishingly firm grip by the little fingers on her glove, and they walked quietly down the staircase and into the street, then around the corner onto Church Place, toward Piccadilly and home.

In the minutes that had seen Georgiana's meeting the child and securing her, there had been no time for any thoughts except removing her from such vile surroundings. She had given no thought at all to her own reception when she arrived at her brother's house, and entered with the child. She did not fear his reaction, but had no idea whether it would be praise or censure. Surely he would be very right in thinking that the preservation of this one child would do no good against the thousands who roamed the streets of London each day. She had her ready reply, "It matters to this one."

And, in her silent dialogue with herself, she steadfastly defended her resolution of keeping the little girl, and bringing her up at Pemberley; it would be the best, she considered, if her brother and Elizabeth were to adopt the child. Or, if their charity would not extend so far—and she had no idea that it would, or if her brother would allow it—it would appear very improper if she were to keep Betsey herself. Georgiana realised, much to her *own* surprise, that she felt herself quite equal to the suppositions that would attend a single woman with a child, but feared for the future of the child under such a cloud of scandal, however misinformed. But, if Betsey could not come to Pemberley as her brother's child, and she were not allowed to bring her up there by herself, Georgiana resolved that she would purchase her own house—and so on with similar bold resolutions and rejoinders. Occasionally, she stopt to see if Betsey were out of breath, or to adjust her burthen of cat and kittens; with such firm sentiments of charity and righteousness did she keep the dirty little hand in hers and cross into Piccadilly. Through her own reflections and the general din of the street, Georgiana gradually became aware of someone calling her name.

Upon Elizabeth's information, it was possible for the Colonel to act, and act he did. The route from Park Lane to Piccadilly was a twenty minutes' walk, but Colonel Fitzwilliam accomplished it in ten. He stopt but a moment to look in at Gunther's, but not seeing her within, strode quickly past. The hour was too late for Georgiana to be in Bond Street, so he made first for Green Park, knowing that she liked to walk about under the cool shade of the trees—but encountered her not. He continued up Piccadilly, tried Hatchard's, and then, thinking she might be having tea, looked in at Fortnum's, without success. He hastened the distance to the circus, and turned back into Regent Street, afraid to go into any of the shops, lest he should be within when she passed.

In a sudden recollection that Burlington's Arcade was opened, he speculated with some certainty that he might encounter her there. As he turned back up the street amidst the usual confluence of walkers, riders, cabs, drays, gigs, stage-coaches, chaises, sedan-chairs, and peddlers' carts, he became conscious of an immense clamour, and found his progress thoroughly impeded by a circus troupe, extending for several blocks in either direction. The number of waggons, carts, horses, musicians, jugglers, animals, and such-like, and the crowds milling around them, rendered crossing the street impossible. He instinctively put his hand into his pocket and clasped his pocket-book, as such a disorder was the delight of pick-pockets. Pacing up and down for some minutes to find a space in the parade, he finally espied a small gap and leapt through it, nearly oversetting a cartful of clown-puppets being pulled along by a great dog, and almost knocking down a man in striped trousers strolling above the procession on a pair of stilts. Without further hesitation, he crossed the street and entered the walkway of the covered arcade.

The place was bustling by this hour, and he was unable to see very far within the length of the building. He pushed along with the crowd impatiently, again unwilling to enter any of the shops for fear of missing her; he made his way up and down the crowded arcade for some several minutes before turning again into the street.

CHAP. 20.

FOR SOME REASON, and without any further plan, he walked back in the direction whence he was come. She was facing away from him, looking up the street for a moment to cross. They were separated by only a few dozen yards, but it seemed to take an eternity for him to reach her. When he did, he stopt behind her, afraid to reach out an arm to her, lest he startle her by his presence or by speaking.

But his agony of indecision was ended because—perhaps she sensed him—Georgiana turned around abruptly, and with no little surprise, addressed him, "Colonel Fitzwilliam!—Viscount—What are you doing here?" Recollecting herself and trying to respond with greater civility, or at least with a pretense to a composure she did not possess, continued, "It is a most unaccountable pleasure to meet you here. How do you do?"

"Who is this?" he asked, dropping down on one knee to speak to Betsey.

"I am Betsey Vale, sir, an' I am goin' home wif' Miss George-Anna."

Seeing the Colonel's startled expression, Georgiana's confusion of mind was increased by the recollection that her own reply would be overheard by Betsey, and needed to be very carefully formed so as not to include anything which might add further wound and distrust to feelings already long-abused. In this, however, Georgiana had underestimated the child's courage; Betsey turned her face up to meet the Colonel's eyes squarely and added,

"We are goin' home wif ' Tabby an' her kit'ns, sir."

Georgiana nodded, still at a loss as to how to explain what was before him. The Colonel bent down and opened his arms to Betsey, and unhesitatingly, she allowed him to lift her up to carry her. Betsey was now near the bundle of Tabby and her kittens, and began speaking to the sack, informing them at length of what had just been told to Colonel Fitzwilliam. Georgiana thought momentarily of her own solitary childhood, and understood the constancy an animal provided in conversation, companionship—and love—and knew that the hours spent in mutual, confidential sympathy with her Tabby was no small portion of whatever little peace and happiness had formed Betsey's days and nights. Comparing also the blessings of her own childhood against the unspeakable misery of Betsey's short life, Georgiana became once again mistress of her thoughts, and her determination.

The Colonel rose up and, as he did so, noticed Georgiana's new locket, and momentarily imagined it to contain a portrait of the Comte. Reminding himself of his hopes formed upon Elizabeth's history, he was determined to have a resolution for his suspense at last, and was about to continue speaking, when Georgiana, seeing his anxiety, forgot her own confusion and lapsed without thinking into her comfortable rôle as his ever-reliable anodyne, enquiring gently, "I understood your father to be well, or I would have called in this morning. And is...?"

Colonel Fitzwilliam interrupted her quite abruptly, "My father? Oh, yes, he is as well as we could expect under these circumstances, thank God! Yes, yes—she is with us, and she is an angel. I could not imagine a more useful, gentle woman—and, so careful of my father's feelings. She grows in my estimation every day. We are truly blessed to have such a woman belong to us. I cannot say that I am proud that it has taken the present calamity to make me realise the extent of our fortune in securing her to our family, but I say it now, and with more conviction and gratitude than I have in better days."

"Oh!" cried Georgiana, her wounded heart so stricken with the injury of what must necessarily follow, that she believed she was in danger of actually being unable to support herself. Fitzwilliam noticed her sudden loss of colour and led her to a near banquette in the church-yard that would do for three. He set Betsey down and relieved Georgiana of her burthen, placing them gently near the seat. "Here is Tabby, Betsey. I think she needs for you to tell her again where you are going and make sure she knows that her kittens will be safe—and that she will soon have her supper."

"I—I am fine, dear cousin. You must not regard me. It is just that there was such a crush of people on the street. I am having a little trouble breathing, that is all. Pray, continue." Georgiana looked all the more unable to continue herself. Her face was positively ashen, and her hands were cold and trembling. Colonel Fitzwilliam instinctively drew near to her, and put his arm around her shoulders to save her from collapsing entirely. Georgiana pulled away, desperate to understand the actual evil before her, rather than endure the constant mischief of her own imagination. She might not be able to adjust her own ideas to endure his news without pain, but, she reasoned, at least she would know what that pain *was*, the sooner the better to find her way to whatever remnant of her happiness remained.

"And Lady Hallendale?"

"Yes, yes—we all are well. Georgiana—"

"You are blessed, indeed, to find such a one. There is certainly no good in these events, but the comforts to be conferred by such a woman are a great blessing. It bodes well for your future happiness that you are so sanguine as to her value. Will Mrs. Darcy and my brother have the honour of receiving her—I mean meeting her—in Park Place to-day?"

"Meeting?" asked the Colonel in some confusion, but then impatiently continued, "No, I think not to-day—too much to do—attending my father—to-morrow." Here he turned to Georgiana, and attempted to take her shaking hands with the hand not already employed; Georgiana resisted but little, her small store of remaining strength and composure having long been exhausted. However, she was still ignorant of the true progress of her cousin's understanding with Miss Crawford, and persisted weakly, but valiantly, to obtain confirmation of the desolation before her.

She was, by this time, forced to rely for her very sustenance on the belief that his brotherly partiality for her would remain to the extent—even in the glow of his present happiness—that he could still feel a disinterested sympathy for her unhappiness, even in the hopelessness and the absurdity of its cause. He would—she could barely reason—even now not wish to see her suffer. "And—am I to—" Georgiana forced herself to continue, adding almost inaudibly, "to wish you joy?—Miss Crawford," and, choking on the last words—if it were possible—was become even more colourless than before, and seemed about to succumb at any moment.

"Miss Crawford? The devil take... Good God! What could I have said that you are thus distressed? Dearest Georgiana... pray..." The Colonel startled himself, as he realised in that moment that Georgiana must have taken her information from his last letters of the month previous! She must, therefore, have been in the most wretched apprehension of his renewing his addresses to Miss Crawford for weeks! Oh! How thoroughly did he regret and repudiate those former sentiments! How abhorrent were those words to him now, which—as he now understood— must have occasioned the most awful sensations of despair and torment to such a trusting, loving heart! Colonel Fitzwilliam had now only to consider himself a great brute and a block-head. It could and should take a life-time of care and tenderness in atonement for his stupidity and unintended cruelty—a penance he was most desirous of securing.

Colonel Fitzwilliam held her hand firmly, and, shaking his head with a very tender smile, he bade her rise and resume their way home. He gently placed Betsey's hand in Georgiana's, and taking up the sack in one arm, took her arm in his other, and directed them out of the church-yard. Georgiana suffered herself to be led through the crowds with her head down, hoping that she was not so much a spectacle as to cause the Viscount embarrassment, in addition to the distress that must necessarily accompany his brotherly care for her feelings. Betsey, gratefully, was yet busily engaged in speaking to the sack. Georgiana, without comprehending where she was or even the direction she was bound, thought only of bracing herself—again—for those words which would seal the close of her hopes and happiness. She began to speak, but Fitzwilliam gently raised his finger to his lips, signalling her to be silent, smiling as if they were at play at a child's game so many years before at Pemberley. She had now nothing with which to resist. She leaned on his arm, tucking her head into his shoulder as she had so often done when she had tired from the running and the games, when the Colonel—as he was then—would read her to sleep. The noise of the city was an indistinguishable hum to her; she closed her eyes, allowing him to guide their motley procession whither he would.

Upon their reaching a quieter corner, he stopt and turned to look directly at her. "Georgiana, I cannot wonder at what you must think of me. I have been a fool of prodigious proportions. In spite of my unworthiness, I have come to ask you to marry me. I have been in love with you—and only you—but had not wit enough to realise it. Foolish and blind I have certainly been. All this time I have been searching for a woman who is just like you, without recognising that in every way my ideal of a wife has been formed by you: your kindness, your gentleness, your strength of mind, your beauty, your grace—your capacity for love. In these past weeks, I have—at last—perceived that you might love me—love me not as your guardian or your cousin, but as an husband. If my past actions—if I am mistaken in this matter— if your feelings have very reasonably undergone alteration these past months, I only ask that you inform me at once, and I shall not speak of this again. Only—I beg you—do not deny me that share of happiness I have long claimed as a brother, because of the mistakes of the past. I would be wretched, indeed, if I lost both a wife and my dearest friend, even though my actions should rightly deny me the regard of both. For the love of God, Georgiana, please look at me! Answer me, if you can!"

Georgiana had always believed that a declaration of love, so ardently expressed, from the lips of the man she loved even better than a brother, would resemble the scenes of a novel, in a secluded glade or atop a wind-swept mountain, rescued from a near-tragedy by the bold, precipitate action of her lover; but in the sight of Colonel Fitzwilliam's stricken demeanour, she found herself growing calm, retreating once more into the familiar patterns of comfort and care: "Hush, Colonel Fitzwilliam. There is no need to speak of alteration to my feelings. There is room in my heart for no-one but yourself." The shy and diffident Miss Darcy looked for the first time into the eyes of the man she loved, to see that love reflected in his whole countenance, and was no longer afraid to believe her ears or her heart. He gently set Tabby down again, and held out his hands to take hers; she never looked away from the diffusion of joy in his eyes, unwilling to deny herself even an instant of the startling joy of this moment, and such unexpected, exquisite felicity!

Carefully resuming his burthen of the dirty sack, the three walked along Berkeley Street, and then turned westward toward Hyde Park. When Colonel Fitzwilliam next spoke, it was in the voice of a man whose happiness was complete. "I have been on tenter-hooks waiting for you to arrive home. I had convinced myself that you would indubitably prefer the eligible Comte—his pretentions and prospects are far superior to my own—and would return having engaged your heart elsewhere. I should deserve nothing less, as we both know. I must learn to be happy in the face of my own undeserved good fortune."

"The Comte is a man of honour and liberality, and one to whom I feel most obliged for his kindness, but there was no danger of his engaging my heart. I believe that my brother and sister took me abroad with the purpose of widening my circle of acquaintance, and, with some good fortune, making my introduction to someone I might esteem as an husband; but they did not apprehend that the only man I could ever love was often right at their door. It has not, though, been a wasted journey, for it is not impossible that my absence taught you to love me. But—Colonel Fitzwilliam—you must tell me of the particulars of your time with Miss Crawford. I have been certain from your letters that you had renewed your attachment to her, and were shortly to make her an offer."

"I will do so, but only if you will agree to call me neither 'Colonel Fitzwilliam,' 'Viscount,' or by any other title other than that of 'Husband,' or 'George.' Do you agree?" Georgiana's eyes and the glow in her smile spoke her agreement to his entire satisfaction. The particulars that Colonel Fitzwilliam then related to Georgiana regarding Mary Crawford were known to no-one but himself and Mr. Gardiner; not even Mr. Darcy knew of her infamy, or the Colonel's acquaintance with her. "I must add, to your certain surmise, that my honoured father and step-mother know nothing of the circumstances I am now—with the greatest imaginable shame—to relate to you.

"After our meeting at Northamptonshire, I did not hear from Miss Crawford for several months. A few days after my arrival at Tunbridge Wells, I was taken completely by surprise by her appearance there. She was come thither with her brother, she *said*, to escape London, but I now know her sole purpose was to reunite with me. Miss Crawford affected not to have known that I was there; still her presence in the town baffled me, for I had informed only my family that I intended to spend my time at Tunbridge before leaving to meet you on the continent. I did not discover the reason for her knowledge of my whereabouts until the investigation was begun into the death of my brother—this is a very shocking story, my dearest, and please stop me at any time if you cannot bear to hear the awful truths."

Georgiana assured him that she was ready to hear anything that was necessary for her to understand the history—his history—and with gentle words and an earnest look of her soft eyes, bade him continue; but before doing so, he stopt to purchase a large, shining orange from a cart on the square, and, removing his gloves, took out his hand-kerchief and wiped off Betsey's dirty little fingers, saying, "I think carrying around a sack of kittens all over London makes one quite hungry, does it not?" And, peeling the orange, he gave it to her. Betsey stared and started away as if she were being handed an hot coal. "Have you never had an orange before, Betsey?" Betsey looked up fearfully at Georgiana for approval. Georgiana bent down and took a piece from the orange and shewed Betsey how to eat it, describing how sweet and cool it was. Betsey took possession of her orange in the proprietary way of children, savouring each slice in turn as they walked along.

"Following my initial acquaintance with Miss Crawford before Christmas, she immediately returned to town after being jilted by another man, the elder son of a baronet from Northamptonshire, with whom she had apparently aspired to marry; there are some particulars I do not need to relate regarding a younger brother, and a serious illness of the older. At any rate, she soon resumed her association with my brother and, before long, they were seen regularly out together in London society. Mr. Gardiner's Bow Street acquaintance discovered that my brother had actually been living in the *same house* with Miss Crawford for some months before he cast her out! The enormity of her conduct might be considered by some as partially expiated by the expectation that he was going to marry her. Unfortunately, my brother was very unlikely to have any such intention, especially given the wretched state of his debts, and soon tired of her."

Here, Georgiana stopt him and asked, "I do not understand—debts? And, if there were debts, was not Miss Crawford mistress of twenty thousand pounds?"

Colonel Fitzwilliam sighed, "Oh, Georgiana, you have not heard—my brother's gaming debts amounted to over an hundred thousand pounds—and that was what Bow Street could *find*. There are doubtless additional debts of honour that will never be discovered."

"But, could not the twenty thousand pounds go some way to appeasing his creditors, and use my uncle's surety to pay the rest?"

"A man of greater conscience might have reasoned thusly. My conjecture is that he did not wish to impoverish himself for life—and in the only honourable light, Miss Crawford—just to pay his debts as would any man of principle. In fact—God knows it pains me to say this!—he was preparing to flee England. I doubt he wanted to be encumbered by a woman, even one with twenty thousand pounds, in his flight.

"It was he who must have informed Miss Crawford of my whereabouts. After she was forced to leave his protection, she journeyed to Tunbridge in order to re-establish our acquaintance. I own that I was entirely deceived by her from the very beginning, and she convinced me to tarry at Tunbridge beyond my inclination—indeed, beyond my own reason—to please her. But, at Tunbridge, there was just that want of proper thought and action that unconsciously kept me from renewing my offer, which was obviously her design. Upon Mr. Gardiner informing me of her history—and I admit to you, my dearest, that, in my shock, I was initially unwilling to credit above half of what he related—my understanding of her true character was complete. I must assure you, my dearest, loveliest Georgiana, that even before the death of my brother and my discovery of their iniquitous affair, she

could

could not have re-engaged my heart. Charming and captivating she might appear, yet at Tunbridge I could no longer be again so infatuated as to reconcile her hardness with my ideal of a wife. That paragon has always been yourself, as I have lately realised, in a most mortifyingly behind-hand fashion."

Georgiana was horrified at the behaviour of Miss Crawford. "Have you seen her since your discovery of her attachment to your brother?"

"I have not. She passed several messages to me through some mutual acquaintance, asking me to see her. I did not. Eventually, shewing a complete disregard for propriety, she wrote me, sending me her condolences on the death of my brother, and insinuating in a most disgraceful manner that his death and my inheritance of the title and estate had secured her affections to myself. I have not responded to her letter, and she does not write again. It must be she now realises that the Runners' investigation must inevitably reveal her history."

CHAP. 21.

THE COUPLE WERE TOO engrossed in their own affairs to consider how strange they would appear, or how they would be received, in Park Lane. Colonel Fitzwilliam entered and asked if the footman might fetch Mr. Simms and Mrs. Reynolds. Elizabeth and Mr. Darcy heard the commotion in the hall and came to meet them from the sitting room, where they had been having their tea. Colonel Fitzwilliam knelt down again by Betsey, and asked if the kind Mr. Simms might have care of Tabby and her kittens, to find them a nice, warm place in the kitchen. Betsey looked as though she wanted to believe him, but knew not whether he was speaking the truth. He staid by her, and said,

"Betsey, Mr. Simms will see that Mrs. Tabby gets some fresh milk and a dish of meat. Cook will give her a bit of a bath, and put her and her kittens in a big basket with a warm blanket. Mrs. Reynolds," he said as she approached the child, "will give *you* a bath, and then you may have *your* supper in the kitchen with Mrs. Tabby. Does this sound like a good plan?" Mrs. Reynolds looked in some doubt as to her opinion of the proceedings, but when Betsey looked up at her and said quite fearlessly, "Yes, ma'am, if you please," every misgiving was done away. She led a staring Betsey up the wide staircase, saying, "Now then, I think we might find some of Miss Darcy's things to fit you. I kept them all quite carefully by in hopes that there might be another Miss Darcy, and here you are!"

Through all of this, Mr. Darcy and Elizabeth remained steadfastly silent. When they heard Mrs. Reynolds at the top of the stairs and the door close, Mrs. Darcy suggested that they all return to the sitting room for some tea, in a tone that indicated that she had no wish their conversation be more generally overheard. Elizabeth bade the Colonel and Georgiana be seated, and calmly began to pour out the tea. As Mr. Darcy closed the doors, he turned to his cousin, saying, "Fitzwilliam—Viscount—George! Are we to have some explanation here? Who is that child, and what is she doing *here*?"

Colonel Fitzwilliam replied in a tone of exaggerated gravity, "Firstly, *Mr.* Darcy, let us establish that I am Colonel George Fitzwilliam, Viscount Dunfield, in that order." Resuming his usual tone, he replied with a laugh, "Secondly, I thought it best that she had a bath and some supper whilst we discuss *exactly* those questions. I assure you, that I am equally ignorant as to those details," as he turned to smile at Georgiana. "However, upon further deliberation, I think that the bath and supper are requisite, but I do not find a need for discussion. Ere long, we will take Betsey back with us into Derbyshire." Elizabeth turned to Georgiana and gave her a wink and a broad, warm, knowing smile.

Darcy stared and replied, "Surely you do not propose taking her to live with Lady Hallendale?"

"I do, indeed."

"And you are convinced that Lady Hallendale will accept the charge of this child, whoever she *is*, and wherever she is *from*?"

"I am, indeed."

"You are certainly sure of *two* things, at least, if I can get nothing else of sense from you," Darcy said, growing a little warm in his reply. Elizabeth was hardly able to keep her countenance, but did not wish to appear to be making light of Mr. Darcy's increasing indignation, wisely deferring that pleasure to the two principals.

"Really, Fitzwilliam, this is the other side of enough! You bring *someone's* child in from the street, and a filthy sack of *something* which you have so generously sent to *my* kitchen, *and* order *my* servants about. You must think very well of yourself, indeed! I am..."

At this point, Georgiana stepped forward and in a very firm and steady voice said, "It is *my* presumption, Brother. Colonel Fitzwilliam—George—," she said with some confusion and a blush, "had nothing to do with this *contretemps*. Your very reasonable imputations arise solely from *my* actions, and are, thus, my responsibility to acquit. I am very willing to tell what I know of the child, and why she is here at Park Lane."

Darcy just stared. At length, he recollected himself enough to look about the room, and discovered—to his annoyance—that he was the only person present not enjoying the exchange. He struggled to keep his temper, asking how Colonel Fitzwilliam could be so very sure of Lady

Hallendale's willingness to take on a child, and one of such unknown history, at that!

Colonel Fitzwilliam just laughed and said, "Because I have asked her."

"How the devil...?" started Mr. Darcy.

Colonel Fitzwilliam had received enough of Elizabeth's hints to bring the delusive exchange to an end, saying, "Darcy, I always believed you tolerably intelligent, but I see I must explicate." Taking Georgiana's hand, he said, "You simply have the wrong Lady Hallendale, Darcy. I have already secured the consent of the lady."

Darcy looked quickly from the Colonel, to Georgiana, to Elizabeth, and back again. In a few moments, he shook his head and laughed, clasping the Colonel's hands and kissing Georgiana. "How is it that I am so stupid here? Elizabeth, do I have your usual prescience in these matters to thank for exposing my imperceptivity so dreadfully?"

Elizabeth replied, "Dearest husband, I did not *know*, but I have *believed* this man here," pointing to the Colonel, "to be both the cause and the cure for Georgiana's malaise, since so long ago as this morning." Rising to kiss Georgiana, and allowing the Colonel to kiss her, she sat back down and said, "May we now discuss the one remaining mystery, and that is, of course, little Betsey. It is certainly best that we all appear in agreement when she comes down from her bath. It would be very unkind to the child were we to seem in disagreement, and she to believe herself the cause."

Again, Georgiana spoke, but in a louder and more determined voice than any present had heard her employ before. Hearing the story of how Betsey was found and the circumstances of her former home, it was impossible to think otherwise than to agree that Georgiana had chosen the only path consistent with both reason and Christian charity.

At last, Darcy spoke again, "But, even if you return to Derbyshire as man and wife, it will look very awkward to be bringing a child with you. Or," he said, turning to Colonel Fitzwilliam, "does your perfect understanding of the world entitle you to an answer for that, as well?"

Colonel Fitzwilliam turned to Georgiana, who replied, "You are right, Brother, to be concerned, but I do not think that the censure of the world could persuade me to any other course. I would be very unhappy were I to find that our feelings on the matter were at variance, but I would be miserable, indeed, with taking any other."

Again, the Colonel stepped into the breach, saying, "Now then, there is no cause for either misery or disapprobation. I will write to-day about taking steps to adopt the child; I am sure Lizzy's Uncle Phillips will be happy to accept such a commission. My family is under such a cloud of humiliation presently, that an extra child here or there will hardly signify, and besides, Darcy," he said, becoming more serious, "it may be the last act of my poor brother's charity that the world at-large impute Betsey's existence to his general profligacy, and decide that the Fitzwilliam family are doing the right thing by the child."

"But," rejoined Elizabeth, "surely there will be the stain of illegitimacy if such a thing is generally believed."

"Indeed, she is *not* illegitimate," said Darcy in a surprising turn of opinion. "Her parents are, as Georgiana related, married. There is no need to enlighten the world as to *who* exactly those parents are, simply that they were married. My cousin was known to be living with a woman. I agree that the best course of action is to engage in the proceedings immediately so as to associate the child's adoption with the general conclusion of the late Viscount's history." Becoming very sombre and deliberate, he turned to Elizabeth and continued, "It is also a kindness to William's memory, my love. He will be regarded as being a man of principle and decency where a man would most wish for such a character—for his child."

The Colonel expressed his heartfelt concurrence with Darcy's way of thinking, adding, "And, cousin Elizabeth, such a blemish is surely diminished by the inference of both her birth, and her future fortune."

Georgiana still looked uneasy. Mr. Darcy, seeing her anxiety, asked what remained of her misgivings. Georgiana replied quietly, "Brother, I accept that this subterfuge is necessary for the good of the child now, as well as her future; and I believe that you and—George— are very properly deciding how to best preserve the honour of my late cousin's memory. I do not know how such a stratagem is to be effected, that is all."

Elizabeth laughed and replied, "Oh, dearest Georgiana! If that is your only vexation, dispense with it at once! It is only necessary that one person whisper it about as a great secret, and it will be immediately and generally believed as a gospel—and *that* hint may surely be arranged with discretion."

At that moment, Mrs. Reynolds knocked and entered with Betsey, clean and in one of Georgiana's old smocks. Her hair was now a beautiful dark golden colour, and she was a remarkably pretty child. She approached Georgiana, and in the voice of one much beyond her years, asked Georgiana if she could "pay a visit to Tabby n' her kittens,

please

please, ma'am?" Georgiana took her little hand and led her down to the kitchen to see the cats and to take her supper. That evening, as Georgiana helped Betsey to say her prayers, she asked,

"Betsey, will you and Tabby be happy living here with me?"

"Oh, yes'm! I asked Tabby, and she is very pleased wif' her basket... but what will you do wif' her kit'ns, Ma'am?" she asked, suddenly becoming frightened.

"Now, now. Tabby's kittens are safe. When they are old enough to want an home of their own, we will find a nice family to take two of them together, and you may choose one to keep here with Tabby. That is a promise, Betsey." She kissed the little head, and produced something from under her shawl.

"This is what I used to sleep with when I was a little girl, and wore the gown you are wearing tonight. Until Tabby's kittens are old enough for Tabby to leave them and sleep with you, would you like to have Miss Kitty?"

Betsey reached for the well-worn toy and said, "Oh! Yes Ma'am!" and tucked the old woollen kitty in next to her pillow. "Now, Miss Kitty, it is time to sleep. Le' me help you wif' your prayers." Georgiana softly closed the door, thinking, "With what different feelings did I leave this house only a few hours ago! In such short time have all my prospects changed—from a life of unremitting struggle against heart-break and despair, to a future of every imaginable blessing! I am truly the most fortunate of mortals; I have not one ungranted wish—no imaginable cause to repine. An husband and a child! Two to bring greater joy with each day, greater tenderness, and greater regard, and who are more deserving than can ever be merited; may Providence grant me the self-knowledge to remember such an obligation. Life is very good, indeed!"

The elevation of wilful deceit is a very poor principle to advocate, especially where at least half the world is imagining some insult to probity where it was neither intended nor found. However, in defence of those involved in this imposition upon the public, the falsehoods of society are more often motivated by malice than charity. In acting to secure the little girl's future, and rehabilitate the late Viscount's past, two wounds were healed with no infliction of further injury.

Georgiana was settled within a very comfortable few hours' drive from Pemberley. Lady Hallendale was able to spend the remaining years with her husband in the enjoyment of a leisure made possible through engagement of a respectable steward, as well as the attentive management of the Viscount and his very capable wife, thus preserving and securing the Fitzwilliam estates for the future. Upon the old Earl's death, upon his widow's blessing, his son gave his cabinets to the nation. Perhaps to be nearer to his collection, or perhaps because she could still be of use, the dowager Countess passed her remaining days at the new British Museum employed in cataloguing the late Earl's specimens, ensuring that his legacy was properly described, and available to all of the interested public.

For Lady Catherine, the prospects were less propitious. The Darcys assisted her in making some improvements to the old dower cottage, and she was given her own apartment in their London house. It was ever unclear, but proceeding from either embarrassment or pride, why she would never consent to visit Pemberley, so no accommodation there was necessary; Elizabeth, in spite of years of insult from Lady Catherine, was as much a friend to her husband's aunt as Lady Catherine would allow. However, whether from preferring the company of strangers to the society of her family, or because she had found someone who was yet gratified by her notice, Lady Catherine rapidly established an intimacy with Lady Brookstone. The former was necessarily content to follow Lady Brookstone whither she would lead, in spite of the latter's gross inferiority of birth, of breeding, and even of beauty; but the cost incurred to under-write both their pleasures was high, indeed, necessitating not only Lady Catherine's complete subordination of her own desires and views to those of her sponsor, but to receive, with an unfailing, cheerful submissiveness, the daily intercourse supplied by Lady Brookstone's superior defects of civility, conversation, and intellect. Accordingly, Lady Catherine spent her time chiefly in Wiltshire or *en route* somewhere, following Lady Brookstone, supplying that constant servility demanded by persons of mean understanding and a proportionally great disregard for the feelings of others. How such a life of obsequiousness and deference—of living to suit the pleasure and convenience of such a one as Lady Brookstone—could be tolerable to someone of Lady Catherine's disposition was a continual wonder. Any rational person must for-ever feel that flattery and servility to another is a very high price for the pleasures so purchased; no reasonable person would willingly choose to live in Lady Brookstone's servitude, as there could be no earthly pleasure worth such sacrifice.

The iniquity of Sir William and Lady Elliot produced such a general disgrace, that neither was ever again noticed by any of the family, this most reasonable recourse leaving the Elliots to their own mutual comforts. Sir William did not, to his surprise, find his wife so silent as formerly. He had charge of only a small share of her fortune—due to the forethought of Sir Lewis—but was required to assume the burthen of Lady Anne, no matter how insubstantial the recompense for his side of the bargain. The Darcys heard that he spent only a few months at Rosings, and had returned again to his own house at Bath and the comforts of Mrs. Clay. Lady Anne was content to spend her time and her fortune travelling with Mrs. Jenkinson.

The felicity of the Bingley family was seldom disturbed; Jane was to produce six little Bingleys, with quite enough fingers and toes to go around, and sufficient disorder and noise to satisfy even their doting parents. Parson Overstowey and his wife were to see an increase in their own family; in addition to Mr. Bennet, they welcomed a little girl and a little boy within a few years' time. Upon the passing of Reverend Franklin, Parson Overstowey succeeded to that living, bringing his family even closer to Pemberley, a circumstance much to the delight of Mr. Bennet, who preferred Mr. Darcy's library, even to his own. Mr. and Mrs. Collins were blessed with a Miss Collins as a play-mate for Charlotte's daughter. As master of Longbourn, Mr. Collins was able to increase his steady friendship with Sir William, spending many agreeable evenings in the company of the neighbouring knight, canvassing the newspapers for information about the titled and infamous.

Perhaps the most unexpected change in the Bennet family circle was the news that the Wickhams were gone off to America. Their reputations not being able to follow them thither, Mr. Wickham at last determined to try his fortune on those prosperous young shores. The Bingleys purchased them a more comfortable passage, and the Darcys assisted with their purchase of a small tract of land in the vast area of Virginia. With the hard labour and œconomy necessary for survival in that new nation, their relations in England were in hopes that the Wickhams' energies would be directed in more useful pursuits, and in accordance with Jane's early prophecy, their characters would find steadiness and respectability, at last.

Those who have persevered to the end of this volume will hear with joy that, shortly after her arrival back into London, Elizabeth was able to inform her husband that it would no longer be necessary to impose upon the Bingleys for an heir. That Christmas at Pemberley was the happiest ever, and when Elizabeth was safely delivered of an healthy boy early in the spring of the next year, the Darcy family circle could now want for nothing, with the possible exception of another Miss Darcy.

The only blessing yet to be desired—considering the negligible success seen by the previous generation in planning the marriages of their infants—was that these children will have less interference in their matrimonial choices. Filial independence in such matters is yet another poor morality with which to conclude; therefore, the happiest, wisest, most reasonable end is to decree that the preferences of all the young Bingleys, Hallendales, and Darcys exactly coincided with those of their esteemed parents.

FINIS.

EPILOGUE.

PUBLISHING A SEQUEL to *Pride and Prejudice* seems to excite the same outrage and opprobrium amongst the cognoscenti as painting a moustache on Peale's portrait of Washington, or, for my English friends, proclaiming that tea is unhealthy. In the centuries that have passed since the publication of what many of us believe is the finest book in the English language, millions of readers have comforted and entertained themselves with their own imagined lives of Mr. and Mrs. Darcys post-*P&P*. To offer something which varies, even slightly, from these innumerable, unknowable "sequels" requires that one, in Mr. John Knightley's words, "think well of himself, indeed." Your humble author begs leave to proffer an alternate explanation.

My love affair with Jane Austen (and no-one who loves her will dispute this metaphor) began in the early 1980s with Masterpiece Theater's airing of the BBC's "Pride and Prejudice," starring Elizabeth Garvie and David Rintoul. This will always be "*My P&P*," and any deviation therefrom is heresy. Period. The only possible exception I can allow is "Clueless," not only because it is a brilliant adaptation that I think would have excessively diverted Jane Austen, but also because it is *not* a remake of *P&P*. I am willing to allow liberties with Emma which I am unwilling to countenance with Lizzy and history's most desirable man.

Nay, dear, gentle readers, my attempt originated from a deep desire for "more Jane." Like many of you, I am not only miserable that she died when there could have been so much more to love, but remain convinced beyond reason that things did not really end on that dark day in July, 1817. In my homage to Jane and her fictional world, I have spent no less than twenty-six years researching and writing this sequel, founded the Chawton House Library and Centre for the Study of Early English

Women's Writing, and donated the many books I have purchased in my quest to honor Austen and her contemporaries—all bold and intelligent women; it has been a task demanded by love and justice, but one driven equally by my belief that the collection of the literature produced by these women, and an unbiased assessment of this long-ignored subset of English literature, is indispensible to the comprehension of Austen's life and times, and hence, her legacy. When this context is unavailable or unreconstructed, I believe, we cannot—despite however many re-readings—know even what we do not know.

CHL was founded at Chawton in 1992 because of my belief—regardless of the fact that we, as readers, read and reread the novels and every other of those precious words over and over again—that we understand little and misunderstand much of what Jane or the other women of her time were saying. I wanted to establish a place where people of to-day could study the complete context of the lives of "our ladies," understanding their world to better understand their words. To do this, I have collected as many of the novels as could be reasonably obtained, as well as other works by women and works about women of our period, roughly 1600-1830.

There has been so much social and technological change in the intervening years that many words have lost any meaning entirely (mantua, manchet), completely changed meanings (exceptional, nice), or simply ceased to exist as concepts for the modern reader (pattens, post*). In other cases, the language has been simply overtaken by events: advances in medicine (aspirin, antibiotics), transportation (motorways, jet airplanes), communication (telephones and (gulp) the internet), domestic comforts (plastic, central heating, microwave ovens), warfare (drones, nuclear weapons), as well as the largely unconscious, daily emotional debilitation of the modern person's ability to find happiness within the constant threat of destruction unimaginable in Austen's time, insatiable guilt over pollution, over-population, and famine on a global scale, and the incessant bombardment with the ever-present baser side of human nature that—incomprehensibly—is used to explain and justify the intrusion of the media and technology 24/7.

In 1994, I presented "Carriages in the Novels of Jane Austen" to the Stanford Jane Austen Society. What I modestly call "Lerner's Theory of Austen" was first publicly expounded in that presentation, and has since been confirmed and refined. In its condensed form, it says, "Whenever Jane Austen uses a *specific* noun, she is making a context-specific, value-laden, descriptive comment about a person or society.

Whenever she is using a word in a *general* form, she is using the word in a value-neutral sense." For example: carriage vs. barouche-landau, out-rider or equipage; and my two personal favorites, mince pies, vs. supper, and landaulet, the latter a *single word* serving—on its own, and without *any* modern equivalent—to redefine Mr. Darcy's character as a pale shade of Captain Wentworth's, and my own firm conviction, that Jane meant, in her last novel, for this to be understood.

Austen has long been praised for her deft use of English in delineating her characters: Mr. Woodhouse's "habits of gentle selfishness, and "Lydia Bennet's "high animal spirits" clearly define the natures of their possessors even to-day. Yet, for all of the beauty and brevity, those characters thus defined are the relatively shallow, less-interesting people of the novels. There are other descriptions, I believe, that we can only correctly conceptualize if we admit, as twentieth-century thinkers, that—in the best case—we don't understand, and, in the worst case, we *misunderstand* what we read. If we thoughtlessly replace eighteenth and early nineteenth century meanings with what we understand to-day, we lose much of the true genius of Austen's language, the intricacy with which she delineates her characters, their relationships to and in a society long-lost, and the enduring contribution of that genius to English literature. If we listen to Mozart without any knowledge of the history and achievements of the Baroque, we can never fully appreciate his genius, the degree to which he changed music—forever—and the great gifts those contributions give us to-day. Jane Austen is the same, yet we read not with any real understanding of what she was *actually* saying, thinking, feeling, writing, and with little appreciation of the nature and scope of her contribution to English literature. Rather, the novels are regarded as exceptionally nice stories (I note that neither "nice" nor "exceptional" means anything even close to her use of those every-day words), external to any context in which her genius and her contribution may be appreciated, or with any accepted notion as to why her writing has persevered so uniquely over the centuries, exciting our love and admiration even through the murky lens of our ignorance.

I believe that Jane Austen endures because she was happy and confident, and wrote with a humour that presupposes universal ideals long abandoned by most modern societies: the purpose of life is to be happy; human relationships end only with life; and, for Jane and her peers, eighteenth century England was simply the best place—ever. She can laugh at her England because she is amused by her world, the world of an English Christian, with no cloud of existential self-doubt or insuperable guilt over relentless images of world-wide suffering. She is undisturbed by the uncertainties of terrorism, Freud, global warming, or getting into prep school. She is alive, living and writing in the moment which she believed—beyond doubt—to be the best of times and places, unquestionably created by a God, who—if not actually English—certainly viewed those of the green and pleasant land as his chosen people: Napoleon was vanquished; Iron Bridge Gorge triumphant; and, the rights of and opportunities for the ordinary Englishman surpassed anything in history. The rules of law and reason united to create a complacency in the English mind that requires a great reach for us to imagine, much less comprehend. It was the England of Reynolds, Newton, Faraday, Byron, Maxwell, Storr, Edgeworth (Richard Lovell), Wedgwood, Fielding (Henry), Gibbon, White, Turner, Priestly, Scott (Walter), Gainsborough, Dryden, Churchill (Charles), Wellington, Fielding (Henry), Händel, Hogarth, Walpole, Vanbrugh, Burney (Charles), Disraeli (Isaac), Burke, Pope, Garrick, Adams, Jenner, and—yes—Moser, LeBrun, Merian, Kaufmann, Cavendish (Georgiana), Fielding (Sarah), Wollstonecraft, Herschel, Burney (Fanny), Siddons, Behn, Bateman and Daughters, Heywood, Scott (Sarah), Sommerville, Edgeworth (Maria), Montagu (Elizabeth), Montagu (Mary Wortley), Churchill (Sarah Jennings)—and, Austen. Not only was England handsome, clever, and rich, but—to a degree unparalleled in recorded history—women shared in the benefits conferred by those blessings. Our failure to understand and appreciate the lives and times of "our ladies" is—in my view—not only to ignore and, thus, be ignorant of several centuries of English literature, but to be blinded to the intrinsic radiance of its brightest star.

Insofar as any actual people, places, or things occur in *Second Impressions*, it has been of paramount importance to write what I believe to be historically, socially, factually, and legally correct for Jane Austen's time. I have read Blackstone and Staves, Pope and Harris, Darwin (Erasmus) and Tomalin, Johnson (Samuel) and Wikipedia, and twenty-six years' reading of relevant materials produced between the centuries that separate them. I have tried to understand and write within Austen's context and her idiom. I have tried to reconstruct a place and time for the Darcys, Fitzwilliams, Wickhams, &c., to continue being themselves. No sane person would aspire to be Austen's equal—all I wish for my effort, (it is not a very enviable one; you need not covet it), is to be a pale shade in the distant glow of that star. There are no references, no glossary, no illustrations, and no video; Jane worked without such *aides à la compréhension*. To what extent I have captured the taste, smell, complacency, security, and questions of her time is not a performance I may decide.

P.S. To those of you about to barrage the website with complaints of punctuation, capitalisation, spelling, the frequent use of the dash, and the ubiquitous comma—now largely forsaken by our collective need to save, perhaps, on virtual ink—this is an effort to plausibly reconstruct the fictional places and people of Jane Austen's novels. Austen used the English language—much like Turner used his brush—sparingly, precisely, intentionally. Language to Austen was a tool, an art form, and a medium, not an artifact of a rigidly defined set of rules. She was concerned with the images she was forming in the reader's mind, not with how those readers might dissect her sentences and pass judgement on their structure. My wonderful editor, Robert Lesman, notwithstanding, I believe she split infinitives, misspelt and inconsistently spellt, and lacked parallel structure without concern. She blithely put punctuation where she wanted to indicate, like a composer uses rests in a musical score, the cadence of her narrative and dialogue. If you disagree with my choices for spellings, italics, punctuation, the rampant substitutions for "s" instead of "z", unnecessary insertion of "u" and a second "l", more commas than in the entirety of Hemmingway's *oeuvre*, &c., you are not alone. There was no way to do this without controversy (now, is that **kon**-tr*uh*-vur-see or *Brit. also* k*uh*n-**trōv**-er-see?); some of today's most justly celebrated scholars of the long eighteenth century are in violent disagreement amongst themselves on precisely these points, so we are in very respectable company.

I pray, instead, that you have read this offering for pleasure and with pleasure, finding humor, a little peace, and some escape from the world as we know it.

---

*My editor begs to remind me that both "patten" and "post" can be found in any good dictionary. However, I assert that the modern novel reader, even reading those words and their definitions, cannot construct an adequate context, imagining a world, in the first example, without sidewalks, pavement (another instance of a changed meaning), or kerbs/rain-gutters to divert the rain off the road, and the economic and psychological benefit pattens conferred against the interminable seas of mud, ordure, and other unpleasantness on the roads, of which there was usually no regular repair. Does the phrase, "ceaseless clink of pattens" convey *any* meaning today? The dictionary provides no indication that pattens were an indication of lower status, as people of means in Bath would have hired a sedan-chair. What made them clink? Why were they ceaseless? What did this "ceaseless clink" say about Bath?

And, in the second example, "post," the regular delivery of mail by professionals was a new concept in Austen's time, as was the use of the mail-carriages as a more "genteel" method of safe, reliable, respectable travel, as opposed to the unreliable, unregulated, and often unsafe public coach services, even the latter of which was unavailable to the great proportion of the populace whose only resort was walking. And, in all of this, what does the Steele's three-person journey with Doctor Davies by *post*-chaise mean? [Ans: impropriety, indecorum (two unmarried females traveling alone with a man, unchaperoned), an utter want of understanding that the relation/admission of this fact conveys the same lowness (not only of means and class, but discretion and sense), and an extremely uncomfortable journey, nonetheless, as a post-chaise is a two-person vehicle.]

Eleanor Tilney's comment to Catherine, "but a journey of seventy miles to be taken *post* by you, at your age, alone, unattended!" [Ans: That General Tilney was grossly cruel and irresponsible to someone else's child, a child for whom he had assumed responsibility, *in loco parentis* (an unconscionable abrogation of parental duty), subjecting not only Catherine's reputation to irreparable harm (a most ungentleman-like action), and, in the best light, her very personal safety to the evils of an entire day, alone, in a public conveyance (*if* she had the means to pay), having to find her way home (having never been away from home before), through many changes of coach, and an exhausting journey of seventy miles (a very real, calculable evil); or, in the worst light, *never* making it home, as he either did not think to give her the money for the trip home (gross insensitivity and negligence), or thoughtfully denied giving her the money for the trip, assuming that, if she did not have the money, she was beneath his concern (grossly heartless and cruel): an abuse of power, privilege, and common decency *for his own mistake*. These were obviously decisive issues to Edmund Tilney, or the ending of *Northanger Abbey* makes very little sense.]

Does any modern definition of the word, "post," convey the meanings of these words as Jane Austen used them? [Ans: no.]